LEONA: THE DIE IS CAST

LEONA
THE DIE IS CAST

JENNY ROGNEBY

Other Press
New York

Originally published in Swedish as *Leona: Tärningen är kastad*
in 2014 by Wahlström & Widstrand, Stockholm.

First published in English in 2015 by Echo Publishing, South Melbourne,
Australia. Published by arrangement with Partners in Stories
Stockholm AB, Sweden.

Production editor: Yvonne E. Cárdenas
Text designer: Julie Fry
This book was set in Quiosco and Founders Grotesk by
Alpha Design & Composition of Pittsfield, NH.

10 9 8 7 6 5 4 3 2 1

LIBRARY OF CONGRESS CATALOGING-IN-PUBLICATION DATA

Names: Rogneby, Jenny, 1974- author.
Title: Leona : the die is cast : a novel / Jenny Rogneby.
Other titles: Leona : Tärningen är kastad. English.
Description: New York : Other Press, 2017.
Identifiers: LCCN 2016055169 (print) | LCCN 2017000228 (ebook) |
ISBN 9781590518823 (paperback) | ISBN 9781590518830 (e-book)
Subjects: LCSH: Crime—Sweden—Stockholm—Fiction. | Policewomen—
Sweden—Fiction. | Robbery—Fiction. | Stockholm (Sweden)—Fiction. |
Detective and mystery stories.
Classification: LCC PT9877.28.O44 L4613 2017 (print) | LCC PT9877.28.O44
(ebook) | DDC 839.73/8—dc23
LC record available at https://lccn.loc.gov/2016055169

LEONA: THE DIE IS CAST

No one had noticed her yet. Slowly and silently she crept along the narrow entrance mat toward the middle of the bank.

Her steps were determined.

Her gaze glassy.

She no longer felt the sores and dried blood on her naked, slender body. Only her heart distracted her. She could hear every beat. 1-2...3-4-5...6...The beats were too fast and uneven to count. She hugged the teddy bear against her chest as hard as she could. The pounding felt softer then.

The fluorescents were harsh and bright compared to the subdued bluish-gray light outside. She squinted. Just a few more steps.

Right...left...right...

She stopped in the middle of the lobby. Without moving her head she looked around the room, taking in the high counters, the computers, the people in suits. She stood still for a brief moment before she slowly and quietly bent down to set the tape recorder on the marble floor. She lightly pressed the play button and straightened up.

A gruff male voice echoed throughout the bank: *"My name is Olivia and I'm seven years old. Now listen carefully and do exactly as I say..."*

ONE

My eyes felt dry. Fixed at a point, as often happens while your thoughts wander. I blinked twice to force my gaze away from the reversed block letters on the glass door to the conference room.

VCD: Violent Crimes Division.

Though renovations had only finished two months ago, the letters were already scratched. Above the words shone the yellow-and-blue police emblem. For my colleagues it stood for a feeling of belonging and community.

Not for me.

To me it symbolized confinement.

Within the walls of authority I could never feel free.

Despite my years as a police officer I had never been able to reconcile myself to being one of them. Just some cop. But work did play an important role in my life. In a way that no one yet understood.

If it wasn't for the fact that I, Leona Lindberg, at the age of thirty-four, knew that my constructed life would soon change, I wouldn't have been able to stand it much longer.

Anette, the unit's admin assistant, looked at me from across the conference table. She smiled. I moved the corners of my mouth. These days it was pure reflex. It hadn't always been that way. Until I was fifteen, I hadn't realized that smiling gave me an advantage. By studying other people I had learned how to socialize. I nodded at Anette, who was pointing at her watch and shaking her head at the fact we all had to sit and wait. The usual weekend's crop of new cases was about to be doled out. My colleagues were chatting. Laughing. A few were complaining about the heavy workload, saying that they definitely couldn't take on any more investigations. I sat quietly, trying to focus on something other than the conference table, but my eyes kept being drawn to the uneven cracks that angrily separated the twelve small tables, which someone had tried to push together into one. There were obvious differences of at least several millimeters in the heights. In more than four places one tabletop stuck out higher than the one next to it. Very irritating. My colleagues grumbled that the room was stuffy, but none of them noticed the gaps and uneven surface of the table.

But I said nothing.

That was the best policy.

I had learned to keep such observations to myself.

I looked out the windows, which ran the entire length of the room. Despite the sky's gray blanket of clouds and the raindrops that were running slowly down the windowpanes, life outside seemed like liberation. Like so many times before, I resisted the impulse to just walk out and leave it all behind.

I stayed where I was.

The door didn't open again until 11:47 a.m., when Superintendent Claes Zetterlund stepped in. He ran his hand through his dark-blond hair and shook his wet jacket vigorously before tossing it over the back of the nearest chair. My colleagues fell silent. Without a word he opened his black backpack and took out a folder. He set it down on the table and took a breath as if to start speaking. But I was there first.

"I'm sorry for being late?" I suggested.

He'd had several seconds to make his excuses. He could at least have mumbled something apologetic when he opened the door. It was only polite—that much I had picked up about everyday social niceties. When he didn't speak I realized that there would be no apology. The look of surprise on his face confirmed my conclusion. He lost his train of thought. Held the inhaled air in his lungs, frowning and looking around to see who had dared to utter such a comment. In a matter of seconds the calm, relaxed atmosphere in the room had become as tense as Claes's moody temperament. Out of the corner of my eye, I caught Anette's quick glance. Everyone was silent. Waiting for Claes's reaction. His piercing eyes finally found their way to me.

"What the hell is your problem, Leona? I've had a terrible morning. The murder last Friday, another rape in Tantolunden, two new cases of aggravated assault on former gang members on Sveavägen, an arson on Lidingö, and another robbery that a bunch of goddamned reporters are terrorizing me about. I'm not in the mood to take shit from anyone in here who doesn't outrank me. Understood?"

I kept quiet. I had made my point. Claes looked out over the conference table. There wasn't a sound. Even a colleague with a higher rank would probably have chosen to keep quiet after that outburst. Claes could really become aggressive.

"We'll start with the robbery."

His voice was still too loud; he seemed to be having a hard time controlling it.

"Robbery, Östermalmstorg. Nybrogatan 39."

I could see that the file he was reading from was thin. Not much had been documented. A statement and an interview or two at most.

Suddenly "Thunderstruck" by AC/DC blared out of his pants pocket. He took out his cell phone.

"Violent Crimes, Claes Zetterlund."

Answering the phone in the middle of a meeting might be considered rude in other professions. In our line of work you were stared at if you ignored calls. The public could be in danger. Claes always talked loudly on the phone. Almost as if he was making a show of it.

"I can't comment on that yet. We have too little informa—… Not yet…No, I said…You can damn well wait until…"

He tossed the phone down on the table.

"Damn it, they're like a pack of dogs, those reporters. Who can take the robbery on Östermalm?"

He looked around the room. No one volunteered, as usual. Everyone thought they had enough to do with their ongoing investigations. Besides, no one wanted to be stuck with a shit case. Giving us the chance to volunteer to investigate the cases that came in, instead of simply doling them out and ordering us to do them, was the department's way of pretending that we had the opportunity to influence our own work situation. But everyone knew that if no one volunteered, Claes would just choose the person he thought was the most suitable.

Claes, who knew that everyone avoided certain types of investigations, had a habit of saying as little as possible about the details of a crime before he assigned the case.

So we were understandably suspicious.

Of everything.

We were especially wary of cases that were being watched closely by the media. So if you didn't know what the case was about, you kept quiet. A robbery on Östermalm could mean anything, from a helicopter robbery to a mugging. Maybe some celebrity had been threatened with a weapon and had their iPhone, iPad, iPod, or some other iSomething stolen, and would now be crying about it in the newspapers, on their blog, and via Twitter and

Facebook. Whining about getting their hair mussed and making sky-high claims for damages that no normal person could afford to pay, especially not the perpetrator. No one wanted to take on a case like that. Especially not now, just after the summer holidays, when everyone wanted peace and quiet to go through the hundreds of emails that came in while they were away.

I was amused by the silence. It was funny that everyone considered themselves so busy, despite the long coffee breaks they took in the afternoons.

Volunteering to investigate complicated cases that others avoided was a good way of gaining points. Unarmed robbery was normally not considered very exciting. The high-status crimes were homicide, kidnapping, aggravated robbery, rape, and other crimes where the victim had been seriously injured. Plus, most investigators hated having the media breathing down their necks. Major media attention on a robbery meant that it must be something spectacular, which interested me for a very particular reason. In a few seconds I would volunteer.

But not yet.

Claes looked around the room with raised eyebrows.

"No one?"

My colleagues were squirming. They looked down at the table. Up at the wall. Everywhere they wouldn't meet Claes's eyes. Everyone knew that at any moment Claes would dole out the case to whomever he liked. If you didn't make eye contact the risk of being chosen was lessened. The performance made me smile. Claes had evidently noticed my smile and stared straight at me.

I cleared my throat.

It was time.

"Okay, Claes, I'll take it."

I sat up straight, to show I was serious. He nodded curtly. Anette, who often mentioned that the distribution of cases should be more even among detectives, looked first at me, then at Claes. "Leona, do you really have time? You already have the murder in Humlegården and the armed robberies from last week." Anette was right. The Humle murder was a big job. Another case the others on the squad had avoided. Claes glanced at her sharply. He pushed the file across the conference table. If not for the uneven tabletop it probably would have slid all the way over to me. Now it stopped about halfway.

I clenched my teeth.

A colleague picked up the file. He handed it over to me with relief in his eyes. Claes looked at me.

"This is a very different case, Leona. You'll really get a chance to show your stuff. Now listen up, everyone!"

It was an unnecessary request. The room was already silent.

"At 10:37 a.m. today a seven-year-old girl went into SEB at Nybrogatan 39. It's one of the few bank branches that still handles cash. Somehow she managed to get five bank tellers to hand over bags of banknotes. None of the eight customers who were on the premises intervened. The girl then left the bank with the money and disappeared."

Claes now had everyone's attention. This was no ordinary investigation. Definitely not a shit case.

"Because of the little girl and the media's interest in the case, the bosses higher up are on the rampage. Their orders are that the case should have top priority," said Claes, looking at me.

"You're telling us that SEB was robbed by a seven-year-old? Was she carrying a bazooka or something?"

Perhaps I shouldn't have said anything, but I couldn't resist pointing out how comical it all sounded.

"Why don't you shut up, Leona, and let me finish."

I often had a hard time comprehending Claes's choice of words and the way he constantly raised his voice. He seemed to have a relentless storm of emotions bubbling up inside him and affecting his mood.

I wondered how that felt.

"No weapon has been reported. The girl had a tape recorder with her and played a message. What exactly was said on it we still don't know. The bank employees are being interviewed right now. According to witnesses the girl is about seven. She was naked and is also said to have had blood on her body. So far we have found no trace of her. She seems to have vanished into thin air."

People were murmuring indistinctly. A little girl had carried out a bank robbery?

Naked.

Bloody.

The team had never faced anything like this before. There probably hadn't been a similar case at any point in Swedish crime history. We had all been involved in strange investigations over the years, but even a few of the older detectives seemed moved. I turned to Claes.

"A naked girl on the streets of Stockholm can hardly have gone up in smoke. Someone must have seen something. Has the dog squad been out there?"

Claes avoided meeting my eyes. He acted as if the question had been asked from somewhere near the ceiling at the far end of the room. He looked up as he answered.

"The dogs behaved strangely and were unable to pick up a scent. According to witnesses the girl went north on Nybrogatan. After that it was as if she was swallowed by the crowd."

"Someone must have picked her up in a car nearby. Or she could have disappeared up a stairwell. What do we have there?" I asked.

"Cars in the area are being stopped. There have been no traces so far. Officers are going door to door. We'll have to see what that produces."

He looked down at his papers.

"The preliminary investigation is being conducted by the police, because so far we have no suspects, but considering the circumstances, with the girl and the media attention, the case will be randomly assigned to a prosecutor."

This was to be expected. Having the police run the investigation was usually simpler, partly because the person in charge was then easily accessible in police headquarters and not at the city prosecutor's office, which was some distance away, but mainly because detectives were more on the ball and aggressive when things got heated. Police officers were more inclined to use force where necessary, while prosecutors were usually more cautious. They were focused on whether the case would work out in the courtroom, and only interested in an eventual conviction.

In this case I saw an advantage in having a prosecutor lead the preliminary investigation rather than a detective. Some prosecutors were relatively passive, which was a good thing, as I hoped to be able to conduct the investigation in my own way, without having to account for every little step. The person in charge of the preliminary investigation was important — they would set the bar for how the investigation would proceed. On a couple of occasions I had refused to take a case because of the person who was leading it. We didn't get along. He kept interfering with my work. I couldn't deal with that. I preferred to work on my own.

"I've put together a team and scheduled a meeting at three o'clock so you can brief them on the case. By then presumably we'll have the prosecutor in place."

He looked at me to gauge my reaction. He knew that I didn't like working with just anyone. I nodded curtly.

"How much money did they get?" Fredrik asked predictably. He was always interested in unusual crimes. He had said "they," which implied he assumed that others besides the girl were behind the robbery. This was a reasonable conclusion, of course, if you ruled out the unlikely possibility of a hyper-intelligent, criminal little girl. If anyone believed that, though, presumably the case would have ended up at the Juvenile Division rather than the VCD. Even so, it was impossible to get away from the fact that it was the girl who had committed the robbery.

"You mean how much did *she* get, that little seven-year-old girl?' I said, smiling.

Claes flung a folder on the table with a thud. He seemed to have had enough of my comments.

"Maybe I can't trust you to be responsible for a case of this importance, Leona. You don't seem to be able to handle it."

I was getting tired of Claes's attacks.

"Not the Humle murder either, then? Or the robberies from last week? You can let someone else handle them, too, if you're suddenly doubting my ability. Why don't you assign the robbery to another detective, if you think there is someone more capable!"

If he wanted a fight, I wasn't going to back down. He stared at me. A flicker of doubt flew through my mind. Had I crossed a line? I had, after all, implied that I was a better investigator than my colleagues. A statement like that was almost a capital offense around here, where everyone was supposed to be equal. No one was allowed to claim superiority, unless they had been promoted to a management position.

The room was again dead silent. Claes stood leaning over the conference table with both hands on the tabletop. He stared at me wide-eyed.

"You're dismissed!" he said.

I stared at him, trying feverishly to read his expression. Was he serious? He raised one hand and pointed at the door with an outstretched arm. I didn't move.

"Are you having trouble understanding, Leona? Get out!"

"But Claes, dear, surely you don't mean that…"

Claes raised a hand to stop Anette, who was trying to come to my rescue. Without taking his eyes off me, he continued to point toward the door. Everyone sat petrified. I gathered up the report and the other documents and stood up so quickly that my chair skidded back with a sharp scraping sound until it ran into the wall behind me. After I had adjusted my shirt with my free hand I walked around the table on hard high heels toward Claes. He was still standing with his arm pointed at the door as I passed behind him. I flung the door wide open and then slammed it behind me.

TWO

Olivia had started shaking. She tried to relax, but couldn't. The rain made everything wet and cold. She itched, too, and her eyes and nose ran. Every time she tried to scratch, it hurt so much it brought tears to her eyes.

She had barely been able to lift the backpack off the floor inside the bank. Once she had it on her back it was fine. But not later, when she needed to take it off. Then she lost her balance and fell right down on the asphalt. The wound on her knee was bleeding and stung much more now than before. The backpack was wet and dirty. She prayed that nothing had broken, because then Daddy would be very angry.

Nothing had been the way Daddy had said. He must have forgotten. Forgotten to tell her that it would be so…scary.

The black rain cape was wet both inside and out. It clung to her body, like an icy blanket on her skin.

It smelled weird, too. And she kept hearing strange sounds. Lots of people. Sirens. They echoed loudly. Cut into her ears even though she covered them. She had also heard dogs. She loved dogs, but these ones sounded so angry. But now all the sounds were gone.

She sang quietly to herself, even though Daddy said she wasn't allowed to. Time went faster then. It was a song that Mommy used to sing to her. She could hear Mommy's voice humming the tune in her head. If only Mommy were here now, she thought.

Daddy was really strange to let her go out without clothes like this. Mommy would never let her do that. If she had only told Mommy right away that she really didn't want to go away alone with Daddy, but she had been so happy that he had chosen only her to go with him. She had danced with happiness around the kitchen table when she'd found out that she would get to go on a boat for the first time in her life. Her whole body had tingled. Even if she'd been a little afraid, she had missed Daddy so much. And he had promised that she would get to see Grandma, too.

The first day of the trip was fun. The boat they were on was the biggest one she had ever seen. It was bigger than their whole building and even had room for a couple of shops. In one shop she was allowed to pick out any candy she wanted. Then they found another shop, where Daddy had bought her a soft teddy bear and a bracelet with white stones. He had been so nice. Let her stay up until ten-thirty and then sleep in a bed that was above the one Daddy slept in. It wasn't scary at all to sleep on the boat, not like her sister had said. She had told her that there would be such big waves that you fell out of bed at night, but it only rocked a tiny bit, like when Mommy rocked her when she was little.

It wasn't until they came ashore that all the scary stuff started. Then Daddy got really mean. That was strange because he was so nice sometimes. She had wanted to sleep every night with the teddy bear that she had got on the boat, but after only one night he took it away from her. He said that it was sick and that he had to spray something on it so that it would get better. That was strange. Teddy bears couldn't get sick, could they? Sometimes she wondered if it was Daddy who was sick, but she pretended to believe that it was the teddy bear so that Daddy wouldn't get mad. He always got so mean when he was mad, shouting and waving his arms.

He used to hit her sister and her Mommy. That was a long time ago, before they moved away from Daddy. But he never hit Olivia then, because she was nice. He was just mean to people who were stupid, he always said. Olivia tried to be nice all the time, but sometimes it was hard because she didn't always know what he wanted her to do. Then he said she was slow on the uptake. So she always tried to think really fast.

Sometimes Daddy said that she had been stupid without her even knowing why. Like today. She must have been really slow, because he had forced her to do such hard things. The backpack was the hardest because it was so heavy. And then it was so cold. But Daddy would pick her up when it got dark. She couldn't wait for that, because she was sure by then he would be nice again.

She crouched down for a while. It was hard to keep standing for so long, but it was too wet to sit down. And there were creepy beetles on the ground. Not the tiny round red ones with black spots that were always on the flowers in her grandmother's summer house. These were much bigger and had long feelers on their noses. Not cute at all. They made a strange scratching sound when they moved, and they could walk up the walls, too. One had run up her leg, but she'd swatted it away, and it had ended up on its back. It lay there, kicking its legs. Two of the others were eating something from the ground.

Olivia was hungry too. Daddy had given her a sandwich and a banana that morning, but she wasn't allowed to eat or drink anymore, because then she would have to pee, he had said. She could almost taste the banana in her mouth. Sweet and creamy. If only she had one now.

THREE

A fleeting sense of freedom passed over me in the corridor as I walked quickly away from the meeting. I reached my arms toward the ceiling and stretched my whole body, then I pulled out my ponytail and shook my head until my hair fell down over my shoulders. I wasn't worried about being thrown out.

On the contrary.

I smiled.

Smiled because I had avoided having to sit there for the rest of the hour. Especially as I wanted to get to the crime scene as soon as possible. I held my ID against the card reader by the glass door and entered the code that would admit me into the corridor leading to my office.

After taking two steps into the corridor I saw it. The picture. It was hanging crookedly. It wasn't much, but it was enough to disturb my enjoyable walk from the meeting. I took hold of one corner of the framed print and moved it up a couple of millimeters, then I stood back against the opposite wall and admired my handiwork. Not that I was the artist, but by making sure the work was hanging parallel with the floor and ceiling I had enabled the artwork to display its full potential. I didn't care much for what the print depicted, but at least now it was in harmony with its surroundings.

I exhaled.

It had been quiet all morning, but when I stepped into the elevator I was reminded of the renovations. The cardboard covering the inside of the elevator made the space feel smaller than usual. Not that small spaces were generally a problem for me, but this reminded me of something. I couldn't remember what. The gravel and the moisture from people's shoes had broken up the cardboard on the floor, creating a musty, moldy odor that made me feel queasy. I swallowed. Looked up to see what floor I was passing. Judging by the elevator graffiti some people were getting tired of the never-ending construction work. "WHEN IS THIS DRILLING HELL GOING TO END?" and "CAN YOU CHARGE SOMEONE FOR POSSESSION OF LOUD POWER TOOLS?" were written on the cardboard walls.

When the door opened, three workmen in blue overalls were waiting to get in the elevator. Out of the corner of my eye I saw them turn around to watch me as I got out. I sighed. The renovations would be going on until next summer, which meant that the workers would be in the building at least until then. Since the Police Department had decided to solve the shortage of office space by expanding the headquarters at Kronoberg so that the whole department could fit under the same roof, the construction workers were unavoidable. In my opinion workmen weren't the most sociable of creatures, so I had been surprised to find that they spoke to me fairly often, asking questions about everything from burglaries at summer houses to who had assassinated Olof Palme. Some of them seemed genuinely interested in the police and saw their work as an important part of the agency's reorganization. They thought it was good that the investigative department was divided into several squads and that VCD sounded "cool, like a crime show on TV," as one of them had put it.

My phone vibrated in my pocket.

"Violent Crimes, Leona Lindberg."

"Hi honey, it's me."

I recognized that gentle tone of voice all too well. What did he want?

"I'm busy — on my way to a crime scene," I said.

I turned onto Kungsgatan in one of the agency's unmarked cars that these days I pretty much saw as my own. The car behind was much too close. I let it be.

"Just one quick thing," said Peter.

Hardly. Quick things no longer existed in our relationship. Simple conversations that we had previously dealt with in minutes had now been transformed into thorny disputes that could end in hours-long discussions.

Though not all at once.

There was never time for that.

Between work, taking the kids to and from day care, shopping, cooking, playing, story time, and bedtime, there was never enough time to do anything for several hours in a row. Instead, we would drag out the most trivial arguments over the course of a few weeks. Peter loved to dwell on things. Personally I saw most of our disputes as completely meaningless.

"Can you pick up the kids at day care this afternoon? Something's come up for me," he said.

I should have known. Of course something would come up for him today, while I was busy with the new case. I glanced at my watch. After I had visited the crime scene the afternoon would be filled with meetings and investigations.

"I can't, Peter. Claes has just put me on a big robbery. I won't have time."

"Well, things are really piling up here too, Leona. You'll have to try to work something out."

"Peter, this is a bank robbery with a child involved. It won't work."

"It's just a job, Leona, try to keep that in mind. Anyway, aren't your own children more important?"

I shook my head, astonished that Peter still hadn't realized that it was pointless to try to play on my conscience.

"They're your children too, remember? And isn't your job *just a job* as well?"

"You know how my boss is. I don't have any flexibility. I'd much prefer to be a stay-at-home dad and take care of the kids full time if we could live on your salary alone, but a single person can barely live on that, let alone a family."

There it was again.

Another jab.

Peter's comments confirmed that our relationship had taken a path I saw as failure. My efforts to create a well-functioning family life had succeeded for years. We lived just like the majority of our acquaintances. For the same reasons that I needed my job, I needed a normal family life. It was vital. It helped me keep my head above water.

But it was wearing me down.

Eating me up from inside.

Soon it would come to an end.

The fact that Peter was trying to make his job at the advertising agency seem of vital importance was pathetic. I had an increasing desire to hang up on him. Let the children rot at day care. When the staff called and asked, Peter could explain why he hadn't picked them up on time. If only the day care staff could learn to call Peter instead of me when there was a problem with the children. There was no equality there.

I didn't have time to pick a fight with Peter right now. Another quick glance at my watch. With a little luck I might have time to pick them up anyway.

"I'll work it out," I said, driving onto Nybrogatan, heading toward the SEB branch at number 39.

There was still a significant response at the crime scene. Two marked cars with blue lights rotating on their roofs were parked on the street. Curious bystanders, journalists, and photographers were crowded outside. Most of them holding umbrellas to escape the pouring rain. I had to squeeze my way to the field commander. I flashed my badge.

"Leona Lindberg, detective. How are we doing?"

He nodded and raised the barricade tape for me.

"Antonsson. The witnesses are being interviewed in the van. No trace of the girl yet."

Antonsson was probably the oldest officer still on patrol duty that I had ever met. His age wasn't his only distinguishing feature; he was also big-boned and a head taller than the rest of his colleagues. His gray-and-white mustache and beard made him look like an old-time constable from the movies.

A male journalist with blond hair appeared and looked at me. "Excuse me, can I get a brief statement? What's known about the girl?"

"I've told you that we can't make a statement yet," Antonsson said to the journalist.

He followed me away from the barricade, toward the bank.

"Forensics?" I asked.

"They're on the scene. No information yet, but you know how Forensics is these days, they refuse to collaborate. I'm just waiting for them to be done so we can pack up. I haven't seen such a crowd of journalists since Anna Lindh was stabbed at NK. This little girl seems to be prime front-page news."

"You can refer all media to me," I said.

On my way to the bank I turned toward Antonsson.

"Could you ask the officers over there to turn off those lights?"

I had never liked the blue lights. Some of my colleagues seemed to love them. They didn't feel like real cops unless they were riding around in uniform in a marked car with the sirens blaring. The louder and more visible they were, the higher their sense of self-worth. It was mainly the younger officers who liked to show off. A few of the older ones who still worked in the field were the very best kind of officers. They were able to distance themselves from their role, and they didn't feel the need to assert themselves or display their authority as soon as they got the chance. Unfortunately there were far too few experienced officers in the field because the work—outdoors, with inconvenient shifts at night and on public holidays—didn't fit with the kind of family life that most officers preferred.

The blue lights were irritating.

"You can get epilepsy from less," I muttered as I approached the entrance.

Just outside the bank I turned around and looked out over Östermalmstorg. The square a little farther away was almost empty. The rain made people move slowly along the building facades. I walked into the bank. A man approached me.

"Gunnar Månsson, Forensics. We'll be done here soon. Not much for us to do, unfortunately."

"The witnesses said the girl was covered with blood. Any traces?"

"Not even a drop."

"Fingerprints? Anything?"

Månsson shook his head. The automatic sliding doors at the entrance meant that the girl hadn't needed to touch the door with her hands. Not that we had any fingerprints to identify her with anyway, as she was too young to be in the print register, but once we found her it would've been nice to be able to make sure it was the right girl.

It seemed extraordinary that both the forensics team and the dog handlers had no decent leads.

"What about shoeprints?"

"It's not clear what she had on her feet. There are no small shoeprints in the usual sense, but we have found traces of a different type of sole in a small size. We'll get back to you about that."

"As soon as possible, I'm assuming."

Despite the intense media scrutiny on the robbery, I knew that it wouldn't be a priority for Forensics. There had been several homicides and other serious crimes lately, and they were swamped. No one had died here. There hadn't even been any physical injuries reported, except for the wounds on the girl, which hadn't occurred at the crime scene. Still, I wanted to reassure myself that the investigation wouldn't drag on, to avoid any unexpected surprises cropping up weeks after the crime had taken place.

I ignored Månsson's snort in response. Instead, I walked around the bank. It was unusually large. After the banks had moved the major part of their operations online, the offices had been shrinking in both size and number every year. But this branch was spacious, with high ceilings and windows all the way along the front wall, facing Nybrogatan. From inside you could see out clearly, but the gray-tinted window film on the panes reflected the light from outside, which meant that during the day it was hard to see in. The five teller desks were placed in a semicircle at the back of the lobby. I counted the surveillance cameras that were mounted on the walls.

"An unusually large number of cameras. Have the recordings been secured?"

"They're working on that now. As you said, there are a lot of cameras, so we should have views from different angles. Someone wanted to make a show of this."

"I want all the surveillance recordings from the past two weeks. Someone may have been here to case the place in advance. The videos from yesterday and earlier can be sent to the Image and Audio Analysis team. I want today's footage on my desk tomorrow morning."

On my way to the exit I saw Antonsson through the window. He was wrestling with a young man with a camera around his neck who had sneaked through the barricade and was heading toward the entrance. I turned to Gunnar Månsson.

"Listen, be careful with the reporters who are sneaking around here. I don't want to see pictures of a blood-covered seven-year-old on the front page tomorrow."

Månsson nodded.

"It would be good if you could have a chat with the bank manager," he said. "He's stressing out about us being here, because he wants to reopen the bank."

I nodded and continued toward the exit. I had nothing against politely but firmly explaining to a suit that this was a police investigation and that he could go home and play with his kids until the forensics team was done. It would liven up the boring drive back to the office.

FOUR

The team that Claes had put together was waiting for me in the conference room when I came back from the crime scene. I was supposed to inform them about the case, but I didn't intend to hold a long, detailed run-through. They didn't all need to know everything. The most important thing was that everyone had enough information to carry out their part of the work. Normally I would have switched to autopilot. Now I had to think a few steps ahead.

I was being watched.

By Claes. By his superiors.

By the media.

"For those of you who haven't met me before, my name is Leona Lindberg. I'm in VCD and I'm handling the robbery that took place this morning, which was committed by a little girl. I've called you here to quickly brief everyone on what we should be focusing on right now. I also wanted us all to meet face-to-face."

I didn't particularly care about seeing people's faces, but anyone who has ever worked within the Police Department knows the importance of personal relationships. Every employee had their own little black book of names of colleagues who were good to work with. Not everyone was. Good to work with, that is.

I straightened two pens that were lying on the table in front of me. Didn't like having sharp objects pointing in my direction. Besides, they were at an angle. As I picked up the pens I noticed that the nail tip on my thumb wasn't properly glued down. My nails had just been done by Madeleine on the corner. She usually did a good job. This time she'd been sloppy.

"First and foremost, I assume that the massive media coverage hasn't escaped you," I said. "There's already wild speculation about the case. As usual, you are not to make statements to the media—just mention that preliminary investigations are confidential, or refer them to our public relations officer. If they aren't satisfied with that, then refer them to me. Has anyone already been contacted by the media?"

Three people nodded.

"Of course I don't need to mention that there should be no information leaks. *None.*"

It didn't matter how often and how clearly you said it, the agency was like a sieve. Individual officers were more than likely paid to give out secret information.

"Without being menacing, I want to remind you that anyone who violates this can expect repercussions."

No one said anything.

A brief vibration made me put my hand in my pocket and pull out my phone. I noted the English words in the text message on the screen. For a moment I was lost in thought, but I snapped back. I would have to wait to answer until the meeting was over.

"Report whatever you come up with directly to me. Always in writing, of course, but call or email me if there's something important. I will also—in exceptional cases—accept a fax, but only if you're sure your information is completely unimportant, and you'd better have a damn good reason for sending it by fax."

A few people smiled. I took that as a good sign. They were with me.

"We're going to be using a scaled-down version of the PMI. Are you all familiar with that approach?"

Some people nodded, but others didn't. Claes had brought in people from other divisions. Even though most were experienced investigators, I knew the importance of establishing a solid framework for the investigation. I hated seeing stressed-out investigators running hysterically up and down the corridors because they had missed important details. Or investigative measures that weren't done at all, or were done at the wrong time. Typical structural problems that shouldn't exist. I wanted to clarify my role in the investigation with extreme precision. I didn't want to be questioned about it later.

"We'll follow the guidelines in the PMI, which stands for Police Methodology for the Investigation of Violent Crimes. It's a refined version of the old homicide bible that I'm sure you all remember. I'm responsible for the case. I will run the investigation, acting as the coordinator, and I'll also conduct some of the interviews."

This was unusual. The person who coordinated the PMI cases seldom conducted interviews personally, usually delegating them to others. That's how I would have run any other investigation.

But not this one.

This one was special.

I picked up the black marker and wrote "Who is the girl?" on the whiteboard.

"Lars, do you have any theories?"

Lars lit up. He was always on the ball, and in contrast to some of the others, he seemed to really enjoy his work in the Criminal Intelligence Service. For a guy who had two school-age kids and a newborn, he looked almost shamelessly alert and well rested.

"Hi everyone, Lars Nyman at CIS. Unfortunately we don't have much to work with at the moment. According to witnesses, the girl's appearance was hard to describe due to all the wounds, bruises, and blood she reportedly had on her body…"

He was interrupted by a light knock. The door opened.

"Excuse me, is this the bank robbery at Östermalmstorg?"

"Nina!" I said. "It is. Come in!"

So she was the one assigned to lead the preliminary investigation. Nina was a very sharp prosecutor from the city prosecutor's office, notorious amongst the police. Claes described her as very meticulous, but investigators were more likely to call her zealous as hell. She didn't give in until you had turned over every stone five times in an investigation.

She stepped in and took off her black trench coat. Her dark hair was freshly cut into an asymmetric bob. Her oval face, pale skin, and stylish glasses, along with her tight, knee-length skirt, blouse, and jacket, made her look like she had stepped right out of the pages of a business magazine.

"Nina Wallin, district prosecutor. I'm the preliminary investigation leader in this case, as of now."

"Have a seat," I said. "We've just started. Lars Nyman from CIS is telling us what we know about the girl."

Nina sat down in an empty chair as Lars continued.

"The girl didn't say a word during the robbery, so we don't know what nationality she is. No Swedish girl with that description has been reported missing. She could be a trafficking victim from abroad, perhaps from a Baltic country. I've asked Europol to look into that further."

"According to the first witness statements she appeared to be approximately seven years old," I said. "What does that tell you, Lars?"

"That I have to get better at disciplining my own kids. I can hardly even get them to make their beds."

I tried not to laugh. That wouldn't be good form. The others looked at each other and at me. No one dared to laugh.

"Yes, I wonder how you get a seven-year-old to do something like this," I said, even though I knew. If in other parts of the world you could turn children into soldiers and get them to murder their own family members, then naturally, with some manipulation, you could get a child to commit a robbery.

"Thanks, Lars. Report to me as soon as you find out anything else. Johan, have you managed to get hold of the surveillance material?"

Johan looked at the others around the table.

"Johan Östberg, Image and Audio Analysis Group. We're in the process of going through all the visual material, which is quite extensive. There is surveillance video from two weeks back. From subways, escalators, stores in the vicinity, ATMs, and inside the bank. I'll get back to you when I know more."

"Thanks, Johan. Robbie, what happened with the dogs?"

"Robert Granlund, dog squad. We didn't manage to find any traces. The handler who was first on the scene called me because his dog was behaving strangely. I got there twenty minutes later and couldn't get a response from my dog either. It was odd, because witnesses said the girl was covered in blood. I suspect that — "

"The two of us can talk more about that later, Robbie. Let's continue."

It was better if I discussed people's personal theories with them separately. I did not want them to race off on wild tangents this early in the investigation.

"We'll need the shoeprints analyzed as soon as possible. Gunnar?"

I looked at the technician, Gunnar Månsson. He seemed to have a hard time keeping his eyes open. His bushy eyebrows were sticking out and his eyelids were almost closed. He cleared his throat. "Umm...Månsson here. The girl didn't touch anything, so we don't have any fingerprints. But we do have some small shoeprints we're analyzing. I'll get back to you on that. There's no other forensic evidence. We took some DNA samples, but it's unlikely they'll tell us anything. It's fascinating, I must say..."

"Thanks, Gunnar. A naked and bloody girl with a heavy backpack can't have gone far. The door-to-door effort hasn't produced anything yet, but we'll keep at it. Once we know what the girl had on her feet you'll need to check where the shoes, or whatever she was wearing, can be obtained. When they were bought and by whom."

I continued writing on the board: "Teddy bear?"

"She had a teddy bear with her in the bank. I want you to ask all the witnesses that you interview to describe the teddy bear as a follow-up. If we're lucky it might be an unusual one. We can't let the interviews drag on, so get going with them immediately and make sure to have the witnesses read and sign their statements on the spot. All memos for this case should be printed out. Nothing handwritten."

Some officers, especially those working in the field, had a fondness for jotting things down on any scrap of paper they could get hold of. Advertising flyers, napkins — I had even seen pieces of toilet paper with notes scribbled on them. These days it wasn't as common for people to bring in handwritten notes, but instead of writing things down for the case files they just called headquarters and rattled off a whole lot of things on the phone. Some investigators thought documenting their findings was tedious, and they hoped that the officer on the other end of the line would do it for them.

"The girl set a tape recorder down on the floor and played a message. We don't have the audio recording yet, but, Johan, you'll need to be prepared, as presumably we'll get it for analysis later."

Johan lit up. He had fought hard for his department, which was formerly only called the Image Analysis Group, to also be able to analyze audio recordings. As more and more people used smart phones to film events with both sound and image, not to mention the large quantity of audio recordings that secret wire-tapping generated, the agency had recognized the need. Johan was proud of his team's achievements, and would be taking over the position as group manager of the Image and Audio Analysis Group at the end of the year.

"I'll take care of it as soon as it comes in," he said.

"All the witnesses will need to be interviewed thoroughly about what was said on the tape. Perhaps there are some leads there about the perpetrator or perpetrators. How did the voice that was speaking sound? Age? Dialect? What can be heard in the background? You get the idea."

I wrote "Audio recording" on the board, and then below it "Weapons."

"There doesn't appear to have been a weapon involved," I said. "Bank customers and personnel did as they were told out of fear that the girl would be injured. But the question must still be asked of all the witnesses."

The last words I wrote down were "Backpack" and "Escape route."

"She was carrying the money in a backpack. Ask questions about it — color, size, brand, old or new, and so on. Obviously the witnesses will also need to be interviewed about the girl's escape route. Someone must have seen where she went. What cars were in the area? Did someone pick her up in a car, and so on. All we know is that she left the bank on foot and went north on Nybrogatan. Any questions about that?"

No one said anything. I looked at Nina, who was sitting quietly taking notes.

"Nina, do you have any other instructions?"

She shook her head. "You seem to have the situation under control. Start that way, and we'll stay in touch."

"I'll call you when I need decisions to be made, otherwise we'll just keep on working."

I watched her reaction to my words carefully. She nodded. I took it to mean that I would work on the investigation without her involvement until I needed decisions about house searches, arrests, or the like. I hoped my interpretation was correct.

Nina looked around the table.

"You can reach me directly if it's urgent, but preferably go through Leona, so we can avoid any misunderstandings."

"You'll have a hard time getting hold of Nina even if you try," I said, smiling.

"However much I want to be available, unfortunately that's true," said Nina. "I apologize in advance if I sound abrupt on the phone—my only excuse is the unbelievable workload we prosecutors are handling at the moment. The best way to reach me is by email."

"Call me instead," I said.

Maybe I jumped in a little too quickly, but I didn't like people going around me and speaking to the prosecutor without my knowledge. That couldn't happen here.

"I'll have a meeting with the investigators every day at three o'clock to go over what we've found during the day," I said. "The rest of you should let me know immediately when you've discovered something. It's great to be working with you all. Now let's see about solving this case."

Everyone got up. I turned to Nina.

"Do you have a moment?"

Nina nodded and remained seated. She looked at me.

"How's everything going, Leona? Stressful?"

Few people noticed the changes in my mood the way Nina did. She knew me well, although there was also a lot she didn't know. I wondered what she was referring to. Did I seem distracted? I had a lot to think about, though nothing I could, or would, reveal to her. Maybe she just thought I looked tired. I decided to go with that and sighed, perhaps a little too deeply, shaking my head.

"It's Benjamin. He's not sleeping."

It was true. Nothing I couldn't handle, of course, but it did wear me out.

"Poor little guy."

"We hoped that the last operation would help, when they removed another part of his intestine that was inflamed. But now the same thing is happening again. I don't know what to do. It doesn't seem right to pump a three-year-old full of painkillers, but he can't sleep without them now."

Life had been so much easier before the children. Not completely without worries, but simpler. It was simpler not to feel. When Beatrice was born I realized for the first time that I actually had the capacity to feel deep emotions.

It frightened me.

Love. An abstract concept that previously lacked meaning for me suddenly had substance when the children were born.

"What do you think about the robbery?"

I changed the topic. I wanted to know what kind of theories Nina had.

"It's pretty spectacular, and would have required a lot of planning. Getting a child to carry out something like that would take a lot of preparation. I don't believe the trafficking theory that Lars brought up. The perpetrator knows the girl too well. Knows how she reacts and what she can handle. It's probably someone close to her. A family member or a relative, perhaps."

Nina was sharp, but anyone could have figured that out. I had expected her to arrive at something more. After a quick look at the clock she got up and put on her trench coat.

"I wish we could have lunch together, but I have to get to court."

It had been a month since we last had lunch.

"No problem, we'll do it next week," I said.

Nina and I had met for the first time seven years earlier, when we were both working on an arson investigation. It was a messy case. In order to have any time at all to eat during the day, we started having lunch together, so we could talk shop at the same time. We had become friends, I guess.

Close friends, others would say.

But I don't really have friends like that.

Nina looked out for me, I could see that. And when she had gotten married four years ago, to a man who started abusing her only a few months after the wedding, she had turned to me. As a prosecutor she had seen many abusive men go free, so she chose not to report it but instead asked for my help "off the record." Of course I agreed. With the help of some colleagues, I made sure to scare the man soundly, so that Nina could file for divorce without having any more problems with him. After that, she had told me many times that she saw me as one of her closest friends.

I had hoped for a somewhat less involved prosecutor. Even though I knew Nina had confidence in my ability to handle the investigation, there was a risk that she would interfere in the work too much. At least she understood I worked best independently. That was important to me. Especially with this case.

As I left the conference room I took out my phone, opened the English text message, pressed reply, and started typing.

FIVE

Journalist Christer Skoog was waiting for the press conference at Rosenbad to begin. As usual, someone had underestimated the number of journalists and had organized the press conference in a room that was much too cramped. There was almost no oxygen.

He was dressed warmly, though it was only early September. It had been a cold summer, and the autumn wasn't looking much better. But the layout of the room didn't really allow the air to circulate, so the couple of open windows didn't make a difference. Christer pulled off his navy sweater and shoved it down into the side pocket of his laptop bag. His wavy hair, which these days displayed a large number of gray streaks, hung halfway down the back of his neck and stuck to his skin. During the two hours he'd been in the room the temperature had risen at least five degrees. He shook his head to get a little air under the hair on his neck.

The press conference's PR officer seemed nervous. Either it was the warm room that had made her face flushed, or else she was unprepared for the large group of journalists that were gathered. Christer didn't care which. He was just waiting for her to leave. Instead she placed herself right in front of all the microphones.

"In view of the accusations directed at the minister for finance, the minister for foreign affairs, and the finance commissioner for the city of Stockholm, a press conference will be held shortly where the attorney general will announce the decisions made regarding the indictment. After that there will be an opportunity to ask a few brief questions."

Christer looked at the clock again. It was really about time they got started.

The buzz in the room was replaced by flashes and the sound of clicking cameras as the attorney general stepped into the room. He walked up to the bank of microphones, standing tall. His suit hung on his body as if it were still on the hanger. He cleared his throat. Christer took a deep breath. It was time.

"The evidence that has emerged in the preliminary investigation of Minister for Finance Niklas Olander, Minister for Foreign Affairs Lars Tranberg, and Finance Commissioner Hans Nordwall concerning accusations of purchase of sexual services has been clear in some respects, while in others it has created such doubt that it has been difficult to assess its credibility."

The attorney general's voice was loud and clear, which was helpful for the audio recording. Everyone was silent. Prepared to bombard him with questions as soon as the decision was announced.

A journalist from *Expressen* turned to Christer, shaking his head and whispering, "What do you think?"

Christer didn't reply. There was no point in speculating. Especially not with competing journalists. Besides, it was impossible to make any meaningful guesses. How the prosecutors reasoned was generally completely incomprehensible. They always found some loophole to allow them to interpret the law the way they wanted to. Christer was still hopeful, however.

He had specifically requested to report on events that concerned the finance minister, but so far there had been very little of interest. Most recently it had been the EU's new banking regulations, which required all member states, even those outside the monetary union, to hold a certain amount of euros in cash, so that citizens would be able to get their money out in a safe currency in the event of a bank collapse. The Swedish banks had protested loudly that it was unreasonable to expect them to hold such a large percentage of their liquid assets in euros, but the finance minister had stood behind the EU's decision. The criticism the government had received as a result of the minister's position was nothing, however, compared to the onrush of dissatisfaction and blame that had broken out now that he and two other politicians had been accused of criminal activity.

No one knew how much Christer disliked the finance minister. Every time he showed up on television Christer saw only the young bully from the Trollboda School in Hässelby. At the time Christer had been a taciturn student, shy and retiring. A tempting victim for Nino, as the finance minister, Niklas Olander, had been known in grade school. As a result of Nino's bullying, Christer had been afraid to go to school, and had eventually been forced to repeat a grade, as he had missed too many classes. Christer had known that Nino had joined a political youth association right after high school, but it was beyond his imagination that Nino would eventually be appointed as a cabinet minister and head of the Ministry of Finance, one of the youngest ministers in the government. When it was revealed that a police report had been made and that several politicians had been accused of paying for sexual services, Christer had reveled in the thought that reality had finally caught up with Nino.

Christer had been sent to report from the annual Swedish Moderate Party conference in Örebro, and by chance had ended up at the same hotel as the politicians. Relaxing with a beer in the hotel bar at the end of the day was the norm. At the end of the second-to-last day of the conference, the three government ministers had gotten drunk and started joking a little too loudly about whether or not they would dare offer a woman money for sex, how much intercourse was actually worth in monetary terms, and tactics for bargaining. The minister for finance had seemed particularly amused by the discussion and started making bets with the other two about how low a price they could get for various sexual acts. Christer had been sitting with his back toward them and had heard the whole conversation. He remembered the feeling. It had been pure pleasure to hear what they were saying to each other. Now he would finally get his chance to strike back for the years of anxiety, fear, and depression he'd suffered as a result of Nino's bullying.

Christer's editor had been dubious about printing the article, but Christer had insisted. The outcry did not take long. Other politicians, feminist organizations, and readers from every corner of the country expressed their opinions. All three politicians denied the allegations in the press, protesting that it was all a lie. They would never even think of discussing something like that, much less act on it, they said. It all probably would have ended there, but one event distinguished this incident from similar ones that Christer had reported on in his career. A prostitute suddenly filed a police report accusing the three politicians of purchasing sexual services.

In the majority of previous cases involving elevated individuals paying for sex, the prostitutes hadn't wanted to report the incidents. The few who had spoken out were given little credence either in the media or in the courtroom, if the cases even went as far as indictment. But this woman was different. Christer had heard rumors that she wanted to stop walking the streets, and that she saw it as her duty to show society what was going on behind the scenes in politics.

He had labeled it the Hooker Affair in his article, and to a direct question the prime minister had responded that the incident had very seriously damaged the credibility of Swedish politicians, both nationally and internationally.

The attorney general's decision today would be momentous.

Christer had demanded a place at the front at the press conference. He came from *Aftonbladet*, after all, not some local rag. He couldn't stand most of his colleagues. Some came directly from journalism school and had no idea how things worked, taking up valuable time by asking stupid questions with no sense for when it was time to back off. Others snooped around in their colleagues' notes or paid for information that they then distorted to fit their angle.

The attorney general continued.

"I have therefore made the decision that the allegations with respect to Minister for Finance Olander, Minister for Foreign Affairs Tranberg, and Financial Commissioner Nordwall do not have sufficient grounds for indictment. The charges against them are hereby dropped."

The room where the press conference was being held went from total silence to complete chaos. Journalists crowded closer, all calling out at the same time.

"Is it true that the prostitute recorded everything?"

"As always I have weighed all the evidence we have received and as I said earlier it has been of variable quality. For that reason I consider that what has emerged so far does not constitute sufficient grounds for indictment."

"Didn't the prostitute describe the bodies of the accused in detail?"

"As I said I have weighed all the evidence and concluded that..."

Christer signaled to the photographer that they should leave. It was pointless to stay. The attorney general was simply reeling off the same response over and over again. Christer squeezed past reporters and photographers to make his way to the exit, shoving aside a young journalist who refused to move, his eyes glued to the attorney general and his body pressing in toward the middle of the throng. Christer's clothes felt too tight on his body and he was having a hard time breathing. He had to get out. Quickly he made his way down the corridor to the doors, stopping on the steps just outside. He fanned his face with his notepad.

"Crowded in there."

The photographer had caught up and positioned himself by the railing, putting his camera back in his bag.

"We don't need any video of that shit. Just send a still picture, and I'll bang out something readable in the car."

As Christer started to leave he pulled out his phone and punched in the prostitute's number. He had been trying to reach her ever since she had made the police report. Without her, the series on the politicians who bought sex would be dead within a week. Just as before, there was no dial tone.

"*The number cannot be reached at this time. Please try again later.*"

SIX

Office after office was empty. The clock in the corridor told me it was only two-thirty and the fluorescent lights were on in most of the offices, which suggested that my colleagues hadn't gone home for the day. I could hear a keyboard clattering from Claes's office, and I positioned myself in the doorway. The windows along the one long side did not admit much light from the autumn gloom outside. He only had his desk lamp on. The yellow glow cast shadows over half his face as he was writing. If he didn't insist on having the curtains facing the corridor closed, the room would feel more open and welcoming.

"Where is everybody?" I said.

Claes looked up. The distance and the low light meant that I couldn't make out his expression. He had the biggest office on the squad. Some thought that was completely acceptable. Others were irritated that the boss sat alone in an office that could hold four detectives while some officers had to sit at makeshift desks in the corridor. A new colleague had suggested at a squad meeting that Claes's office could be divided up for newly hired detectives to sit in. Claes hadn't even bothered to comment on the proposal. His look and loud snort let everyone understand that it was completely out of the question. Personally I had been amused by the new guy's naive conception of workplace hierarchy.

"Come in, Leona."

He looked at the long and narrow calendar on the desk.

"Tuesday, September 3 — all of them are at the narcotics seminar. Did you miss that email?"

His voice was flat. I tried to interpret his mood without success. After the squad meeting yesterday, I didn't know where I stood with him. The other officers had sat in silence, seemingly shocked that I hadn't backed down when he got going.

I'd always thought that there was something peculiar about Claes. There were rumors that he was the kind of officer who didn't always play with a clean deck, but those kinds of rumors circulated every now and then about various colleagues. What fascinated me was that he, more than anyone else, seemed to act based on emotional impulses. He flared up easily and often made decisions in an agitated state. As a relatively young, recently appointed squad chief, he had managed very quickly to gain power through methods that were not particularly appreciated by some of the staff. During the last nine months alone he had transferred three investigators on the basis that they had "problems with authority." He amused himself by moving those of us who were left between various offices along the corridor as it suited him. He and I had clashed before, and I was convinced that I was now at the top of his transfer list. Despite this, I couldn't help being amused by his way of making unpopular decisions. My colleagues complained that they didn't have time to "settle in" and have peace to work because they were constantly being shuttled around between various office spaces. Personally, I didn't care. I didn't understand how they could become so attached to a certain office. All the offices were the same — the same white, sterile walls, the same shelves, the same desks. In fact, they resembled the nearby jail cells.

Police and criminals, locked in, just in different ways.

Almost wall to wall.

The irony of fate.

It didn't bother me that Claes had scolded me in front of my colleagues. I found it stimulating, oddly enough. Flattering actually. His intense reaction to my comments gave me a kind of satisfaction. It convinced me I meant something to him.

Claes got up. He nodded at the chairs around the conference table at the other end of the room and calmly closed the door, as he always did when he wanted to indicate that something was serious. I quickly smoothed out the tablecloth before I sat down. I studied him carefully. He went back to his desk and leaned against the edge. His choice to stand when everyone else was seated wasn't unusual — the height difference gave him the power. Last week at the two o'clock break, when everyone was sitting down in the circle formed by the couches and armchairs, he had positioned himself in the center and rattled on loudly, at the same time gesturing expansively with his arms. At the team meetings he often looked out over the heads of everyone like a president speaking to a crowd of people. He truly did not apologize for himself, Claes. Some people were bothered by that. I saw the whole thing as theater and was amused by the scene he performed.

He crossed his arms.

"What the hell kind of maneuver was that at the meeting yesterday?"

So that's what he wanted to talk about. I shrugged.

"You were late and I pointed it out, that's all. The rest was your doing."

He took a breath and started pacing around the room.

"You should be very clear that I won't accept that kind of attitude, especially not in front of the whole squad."

Why on earth was he harping on about this? Could he really have taken it so seriously? The two of us had treated the others to a show, and they were probably happy that someone had managed to inject a little drama into the meeting, which was usually deadly boring. The only thing I would have wished was that the door had made more noise as I closed it behind me. The hinges on the glass door were designed to close quietly and had eliminated any dramatic effect. Other than that, I had been pleased with the drama of our performance. Claes should be able to take a few taunting remarks. Especially because I was right. He had arrived late to the meeting and hadn't apologized.

"I think you should keep in mind who it was that got you to where you are," he said, crossing his arms.

As usual, superiors within the police seemed to believe that everything good in the world was their doing and everything bad someone else's. I let him have his way. He continued to scold me.

"You've been damned awkward for a long time now, Leona. If this continues then I won't have any choice but to move you."

Now I had to bite my tongue. This wasn't the first time he made threats about transferring me, but they had never been this direct. Previously he had phrased it differently, saying that he would be "forced to take measures" if I didn't stop challenging him. Even though my pulse rate was rising, I did my best to hold back my impulse to put him in his place. I didn't have anything to gain by fighting with him. The only way to turn the whole thing around was to try to warm up the frosty mood.

"You're making a mountain out of a molehill, Claes. But I'll try to think of a way to make it up to you."

It was a line from a B-grade movie, but along with a smile it sounded good, I thought. It would probably work. I got up and slowly walked closer. He looked me right in the eyes, searching. As if he didn't know what I intended to do. I stood in front of him and carefully put my hands on his shoulders.

"You're stressed, I can feel it," I said, lightly rubbing his shoulders. "Negative stress isn't good for you, Claes. Two minutes of relaxation can do wonders."

He offered no resistance, and his shoulders sagged noticeably toward the floor. While I worked his tense neck and shoulders with my hands he sighed deeply and closed his eyes. I stood closer. My legs on either side of his. I could smell his sea-scented aftershave. I saw out of the corner of my eye that he was slowly opening his eyes, just a little. He looked at me. I continued massaging, pretending not to notice. Let him look.

We'd had sex once, Claes and I. It was the last time he'd threatened to transfer me. Afterward he'd felt so guilty about his wife that it had never happened again, which was fine with me. I'd achieved my goal—I got to stay. If I had been an emotional person I probably would have felt guilty about Peter. Although intellectually I could understand the concept of guilt, I had never experienced it. I'd often wondered why I wasted so much energy trying to feel things. Was it really something to strive for? Most people who did so seemed unhappy anyway.

Sex wasn't interesting to me. I thought it was mostly awkward and uncomfortable. I'd never understood people's obsession with it.

I moved even closer to him and stood there as the phone on the desk let out a loud, piercing sound. He flinched. Leaped up quickly and went around the desk, sitting down in his office chair.

"Violent Crimes, Claes Zetterlund…Then I'll arrange it so you have it tomorrow morning…No problem…I'll handle it."

He hung up. His facial expression and a whispered oath showed that he wasn't at all pleased by the phone call.

"Just a lot of fucking demands, but never anything reasonable on payday. Really makes you wonder why we keep on with this."

"I would have thought you had a decent salary," I said.

Claes let out a sarcastic laugh.

"We're done, Leona. I'll make a decision about you later. I have to get this done before tomorrow morning."

He nodded at the computer screen.

"Seriously, Claes. I want to keep going with the bank robbery. You know what I can do. I'm going to solve it."

"Okay, see that you do. The higher-ups have their eyes on you, just so you know. And listen—no more crazy outbursts at meetings. I have more than enough shit to think about."

"Okay, okay," I said, throwing up my arms as I walked toward the door.

I needed to be more careful with Claes. He was capricious. I couldn't risk being transferred. Not now.

My phone vibrated in my pocket as I left Claes's office.

"Christer Skoog from *Aftonbladet*. You know why I'm calling, don't you?"

It was typical of a reporter from *Aftonbladet* to open with that line. Didn't they understand that their whole manner doomed the conversation right from the start? If there was anything I had learned about communication with other people, it was not to start a conversation by making the person you wanted to talk to angry. Especially not if you wanted to get anything useful out of the conversation.

"How should I know that?" I said, even though I knew.

"The little girl robbery," he answered, as if it was obvious.

So they had already given it a name in the press. The Little Girl Robbery. If you didn't know what it was about, your first thought would be that it was a girl who had been robbed.

I realized that the case was of interest to the media, but their unrefined methods of obtaining information irritated me.

"I don't have enough info to give you anything of value, unfortunately."

I pretended to be sorry, exaggerating a bit.

"I can judge the value myself. Why unfortunately?" he said.

"Otherwise obviously I would have gladly given you all the information we have. Any other confidential investigation you want to know about, since you're calling anyway?"

"I'll call you again in an hour."

His tone was abrupt. Evidently he did not appreciate my sarcasm. Didn't they have a sense of humor at *Aftonbladet*?

"You're more than welcome to contact me any time you—"

Christer Skoog had hung up.

SEVEN

Olivia pressed her finger against the blue-striped foam mattress. Blue had always been her favorite color. Not anymore. The thin mattress on the floor didn't even hold up her light body. She had to roll over all the time so it wouldn't hurt.

Besides the mattress, the only other things in the room were a desk and a Windsor chair. Not at all like her room at home with Mommy. The walls were worn, with peeling paint. She wondered who lived there when she and Daddy were not there. Probably no kids.

Daddy had been talking on the phone a long time now. He sounded angry.

She angled her head, but she still couldn't see whether the heater was turned on. She huddled up, trying to keep warm. She had made a little tunnel from the blanket that had become her own little hut. There she could hum quietly without Daddy hearing. Before she used to sing on top of the covers because it echoed so funnily in the room. She wouldn't dare do that now. Not when he was home.

Olivia had been clever and done well, she knew, because now Daddy was being nice. He had given her food and a bath, letting her bathe as long as she wanted in warm water. It had been scary in the bath. The water had turned red when Daddy scrubbed her. Like in a horror movie she had seen at a friend's house once. The friend's big sister had shown it to them when her parents were away. Olivia had hated horror films after that.

It stung a lot on her back and arms when she was in the bath, but that didn't matter. She just hoped that Daddy would keep being nice for a long, long time. But he had started drinking beer, and she knew that soon he would get mean and make a mess of the apartment. There were lots of beer cans everywhere, and he put his cigarette butts in them when they were empty. He coughed a lot when he smoked. Loudly. Olivia would start coughing too, because the smell was so strong. Once Olivia had opened a window to let out all the smoke. It had made Daddy furious. He'd hit her in the stomach and screamed that she must never go near the window.

Daddy had a friend. The quiet lady. She had been there two times and when she came she would throw away the beer cans and open the window. Olivia had seen that when she peeked out through the keyhole. The lady talked so quietly that Olivia could barely hear what she said, even though she put her ear against the door. Daddy said that Olivia had to stay in the bedroom and have the door closed while the lady was there, and she did as she was told. The quiet lady never came into the bedroom. She probably didn't want to see Olivia. She must have thought that Olivia was ugly. She was, too. She knew that because Daddy always said so.

Olivia wished her hair would dry. The pillow was so wet and cold from the water. Luckily she didn't have to wear the wig any more, the one the quiet lady had left. Daddy had hung it over the back of the chair by the desk. What if her friends at school had seen her in it? Some of the girls' mothers let them dye their hair, but Olivia wasn't allowed. She had to wait until she was fifteen, Mommy had said, which had made Olivia think that Mommy was the meanest person in the world. Olivia had always wanted to have blond hair. She didn't want that anymore, though. The quiet lady's wig had turned completely red and the strands of hair had clumped together strangely. She never wanted to look like that again. Besides, the wig was too big, and it itched. Daddy had taped it on the back of her neck with brown tape. It burned and stung when he pulled it off afterward. She never wanted to wear the wig again.

Olivia listened. Daddy was still talking on the phone. She gathered her courage and sneaked carefully up to the radiator that was on the wall below the window. Her whole body shivered when she touched the cold metal. The knob that controlled the heat was firmly in place but she turned it as far as she could and hurried back to get under the blanket again.

Even though Daddy had been nice and let her bathe in warm water, she was shivering with cold. She turned over on the mattress, but she had to lie a certain way so that it wouldn't hurt. She missed her teddy bear. Daddy had sprayed it and hung it up in the bathroom. She stood up as quietly as she could. It had gone well. She was clever. She could sneak like a cat. When she put on her socks and walked on tiptoe she didn't make a single sound. She didn't dare turn on the light until she had carefully closed the bathroom door — not too slowly, because then it creaked. The light blinded her when the bulb flicked on. The walls were white and made of shiny squares. She stood quietly awhile and listened, making sure that Daddy hadn't noticed anything. He was still talking.

Olivia looked at the clothesline above the bathtub. No teddy bear! Suddenly it was hard to breathe. She quickly scanned the room. Then she saw it. It had fallen down into the bathtub and was lying upside down with its legs against the edge. It was looking at her. She took the bear into her arms and hugged it as hard as she could. Then she heard Daddy speaking louder.

"Yes, I understand Swedish. I'm not completely...damn it!"

Not a sound. He must have hung up. Olivia cracked open the bathroom door. She couldn't see him anywhere, so she hurried into the bedroom, moving quickly and quietly. Just as she crept under the blanket with the teddy bear, Daddy opened the door. He had a big crease between his dark eyebrows. She knew what that meant. He was angry. Olivia crept even farther down under the blanket and peeked out with just one eye. He was searching around with his eyes as if he knew that she had done something that she wasn't supposed to.

"We're going to do it again, Olivia, you may as well know it now," he said.

Olivia tried to say something but could not. She was having a hard time breathing again. She couldn't make a sound. Her stomach hurt, too. Not like when she got hit, more like from inside. He had promised. Promised that it would only be the one time and then she would get to go home to Mommy.

She didn't want to cry, but she couldn't stop the tears from coming. She tried to hide it from Daddy. Normally she would have just looked down as much as possible, and then he wouldn't have noticed anything. But now she was lying down. She couldn't pretend to be sleeping, either, because then he would just come and shake her. She pressed the teddy bear hard against her body under the blanket.

"What have you got there?" said Daddy.

He came up to the mattress. Pulled off the blanket.

"What the —?"

He tore the teddy bear out of her arms. She wanted to scream at him to be careful, but she didn't dare.

"What have I said about this fucking teddy bear. You can have it the next time we work. Until then just leave it the fuck alone. Do you hear me?"

He stormed out of the room and into the bathroom. She heard the teddy bear thump down on the cold hard bathtub and then he started spraying it with the bottle again. The teddy bear's fur had already gone rumpled and stiff from the spray.

"Sorry, Daddy," she called.

Now you could hear that she was crying, even though she was trying not to show it. Maybe he hadn't heard that from the bathroom, though. She pulled the blanket up over her head and closed her eyes as she heard his steps approaching.

"Get up!" he said.

Olivia's whole body became rigid. She could barely breathe. When he sounded like that she didn't know what was going to happen. She wanted to do what he said, but she couldn't move.

"*Get up, I said!*" he shouted.

She tried to move, but now her whole body was shaking. She hated it when her body didn't do what she wanted. With one arm she lifted part of the blanket but when she tried to get her legs out they'd turned soft.

"Damn it, you're so slow."

Daddy took hold of the blanket and tore it away, then grabbed her arm and pulled her up from the mattress. Her arm made a strange sound. It cracked. Now she started crying even more, even though she didn't want to. He took hold of both her arms and shook her back and forth.

"I've told you that you can't have the teddy bear! Why the hell did you go and get it anyway?"

She didn't know what to say that wouldn't make him angrier. Nothing came out when she tried to talk. Something in her throat had swollen up, and her nose ran.

"It's because you're stupid. You can never have a stupid girl with you on a trip. Maybe you want me to leave you here alone?"

Olivia shook her head as hard as she could.

"Well, then that was the last time you do something you're not allowed to, do you get that? I don't have time to keep track of you all the time. As of now you will do exactly as I say and nothing else."

She could not think of anything except that she wanted him to let go of her arms, which had started aching. His hands were so hard. The cut on her shoulder was throbbing even more now. Something wet was seeping out from it too.

"Your sore is full of pus," said Daddy. "Wipe it off, for God's sake."

He let go of her arm. The tears stung her cheeks. Her eyes ached. She felt snot running down toward her mouth.

"Jesus, you're so disgusting! Gross!"

He pushed her down onto the mattress and went out. She pulled up the blanket and wiped her arm and the snot so she wouldn't be so disgusting. Now that Daddy was gone she could cry all she wanted, but no more tears came. She was so tired. Her body ached. She turned her head toward the wall to avoid seeing the lady's wig, which had fallen on the floor. It reminded her of everything that was scary. She closed her eyes and pretended that she was at home with Mommy.

EIGHT

The electric toothbrush emitted a buzzing, pulsating sound, signaling that I had completed the two minutes required to maintain good oral hygiene. I rinsed off the brush and spat out the foam. There was less risk of periodontitis with an electric toothbrush than an ordinary one, Peter maintained. I didn't care either way. I used the brush for the sake of domestic tranquillity. I refused to use the new toothpaste he insisted on, though. The husband of one of Peter's colleagues was a dental hygienist and had recommended a toothpaste made from herbs. It looked like liverwurst, tasted salty, and produced no foam. There was a limit to what I would put in my mouth. Now we each bought our own toothpaste.

I spat out the last of my mint-flavored Sensodyne super-blue gel with extra whitening and made sure all the foam drained away before I turned off the tap. I removed my makeup and went into the bedroom.

Peter was reclining under the covers with his computer on his lap. He didn't react when I came in. After combing my hair at the dressing table we had inherited from Peter's mother I got into bed, reaching for the light switch on the nightstand.

"I've found a few here that are probably worth looking at," Peter said.

I sighed inwardly. No matter how late it was, he always managed to find the energy to look at real estate ads. Our tiny five-room apartment on Allhelgonagatan in Södermalm was possibly a bit cramped, but living in the suburbs wasn't an option. Södermalm was always humming. The outdoor cafés and the parks in the summer gave the area an atmosphere you couldn't find anywhere else in Stockholm.

"A pretty big terrace out the back," he continued. "No southern exposure, but the price is reasonable. We should look at this one."

Looking at houses wasn't only remarkably boring, it was also completely pointless, because I didn't have the slightest intention of moving. Having to put up with a young brat in a pink shirt with slicked-back hair, who showed up in a brand-new BMW three minutes before the start of the showing, completely irritated me. The real estate agents were always poorly informed about the houses they were selling and referred you to the seller as soon as a question was asked. At best they knew whether the house had any damage, but in those cases they generally kept quiet about it unless they were asked a direct question. At a previous showing Peter had nagged me into attending I had pointed out some obvious water damage. The agent stood there like a fool and mumbled that the wallpaper was probably just a little discolored.

Despite all this, I went to the showings. I picked my battles with Peter.

"Mmm."

"I'll add it as a favorite on the computer in the guest room along with the other interesting showings so you can look at them later. It's in Spånga and has..."

I tuned out. I only used the desktop computer in the guest room at night, and for a completely different purpose. One night Peter had stuck his head into the guest room when I was in the middle of something. I had explained that I couldn't sleep so I'd gotten up to check a few real estate ads. He'd been happy with that response and had gone back to bed without any further questions.

"Can we turn out the light, do you think?" I said in a gentle voice.

Peter shut down the computer and turned off the bedside lamp on his side. He lay down close beside me with his arm around me. After only a minute or two his breathing became heavy. I never knew anyone else who fell asleep as quickly as he did.

I carefully moved his relaxed arm away and slipped out of bed. He never woke when I got up at night, but because he had just fallen asleep I was particularly cautious. He was completely unaware. If he suspected something, he never said anything.

I put on the champagne-colored terry cloth bathrobe he'd given me for Christmas last year. Moved soundlessly across the floor. By the dresser there was a spot where the wood always creaked. I stayed clear of it.

I had been looking forward to this all evening. Longed to flee into a world that was only concerned with the present. A place where I could feel the same rush I used to get at work, but which lately had become harder and harder to achieve.

A world of thrills.

Where everything around me disappeared.

NINE

I didn't get much sleep that night. As usual I had been so consumed that I didn't notice as the hours flew by. The morning at work went okay. The afternoon was harder. At the two o'clock break I knocked back three heavily sugared cups of coffee in a row to get the caffeine and sugar hit I needed to conduct the interview I was about to hold.

The woman who had been closest to the girl inside the bank hadn't been questioned at the scene. Reportedly she had been too overwrought to talk about what she had witnessed. For me that was just as well. If she had noticed anything that the other witnesses hadn't observed, I wanted to be the first to find out about it.

"Birgitta Rosenqvist," I called loudly.

As always there was a hodgepodge of people in reception. There were people waiting to be interviewed, making police reports, or applying for new passports, as well as some people sitting there just to warm up, and others simply for the security of being in a police station.

"Birgitta Rosenqvist!" I called again.

Louder this time.

Why were people always late? I took my phone out to check the time. The display showed that I had an unread message. I clicked on it and read, "I'm waiting."

"Over here!"

At the other end of the room an elderly woman with a shrill voice raised her hand, trying to get up from her chair. I quickly put the phone back in my pocket, went up, and greeted her.

"May I help you with your coat?"

I caught myself speaking with exaggerated politeness. The woman's elderly appearance seemed to warrant it.

"Thank you, that's very kind. I don't know whether to put on a fall coat or a winter coat when I go out at the moment. The weather is so unpredictable this time of year."

With the support of the cane that had been leaning alongside the chair she walked slowly behind me. She was breathing heavily and stopped to cough a couple of times along the way. That gave me time to answer the text message. Even though she was limping, she wore shoes with heels. Not particularly high, but still tall enough that they looked uncomfortable. A flowery scent of perfume floated along the corridor and made a couple of oncoming colleagues turn around and look at us.

I opened the door and turned on the light in the interview room.

"I never thought I would end up at the police station. Not at my age. But I'm glad I could come."

I had offered to hold the interview at her home, but she insisted on coming to the police station. Needed to get out of the house, she said.

I hung her black coat over the back of the chair in the interview room. Under it she had on an all-black pleated skirt and a black jacket. The only deviation colorwise was a flowery blouse and a red-beige-and-white silk scarf tied around her neck.

"Would you like something to drink? A cup of coffee perhaps?"

I had started to sound like a waiter at a nice restaurant.

"Oh, no thanks, it's much too late in the afternoon for that."

I noted the time for the sake of the written report: 3:13 p.m. It had taken thirteen minutes for us to make our way from reception to the interview room. I would need to start the interview immediately if I was going make it to day care on time.

"Birgitta, I want you to think back and in your own words tell me in as much detail as you can about what happened at the bank. After that I'll ask you a few questions."

Without answering me, Birgitta closed her eyes and sat quietly for a long time. I was astonished to see how much makeup she was wearing, despite her advanced age. A thick layer of foundation had settled in the folds of her face. She was wearing light pink lipstick, rouge on her cheeks, and her eyebrows were darkly painted. Apart from the lack of jewelry, she was the spitting image of an elderly upper-class lady.

She kept her eyes shut. Closing out immediate visual stimuli was good when you were trying to remember an incident. I used to be able to sit quietly for a long time and wait out interview subjects who for various reasons did not speak, but Birgitta had been silent an unusually long period. I was just about to say something when she started talking, her eyes still shut.

"I went into the bank to take out some money, as I always do on Mondays. I took a queue number and was about to go and sit down when…"

She fell silent, shaking her head slowly.

"The strange thing was…I didn't see the girl come in. Suddenly she was just standing there…right in front of me…just a few meters away. Heavens, she was completely covered in blood, the poor child."

Birgitta opened her eyes and frowned. She didn't seem to want to keep picturing the little girl.

"I thought I was seeing things. I looked around. Thought it was strange that no one reacted…I simply couldn't understand…it was like seeing…a ghost."

There was silence again. She looked blankly around the interview room.

"When I came to my senses I started walking toward the girl to help her, but then that voice started. I didn't know what to think…I understood that someone had already injured her and could do it again, exactly as he said. I was so afraid that something else would happen to that poor girl."

I made a note of what Birgitta was saying. She turned her eyes to mine.

"You don't forget when you see a child mistreated. I've never been involved with anything like it…And in broad daylight too. I don't know, it made the whole thing so…so macabre. Heavens. Could I please get a glass of water?"

"Of course. I'll leave you for a moment and get it."

I left the interview room. The lady was still very shaken. A child could truly stir up emotions. Of course, it was carefully thought out. With an injured, threatened child no one in the place had dared to try to stop the robbery.

The break room was dark and empty. Rain was running down the windowpanes. Autumn had definitely arrived. I poured a glass of water. When I came into the interview room again the old lady was holding a phone, tapping at the buttons. Unusual for a lady of her age.

"Did you have your phone with you at the bank?"

I set the water glass down on a napkin on the desk. She shook her head.

"My daughter gave it to me, but I rarely have it with me when I go out. Now I guess I've realized the value of it."

She pressed a few keys on the phone, which beeped with every tap.

"If only I understood all the functions on it. My daughter just sent one of those text messages to me. I'll try to call her as soon as I'm done here so she can meet me."

"It's good that you'll have company on the way home," I said.

"I've never needed help with anything before, but now I prefer not to go out by myself. Not even on Karlavägen, where I always felt so at home."

She looked down.

"To think that the world has become so...so..."

I handed her a tissue. Birgitta took off her glasses and let them hang on a cord around her neck. Dabbed the tissue below her eyes, careful not to disturb her makeup.

"I understand that it must be difficult for you to talk about this, but your information is extremely important to us, primarily because the child is involved."

I wanted to shift the focus from the woman's own fears. If they took over it would be more difficult to get the information I needed.

"Oh, yes, of course. The poor girl must be taken care of. I'll be all right, don't worry."

She put the phone into her handbag with lightly shaking hands. Her fingers were wrinkled. The nails painted with a light-pink nail polish. Although her skin color was uneven and pigmented, I could clearly see light circles around her ring finger and the index finger on her left hand. She must have seen me looking at her hands.

"I don't dare have my wedding ring on anymore. What if I got robbed? I remember my husband proposing to me like it was yesterday. He was unusually romantic. Got down on his knees, of course. I was on cloud nine. What a marvelous marriage we had. He was so kind to me, he didn't drink and he was never violent."

Women didn't have high expectations back then. As long as the guy didn't booze or hit you, then...

"How I loved that man. I still do. If only he hadn't passed away so soon. But you know, men are so much weaker than us. They quickly become frail when they get older."

I sat quietly, trying to work out the best way to get her back on track.

"Of course they're weaker. My husband had the flu a week ago, and you've never seen anything more pitiful," I said.

Of course it was insensitive to compare the flu with her husband's passing, but I was starting to get tired of the woman, and I needed her to focus on the robbery. It was sink or swim.

"Oh, yes, and then they're very happy to have a strong woman to take care of them."

She smiled and reached for another tissue, excusing herself politely before she blew her nose. My tactic had worked.

"Birgitta, I need you to describe the little girl in as much detail as possible."

"The voice said that she was seven, but I thought she looked younger. She was so small and thin. Her skin was quite pale, the poor girl. Blond hair, but I could see she was wearing a wig. The kind of thing you need when you get to my age."

A wig. None of the other witness had mentioned that. It didn't seem to have been spotted on the surveillance video either. I refrained from writing that down on the interview report. Perhaps the old lady was a little confused.

"And then she was so horridly covered with blood. I don't understand who would want to harm such a little..."

"Did you see where the blood came from?"

"It was probably from her wounds."

"Could you see that she had wounds?"

"Dear, it's obvious she must have had wounds. Where else would the blood have come from?"

It was always hard to get witnesses to understand the difference between what might have happened and what they had actually seen. The brain has a way of putting together familiar images and events to create context that is often misleading. A person might believe they'd witnessed a series of actions, when in reality their brain had just joined together various remembered images to create a unified picture, and he or she had really not seen all the parts of the event, but only assumed it had occurred a certain way. The lady had seen blood and therefore assumed the girl had wounds, even though she hadn't seen any.

"Okay. Do you remember what the wounds looked like?"

"I guess they were ordinary wounds."

"Could you describe them?"

"Dear, I'm sure you know what a wound looks like. Like when you cut yourself?"

"Did it look as though she had cut herself?"

"Not her. He must have done it."

"Who?"

"The man who talked on the tape. He must have cut her so that she was bleeding so terribly. Heavens, how awful that was."

I didn't want to give the lady any more elbow room. To avoid her raising more loose assumptions I needed to ask her about something specific. Something she should be able to answer without guessing.

"You said that the girl was bloody."

"It was so terrible. Her whole —"

"Can you describe the blood on the girl's body?"

I wanted to know whether Birgitta had noticed anything in particular about the blood—if it was light red and fresh, a congealed dark red, or something else.

"Red."

"Did you notice what shade of red it was?"

"No, heavens, I can't think about something like that. It was bad enough having to see all that blood on a little child. We women are used to seeing blood, of course. We've had to put up with it every month, ever since our teens. But seeing blood on a little girl like that. That was completely...completely awful... terrible."

She stopped. Few people were comfortable talking about blood. Plodding on about it wasn't necessary.

"She didn't have any clothes on, either. Goodness, how cold she must have been."

"Do you remember whether she was carrying anything?"

The lady looked up at the wall while she thought.

"She was hugging something...a stuffed animal...yes, that was it. I wonder if it wasn't a teddy bear. Pretty battered, I seem to recall."

"Did it have any specific characteristics? Some markings perhaps, or a brand?"

Birgitta shook her head.

"It was an ordinary brown teddy bear. But I remember that there was blood on it."

I had already instructed the investigators to search for possible purchasing locations as soon as they got detailed information about the teddy bear, but in the present situation there was no point. A brown teddy bear could be acquired at any toy store, anywhere.

"Was that all she had with her?"

"She had a tape player too. Not one of those old transistor radios we had when I was young, no, this was a neat little thing. Fascinating that so much sound can come out of such a little..."

"What kind of sound came out?"

"It was a man, claiming to speak for the girl, as it were. He spoke as if the words were coming from her. He had a Finnish accent, I remember that clearly. Finnish-Swedish, which usually sounds so lovely, but what he said sounded so awful. Then there was another person who also came in at the end of the tape or...I may have been mistaken. We were forced to do exactly as he said, anyway, otherwise the girl would..."

She fell silent.

"What?" I said.

The lady has fixed her eyes on the wall by the side of the desk.

"Birgitta!" I said firmly.

"Yes, I'm sorry. What was it?"

"What would happen to the girl if you didn't do what the voice said?"

"She would..."

Tears started running down Birgitta's cheeks. She let them run unchecked and said quietly, "It was lucky my husband didn't have to be part of this. You know, he's no longer with us, but in some ways he is still present."

"Okay, Birgitta. I want to thank you so much for telling about your observations."

"I'm happy if I've been of any help. May I ask? Have you found the little girl?"

"Unfortunately we haven't, not yet. We're working on it."

"The poor child. I hope she's found," she said, drying her cheeks with the napkin. "Her parents must be beside themselves with worry. We're lucky that the police are around to take care of this sort of thing."

I got up and helped the old woman with her coat. The walk back through the corridors to reception felt like ten kilometers. I walked faster now – I didn't have time to take thirteen minutes to see her off. She hobbled along after me as fast as she could.

"Thanks so much for coming, Birgitta. Take care now. Please call your daughter. It's good to have family near you after an incident like this."

"Thank you so kindly. You police are doing an amazing job. The things that you're forced to deal with…"

"It's no problem, Birgitta. It's our job."

I left Birgitta feeling a sense of relief. If I'd known she had no more information than that I would have turned the interview over to the other investigators. My body had itched with frustration having to sit and listen to her digressions. The interview had been necessary, though, as she might have made some important observation. But besides some uncertain information about another voice on the tape, and a wig, there was nothing new.

TEN

Christer Skoog had been trying for months to get an interview with the prostitute, without result. But now, the day after the prosecutor closed the preliminary investigation of the politicians, she had made contact with him voluntarily. He understood why. Even if many thought the decision by the prosecutor not to indict the men for buying sex was wrong, some had also been critical of the woman who had made the allegations, saying that she was a gold-digger who had made the whole thing up.

"Why would I want to publish your version now, Dina? The story has gone cold," said Christer.

He had been sitting in an editorial meeting when she called and had been close to declining the call. When she said her name on the phone, though, he had literally run out of the conference room. Now he was in the bathroom, to avoid being disturbed by loud colleagues. He was still eager for the interview, but the power dynamic between them was reversed now that she was the one who'd called him. It was in his interests to seem a little reluctant. If he appeared skeptical, she would presumably try harder to convince him of the value of her story, and perhaps be more willing to give out detailed information.

"It's so frustrating that they won't even be indicted. I want to tell everyone what pigs they are," she said.

That she had turned to him in particular was an obvious choice, since he was the one at *Aftonbladet* who reported on the incident initially. He agreed with her that the truth about the politicians should come out and was thrilled that now she'd finally let herself be interviewed.

"I understand, but it's a little late. I've been looking for you for months for an interview. Ever since you made the police report."

"What if you're allowed to use my name and picture?"

Now they were starting to get somewhere. Christer heard her puff on a cigarette as she was talking.

"I'll need new information too. It won't work to publish old leftovers. You'll have to be prepared to give details. Intimate details."

"As long as I don't look like a publicity-hungry gold-digger. Can we meet tomorrow?"

"Sure. Where would suit you?"

He let her decide the location for purely selfish reasons. It was important that she was in an environment where she felt comfortable revealing sensitive details.

"Rival, at Maria Square. Three o'clock tomorrow."

He nodded to himself and ended the call. Finally!

ELEVEN

Five DVDs of surveillance video were sitting in my in-tray when I arrived at work the next morning, all marked with the Image and Audio Analysis Group's label. I turned on the radio, opened the desk drawer, and was about to toss in the DVDs when Claes knocked on my open door.

"Surveillance from the robbery?" he asked, looking at my hand.

I'd already started to shut the drawer and saw no point in stopping. I had no intention whatsoever of looking at the footage of the robbery with Claes breathing down my neck.

"Go ahead, put it on. I want to see," he said, stepping in.

I slowly opened the drawer again and picked out one of the disks. On the radio news broadcast they were talking about the robbery. A psychologist was being interviewed about the possibility of children committing criminal acts.

"My computer has been on the blink lately," I said.

The screen was completely dark. You couldn't tell that it was switched on, because I had put the computer itself under the desk. I had removed the usual screensaver with the police logo long ago. Seeing the emblem float around on the screen only irritated me. I leaned down under the desk, realizing that Claes was looking at me from behind. He could look all he wanted. It wasn't going to go beyond that. I pressed the power button, so that the computer actually turned off instead of on. Claes didn't seem to notice the difference.

The child psychologist on the radio was speculating that the girl had been coerced into committing the crime, and that she had likely been traumatized by the event.

"Have you interviewed the witness who was standing closest to the girl inside the bank?" said Claes.

Before I had time to answer my phone buzzed on the desk.

"Excuse me, Claes," I said.

I heard Anette's voice through the receiver.

"Leona, a man who won't give his name wants to talk with you. I'll transfer the call."

I waited. There was silence on the line.

"Hello?" I said.

Someone was there — I could hear them breathing on the other end of the line. I pushed the phone closer to my ear to hear better.

"I know."

The deep male voice said the words quietly. Almost whispering. The voice was familiar, very familiar, but I couldn't place it. The man hung up. I looked at Claes and shook my head.

"No one there."

"Are you getting the video started?" he said, looking at the black screen. "And what did you say about the witness inside the bank?"

"The woman has been interviewed, but there was nothing new," I said.

"Claes, do you have a moment?" said Fredrik as he passed by in the corridor.

"Use my computer to check the video if you can't get yours started," Claes said to me, going out to Fredrik.

In the doorway he turned around.

"And keep me informed about what's going on in the case. The bosses higher up are pressuring me about this."

When Claes left I turned on the computer again. The news announcer on the radio ended the interview and started reading the weather report. I took a gulp from the water glass on the desk.

Tried to remember why I recognized that voice.

TWELVE

Christer Skoog was sitting at Rival on Maria Square with an espresso. He had already decided how he would structure the interview with Dina. He knew she wanted to talk so he would be able to lean back a little. Just be sure not to interrupt her. Normally he would have chosen a table by the window, but for Dina's sake he chose a seat toward the back. The cloudy gray sky and subdued lighting made the place seem dark. He took a candleholder with a tea light from the next table and set it on the one where he was sitting. He'd already had two espressos. Maybe he would have time for one more before she came.

Christer hadn't seen Dina since she had testified in another prostitution trial three years earlier. He was actually not particularly fond of people in the lower social strata. He thought they were mostly whiners who saw themselves as victims instead of doing something about their situation. Admittedly he himself came from an academic family, but his father had died when Christer was young and he had grown up with only his mom for support, and had a very tough time in school besides. Despite that he'd managed to pull himself together, caught up on what he had missed, and hadn't asked for any help from society. It was an example for others to emulate, he thought. Dina, for example.

Dina moved in the lowest level of society but to some degree she impressed him anyway. During the hearing in the case three years ago she had spoken clearly, in a steady voice, and hadn't hesitated on any details, even though the defense attorney had done everything in his power to make her lose her composure. That alone made her unusual. She was well dressed, besides, and appeared conscientious. When the defense attorney had asked what kind of work she did, she had answered, "Sex worker," without any embarrassment. She had said then that she wanted to quit but didn't have any opportunities to get alternative work. Dina had stated clearly that she did not abuse any form of drug, neither alcohol nor narcotics. On the contrary, she drank lots of herbal tea and always asked her customers to buy her a cup before it was time, otherwise there wouldn't be any "action," as she had put it. Her open, humorous manner had succeeded in getting both the judge and jurors to smile. That was the first day in court.

The second day, though, she had been completely different. Taciturn, barely answering the questions she was asked, and even retracting several of the statements she had made the day before. The prosecutor had become very worried and tried to get the court to realize that something strange had happened since the previous day. It had been so obvious that the prosecutor even asked flat out if someone or something had influenced her to change her testimony. When Dina answered no, the defense attorney had almost rubbed his hands with glee. Naturally no one was particularly surprised when the bank official was acquitted. Few were convicted of paying for sex if they were not caught in the act. The class difference between those involved did not make it any easier.

It was now a quarter past four. Was Dina just late?

When the accusations of paying for sex against the minister for finance, the minister for foreign affairs, and the finance commissioner became public, all three had been forced to take a break from politics. Coming back would probably be impossible for them after Christer had published Dina's version.

He picked up his phone. Entered Dina's number. She answered immediately.

"I'm sick. Can't come."

He heard nothing in her voice that had changed since yesterday's conversation to hint at any sort of illness.

"We can meet tomorrow instead," said Christer.

"I'll probably be sick then, too," Dina said.

How can you know that? thought Christer. If she didn't see so many customers maybe she would be able to get herself out of the squalor instead of diving deeper.

"I can come to your place instead, and then you won't have to go out in the cold," said Christer.

"I have nothing more to say other than what I told the police before."

"But, what…? You were the one who wanted to meet me!"

"There's no point in meeting."

She hung up. Damn it! She had seemed so determined the day before. This made it even more important for him to speak with her. He just didn't know how to make that happen. According to his sources she had no permanent address, but moved around among friends instead. If he could just see her he was convinced that he could get her to talk. If there was anyone who could get a legal action against these big shots, it was her.

He couldn't back off now. Felt uneasy just thinking about all the years of anxiety the finance minister had caused him. Christer could not tolerate the fact that a bully who became a person who bargained and paid for sex with prostitutes was one of the most powerful figures in Sweden. He couldn't stand the fawning, well-polished smile that appeared as soon as he knew he was on camera. He had been waiting for an opportunity like this to put Nino in jail for years. It was unlikely he would ever get a better chance than this again. It had to happen now. He needed to quickly produce more information about the case. As luck would have it, he had a trump card he'd been saving for a while.

Now was the right moment to use it.

THIRTEEN

My eyes were drawn to a large, framed photograph on the wall inside the dog handler's office. It depicted a German shepherd sitting at a firing range, wearing a police cap on its head and carrying a medal in its mouth.

The place looked more like a changing room than an office. There were cabinets along one wall, and hangers with leashes and other equipment. Farther in was a glassed-in room with four desks. Like most other departments they'd had to move recently and were now located not far from reception. The room was empty. Evidently everyone was out on assignment.

"He was my absolute best."

I turned around. Robert Granlund was standing behind me, looking up at the photo.

"He's been in dog heaven since last spring."

"That's too bad," I said.

I put my hand under my hair and lightly massaged my neck. The hours in front of the computer at the office last night had given me a tension headache. Peter's tone had been curt when I called at midnight and said I had to work late and would have to sleep over in one of the squad's break rooms.

"I just about cried myself to death, you know. He was my soul mate. Better than a woman. It was love until death did us part."

I understood what he meant. As a child I had loved animals. Wanted a pet, but my parents wouldn't let me have one. They said I wasn't capable of taking care of an animal. That I was cruel to them. One time I had sneaked an injured young bird into the house by wrapping it in my cap and hiding it inside my jacket. I was punished, of course.

"Would you like a cup?"

Robert went over to the coffee machine that was found in every break room in the agency.

"Thanks, I don't have time to stay. I just wanted to hear what ideas you had about my case."

Robert had a worried look in his eyes.

"Right, that. The dogs behaved extremely strangely. They mostly wandered around without picking up any trace. The first handler was on the scene just fifteen minutes after the alarm came in so the dog should have found something, either via tracks or airborne scent. Because the girl clearly was naked and bloody, the whole thing is really strange. I'm almost starting to suspect…"

"Leona Lindberg, is that you?"

I turned around. A young patrol officer stood in the doorway.

"A guy was just here and left this note in reception. Said it was for you. I heard you were here."

She handed over a folded piece of paper with my name on it. It was torn from an ordinary lined college notebook and held together with a piece of tape.

"He wouldn't say who he was. Looked to be between eighteen and twenty. Short, brownish-black hair, slender, about 175 centimeters tall, black clothes."

I unfolded the paper. When I saw what it said I quickly got up and started running out toward reception.

"Thanks, Robbie, I'll be in touch later," I called from the corridor.

I tore open the door to reception and ran outside, my eyes scanning up and down the street. An elderly woman on the other side of the road was hauling a floral shopping bag on wheels behind her. A girl with an unruly puppy tugging on the leash was at the crosswalk farther up. Down by the park by City Hall, I saw a guy who matched the description. He cut quickly down toward the park. I ran after him, but he had a good head start. By the time I got to the park he was gone. I could no longer see him, so I stopped. Looked around. Silhouettes of people, the dark-green trees, and the lights from cars driving on the street next to the park. I was about to give up when suddenly I saw him go into an entrance far down on Scheelegatan. I ran toward the building and tore open the door. A narrow passage led up to a large darkened room with a short counter along the left side. In the room row after row of computer screens were set up. In front of every computer were young guys with headphones on. The only person standing up was the guy behind the counter. He too was staring at a flat screen. No one appeared to have just come into the place and thrown themselves down in front of a computer to blend in. I went over. Showed my badge.

"Where's the young guy who just came in here?"

The guy did not raise his eyes but instead stared in concentration at his computer screen and briefly shrugged.

"Only young guys come in here."

"But damn it, he just came in. Where did he go?"

The guy looked up with tired red eyes. He was probably high. He nodded toward a narrow staircase on the other side of the room. I ran up the stairs. The staircase was covered with wall-to-wall carpet, which dampened the sound. The room one flight up looked similar to the one below. Lots of computers in long rows. Pale boyish faces with dead eyes staring into the flickering screens. From the bluish-white light from the computers it was impossible to differentiate between them. Besides, I had only seen the guy from behind. They all seemed to have dark clothing on. I gave up. It wasn't worth turning the place upside down to find a snot-nosed teenager. If the guy wanted something from me, he would be in touch again. I went downstairs and out on the street. For the first time in a long while I felt really old. Was this how young people occupied themselves all day and night? I took the paper out of my pocket and unfolded it again.

I know something that you want to know

The text was handwritten; tilted and a little sprawling. A young man's handwriting.

What did he want?

FOURTEEN

When I got back to the agency, I could see from a distance that someone had set something on my keyboard. I walked into the office, unbuttoning my jacket. Another note. Handwritten in pencil on lined paper from a college notebook. The same sprawling handwriting as before.

I know

I looked out into the corridor. I had always known that security at the police station was poor. They were always trying to improve the systems so that unauthorized people couldn't get in. Staff usually had reasonably good knowledge of who was moving around in the building. At least you generally kept track of your own corridor. Plus nowadays everyone was required to wear their badge or ID plainly visible outside their clothing while inside the building. People from outside had to sign for a visitor ID on entry. So who had managed to get into my office? My thoughts were interrupted by the ringing of the phone on my desk. I looked at the display. Blocked number.

"Violent Crimes, Leona Lindberg."

"You got the message. Meet me at Norrtullsgatan 19 in an hour."

The caller hung up. It was the same familiar voice as earlier. I'd heard it before, more than once. If only I could place it.

We didn't have a tradition of practical jokes in our squad, but I couldn't be sure it wasn't something like that. There were probably a couple of officers who would think of something like this as a joke. Still, I was too curious not to go. Perhaps the person had information about the girl robbery.

I went slowly out into the corridor. Looked around. Empty. I took a turn past the administration office to check that it was staffed. Anette was sitting in her office and looked out when I went past. So that it didn't look as if I was snooping around I asked whether the report I was expecting from the forensics lab had arrived. Anette shook her head.

"No mail for you at all today."

"Okay. By the way, Anette, I'm going out to interview a witness. It may drag on so I probably won't be coming back at all this afternoon."

Anette nodded. I headed back toward my office and ran into Claes in the corridor.

"Claes, have you seen anyone go past my office recently?"

"I just came back from lunch," said Claes. "What do you mean, has there been an unauthorized person in here?"

"I'm sure it's just someone who's trying to play a joke. I already see a suspect."

I laughed and pointed at Fredrik, who had opened the glass door at the far end of the corridor. He would never do anything of the sort, but I didn't want to worry Claes unnecessarily. Claes smiled and went into his office.

I looked at the note again. Someone had taken a risk to enter the police station, through the locked, alarmed doors, and leave the note for me. Or more likely, they had managed to pay a cleaning person, mail carrier, or someone else to put it in my office.

I decided to drive early to the address, stay in the car, and see who was standing there. If it was another officer playing a joke I could drive away and act as if nothing had happened. But somehow I knew that this was not a joke.

It was nearly one-thirty—time to go. To be on the safe side, I put on a bulletproof vest. I had my service pistol with me as always.

Even though it was no longer lunchtime, there was still a lot of traffic. Sveavägen was packed with cars. I turned left on Odengatan up toward Odenplan, parking a short distance away on Surbrunnsgatan. I positioned myself so I had a view of the meeting place. Waited. And waited. A lot of people went past, but no one stopped.

I had a creepy feeling.

Something wasn't right.

After sitting there for more than fifteen minutes without seeing anyone I recognized, I got out of the car. Presumably the person was sitting in another car in the vicinity waiting for me to show myself. I locked the car and started walking toward Norrtullsgatan. As I approached, a man came up behind me.

"Leona."

The same voice as on the phone. I turned around. A man aged about thirty-five or forty with longish, dark-blond hair was walking beside me. He was wearing a dark-green parka and jeans. I looked at him. I had no idea who he was.

"Christer Skoog, journalist," he said without stopping.

It was him. One of the journalists who kept calling and terrorizing me about the girl robbery. I suddenly became irritated, almost furious. I had set aside my work to play cat and mouse with a persistent journalist who had thought of a new tactic.

"If this is your new way of trying to get information about the girl robbery you can forget — "

"Knock it off, Leona! You're the one who's going to get information. Information that I know you will be extremely interested in. We can talk in your car."

Without looking to see whether I was following he turned around and started quickly walking back. His confidence made me even more suspicious. I didn't like his tone, either. It wasn't impossible that he had managed to sniff out something about the investigation that I didn't know; journalists were good at nosing around where they didn't belong. But why did he want to give the information to me this way?

"So you were the one who bribed some snot-nosed kid to leave notes for me at the station. Is that *Aftonbladet*'s new strategy?"

"You don't answer the phone or email," he said. "This worked."

I had no desire to play into his hands. At the same time I wanted to find out what this was about. I walked a couple of meters behind him back to the car. I didn't want to be seen walking with a journalist. That wouldn't look good. Someone might get the idea that I was leaking information to the press.

"Drive!" he said as soon as we were sitting in the car.

"Who the hell do you think I am, your private chauffeur?"

He didn't answer. I didn't like him dictating the conditions but I let him have his way and started driving north, out of the city. We drove past Karolinska Hospital and out toward Haga Park. Neither of us said a word. I glanced at him. He mostly sat staring straight ahead. I noted his laptop case, which he held tightly between his legs on the floor in front of him. At an empty parking lot at Haga Garden I drove in. Turned off the engine.

"I hope you have a damned good reason why I've devoted my valuable work time and taxpayers' money driving you around in a police car. If you'd hoped to get to ride in a marked car I'm sorry to have disappointed you."

He didn't reply.

"What was your name again?" I asked.

"I must've left more messages than anyone else on your voice mail in the past few days, so it's strange that you don't remember the name. Christer Skoog."

"You'll have to excuse me, but you actually aren't the only journalist who calls me. You're swarming around me like flies."

Christer picked up the laptop case from the floor. He took out a folder, from which he pulled out a photograph. It showed me walking on a sidewalk in the city. I raised my eyebrows.

"I see, you've taken a picture of me when I'm out walking? Flattering. Your hand seems to have been a little shaky, because it's not very sharp, but otherwise, a completely okay picture. I looked good in that coat, by the way."

I was trying to be funny, but in reality the whole thing was starting to become unpleasant. He didn't say anything, he just watched me. This did not seem to be about information that would add anything to the investigation.

"Honestly," I continued. "I got up early this morning and I'm starting to feel really tired. If this is all you have then you'll have to excuse me, but I have more important things to do than play spot-the-difference with a journalist."

"You know very well where that picture was taken," he said.

His voice was calm. That worried me. I pretended to look at the picture more carefully. You could see the Östermalm Food Hall in the background farther away.

"It's me taking a walk on Nybrogatan in Östermalm. Where are you going with this?"

He took out another picture. The picture showed me stepping through a doorway.

"I'm probably going into a store or something."

I did not like where this was headed. Christer took out yet another photograph from the folder. Now my mouth was starting to feel dry. When he took out another photo, showing three people in a car, my whole body turned cold. Where the hell did he get hold of that? I stared at the photograph. There was no doubt that I was the one sitting in the passenger seat. At the wheel sat a man and in the backseat a small, dark-haired girl could be seen. It was dark inside the car and the picture was grainy, but a trained eye would easily see that it was the same girl as the seven-year-old who had robbed SEB. Christer Skoog knew.

I couldn't produce a sound.

My heart was pounding.

I swallowed.

Sucked in air and pressed it down into my lungs. I tried feverishly to work out how to handle the situation. I had only seconds to decide on a strategy. Should I threaten him? I was the one carrying a gun after all. But I would still never be rid of the knowledge that he could release the information that he was now showing me at any time. I rejected that option. He was not some Joe Average you could threaten in any old way. With a journalist it was much too risky—he could do far greater damage. There was no point in flatly denying it either. I breathed in. And out. Slowly, gaining a little strength and calmness. Without looking at him I said quietly, "What do you want?"

"Information."

I was surprised. I had expected he was after money. I looked at him with raised eyebrows and he repeated, "Information. About the Hooker Affair."

"What? I'm not investigating that case. It's not even in my squad. I don't know anything about it."

"Then you'll have to find out. I want to know what happened in that investigation, and what is required to put those big shots away. You can reach me here."

He handed over a business card. I took it reluctantly. He smiled.

"It looks like you'll be the one chasing me on the phone from now on, Leona. I'll expect the first call in a few days. If I don't hear from you then I'll assume you think it's okay that the information I have here goes to press before next weekend. I'm convinced that your bosses and your family would find this information very interest—"

"I get it, asshole. Get out of my car!"

I was suddenly furious. Couldn't even look at him.

"I'm not getting out here. You'll have to drive me into town again."

"*Out!*"

I heard myself scream. I seldom had such outbursts. But now—now everything was at risk of being destroyed. I had planned this for far too long to let a lousy journalist mess it up for me. If he did not get out of the car fast enough, I would draw my weapon. Aim it at his head. Without hesitating. I couldn't stand this idiot.

He opened the door and got out. I stepped hard on the accelerator, making the car jerk forward and the door slam shut. I spun around, the gravel spraying up and hitting the underside of the car, and then I tore off down the highway. In the rearview mirror I saw Christer Skoog hold up his phone and shake it back and forth in the air. Fucking idiot! How the hell did he get hold of that information!

I turned off at the next exit and stopped the car. I didn't want to admit to myself that I was really shaken. I had counted on someone suspecting something.

But not so soon.

And not a journalist, of all people.

It was the worst possible scenario.

Still, it would have served no purpose to play dumb. Christer seemed much too bloodthirsty. I could not risk him publishing the pictures or reporting me. Too much was at stake.

The question was, how the hell was I going to get hold of information about the politicians' case? Officers on different squads didn't talk to each other about their investigations. And what if I got hold of the information? How great were the risks of giving it out? I would be the kind of police officer that everyone despised.

A leak.

Leaking information that other officers had fought hard to bring in was worse than committing a crime. You no longer stood behind the force and its values. You were a rat, a traitor. Of lower standing than a crook.

I closed my eyes and took a deep breath. Would everything fall apart now? Now, when I had finally started to be true to myself. Now, when I had finally realized that the existence I had been striving toward for so long was not a real life. That I was not free. Not alive. That I was trapped instead inside daily schedules, patterns, routines.

It was a jail without bars.

Should I retreat, get back in line again, act like everyone else, and endure the tedium of everyday life? No, that wouldn't work. I couldn't live that way. Just as I had created my own schedule-driven life, I had also started the journey out of it. I owed myself this. No one else could do it for me. But who would be hurt along the way? I pictured my family. My job. My reputation. I risked losing everything. I wanted to get away from it, but not like this. Not by being exposed.

With clenched teeth and fists I tried to halt the fluid that spilled out from underneath my still-shut eyelids. Negative thoughts whirled around in my head. I had to turn them around. I had to. Now! It wouldn't do to sit here and feel sorry for myself. That wouldn't help anyone. I told myself to get a grip. Blinked away the tears and opened my eyes. Had to start thinking clearly. I knew one thing. Whatever I thought or did, I couldn't go back now.

Everything was already in motion.

The die was cast.

FIFTEEN

Deep down I had probably always known that an average life would be impossible to maintain. That I couldn't cope with living within the confines of normality.

For years I had struggled, repressing the real me. I would wake up in a cold sweat, feeling as if a noose was tugging at my neck. I was caught in my self-created, structured world. But it was no longer possible to ignore who I was. Once I started to question my own desire to be like other people, everything became clear. Then there was no longer any choice.

I had to be free.

I didn't make the decision until I was thirty-two years old. I would stop fighting it. Stop striving to be like other people. Only then, finally, did life have real meaning. But suddenly I was faced with a new challenge. I needed to learn to live without being able to lean against everything that was conditioned, accustomed, structured. I would be forced to risk a lot to get where I wanted. To make difficult, daring decisions. From that moment on, I began to grope my way toward existence.

I was a newcomer in an unfamiliar world.

My own.

A week had passed since the robbery. It was seven-thirty. Half an hour earlier than I usually got to work in the morning. I went in through the long, grand entry in the older part of the police station, which had been preserved during the renovations.

Everything looked different now. Distant, somehow. I felt like I was being observed. By someone who knew that I never really had been one of them.

That I didn't belong here.

That I shouldn't be allowed in.

The guards who always sat by the entrance to the security passage looked at me for longer than usual. Or was that an illusion? I swiped my card to open the security passage. The first door opened. I went in and it closed behind me. It would take a few seconds before the next door opened. It always did. Several seconds passed. Nothing happened. Everything was quiet. Silent. I felt as if my ears were blocked. A vacuum. I could feel a faint pressure inside my head that was increasing. Drilling itself in. Then came a sound. A very high and distinctive sound. I put my hands up to my ears to muffle it. Opened my mouth to try to force air down into my lungs. I felt the blood rushing to my head. My forehead and cheeks were hot. I couldn't get any air, and the sound was insufferably loud now. I turned around. Saw the guards sitting with their backs to me. Went closer to the glass to make them aware that something was wrong with the passage. Suddenly the door opened on the other side. I quickly stepped out. Into the corridor. Into the inner courtyard.

Stopped.

Breathed.

Hyperventilated.

I tried to take long, deep breaths. To calm down. I must remember to report that the security passage needed to be inspected.

I continued toward the escalators, through the corridor and into the elevator up to the squad office. I positioned myself with my back to the mirror. To avoid looking at myself.

Even though I was walking quickly I was experiencing everything in slow motion. A colleague came toward me in the corridor and opened his mouth, but no sound came out. Had I lost my hearing? I think I said "Good morning," but I couldn't be sure. I arrived at my office. Remained standing in the doorway. The room looked empty. Soulless. As if I had already left it for good. I went up to the window. Opened it. Closed my eyes and breathed right out into the nothingness. The cool air rushed deep down into my lungs and balanced me. I had to pull myself together.

With closed door and drawn curtains I put the first disk of the surveillance footage into the computer. Even though the police who had been first on the scene hadn't been able to identify the girl on the video, I needed to reassure myself that no details could lead to me. I couldn't afford to make any mistakes now.

I sat up straight in the chair. Opened my eyes wide. Forced myself to concentrate. The first image I got up was from a camera angled above the entrance and aimed at the door to the bank. The image quality from surveillance cameras usually varies considerably, and I had seen both better and worse. The image was in color, but grainy and choppy because of the inadequate frame rate. A clock in the upper left-hand corner showed the time.

A few people went in and out of the bank. Mostly elderly people, as I had expected. Not many younger people went to the bank these days. The timing had been carefully chosen. Some senior citizens had the habit of waiting in the morning by the locked doors outside stores and banks, so right at the ten o'clock opening time would not have been a good choice. Not too close to lunchtime, either. I skipped forward a little. The people were moving quickly across the screen. From that angle I could see a short distance out onto the sidewalk. As always on Nybrogatan the cars were parked very close together. The girl had been instructed to walk as close to them as possible the short way she had to go to and from the bank. Then she was less noticeable.

When the doors opened I could see more of the outside. I was struck by the gloominess and darkness. Autumn was the worst time of year, with the long, dark winter waiting just around the corner. In this situation, though, autumn was my friend. Gray, rainy weather was a prerequisite to the whole thing being carried out. If it had been sunny I would have been forced to cancel everything and wait a day or two. But the weather that Monday had been as gloomy as usual in autumn.

The passersby wore light coats, huddled against the wind and rain. They held on to their umbrellas and angled them downward so they would not be bent back by the wind. People looked down at the ground as they walked quickly past. They only wanted to get from place to place as quickly as possible, not looking at anyone or stopping for anything. No one would notice a girl in a black rain cape walking past on the street.

There she was. When the doors to the bank opened again the girl was standing there. It was strange to see her that way. Judging by her appearance and posture she looked closer to five than seven. She was very slender, and she was hugging the teddy bear. I paused the video and sat with my head bent down and my hands against my forehead. I squeezed my eyes together as hard as I could, as if that would make everything disappear.

The girl looked so vulnerable.

What had I subjected a child to?

The whole thing was surreal. I had watched many surveillance videos at work, of fistfights, knifings, rapes — even murder. But nothing like this. I was seeing strange images in my mind. I saw myself there, as a little girl.

I got up and walked back and forth around my office, drinking from the bottle of mineral water that was on the desk. I had to pull myself together.

I knew.

It wasn't real.

It wasn't me.

And the girl was not injured.

But everything looked so realistic, with wounds and the blood, that even I almost believed it.

After a few deep breaths I sat down again. Browsed through the other disks. Searched for a camera that showed the whole place from inside. Preferably with the girl in front. The videos weren't labeled by camera angle, which meant that everything took even more time than I had thought it would. I looked at the clock. Ten minutes left until the morning meeting. I had to be there.

To keep up appearances.

In went another disk. Same procedure. This camera showed the angle seen from one of the tellers. From there I could look out over almost the entire floor inside the bank. The queue ticket dispenser. The windows. The big potted plants. The chairs for waiting customers. Everything. I skipped ahead to 10:37:40. The girl came in. Positioned herself in the middle of the floor. I tried to see her face. The camera angle was better but the image was still grainy and choppy. The backlight from the windows behind made the girl's front side dark, which I had been counting on. Just as planned, she positioned herself right under one of the spotlights that lit up the space from the ceiling, forming deep shadows on her face. It was impossible to get a clear image of her. I could make out darker patches on seven places on her body, the bruises or wounds from which the blood appeared to have run. Just as the officers had said, it was impossible to see the girl clearly enough on the surveillance video to identify her. There were no other leads either, as far as I could see.

That was good.

Everything would work out.

SIXTEEN

As usual a heavy, gloomy fog hung over my parents' villa out in Bromma. Everything was quiet. The children were not even running around Mother's painstakingly set dinner table. I tried to breathe calmly. Normally I would have enjoyed a quiet dinner, but not now. Not here.

Months had passed since I had seen them. My brothers Stefan and Samuel came here often for dinner. I had to force myself to go.

For the children's sake.

For normality's.

As always my parents' home, and everything else about them, was polished on the surface. The decorative objects were dusted and set up in rows on the shelves, the curtains were hanging in straight lines, and the pillows were placed precisely on the couch. Even though some of the furnishings had been replaced since I was young—to lighter, warmer tones—the old, dark, closed-in feeling was still there. Wherever I looked memories flooded me. The dark stairway to the top floor. Mother's embroidered Bible quotations framed on the walls. The door that led down to the cold, damp cellar. A musty, suffocating odor of mold and earth spread from the cellar up to every corner in the house. It made me lose my appetite. I clenched my jaw. Tried hard to rid myself of these feelings. At the same time, though, part of me wanted to keep feeling them, because it astounded me that my parents and their home could evoke emotions in me.

I was five years old. Even though I had been made to stay alone down in the cellar, I remember the warm feeling in my body. Nothing was like when I had just finished my favorite dish, lying under the blankets, able to make out stars in the sky through the little cellar window.

They were there then.

The emotions.

I remember how they filled me up.

Real emotions that flowed through my whole body. Warmth. Anger. Sometimes mixed together in a single mishmash of indefinable assaults, impossible to control.

Stefan, my brother, always loved to tease me. He often stared at me from the other side of the dinner table, making faces when Mother and Father weren't looking. The fork I flung across the table hit Stefan's eyebrow before it slammed down on the plate in front of him and then fell to the floor. The satisfaction of hitting him made me laugh loudly and uncontrollably. Stefan's reaction was not long in coming. After a contorted facial expression he was carried away howling by Mother up the stairs to his room. I did not stop laughing until Father struck his fist hard on the table so the porcelain clattered against the tabletop.

I knew what was coming after that. I looked out the window in the dining room and up toward the sky. It was dark. That was good. Then I could see them. The stars. I talked with them out loud, explaining to them that soon I would be coming down where we could be together. At the same time I watched Father as he went over and unlocked the wooden door down to the cellar.

"Quiet," he said to me.

I kept speaking. Couldn't stop myself. Instead I was talking even faster, telling the stars that they had to promise not to go out because I had so much to tell them. Father opened the door. Looked at me, shaking his head. I went down the stairs voluntarily. Knew there was no point in making a fuss. I was used to the cold that struck me and the dampness that slid over my body with each step I took. And the smell. A musty smell of dirt and mold.

I was down there. The cellar I had screamed in so many times, that I had wept and thrown things in, had now become my refuge. My escape from reality. It was there that I could simply be.

To think.

To dream.

Of another life.

Then it didn't matter that I had been punished with solitude in a dark stone cellar and that I didn't get to eat with the family up in the dining room. That water dripped in along the stone wall or that the cellar window was so full of earth and dust that it was barely possible to see out. None of that had any significance as long as I could see the stars. Sometimes they were like white, sparkling contrasts against the dark night sky. Sometimes they were blurry through a rainy, dirty windowpane.

They could see me too, I knew that. They winked at me. Talked with me. Never corrected me. Never said that I had done wrong and never punished me. I talked with them often. That was why I couldn't be around people. That was what Mother said to me anyway.

I was different, she said.

I talked to myself.

I explained that I was talking with the stars, but she never understood. She didn't want to listen. When I stopped doing that and learned to behave, then I would avoid being punished in the cellar, she said.

It never turned out that way.

"So Peter isn't coming tonight at all?"

Mother adjusted the coral-colored shawl around her neck. Under it hung a small gold cross on a simple gold chain. She looked at the unoccupied table setting and then at me.

"He'll be late. He's in the middle of something at work. Advertising is evidently more important than murder and robbery, which I work with."

Father reacted quickly to my sarcasm, lowering his head and looking at me over his reading glasses.

"Peter has an important job. And it brings in good money."

As always. Mother and Father always took the other party's side ahead of mine. Usually it was my brothers', but also Peter's or the children's.

"You should be happy you have Peter," said Father.

Love. Till death do us part. Peter talked a lot about those words after we got married, repeating them like a mantra. Said that what we had done was the greatest thing that had ever happened in his life. I remember when we were standing there in the church. In that moment, more than at any other time, I wished I could feel like him. Sure, I felt, but in my way. I felt pleasure and satisfaction that I was a major step closer to the life I had decided to live. But love, no.

"Dinner's ready, everyone," Mother said with a smile. "Help yourselves now. You never know when there will be food again."

My stomach knotted. I had heard that expression so many times. So many times I had to wait before I was allowed to eat. Anyone incapable of behaving like a civilized human being couldn't eat with other people, that was the rule at our house. I took a deep breath. Memories fluttering past like images on a screen. Mother's submissive, nervous smile at Father. Stefan's and Samuel's teasing looks. Father getting louder and more dominant the more he drank. For Father, discipline was everything. Without that you got nowhere in the world, he always said. Neither he nor Mother tolerated anyone or anything that deviated from what they considered to be normal. When I made a mistake I was supposed to sit in the cellar and think about how stupid I had been so that I could do it right the next time.

I understood early on that I was not as important as my brothers. I had often heard my parents' proud voices when they talked about their two boys. If I was even mentioned it was more likely as the problem child.

"Watch the glass you're holding, Bea," I said.

Beatrice, who was about to spill the milk she had just been given, heard me and at the last moment managed to balance the glass in her hand and keep it from spilling on the white, embroidered tablecloth.

I saw Father's look. Knew that he thought I should be more authoritarian toward the children. Mother looked worriedly at the table to see whether a drop had landed on the cloth. Then she opened the lid of a little bowl that was sitting next to Benjamin's plate.

"There is some extra good special spaghetti just for you in here, Benjamin," she said, starting to ladle pasta onto Benji's plate.

"I want special spaghetti too," said Bea, pointing at the bowl.

"We've talked about this, Bea," I said. "You know that Benji has to eat special food. You get the same as the rest of us."

Beatrice let out a loud howl but fell abruptly silent as she was drowned out by my father pronouncing her name in his deep rumbling voice.

I felt a vibration in my pocket and took out my phone, excusing myself as I got up from the table. A journalist on the other end asked whether he could ask a few questions about the robbery. I said no firmly and referred him to our public relations officer.

"Are you having a rough time at work too, Leona?" said Mother when I sat down again.

"It's the bank robbery at SEB with the little — "

"We're eating now, if you were thinking about bringing up a lot of unpleasant cop stories," my brother Stefan interrupted me.

As long as I could remember the two of us had disagreed about everything. Since he had started working as a stockbroker he had become completely insufferable. A conceited ass in a shirt and jacket who refused to take off his tie, even at our parents' house. Mother and Father were extremely proud of his choice of occupation.

"I neither can nor want to talk about such things, especially not to weak, sensitive people like you, Stefan. You'll have to hear it on the news instead."

Stefan snorted at me and took a sip from the wineglass in front of him.

"If it's a problem to listen to something that has to do with me, perhaps these dinners don't suit your distinguished persona," I said quietly.

"Mommy, what does 'stinguished persona' mean?" asked Bea.

"It means that a person is completely full of himself and looks down on other people, dear."

Mother cleared her throat.

"Leona, will you please pass the salad?"

She reached out her arm toward the salad bowl. I glimpsed a thick Bismark chain along with the gold watch around her wrist.

"Your brother is just worried about you. And I agree that it's not good to work with robberies and ghastly things like that.

Especially not when you have small children. What if something were to happen to you?"

For all these years Mother had tried to get me to change occupations. For my own safety and for the children's sake, she said. In reality it was about something completely different. It wasn't acceptable among their fine college-educated friends to have a child who was a police officer. Especially not a daughter.

"I can't bear to discuss this again, Mother."

The piercing sound of the doorbell interrupted me. It was the sound I had heard so many times from the cellar, and longed for.

Hoping that someone would come.

That someone would discover what was going on.

"Oh, how nice! Now he's here," said Mother, walking quickly out toward the hall.

When she left there was silence at the dinner table. I glared at Stefan. He responded with a shrug. He didn't seem to think it was worth even opening his mouth when Mother wasn't around. Samuel sat occupied with his phone, uninterested in communicating. The two of them behaved exactly like when we were kids. Father finished his third glass of wine and got up to get more.

We could hear Mother's voice in the hall.

"Peter, how nice that you could get away from work after all. Oh, you didn't have to buy flowers."

Flowers for Mother. Pathetic. My parents were pushovers. They probably realized that Peter was only showing off, but that was how you were supposed to behave when you visited the family for dinner. Then you were welcome in the Lindberg family home.

"Nice to see all of you. Sorry I'm a little late."

A little? An hour and thirteen minutes had passed. Peter had evidently had time to go to the hair salon, anyway. His dark, wavy hair was trimmed at the neck and shorter than this morning.

"No problem, Peter," said Father, who came from the kitchen with the wine bottle in hand. "Leona told us that it's stressful for you at work. It's tough being the family breadwinner."

Father set down the bottle and shook hands with Peter as if they were best friends. It was true that Peter earned more than I did, but he was hardly the sole family provider. In contrast to the men I had previously been involved with, Peter was relatively uninterested in money. Ever since we had moved in together I had been the one responsible for our joint finances. As long as he knew there was enough money when we needed to buy something, he was happy.

"Wine?" Father asked, reaching toward Peter's glass.

"Thanks, but I'm driving, so if there's something else..."

"How nice that you had time to get a haircut," I said.

Peter walked around the table and over to me.

"I went to the drop-in salon on the way. Wanted to look good for my darling," he said, giving me a light kiss on the cheek. "Nice that you could pick up the kids."

"Of course she could," said Mother, pouring mineral water in Peter's glass. "Picking up the children at day care is marvelous. I remember when we used to pick up the boys at — "

"Mother, please, knock it off," I said.

She fell silent and looked down at the table. She was good at playing the martyr. I was tired of the stories about when my brothers and I were little. Stories that always ended with me having done something stupid that everyone laughed at. Peter tried to salvage the situation.

"Yes, of course, it's sweet. I love picking them up. Have you told that we're thinking about having..."

He stopped when I stared at him.

"Oh," said Mother, lighting up. "Are you thinking about an addition to the family? How nice!"

Peter avoided my gaze. Mother seemed to have understood what was going on.

"Leona, that's not anything to keep secret, is it? You already have two wonderful children, a third will be yet another gift from God. Just like when we had you."

Mother smiled. Out of the corner of my eye I saw Peter looking worriedly at me, but I avoided catching his glance. Father did not take long to pick up on Mother's happy act.

"Nice to hear, Peter. Oh yes, Marita nagged about a third child until I gave in. And we haven't regretted it, even if the boys got a little wildcat to share. A real little lion."

Father laughed and winked at Peter. I said nothing. Peter accidentally mentioning something that we hadn't agreed on at all was one thing, but for Mother and Father to try to pretend that they had wanted three children made me mute. They had always treated me differently from my brothers. Even with my name they had marked me as different. Stefan, Samuel, and Leona. "Leona, the little lion," Father always said. People laughed and thought it was sweet. I knew that he didn't mean it in a positive sense.

"Excuse me."

I got up and went quickly into the bathroom, locking the door and positioning myself with my back against it. I spoke softly to myself: Breathe. Breathe. My collar felt tight around my neck and I pulled on it, panting. I thought of them sitting there having dinner at the table I had been sent away from so many times as a child. I got a strange impulse to go out and attack them.

Pay them back.

For everything.

I took a few deep breaths. I needed to calm down. Nausea was bubbling up inside me. My face was hot. I went over to the sink and splashed my face with the ice-cold water. The cold calmed me. I sat down on the toilet seat. Took a towel from the hook and held my head in my hands. It wasn't the first time I experienced these feelings at home with my parents as an adult. The same brief emotional outbursts, just like when I was a child. After a quick look in the mirror I unlocked the door and went out in the hall. I dug out my shoes and started putting them on. Mother came after me.

"But what...?"

"I'm not feeling well. I have to go home," I said.

"It's not the food, is it?"

When I didn't answer she smiled and looked meaningfully at my belly.

"Maybe you're already...?"

"No," I answered curtly, rummaging around among the jackets. "I just need to rest."

"But dear, Peter hasn't even finished eating," said Mother.

Before I put my shoes on I went into the dining room.

"Children, you can come home with Daddy. Mommy is tired and has to go home and rest."

I did not even look at Father and my brothers. After a glance at Peter I went quickly back to the hall and out the door.

The cool autumn air that struck me was liberating. My previous fixation with maintaining a normal life, and all that involved, seemed more and more incomprehensible. I walked quickly over the gravel toward the car. I backed out onto the little road that I used to bicycle back and forth on when I was little. Then, casting a final glance toward the house, I took off.

It was the last time.

SEVENTEEN

Neither of us had said a word to each other after the dinner with my parents. Peter put the children to bed while I sat in the guest room in front of the computer for the rest of the evening. But I was too tired to stay up. Peter had just gone to bed. I quickly twisted my hair into a braid and hoped I would be able to slip down under the covers, mumble a "good night," and turn off the bedside lamp without needing to initiate a conversation. Or any other activity either, for that matter. Since Peter had got it into his brain that we should have more children, he had initiated sex at least a couple of times a week. I ducked and avoided his advances, as well as the harping about more children.

"I shouldn't have brought that up at your parents'."

I turned off the lamp. The last thing I was in the mood for now was to spend half the night talking about whether it was right or wrong of him to do one thing or the other. I had learned to be curt so as not to encourage a discussion. I settled down with my back against Peter and pulled the covers up to my chin.

"It's okay."

I meant it sincerely. The question was whether he would be content with that. There was silence for a moment.

"I thought we were in agreement about having one more," he continued, but he did not sound particularly convinced.

I didn't intend to fall into the trap and start arguing with him.

"Mmm."

"Weren't we?" he said.

When I didn't answer he continued.

"It would be so sweet. And when we move to a bigger house it won't feel as cramped and inconvenient as here. I have several colleagues who have three children and they're very content with that. You're a third child yourself. You heard how happy your parents sounded when they talked about the three of you."

"Peter, I'm really tired."

I didn't expect Peter to see through my parents' happy act, but somehow his naïveté irritated me more than usual. I saw their claim to have wanted a third child as a mockery aimed directly at me. Peter knew very little about what it had been like for me as a child.

I was six years old. I had never heard them say the words before. Not in sequence. It was Father who said them. We had come home after having dinner with Aunt Anna and the cousins. Father was drunk, as usual for a weekend evening. Mother was quiet. My brothers quickly disappeared up to their rooms.

Like so many times before, I didn't understand what I had done wrong. I had been having fun. Stefan, Samuel, and I had gone with one of our cousins into his room. He had a remote control car that the others took turns playing with. I wasn't interested. I thought cars were boring. It was when I was looking around among the things on the bookshelf that I caught sight of it. Far back on one of the shelves was a box. I quietly picked it up and opened it. All the small sticks in the box were lying in the same direction, except one. It was not meant to be with the others, I understood that. I picked it up.

I knew what to do. I had seen Mother do it many times. I sat down. The wooden floor was covered by a big fluffy rug that was soft to sit on. I did what Mother always did. With the box in one hand and the stick in the other I pulled it with the tip along the side of the box. When it got warm in my hand I let go of the stick, which quickly fell down among the fluff in the rug. At first nothing happened. Then a little yellow flame came up. It flickered. Changed color. I wondered how it could do that. Become a different color like that. When it got bigger I was forced to move back. I met Stefan's terrified gaze before the three of them ran out of the room. The rest happened quickly but still as if in slow motion. Mother, Father, and Aunt Anna came running. Someone grabbed hold of me. I did not want to go. I wanted to stay. To see all the colors.

A large black stain on the floor remained after Aunt Anna had poured several pans of water on it, and thrown out the rug. I wondered how all the pretty colors could turn to just black. Father scolded. He yelled that he did not understand what was wrong with me. That they couldn't cope with me. Aunt Anna swore and said that I had always been a problem.

When we got home Father did as he always did when I had done something wrong. He unlocked the door to the cellar and forced me down. While I was on the stairs he shouted to Mother that he was tired of this shit. That it was enough now.

It was right when he locked the door behind me that he said those words: "We have to give her away."

"Everyone wants three children, Leona. Children are the most precious thing we have," said Peter.

I didn't answer.

We have to give her away... We have to give her away... We have to... The words repeated themselves in my head. Give me away? Where to? I didn't understand. The one time I had heard about something like that was when Mother said something about people

who had left their cats behind in the country after summer vaca-
tion, and the cats didn't survive.

They died.

I remained standing on the stone floor in the cellar, without
turning on the light. I just stood there, holding fast onto the rail-
ing. My whole body felt heavy. Everything was dark now. Not even
the glow of the stars enticed me to the window. There and then I
realized.

I had to become like them.

Like everyone else.

To survive.

"Good night," I said.

The only thing we actually had in common, Peter and I, were
our feelings for the children. At the beginning, a family with two
children had been a must for me. It was yet another step toward
being the person I had always strived to be.

The ordinary family.

The ordinary life.

With Peter I had achieved that.

No other person would think that having feelings for your
children was strange. But I could not stop wondering at it. For
my entire life I had sought, searched for, and tried to imitate
real emotions. Sometimes I got the idea that they were there,
but deep down I had always known that they had never actually
materialized. Then the children arrived and a storm of emotions
washed over me. A part of my inner emotional world opened
up. An extremely limited world, but nevertheless a world that
seemed to exist after all.

When Beatrice arrived I couldn't take my eyes off her. I was
fascinated and in love with this little creature who clung to me

so tightly. I found myself feeling a strange rush of emotions. Beatrice and I became as one. Her needs were the only thing I cared about. And she had needs which only I could satisfy.

But then it changed.

By the time she was one she had already started to turn more and more to Peter. I couldn't put her to bed or console her any longer. If I tried she cried even more. It was just Daddy, Daddy, Daddy.

I heard that I shouldn't worry, that some girls early on turn toward their fathers, that it would change. But it never did.

I wanted another child. I hoped for a boy this time. He would attach himself to me. Then I could show that I was a good mother. A mother who loved her child and was loved by her child. When Benjamin was born the same strong emotions poured over me.

He was perfect.

Two children was perfect.

A happy family just like all the others. Neither more nor less, just as I had always striven for. But that was then. Now everything was different.

EIGHTEEN

Pelle was sitting in front of a computer screen at the far end of the room. I didn't understand why so many of my colleagues chose to sit with their backs to the door. Personally, I hated the idea of not knowing who might come in while you were concentrating on the screen. For someone like me, who played poker during work hours, it was inconceivable to have the screen turned so that it could be seen from the corridor.

"Are you sitting there pretending to work again, Pelle?" I said, trying to sound cheerful.

He turned around and grinned.

"Leona! It's been a while. Great to see you. Come on in."

I went in and looked around. On one wall was a framed picture of Pelle holding a globe-shaped trophy, while on the bulletin board a number of medals were hanging from a cord. I had never understood bowling. I thought it was only retired people who were involved in that kind of thing.

"More medals have been put up since I was here last."

Many officers brought medals and trophies to work. Considering how much time we spent at the office, perhaps it was a way of enjoying what you had achieved while at the same time displaying your prowess to others besides your partner and your children. Personally I preferred a tasteful office without a lot of clutter on the walls. Apart from a photograph of the children, I had almost no personal items in mine.

"There's been a lot going on up here lately," said Pelle. "The politician case has taken the life out of us. It's sad that it was closed, but at the same time it's nice that it's finally over."

I was grateful that he had mentioned the case, because I had had no idea how I was going to bring it up.

"It was surprising that no one was indicted. It felt like a pretty sure thing, huh?" I said.

"We knew what was going on but the prosecutor didn't think the evidence went far enough. Unfortunately the whole thing smelled rotten. There was a rumor that the government was putting a lot of pressure on the prosecutor. That there could be a snag there. What it was I don't know."

So it was just as Christer Skoog had suspected. Something wasn't right about the investigation. I had also heard the gossip, but I hadn't known whether there was anything to it. Investigators were normally very careful about speculating about complicated cases, so when there were those kinds of rumors floating around there was usually some truth to them.

"The prosecutor, who is otherwise extremely capable, screwed up big time. Intentionally, in my opinion," said Pelle.

"Was it true that the prostitute described the course of events in great detail at the hearing?"

I hoped that my curiosity wasn't too obvious. I decided to tone down my questions.

"I was the one who questioned her. The woman was telling the truth the whole time, I'd bet my left hand on it."

"And then you have to remember that you're actually left-handed," I said, smiling.

"You bet! Why use your right hand when the left is so much better," said Pelle, winking.

He got up from his chair.

"Damn it, Leona, we had a good time together before we both sat down behind our desks and became pen pushers. Why don't we run off to a desert island together?"

That was my cue. Pelle was nice, but a little too familiar at times. I headed toward the door.

"You'll have to stop by and say hello some time. If I'm not in my usual office, search around in the corridor. Claes has fits sometimes and rearranges us like little puppets down there," I said.

"Ah, we should go out. We can have dinner this week and talk old memories, my treat."

"Sure, I'll be in touch," I said on my way out.

I sighed. The risk was now imminent that Pelle would be hanging at my heels for the next few weeks, just as he did last time we happened to run into each other at a half-day conference. In any case, though, what I had found out showed that Christer Skoog was on the trail of something. I didn't have much to give him, but a little at a time would hopefully keep him calm. I entered his number.

"Christer Skoog."

"I have your info," I said.

"One moment."

I could hear that he was with other people. After a rustling sound a door could be heard closing on the other end.

"Okay. What have you got for me?"

Now Christer sounded completely different. His abrupt, caustic tone made it clear which of us had the power.

"This definitely appears to have something to do with corruption. The government has put some kind of pressure on the prosecutor."

"Damn, this is going to be good. More?"

"The investigators are convinced that all three are guilty."

"Why?"

"The prostitute was highly credible in their eyes."

"Okay. More."

"I don't have more. What the hell, I'm not a fucking reference book," I said.

"I would skip that attitude if I were you, Leona, and remember what kind of information I have on you. I need more information, do you understand? You'll have to see about bringing something more next time you call—that is, tomorrow."

Christer Skoog hung up. Damn it. I was going to have to search in our databases for their names. Already by doing only that I risked being fired. The politician investigation was access-protected anyway, so that curious police officers couldn't go in to read—and leak—sensitive information. Requesting all the investigation's documents from the archive wasn't an option. For one thing all inquiries were registered, and besides, the amount of redacted material in this kind of sensitive investigation wouldn't leave much valuable information. I would have to find a different solution.

NINETEEN

Olivia must have fallen asleep, because she woke up when the door opened. She squinted toward the glow from the living room that lit up the bedroom and saw Daddy's large silhouette. He went up to the mattress and pulled her close. He was probably being nice again now. It was only when he was nice that he took hold of her slowly and gently like that.

"Now you're going to make your Daddy really happy. We are going over all of this carefully so there won't be any mistakes. Because you know what will happen if something goes wrong?"

If only he could always be this nice. This time she would not make a single mistake. Daddy would be so proud, and he would take her home to Mommy again. He would tell Mommy how good she had been. Olivia sat up.

Daddy turned on the ceiling light and spread a big map out on the floor alongside the mattress. Olivia was tired but tried to look carefully anyway. There were lots of lines and dots and patterns in all directions.

"Look carefully now. Here is where I let you off."

He drew a cross on the map with a red pen. She had got one like that from Grandma as a Christmas present once. She had drawn a pretty red sun with it and a lamb that lay and basked in the sunshine. Mommy had been very happy when she gave it to her.

"Then you walk straight ahead on that street, and around the corner, and a little on that street, and then you're there. Do you understand?"

Olivia nodded, although she didn't understand completely. There were so many roads. At a lesson in school the teacher had shown her a map but it didn't look at all like this one.

"Daddy, how long are we going to be here?"

It was only now that his frown was gone that she dared to ask.

"Concentrate now, Olivia. We're going to be here until you've done this completely right. Put on your clothes, and then we'll go."

This was not the first time she and Daddy had been out driving in the middle of the night. It was the only time that Olivia got to go out. Apart from when she had done her assignment, but she had only done that once since they came here. It was cold, but she still liked getting out of the apartment. Daddy let her sit in the front seat, though only if she sank down so she wasn't as visible. The streetlights and headlights of other cars moved past and lit up the inside of the car. She looked at Daddy. He still looked nice.

Olivia had no idea where Daddy was going.

"Here it is," said Daddy, stopping the car by the curb. "Do you see?"

Olivia nodded. She saw a narrow street with only two cars and a sidewalk with a lot of cobblestones. There were a few small shops and a restaurant, too.

"I'll let you off here and then you walk just the way we practiced in the apartment. A little hunched up and looking down. And keep the hood of the rain cape a little over your face. You absolutely mustn't talk to anyone and not stop for anything, just like the last time, do you remember?"

Olivia nodded again.

"Olivia, answer, damn it!"

"Yes, yes, I remember, Daddy."

Now she had to listen carefully because Daddy was starting to get angry again.

"There are going to be a lot of cars here and you will need to walk as close to them as possible right up to the corner over there. Then you go to the right."

Daddy pointed. Olivia had learned right and left long ago but Daddy probably didn't know that. He started the car and drove up to the corner where he turned right.

"Then you continue here, down to here."

He stopped outside a large entry where there was a yellow-and-black sign. Olivia could read what it said.

"F-o-r-e-x. What is that, Daddy?"

"Listen now, Olivia. You go up this little stairway to the entry, and open the door. Inside it there are a few more steps before you get in. Then you do exactly like before. When you come out again you keep going up this street. Between these planted trees and the parked cars. Then into that narrow street."

He drove up to a dark, narrow street.

"Here. Do you see? Then you do exactly like before."

It did not look hard at all. She knew that she had to do everything right. Like Daddy said, it was her own fault that she had to stay. If she had only understood faster and been nice the whole time, she probably would have been home with Mommy already.

Daddy said that they were done.

"And Olivia, you know what to do if something goes wrong."

Olivia knew that she was not allowed to talk to anyone other than Daddy and the quiet lady. Daddy had said that someone might come and take her away if she wasn't good and didn't do as he said. Olivia didn't know for certain what he meant by that. You might end up in jail if you did stupid things, she knew that, but Daddy said that they were not doing stupid things, only nice ones. She was still worried about ending up in jail, though. Once she had asked Daddy about it and he had got angry and hit her right in the stomach so that she couldn't breathe. After that she did not dare ask again. If she was good and did exactly as he said she would probably not end up in jail.

TWENTY

As usual in the evenings I lay in bed waiting for Peter to fall asleep. It seldom took long, which was particularly important now. Tonight I didn't have many hours to myself. I had to get up early in the morning, but I had already prepared everything.

He didn't wake up as I tiptoed out of the room. I had left the computer on so that it would be quick to log in. When I moved the mouse the screensaver disappeared. I opened up a window and logged in. People from all over the world were logged in too. Twenty-four hours a day. We all shared the same interest.

Poker.

Money.

At the beginning my interest didn't have that much to do with money. It was the excitement, the kick, the challenge. During the time I had been playing I had both lost and won. In the beginning, it was slow. In my good moments I thought I probably broke even. In reality, that was far from the truth. To be honest I hardly understood how it was possible to have lost so much money as I had in so little time. As luck would have it that had turned around and now it often went really well.

I played both cash games and tournaments. There were a lot to choose from, some with several thousand players. Even though I chose tournaments with only a couple of hundred players it often took several hours before they were done. I had been depositing a few thousand at a time into the gaming account for several months. Last month it had been going so well that I had now started playing for higher stakes. Every time I won a tournament I cursed myself that I hadn't bet even more. Now it was time to raise it one more notch. Increase the stakes.

I scrolled around among the virtual tables on the screen, found one that was suitable, and sat down. I looked around. There were eight people, plus me, at the table. Everyone had their own avatars except one. I called myself Modesty and put in a picture of the cartoon character Modesty Blaise. It was completely trite and silly, but here you could be who you wanted without anyone caring. Somehow the character and the name suited my playing style—tight and aggressive. I had quickly learned to play tight after I realized I had been making the biggest beginner's mistake in poker: being too eager and willing to stay in the game despite having a poor hand. The times I took a chance and went in with low or medium cards I went out headfirst. The past month I'd had the patience to wait for high cards. Once they came, I played aggressively, with high amounts.

The table had a mahogany border and was covered by a green cloth that was supposed to represent velvet. I wondered whether the poker tables really looked like that in a live casino. I had been at Casino Cosmopol a number of times on duty, but strolling in there and sitting down at a poker table was inconceivable. No one knew that I played. Online I was completely anonymous.

Around me at the table were patrom29 from Uruguay, knightride2369 from Jamaica, nikolai5350 from Russia, a Canadian, two Italians, a Frenchman, and a Chilean. A real mishmash of nationalities, which made it even more interesting. It was as if the whole world was in my guest room.

Even though I had been warned against it, I always chose to play in "turbo." At that speed you had less time for reflection. If you hadn't made a decision before the seconds ran out, your hand got folded automatically. That suited me perfectly. At a normal pace it took much too long. I hated sitting and waiting for people to decide. There weren't that many choices to make, after all. Either you bet, passed, or folded. In turbo you could play one or two tournaments and still get a few hours of sleep.

The recent wins had made me more self-confident and accordingly more daring in my play. I always played Texas hold 'em, and always "no limit." In no limit I could go all in, betting everything I had on a single hand. I risked losing the whole stake in one go, of course, but the possibility of winning a large sum was greater. I hated being limited in how much I could bet.

It was all or nothing.

It was breathtaking.

The tournament was progressing. As usual I had to restrain myself so I didn't get too eager. Patience was the most important thing in poker. I waited.

Folded.

Waited.

Folded.

I amused myself in the meantime by studying the other players. At least three of my opponents seemed relatively new to the poker world. They played almost every hand, bluffed wildly, and were revealingly inconsistent. Two players, on the other hand, seemed to be strong. One of them was the Frenchman.

After many rounds without good cards I started to get impatient. King of diamonds and queen of spades. No top cards. Not even the same suit, but that would have to do. Sometimes you needed to take a few risks. Three of the players threw in their cards immediately. I chose to bet properly. No point in holding back once I had entered the game. One of the players raised high. It was the Frenchman. Not a bad stake. The community cards dealt face up on the table, that you could count with your own, showed the three of hearts, nine of spades, and king of clubs, which meant that I had a pair of kings. I knew that I had the highest pair, as long as no one was sitting with two aces in their hand, which was unlikely.

Of course the Frenchman could have two pairs, but that was not very likely either. Possibly he was also sitting with a king and then the other cards were important. My queen ought to do very well in that case. Maybe he was bluffing. One more player dropped out. And another. Only the Frenchman and I were left.

I was first out on the new round. I checked. Waited. The Frenchman took his time, using all the seconds he had. Right at the last moment he checked too. The last card was laid out on the table. Damn it! If the Frenchman had a ten that meant three-of-a-kind for him and I would be burned. I had to be careful in this situation. I checked. He did the same. We showed our cards — I won the round. Yes! This was important. I was in first place in the tournament now, but there were still 119 players left. I was so into the game I didn't notice that the door to the guest room had slipped open. I only heard a thin voice.

"Mommy, I can't sleep."

Beatrice had started getting up at night now and then. This I definitely did not have time for. Especially not now when I was in such a good position. I quickly looked at the clock. In just a few seconds the tournament would take a break. A five-minute break every hour was standard for all tournaments. In that time I would probably be able to get her back to bed again.

"Honey, shall I warm some milk for you?"

She nodded. I led her quickly into the kitchen. Took out a mug and poured so that the milk spilled over the edge and down onto the floor. I swore silently to myself and wiped it up with a paper towel. I looked at the clock. A minute had already passed. I put the mug in the microwave. Twenty seconds, that would be enough.

"Come on, I'll go with you to your room while the milk gets warm."

If she was lying under the covers there was a greater chance that she would fall asleep. I did not want to miss the start after the break.

"I want to be with you, Mommy. I want to play computer too."

"But I'm going to go to bed, honey. You have to lie down in bed at night. Come on now."

I pushed her gently ahead of me on the way to the small bedroom that we had recently repainted in a warm shade of yellow. Bea slid into bed without further protest. I tucked her in and sat on the edge of the bed.

"Ah, it looks really cozy. Do you want Mickey beside you?"

Bea nodded. I got the cuddly toy from the armchair and tucked it beside her under the covers. The microwave beeped in the kitchen.

"Lie here and cuddle with Mickey and I'll fetch the milk."

I walked quickly out to the kitchen and looked at the clock. Now there wasn't much time. I took the mug out of the microwave. A film had formed on the milk, which I knew that children loathed. To avoid complaints I opened the top drawer, took out a teaspoon and skimmed the film from the surface. I tried the milk to see if it was warm enough and then bounded to Beatrice's room with the mug in my hand.

"Here is some lovely warm milk for the finest girl in the world. When you've finished it you're going to fall asleep in a second. Drink calmly now and try not to spill, okay?"

She nodded.

"Mommy, don't go."

Kids had a strange ability to pick up on when you were stressed.

"I have to sleep too, honey. Otherwise I'm going to be grumpy tomorrow. You don't want that, do you?"

I made a face to Bea, to show how I would look if I didn't get to sleep. Bea laughed.

"Noooo, not grumpy."

I leaned down and gave Bea a kiss on the cheek.

"See you tomorrow morning, honey. Sleep well now."

I went out. Closed the door behind me. Quickly moved back into the guest room. The tournament had started. I didn't know how many rounds I had missed, but I hadn't lost that much. A few people had managed to pass me, which was irritating. I was in fifth place, but there were still so many players left there was plenty of time to come back. I went ahead with the same strategy.

I lost a few big hands but managed to win some back. This time I would win, I felt it. My confidence increased with every hand I won, which made me more and more daring. The two players who were left were fairly capable. I couldn't do the usual tricks of stealing blinds or betting low when I had a good hand to lure them into raising ahead of me. They saw through that sort of thing. Now we were playing with high denominations, which meant that the game fluctuated a lot.

The players had thinned out. Only my table was left in the tournament, and there were only two players left besides me. The Frenchman, who had been there from the start, and a Brazilian who had come in when people left and tables were combined. The Frenchman played steadily and methodically. The Brazilian was more daring.

Suddenly the Frenchman went all in, betting everything he had. It was the first time during the entire tournament that he had done that before any cards had been dealt face up. Either he was bluffing or else he was sitting with a high pair. It was a strange move by the Frenchman, as he had played so carefully until now. Taking too big a risk in the tournament when you had played for several hours and were so close to the end was a dangerous strategy. If it worked, it was a winner. Since I had followed his methodical playing I didn't dare bet against him, so I folded instead. The Brazilian bet against the Frenchman, which in a way was good for me. One of the two would lose the round and leave the tournament and I would stay in and play against the winner.

When the cards were laid out on the table I wished I were at a live casino and could see whether either of them batted an eye. Both bet everything they had, and were only waiting for the last card to be dealt. An ace! The Frenchman's three aces would have been a winning hand if the Brazilian hadn't turned out to be sitting on a four and a five and along with the cards on the table managed to put together a straight.

The Frenchman left the game after writing something in French in the chat field. I suspected it included some swear words because he had gone out with such high cards. The official language in the poker space was English but some still communicated in their own language.

In a way I had wanted the Frenchman to be the last left with me because I'd had time to understand his playing better. The Brazilian seemed completely wild. The fact that he went all in with a four and five in different suits at the end of a tournament was almost madness. That he had put together a straight was nothing other than pure luck. At the same time, it was good that

I now knew he was crazy. It was just a matter of making sure to keep myself above the surface until I got really good cards, and then run over him like a bulldozer. He was eager, it was noticeable. But I did not intend to let myself be dragged along in his attempts to entice me to raise with a crappy hand.

It was the last round now, and I had my chance. With two kings in my hand. I didn't intend to back down. I raised immediately. He bet. I had a desire to raise again but abstained. Didn't want to make him so suspicious that he folded. An ace was dealt face up. Damn it! If he had an ace in the hole he would win unless the last card showed a king, meaning I had three kings. He bet. I became suspicious but decided the only thing to do was to keep going. It was sink or swim.

I went all in.

Held my breath.

I assumed that he would bite. He seemed to hesitate, using all of his seconds to think. Would he chicken out now? Hardly. He went all in too. Now the game was almost over. We were just waiting for the last card to be laid out on the table. As usual it would decide everything. It could reverse the game completely.

My heart rate increased.

The last card now.

A king. Yes! I had three kings. I had won! The Brazilian chose not to show his cards. I was curious, but it didn't matter now. It was over. I stood up, reaching my arms toward the ceiling. If the family hadn't been asleep I would have yelled out loud:

Yesss!

TWENTY-ONE

It was as if the red digits of the clock radio had forced their way in through my eyelids and even while sleeping I knew the alarm would go off in two minutes. I turned it off and looked up at what it said. Tuesday, September 17, 4:58 a.m. More than two weeks had passed since the first robbery.

It was time again.

I had explained to Peter that I was going to work early. That was not unusual. I turned and looked at him sleeping peacefully, as if he didn't have a care in the world. Perhaps he didn't. He seemed so carefree. So content with his existence. Sure, he wanted to move to a big house and have another child, but in general he seemed happy with his life. Our life. I envied that. I looked at him. His face calmed me. I remained lying with my head close to his a little while before I quickly got dressed. Did the morning chores.

Quietly.

Mechanically.

Everything was prepared. The clothes. The equipment. Everything. When I was ready I took out the sandwich wrapped in plastic that I had set in the fridge the night before, put it in the bag, and went out as quietly as I could. The damp air penetrated my clothes on the way out to the car. The seat creaked loudly when I sat down. I tried to focus on other things. I looked around. Was anyone following?

I parked a couple of blocks away from the apartment on Sandhamnsgatan at Gärdet and walked quickly toward the entrance. I entered the four-digit code and slipped in. Two floors up. A quiet knock on the door. Ronni answered. The lighting in the hall cast shadows on his face that made him look at least ten years older. He was pale. Dressed completely in black. He hardly looked at me, instead walking right back into the apartment. His short, dark hair hadn't been tamed and even though it was short, it managed to look disheveled. The apartment smelled strongly of smoke. I took off my shoes and hung up my jacket on the coat stand. Besides that there was no furniture in the hall. I followed him into the kitchen.

"Is the girl asleep?"

"You can wake her," Ronni answered.

I stared at him. He knew what the rules were. He was the one who would take care of the girl. When he saw my expression he left the kitchen.

I took out the sandwich and looked around for a cup. The electric kettle was already full of boiling water. I took a bite of the sandwich and scooped a couple of spoonfuls of instant coffee into the cup, pouring the water in a little too quickly, so that it spilled over on the other side where I was holding my hand.

"Damn it," I whispered to myself.

I dried the back of my hand on my black jeans and looked at it. The skin was hot. I turned the faucet to cold, put my hand under the flow and held it there. Ronni came into the kitchen, dragging the girl. She had pajamas on and looked like she was still asleep. Seemed barely able to hold her head up.

"Damn it, Ronni, let her wake up properly before you force her out of bed," I hissed with my hand under the water faucet.

Sometimes I wondered what made him tick. He took the girl back to the bedroom. I avoided having anything to do with her. I never talked with her. It was simpler that way. At the same time I felt compelled to be there to make sure that Ronni held up his end of the deal.

I had my doubts about Ronni. He had a formidable record in the crime register, everything from misdemeanors to felonies. I had first met him seven years ago, during an investigation where he and two other men were convicted of arson and criminal conspiracy after setting fire to a restaurant belonging to one of the men. An insurance fraud that had not played out as planned. The man who set the fire was burned severely and told me during an interrogation from the hospital bed that Ronni was the one who planned the fire and was also on the scene when the man set it. Ronni was sentenced to four years in prison.

My hand was starting to feel numb from the running water. I turned off the tap. Dried my hands, and began unpacking the bag on the counter. I set out the spray bottle, the child-size plastic gloves, the makeup. I sat down at the kitchen table with another cup of coffee and continued eating the sandwich. It was almost impossible to swallow but I had to try to eat. I forced myself to eat the last dry bite, chasing it down with the warm coffee.

In the first interview I had held with Ronni he had made it clear to me that he did not intend to talk. He refused to talk about the fire, mostly just sitting and shrugging, but he did tell me that he and his girlfriend had recently had their second child. A girl named Olivia.

It wasn't until I brought him in for questioning after a bar fight over a year ago that I'd realized I could actually make use of Ronni. By then he was separated from his girlfriend, who had moved to Finland with both of their girls, which Ronni was angry about. He drank too much, fell out with the wrong people, and had big debts, both to other criminals and to debt collection agencies. He was at rock bottom.

Claes, who due to summer vacations and a personnel shortage had served as the leader of the preliminary investigation for the bar assault, closed it for lack of evidence. I could clearly remember Claes muttering that it was frustrating that people like Ronni wandered the streets, and even worse that he had two little girls, just like Claes himself.

Ronni was not a nice person and he was not particularly sharp, either, but all this made him suitable for my plans. He already had an extensive criminal record, he was in desperate need of money, he had messed up his personal life and lost his family. Most importantly, he had a daughter at the right age and, as it turned out, was disturbed enough to drag his child into his own criminal activity.

There were risks in collaborating with Ronni, I was fully aware of that. I also knew that risk-taking was necessary if I truly wanted to change my life. I couldn't expect to take the safe route. I had to throw myself out into the unknown.

I was prepared for that.

Even excited about it.

Although at the beginning I had doubted Ronni's abilities, he had, after all, managed to get the girl to perform her part exactly according to my instructions. She had conducted herself faultlessly during the previous robbery. The girl was special. Reminded me of myself when I was younger. At her age I would have been thrilled if I'd been asked to do what she'd done—to be given a task. Be needed by someone for an important mission. The only thing that worried me was that she did not look quite healthy. Maybe it was the dim lighting that did that, though, and presumably she was just tired. Any seven-year-old would be tired at this time of the morning, after all.

Ronni came into the kitchen without the girl.

"Have you gone over everything carefully with her?" I asked.

"I don't get why you needed to come here," he answered, lighting a cigarette. "I have everything under control."

"Do you think you succeeded with the crimes you committed before I came into the picture?"

He didn't reply.

"You see, then," I continued. "Your job is to look after the girl. The question is whether you will even be able to manage that. What have you done with her? She looks almost drugged."

"You are so fucking naive, Leona. Try to get a kid to do a thing like this and you'll see for yourself. She's just tired in the morning. Damn it, it's only six o'clock."

His attitude irritated me.

"I'll get her ready today. You'll have to arrange the car instead," I said, getting up.

I poured the rest of the coffee out into the sink, fetched the girl, and went into the bathroom.

TWENTY-TWO

Olivia stood in the bathtub while the quiet lady combed her hair straight back. It was time again. The lady held her head with one hand and combed with the other. Her hair was tangled after sleep. The lady didn't tear at it the way Daddy always did. She had much softer hands. She looked at the lady's head. Her hair was brown, curly and fluffy. Like angel hair. Olivia wished she had curly hair like that, not straight like her own. Daddy always said that it was spindly. The lady probably thought it was ugly too, because she wanted Olivia to wear that matted wig again. Olivia had tried to comb it one time but then Daddy tore it away from her and said it was not a toy. They must have thought it was good that the strands of hair hung together like that in clumps. Olivia had never seen anyone with a hairdo like that.

The lady turned her and started gathering the hair at the back of her neck with a hair band. It was warm in the bathroom and as long as she had her pajamas on it was fine. But Olivia knew it would be cold later. She hoped that the quiet lady would not see that she had bruises and wounds on her body. She mustn't show them to any-one, Daddy had said. Otherwise he would get really mad. As long as Olivia had on her pajamas the quiet lady would probably not see.

"Can I have clothes on this time? It was so cold before," Olivia said.

The lady stopped and looked at her. Olivia became worried. Had she been stupid again? Without saying anything the lady got up and opened the bathroom door.

"Sorry. Please don't tell Daddy."

It was too late. The lady had gone out and closed the bathroom door. Olivia climbed into the bathtub. Curled up into a ball. She didn't know what to do. Why had she said that? Daddy would come in any moment now and he would be furious. She closed her eyes. If only she had the teddy bear.

The door opened. Olivia didn't dare look up. But it was not Daddy, it was the lady. She set a pair of blue underpants and a white undershirt on the toilet seat. Olivia was unsure. Did the lady mean that she got to wear them?

The lady told Olivia to sit on the edge of the tub and then she slipped on the strange cap that Olivia had to wear under the wig. Oh, if she only didn't have to wear the wig. It was so prickly. Before she had time to think more about it the lady had put it on her and taped it to her neck.

"You can change," said the lady, opening the cabinet above the sink.

The lady moved Daddy's toiletry things back and forth. Seemed to be looking for something. She swore quietly and went out.

Olivia didn't know what she should do. She didn't dare take off her pajamas. She just stood there.

The lady had left the door open, so Olivia could hear what she and Daddy were talking about.

"Where's the blood, Ronni?" said the lady.

"Damn it, I forgot," Daddy answered. "I used the whole bottle last time. I was going to buy more but…"

Daddy fell silent. The lady didn't say anything either.

TWENTY-THREE

I couldn't believe it. I knew that Ronni wasn't particularly clever, but I hadn't taken into account that he could be this incompetent. The girl was supposed to look bloody, that was the whole plan from the start. Her vulnerability would terrify the people around her, which was a prerequisite for her being able to carry out the robbery. If people thought someone had injured her they would quickly understand that this someone could injure her again if they did not follow the instructions on the tape. For that reason no one dared approach her during the robbery. That was the key. No blood, no robbery; it was that simple.

I stood in the kitchen and stared at Ronni. He stared back with a hollow, vacant expression that didn't exactly make his pale, stubbly face look any more intelligent. I looked at the clock. Ten minutes to eight. We wouldn't be able to get hold of any blood until the stores opened at ten, and by then it would be too late.

"We must be able to get hold of it somewhere," said Ronni.

I looked away. I couldn't bear to look at him. The only person I knew who maybe stocked blood was Madeleine, the nail technician near work. She had mentioned that she brought in seasonal makeup to beef up sales. I had seen other Halloween items on the shelf when I had been there to have my nails done, and though I couldn't remember if there had been any blood, there probably was. It was a gamble. Madeleine opened at eight in the morning.

"You'll have to run over to Madeleine on the corner and buy some."

I wrote down the address. Ronni looked at the slip.

"Damn it, that's right next to the police station."

"Shut up! You're going! She knows me. You'll have to say you're buying fake blood for your kids who are going to a Halloween party or whatever. Improvise, Ronni. But be damn sure not to fuck this up too. I'm starting to get really tired of your mistakes."

Ronni threw on his jacket on his way out. God knows what he would have come up with if I hadn't been there.

"And listen, let the girl have some underwear on this time. I've set them out in the bathroom."

I went to work. I had intended to get the girl ready completely but I didn't have time to wait for Ronni to get back. There was nothing more for me to do until tonight.

TWENTY-FOUR

Olivia was in place. She had walked exactly the way that Daddy had shown, up all the stairs and in through both of the doors. She had dropped the rain cape and backpack right inside the door. Now she was standing in the middle of the room looking up toward the high counter. The room was small. Smaller than last time. It was like a bank but somehow not. There were stronger colors, yellow and black. Daddy had gone and bought that red stuff and covered her with it. Then he sprayed her and the teddy bear, just like last time. She had gloves on too. Not warm, furry winter gloves but thin plastic ones. They smelled funny. And they were too big. Not comfortable at all. It was like having bags on your hands, but Daddy said that she couldn't take them off. It was something about the door handle, he said. Last time when the doors opened by themselves it went much better. This time there was first a little stairway, then a heavy door, and then another stairway and sliding doors before she came to the right place. Daddy had shown her which way to go. They had practiced two nights in a row.

The ladies who were working sat behind a high counter. They were completely glassed in, too. They almost looked like dolls, sitting completely still. Just like Daddy told them to do on the recording.

If Olivia only managed this she would get to go home to Mommy. She had to manage it. Daddy had said this time would be harder than last time. If anything went wrong she should not say a word. She was good at that. She didn't like talking that much anyway. She mostly liked to sing. But nothing could go wrong. Not now, when Daddy had been so nice. He had let her wear the clothes that the lady had given her. Her favorite undershirt and underpants. And then the rain cape on top. But it was still cold.

There were only two customers inside. A lady and an older man. They did just as Daddy said. Olivia was just about to put everything in the backpack when the man approached her. He whispered, "What's your name, little girl?"

Olivia continued to put the bags into the backpack.

"Who is doing this to you?" he said quietly.

Olivia looked quickly at the man. He looked nice. Not stupid like Daddy had said all men were. It couldn't do any harm if she just said a word or two, could it? Now she was done. She had put everything in the bag. Maybe the nice man would tell Daddy how clever she had been. That she did everything just right. Because if Daddy only knew that, then she would get to go home.

The man leaned over.

"Little girl. You look cold and tired. Have you had anything to eat?"

Olivia shook her head.

"You know," he whispered, "I live very close by. If you want you can come up to my place and warm up a little. I have hot chocolate and sandwiches. Would you like that?"

The man leaned on a cane. He looked at her with warm, kind eyes. If she had a grandfather she would want him to be just like the old man. Hot chocolate was the best thing she knew.

"My dear, you're completely covered with wounds."

The old man came closer. Olivia backed up. It was a reflex. Suddenly she could hear Daddy's words in her head: "If you make a mistake you will never go home to Mommy, do you get that?"

She picked up the rain cape, slipped it over her head and was about to pull it over her body when she felt a hand on her arm. A big, warm hand. It was soft against her skin. Not like Daddy's hard, scratchy hands. She looked up. It was the old man who had taken hold of her. Her heart started to pound. She had to get out. Quickly. She drew her arm out of the old man's grasp, picked up the backpack, and ran to the first door. It opened automatically in front of her. She pulled the pack up onto her back as she ran down the steps to the main exit. With the gloves on she pushed as hard as she could on the door and ran out. The cold wind struck her, pressing the rain cape along one side of her body and the hood against one cheek. She bounded down the steps to the street. With both hands she adjusted the hood around her face and turned around. The old man was not coming after her. She walked as quickly as she could up to the ornamental trees that stood in rows along the sidewalk. She was supposed to walk between them and the parked cars. She was not allowed to run because then people would be more likely to notice her. And she might fall. She did not want that to happen. Not on the hard cobblestones. It hurt to walk on them. But she didn't have to go far. When she came up to where she was supposed to turn she stopped by a tree and looked around as Daddy had said. Everything looked different when it was light. She could see the subway going past far away on a bridge over the water. In the other direction she saw a lady walking a dog. When they disappeared she walked just as fast as she could into the little narrow street. There were no people, only cars parked on one side. She slowed down. Just as Daddy had told her, she crouched down and kept as close to the cars as she could. But she didn't touch them. She searched with her eyes along the sidewalk. There it was! Right below the curb between the next two cars. She slipped in and crouched down even more between the cars. She wriggled off the backpack, then she cracked open the grate to the storm drain and let the backpack fall down. The thud was delayed. It was deep. She looked around. Far off, on the street, she could see two ladies walking on the sidewalk. She pressed her fingers down through the grate and pulled it all the way to the side over the cobblestones on the street. The grate was just as light as last time. She huddled up and set her feet down on the hard, bent iron rungs that were the ladder down into the drain. She could hear that the ladies were coming in her direction. She pulled on the rain cape to get everything down with her and carefully climbed down the ladder. She must not fall. Putting the grate over her head was easy as pie. She stood completely still under the grate while she heard the ladies pass by on the sidewalk. She had done it. Now she only needed to climb down to the bottom and wait for the evening. Until she heard Daddy's three knocks on the grate. Then she could come up.

It was cold this time, too. Even though the quiet lady had let her put clothes on. But when Daddy came he would put a blanket around her and drive her to the apartment. Then he would be nice and think that she had been clever. Then she would get to bathe in warm water again. For a really long time, now that she had done it completely right. She longed to be able to show how clever she had been. And she wouldn't say a word about what had happened with the old man. Ever. That was her own little secret.

TWENTY-FIVE

Fredrik nodded to me when I got to work. Was that a normal nod? The others were looking as well. Did they really always keep their eyes on me that long? Study me up and down like that? I observed them more carefully now, to see whether they were watching me. Maybe I just looked tired. Considering how little sleep I had gotten lately, and that I had been up since five o'clock in the morning, that wouldn't be surprising. I should've worn more makeup.

As usual, the discussion in the break room was meaningless babble. The same conversations, just like so many times before. One officer was complaining about a difficult suspect, while another had witnesses who refused to appear for questioning. A few people were running around in the corridor with phones to their ears.

I went over to the coffee machine and poured myself a cup. Sat down in one of the armchairs. Claes was sitting on the couch opposite. He seemed to be having a hard time keeping his eyes open and he yawned widely behind his hand. He seldom took a coffee break. When he did, it was obvious that he was only there because he knew he should be a little more social with his staff. The atmosphere in the break room was different when he was there. Stiffer. People tried harder to be noticed. If they didn't talk about work, they told stories about how diligently they had been working on their gardening, or floorball, or whatever else they did in their spare time. Claes didn't seem particularly amused, though. He mostly just sat staring straight ahead. Joined in on the conversation only when there was an opening to talk about cars or boats he would have bought if he'd had the chance. He took his phone out of his pocket and answered it.

"I'll be damned! You have the situation under control, right? I'll send the investigator over."

Claes looked over the room. Stopped when his eyes found me.

"Leona. There's been another girl robbery. At Forex in Old Town."

"What?"

I stood up.

"They think it's the same girl as in the previous robbery, but evidently the alarm came a while after she got out of there. The response team seems to have done a good job and Forensics is on the scene. You'd better head over there now."

I drained the cup of too-hot coffee and jogged toward my office.

"You need to solve this case as quickly as possible. The newspapers will go crazy," Claes shouted after me.

I closed the door. My phone was buzzing in my pocket. Now the media circus was in full swing again. I didn't answer. I picked up my things and turned on the radio.

The Forex currency exchange office at Kornhamnstorg 4 in Stockholm's Old Town was robbed this morning by a young girl. According to witnesses, the robbery has similarities to the bank robbery that occurred at SEB just over two weeks ago, where a young girl managed to get away with a large amount of cash in a similar way. The police have not confirmed whether the same girl was involved in both robberies. She was reportedly unarmed and had large wounds on her body. The police have not released many details about the circumstances surrounding the two

robberies, but so far have found no trace of the girl. A witness from inside the bank is said by his own report to have touched the girl, who was covered with blood. The man was too shaken to speak further about the incident. No arrests have been made.

What? I stopped suddenly. A man had touched the girl. I swore to myself. I was worried this would happen. It was a mistake, letting the girl have clothes on. The Forex office was small, so the girl ended up closer to the customers. With clothes on she didn't seem as vulnerable. I should have realized that some fool would try to approach her despite the threats from the recorded voice. What kind of crazy person would dare jeopardize a child's safety like that?

The phone rang for the third time. I tore it out of my pocket. "*Yes!*"

I curtly answered several questions about whether there was a crime wave of robberies with young perpetrators, whether the girl had been armed, and if there might be some criminal gang that had started to involve children in their illegal activities. I was amazed at the journalists' inventive theories, but I didn't have time to sit and chat on the phone. It wouldn't be long before Claes started asking questions about what I had produced in the investigation. I needed to make it seem as if I was working hard to solve the two robberies.

Producers from *Sweden's Most Wanted* had called a number of times after the first robbery, wanting to have the case on the program. I'd firmly said no, but now it was time. It would be a clear sign that I was doing everything I could to help the investigation. I picked up the phone and was connected to the production director, who explained that the week's program was full but that he could postpone another feature to include it.

"Is there any surveillance video we can show?" he asked.

"A bloody, naked seven-year-old is not something we can run in prime time," I answered. "It will have to be without."

As usual they wanted to have the investigator on the program. I wasn't keen on the attention, but it was important to show outwardly that I was doing everything I could.

It was not the first time I had been on *Sweden's Most Wanted*, so I knew the procedure. First a short clip would be shown of the investigator talking about the crime, followed by the program's own pieced-together reporting on the event. The reporting was often ludicrous in its desire for excitement and drama à la *CSI*.

I had never liked the idea that the government, week after week, supplied a commercially funded channel with information that meant they brought in enormous sums in advertising revenue. I had nothing against the program as such—it was a good way to get the general public involved and to find individuals willing to help solve crimes—but it shouldn't have been shown on an advertising-financed channel.

For my purpose, however, it was fine. The reporter wanted to meet me the next day in the Old Town, outside the Forex office that had been robbed.

Claes stuck his head in my office.

"Leona, you haven't left yet. What are you doing?"

"I was just contacting the producers at *Sweden's Most Wanted*. They won't have time to feature the girl robbery tomorrow, but it'll be included on the show Wednesday next week. We'll need the general public's help, and at the same time this will show that we're treating the case seriously. Obviously I'm putting most of my energy into finding the girl."

I threw on my jacket, grabbed hold of my bag, and headed toward the corridor.

"Good. You need to start getting control of this, Leona."

Appearing on *Sweden's Most Wanted* now was perfect timing. From sheer reflex, I pressed the answer button on the phone without looking to see who was calling.

"Leona, it's me, Christer."

Damn it, not that too.

"I can't talk right now. I'm sure you understand that I'm really busy."

"That's why I'm calling. Another girl robbery, are you out of your mind? That little girl…"

"I'll call you later. I have information for you but can't talk right now."

I hung up. Hopefully he would stay calm for a while. Right now I was thinking about the witness who had touched the girl.

TWENTY-SIX

After a quick stop by Forex in Old Town I was on my way back to the office. If there had been a lot of media with the first robbery, that was nothing compared to now. My colleagues at the crime scene had plenty to do just keeping journalists away. My phone was ringing nonstop.

The commander had confirmed that a witness had touched the girl and got blood on his hands. The technicians had taken DNA and sent the blood for analysis. Otherwise there were no traces of her. Ronni seemed to have done his part.

The results would show that the blood wasn't real, but that didn't matter too much. There was still no information that would reach the general public or create other problems. There was nothing else to do at the crime scene, so I headed back to the office.

I had just opened my email when Claes appeared in the doorway with a big, cheerful smile on his face.

"Leona, here come reinforcements!"

I immediately realized my mistake. If I'd had the door to my office closed, indicating that I was occupied, I could have sat and thought over my next move in peace and quiet. Avoided what appeared to be really bad news. More investigators on the case was the last thing I wanted right now.

Next to Claes stood Minna Nordin and Sam Friberg. They were new to the squad and as far as I knew they had previously been stationed in Property Crimes, where simpler cases like bicycle theft, property damage, break-ins, and other low-level crimes were investigated. They were hardly suitable for this type of investigation. Why was Claes foisting these two on me right now? After a quick look at Claes I turned my head back to the screen. I tried to ignore them. Simply pretended that they weren't standing there.

"Thanks, but I'll manage," I said with my eyes fixed on the screen.

All three remained standing like statues in the doorway. I hoped Claes would realize that his plan was unwelcome, and that he would need to change tack and find some other task for them. I had neither the time nor the desire to babysit those two.

"The case is too big to run on your own, Leona. You need more help."

"I have the investigators you gave me from the start. I'll manage fine with them."

"They're needed for other things. The three of you will have to work together on these robberies starting now. Be sure to summarize the case for Minna and Sam and put them to work. They'll have to share your office for the time being."

"Excuse me?" I said, staring at Claes.

"It'll be more efficient that way. The case is a priority, and the investigation can't drag on because we've been inefficient. Besides, there are two robberies now."

"Can you excuse us a moment?"

I closed the door on Claes and me. Pulled the curtain on the window that faced the corridor. Minna and Sam remained standing outside. I turned to Claes.

"What are you up to? Those two are still wet behind the ears."

"Everyone else is busy with more serious crimes. You understand that I can't just pull a few officers from one of our homicides to investigate two robberies."

"If the robberies are so unimportant, let me run the investigation by myself. You know I can manage it."

He shook his head.

"This comes from above. Management has been dragged into the media circus. The case is sensitive because of the little girl. I have to show that we have people working on it."

"So what do you want me to do with them? Or more precisely, what could they do for me? And that thing about them sharing my office—ha! How funny you are, Claes. Forget it, I won't have it."

I was furious, but I managed to squeeze out a fake laugh so he'd understand how absurd the whole thing was. Being forced to have two bureaucrats at my heels intervening and questioning every detail was definitely not something I wanted.

I didn't have time for that.

And I couldn't afford it.

"Be sure to put them to work. You won't get any other help. After all, these are only two robberies, and no one was injured."

He repeated it like a mantra.

"The little girl was covered with blood, Claes," I said. "As far as we know she might be lying dumped in a container somewhere in Frihamnen right now."

Or else she's asleep on a mattress in an apartment at Gärdet.

"This is a serious case, Claes, and I don't want anyone to mess it up. I'd prefer to work on it myself. If we're so overloaded, can't you find a use for those two somewhere else?"

Claes looked at me. He must've realized I was right. "Look, I'll make sure they get a different office, but you'll have to put up with working with them. They need someone to learn from. Keep in mind that you were new once. It's time to share your knowledge with others, Leona. You'll probably make a good team, you'll see."

Team? I despised the word. I was definitely not a team player. I preferred to work by myself, without having to debate every little investigative measure. The agency had never been good at training new personnel, learning by doing always applied. It had always been that way. It wasn't really the best way to learn the job, if you asked me, but it was hardly my responsibility to cover up for the agency's lax attitude where reasonable orientation programs for new police officers were concerned. Claes, however, seemed to have made up his mind.

I would have to put up with them.

TWENTY-SEVEN

When I turned off the engine, everything was quiet. It was strange how few people were outside at night. I looked at the clock. He wouldn't be here for another three minutes. I had arranged the meeting at lower Gärdet. Here, it was calm. Far ahead of me, almost as an extension of the street, was the illuminated Kaknäs Tower. Peter had treated me to dinner in the restaurant there many years ago. It was beautiful to see the illuminated tower against the night sky. One minute to go. I made a U-turn so that I was on the right side of the street.

I turned on the radio, scanning among the various stations without finding anything to listen to. I couldn't stand the uninteresting babble, so I turned it off. I looked at the clock again. He ought to be here by now. Ronni.

I had made it clear to him that I didn't intend to wait more than five minutes after the scheduled time. After that I would assume he had crossed me, and he could expect major repercussions. His reaction, when I had said that, showed that he took me seriously. He respected me, and rightly so. Even Ronni understood that it would mean big problems to double-cross a police officer with good insight into the criminal world. Too big to be worth taking any risks. The previous handover had gone flawlessly.

There was a flash in the window. I looked up. A car was coming. I couldn't make out if it was him or not. I sat quietly as the car came closer. It was him. He slowed down until he was right alongside my car. I rolled down my window. He rolled down his.

Without a word he handed me the backpack with the money. I noted that he had gloves on this time. It was one of the strange things about Ronni. He managed to do the most important things really well.

I pulled on my gloves before taking the backpack. Ronni stayed in the car. After pulling open the zipper of the large compartment, I took out the plastic bags, quickly looked inside them, and then set them on the floor by the passenger seat. I nodded to Ronni and handed him the backpack. He drove off. I pulled out a black bag from the backseat and put the bags of money inside before driving home.

With one hand on the steering wheel, I dug in my pocket for the phone. I quickly wrote "number two done" and sent the text message. I had already told Peter that there had been another robbery and that I would have to work late that night. When I opened the door it was dark in the apartment. I slipped quietly into the larger bathroom in the hall, carrying the bag. The hatch in the bathroom ceiling, where the valves were, was an excellent space that was never used other than when the water needed to be shut off. I got on the toilet seat and reached up. Opened the hatch and pushed the bag in alongside the one that was already there. After that I locked the hatch and started brushing my teeth.

TWENTY-EIGHT

I heard screams from far away. The sound was faint but still jarred in my ears. I'd heard it many times, yet I didn't understand what it was. I looked around, trying to find where the sound was coming from. Now it had become so loud that I had to hold my hands over my ears, but it didn't help. It came closer. Got louder.

When I opened my eyes I could hear Benjamin crying hysterically in his room. I pulled off the covers and quickly got out of bed. Tripped on the rug and almost fell on my way out of the bedroom. Benjamin was lying in bed curled up in the fetal position, his face damp with sweat. The stomach pains seemed to get worse when his little body was stretched out. I sat on the edge of the bed and held him. He was inconsolable. I rocked him, stroking his forehead.

"Shh, shh," I whispered quietly. "It'll be over soon."

"Knives, Mommy. Knives."

I knew what that meant. Hearing my own child say that it felt like knives in his stomach was almost more than I could bear. I felt a lump in my throat. I closed my eyes. Kept rocking him.

"I know, sweetheart, I know. It will be over soon."

The camisole I usually slept in had become damp from his little body. Our skin stuck together. I looked up at the ceiling and felt tears forming. Quickly wiped them away. I needed to be strong for his sake. For almost twenty minutes I rocked him before the pain subsided. I tried carefully to get the wet pajama top off him. He whined and complained.

"Yes, we have to, sweetheart. You can't sleep in a wet top."

After some struggle I managed to get a dry pair of pajamas on him.

"Daddy, Daddy," he said between sobs.

"Daddy is sleeping, Benji."

He started crying more. I carried him into our bedroom and set him down on the double bed beside Peter, who woke up and looked up at me.

"His crying woke me up," I said. "It's better now. Will you take him while I put clean sheets on his bed?"

Peter embraced Benjamin in the bed. I could no longer stop the tears but instead let them run down my cheeks, chin, and down onto my chest while I changed the sheets. I thought about all the doctors we had been to who squeezed and took samples while Benjamin cried hysterically. When we finally found out that he suffered from Crohn's disease his condition had become so serious he had to have part of his intestine removed the week after the diagnosis. After the operation he had been better for a while. In the past six months, though, it had turned for the worse again. Soon we would get the results from the latest tests.

After I changed the bed I could not get myself to lie down. Instead I remained sitting on his bed. Didn't feel I was worthy of sleep when I knew he wouldn't get any.

It worried me that Benji had started asking more and more for his father. Just like Bea did.

I looked up at the photograph we had framed and placed on Benjamin's nightstand. His favorite nurse held her arm around him at the hospital, on the day we got to go home after the latest operation. Benjamin was smiling but pale and thin. It was no life for a little boy.

I fell asleep with my head on his pillow.

TWENTY-NINE

It had become really cold in the ten minutes and thirty-five seconds I had been standing waiting for the reporter from *Sweden's Most Wanted*. Waiting for people was one of the most frustrating things I knew. I would rather have been sitting at the office reading through interviews and memos. Many documents had come in but so far there was nothing I needed to worry about.

It struck me how my job had changed. Investigating your own crime was relatively calm work. I avoided most of the usual tasks like organizing surveillance on various suspects, searching houses, wiretapping, assessing information that came from colleagues' investigations and interviews, searching various registers, and mapping various individuals' contact networks and family relationships in a constant struggle against the clock. Now it was more about lying low. Making sure that none of my colleagues started digging too deeply into anything. Only doing what was absolutely necessary. Appearing on *Sweden's Most Wanted* was perfect. That way I was showing that I was doing all that I could, while also being the one who received and assessed the credibility of the tips that came in. I got tired of waiting and started to walk back to my car when I heard someone calling.

"Leona?"

I turned around. A dark-haired young woman with her hair in a ponytail came running toward me.

"Maria Tillström. I'm sorry we're late. I didn't know about the roadwork here. We had to park so far away..."

"Okay. Let's just get started. I have to be back at the station as soon as possible."

I nodded at the photographer who had followed and started rigging up the tripod and camera. Maria told how she envisioned the whole thing. I couldn't bear to listen. Mostly I was annoyed because it was always so windy around Slussen. My cheeks felt numb.

I had already prepared what to say, so when the photographer was ready all that was left to do was go for it. The camera was aimed at me where I stood in front of the exchange office.

"Here behind me, at Forex in the Old Town, is where the robbery occurred last Tuesday, when a blond girl about age seven carried off a large sum of money. Judging by the evidence the girl was forcibly compelled to carry out the robbery. Out of fear that she would be subjected to more violence, staff and customers did not intervene. The girl left the exchange office in the direction of Lilla Nygatan and since then it has not been possible to trace her. This crime is very similar to a robbery at SEB on Nybrogatan earlier in September. We are now searching for the little blond girl who is believed to have been involved in both robberies, but we are also seeking other information that may help us solve the crimes. The girl is presumably traumatized, and it is of greatest importance that we locate her as soon as possible."

"Very good," said Maria Tillström. "I have what I need but we'll do it one more time to get more camera angles."

The photographer moved the camera and tripod a little farther away to film from a different direction. I quickly ran through the same spiel one more time and then took the car back to the police station. It was Friday, and I hoped that most of my colleagues had already left for the day. I thought I'd have time for a short tournament before I needed to pick up the kids at day care.

THIRTY

There were more enjoyable things to do on a Sunday afternoon in September than traipsing around Spånga to open houses, along with two hyperactive children and a husband who saw the possibilities in a house's every flaw. Peter had found two open houses that he desperately wanted to go to. One was in Spånga and the other in Aspudden. Even that was telling—one north of the city, the other south. Peter didn't seem to know what he wanted. He had grown up in an apartment himself and often talked about how he envied classmates who could have a barbecue in the garden or play soccer with their parents outside the house in the summer. Personally I had no such memories of my upbringing in a single-family house.

It was light outside even though it was seven o'clock in the evening. I was fourteen. I sat in my room, looking out at the well-tended lawn and the flowers that Mother had planted. My siblings and I were not allowed to play in the garden as children. In our teens none of us was interested in using it. My brothers were almost never at home anymore. I was not allowed to go anywhere after school. It was best for everyone that I stayed at home, Mother always said. I had started to agree with her, and spent most of my time in my room. Still, I dreamed of being somewhere else.

There was a lot of time for thinking in my room. I had stopped talking with the stars long ago. Had learned to talk inside my head instead, so that others did not hear. The emotions that previously stormed inside me had stopped.

Perhaps I had learned to restrain them.

Perhaps I had lost the ability to feel them.

I didn't care which was true.

The main thing was that I didn't have to go into the cellar. Father had stopped sending me down there. I was too old and in any case I had started to understand how to behave, he said. When Father did punish me, I had to go to my room instead. I was quite happy with that. I avoided the rest of the family anyway. Preferred to be by myself.

But this day Mother had been really angry at me. We'd had a theme day at school—uniformed occupations. We'd watched a film about how the fire department, military, and police worked. One person from each service had come to speak to the class. I was completely fascinated.

Not by the military officer.

Not by the fireman.

By the policeman.

What he'd said sounded action-packed and intense, like a Hollywood movie. I wanted to be like him. He was calm, but he talked about the most exciting things. I wanted to be just like that. I danced home in a rush. Told Mother I'd decided to spend my future working life in uniform. I would learn to fight. Shoot. Chase bad guys. Fight against evil. In a bulletproof vest. With a baton. With a pistol. With all that great stuff.

She looked at me and said that I should stop thinking along those lines at once. Someone like me wasn't suitable to work as a police officer. I didn't let myself be swayed but instead continued to talk more and more excitedly about everything I had heard during the day. When Mother sent me to my room I continued to dream myself away. Away from Mother and Father. Away from the house.

I would become a police officer.

"When will we move to the big house, Daddy?" Beatrice called from the backseat.

I looked at Peter, who was sitting next to me, keeping an eye on his phone's GPS. He looked up.

"Well, it's no secret we'll be moving soon, is it?" said Peter.

There was no point in making a comment.

"When, Daddy?"

With her shrill voice Beatrice had excited Benjamin, who started singing to himself.

"You did look through the descriptions of the houses I set up as favorites?" Peter said calmly to me while Beatrice started kicking against my back support.

"Hmm…Five rooms, right? Should we turn here?"

"Four. A townhouse, but pretty nice, I thought," said Peter.

"When Daddy, when Daddy, when Daddy, when Daddy…"

"Damn it, be quiet, Bea, and stop kicking."

I yelled at her. Regretted it immediately. Sighed. She turned quiet. In the corner of my eye I saw Peter looking at me. I gripped the steering wheel, my eyes straight ahead. It bothered me that I wasn't as calm with the children as he was.

"The house has a pretty big patch of lawn out the back."

I didn't understand the point of moving from a small five-room apartment in the city to a four-room townhouse in the suburbs. The one thing I definitely didn't want was to be a suburban mom in a crowded townhouse area. I could hardly imagine anything worse.

"Stop," said Peter. "We drove past the turnoff. You'll have to turn around."

I clenched my jaw. Felt my irritation growing. I made a quick U-turn over the double line, making every loose object in the car rattle around. Then I accelerated back.

"It must be here," said Peter when at last we came to a row of blue wooden houses.

It was one of the gloomiest areas I'd seen. Rows of identical wooden buildings all joined together. I shuddered.

"You can get out, I'll go and park the car."

As far away from the house as possible, I thought, so it would take a while for me to get there, and Peter would've already had a look.

"You can probably park in the driveway," said Peter. "It looks like that family is leaving."

We were barely inside the door before a cheerful agent's assistant demanded our names and telephone number.

"Let us look a little first," I said and was about to squeeze past. He looked at Peter who came after.

"Peter Lindberg, hi there." Peter was polite, as always. "What a nice house this appears to be."

I went in while he gave his phone number to the agent's assistant. In the kitchen I was met by an energetic real estate agent who pressed a prospectus into my hand.

"Welcome! I'm sure it was easy to find? Did you come by car or did you take public transport?"

I couldn't bear to answer.

"There are very good connections into the city from here. Here you see the kitchen, an extremely roomy kitchen that's well suited for a family of..." The real estate agent looked for the other members of my family, who had now made their way into the kitchen. "Four. Even five will be just fine if you're planning more."

He winked at Peter and laughed. I didn't smile. Peter looked at me worriedly, as if he expected an outburst. I didn't intend to offer him that.

I looked out the window. The patch of grass that Peter had described as "pretty big" wasn't even worthy of being called a patch. It was no bigger than a terrace. There didn't appear to be grass on all of it, either. Parts of it were brown-spotted, and in certain places it was just dirt. I took a quick look around on the top floor, mostly for the sake of appearances. I looked the way you look out the window from an express train—looking, but seeing no details. I tried to keep from imagining what it would be like to live there and went downstairs again. Peter was standing by the window and seemed to be having a conversation with the children about whether they could place a swing set on the left or right side of the dirt pile.

"Are you already through looking?" the real estate agent asked when I was on my way out.

"I want to see the yard too."

I went straight to the car. When Peter finally came out with the children he was clearly irritated. He didn't say a word but instead put the kids in their car seats in the back and got in.

"I think it's way too small, Peter. If we're going to move we need at least a five-room place."

He stared out the window without showing that he had heard me.

"By the way, I have to go past the office," I said. "Can you go by yourself to Aspudden? I can go to the extra showing tomorrow if you think I should see the house."

Peter didn't reply. I stopped and got out at work. Let him take the car. He went around the front of the car, got in the driver's side, and slammed the door.

THIRTY-ONE

I picked up two cups of coffee on my way to the conference room. I must have turned off the alarm clock in my sleep that morning. Peter and the kids were gone. Presumably he had gotten up, fed them breakfast, and taken them to day care. I jumped into the shower and drove straight to work. Not a good way to start the week.

I was still annoyed at Claes for ordering me to work with Minna and Sam, but I promised myself I wouldn't take it out on them. Hopefully they were enthusiastic and eager to work, so I could toss them a few unimportant tasks.

I stepped into the conference room. My new associates were already there. On time. Heavens, they looked so young. I hadn't taken much notice of them before, although they had been on the squad for at least a couple of weeks. They looked innocent and undisturbed, somehow. I had learned, however, that it was dangerous to make conclusions based on appearances. Several times I had worked with colleagues who looked as friendly as anything, but in the field they turned into real monsters at the slightest provocation.

The conference room was cold, but the cardigan I needed was at home. The thin turtleneck I had on would hardly be warm enough for an hour in a cold conference room. It would have to be a short meeting.

"This is a special case, you understand. I assume that like everyone else you've followed it in the press," I said.

Minna and Sam nodded. God, what sleepy puppets. Shouldn't the new, young ones be a little more alert and hungry?

I'd heard rumors that Sam was perhaps not the brightest of colleagues. He had been transferred, which meant that he hadn't fitted in at his previous squad. This didn't necessarily indicate that he was completely stupid. Being a little different could be enough for certain managers to think that a person didn't fit in. Even so, judging by what came out of his mouth at coffee breaks and meetings, I had detected a certain lack of intelligence. He said things like "That crook is gonna get it" and "You know what that sort is like." Minna, on the other hand, appeared to be his exact opposite. She was quick-witted and sharp. When she opened her mouth, something relevant usually came out. I would need to keep an eye on her. At the moment they were both sitting quietly, waiting for instructions.

"I want you to drop by the Image and Audio Analysis Group and pick up all the video surveillance both from SEB and from Forex. They're probably looking at it right now but I want *you* to look through everything instead so that nothing gets missed. Start with SEB."

I had complete confidence in the Image and Audio Analysis Group. They were efficient and professional. The reason I wanted Minna and Sam to look at the surveillance material was because I wanted them out of the way of the investigation.

"It's a lot of hours to watch, so you'll have to stock up on popcorn and Coca-Cola. Keep an eye on people who stay a long time on the premises or seem to be casing it. Note if anyone returns often, or if some people are seen at both crime scenes. In that case, identify them. Report back to me as soon as you see anything unusual. And by that I don't mean every person who looks a little different, just when you've found something of importance to the investigation."

I was tired of overly sensitive, hyper-suspicious colleagues who were convinced that everyone who looked different from the average Swede was a criminal.

"As I said, don't bother me with a lot of unfounded guesses."

"Was that all?" said Minna. "We've been told both by Claes and by the head of investigations that we should be involved in the whole investigation."

I stared at her, over to Sam, and then back at Minna. Leaned slowly forward over the table, keeping my eyes on Minna.

"Let's be clear that I'm the one running this investigation. The only reason the two of you are here is that I've given my approval. The slightest fuss or mistake from you and I'm going to see that both of you go back to Property Crimes. Is that understood?"

It was an act from my side. But showing clearly that they shouldn't even think about starting to mess with things behind my back was important. Maybe I had overdone it, but it seemed to work. Both of them were staring at me goggle-eyed.

"Understood?" I said, raising my eyebrows, my eyes fixed on Minna.

"Of course," said Minna quietly, looking down.

That was enough. I softened my tone.

"Believe me, you're going to be busy. There are hours and hours of video. There is also footage from the nearby subway entrances, escalators, platforms and even from inside the subway cars, if you start to think that the girl might have taken the Red line to the bank."

I would have expected a little smile, but the goggle-eyes only stared vacantly at me.

"Right. There were a heap of interviews with witnesses who were around the crime scenes. Quite meager. Go out and hold supplementary interviews with the ones who gave vague information."

Sam did not appear to be listening.

"Listen up, because this is the most important thing of all," I said. "If anyone contacts you from the media, refer them to me, for God's sake. Believe me, you don't want to risk making a blunder."

They could not so much as breathe a word to the press. Police were generally unwilling to make statements to the media, but you never knew with new colleagues. They might get the idea that they would be noticed within the agency if they stuck their neck out and made a nice-sounding statement. They were probably unaware that it was impossible to get a nice-sounding statement published by the press. The newspapers always twisted and turned every word, so that when all was said and done, the credibility of the whole agency could be jeopardized by one little quote. And the credibility of the agency was sacred. What was left of it, anyway. Not that it had any great significance to me. I just didn't want any information about the case to get out.

"Questions?"

"Are we going to share your office?" asked Sam.

Hardly, I thought. And here I thought I wasn't very perceptive. This guy was a joke. I raised my eyebrows. Pretended to be shocked.

"What? Ha! No, no."

I started gathering my papers.

"You can hold the interviews out where the witnesses are or in the interview rooms. Surveillance video you can look at wherever there's a computer available or in the video room. If you need space beyond that you can speak to Claes."

"But it was Claes who said that the three of us should—"

"Is that understood?"

I looked at Minna, who had already started squirming when Sam had asked the question. Both nodded quietly.

I left the room. It was nice to have gotten them out of the way. It would take them at least a week to check through all the sur-veillance video and interview the witnesses, and in the meantime I could continue working in peace.

THIRTY-TWO

"Leona!"

I turned around. In the drizzling rain I saw Gunnar from the forensics team come running across the inner courtyard inside the police building. It was a sight I had never seen before. He was big and tall. Lumbered along. I couldn't help smiling; it looked too funny.

"Oh, I'm too old to be running after the ladies," he said. "The smallest effort gets me out of breath these days."

I smiled. He had a sense of humor and self-awareness, anyway. He walked beside me on the flagstones, toward the entrance.

"I have some info for you about the girl robbery. One is that the shoeprint we found turned out to be from a plastic sole. You know how kids always used to wear something called slipper socks. It was a pair like that, children's size twelve. Unfortunately I don't think that will help you at all because you can find them in quite a few places. But there was another thing that was interesting. We found fibers on the floor of the bank that proved to be fluff from fabric. I read that she had a stuffed animal with her. It might very well be from that."

"Yes, the girl had a teddy bear with her."

There was nothing new here, I thought.

"The interesting thing is that there were traces of an odor-eliminating substance."

I stopped and looked at him with raised eyebrows, trying to look perplexed.

"It's a chemical mainly used to cover a person's or an object's own odor."

I frowned.

"How does it work?" I said.

"Either you dip the object into the agent or else you spray it on directly. These products are not usually very high quality but there are some that work surprisingly well."

"Where do you get hold of such things?"

"So far none has been approved by the EU, so they're sold over the Internet. In the US, though, they sell a lot of them. They're mainly used by hunters who want to hide themselves from animals in the woods."

Gunnar slowly shook his head and looked at me.

"It doesn't appear to be amateurs you're dealing with, Leona. If it was bad weather besides, windy, it would be hard for the pooches to pick up any trace."

I looked at him and nodded.

"Now a starving man is going to get some lunch," he said. "I'll send you the forensic report later. I just wanted to tell you as soon as possible."

"Thanks, Gunnar. Give me a call if anything else shows up."

THIRTY-THREE

With one hand around a paper coffee cup, I called and listened to my voice messages.

"Leona, this is Stina Hedlund from the Myggan day care center. It would be good if you could come and pick up Benjamin as soon as possible. He has stomach cramps again."

I sighed. Stina sounded irritated. I had wanted to change day care centers for a long time but Peter had insisted that the children should stay where they were. According to him it was the most practical choice, because Myggan was closest to home. Personally I thought that what was most practical was someplace that didn't irritate and upset me as soon as I had to deal with it. Stina and I had never gotten along. She was probably good with the kids, but she didn't seem to like adults. Possibly that said something about the level of her intelligence. On the other hand, she seemed to like Peter. I didn't understand why Stina hadn't called him instead. I had lots of work to do, but I didn't have the energy to call and argue with Peter about going to pick up Benji, so I got into the car and drove to the day care center.

Next week we had an appointment with Benjamin's new doctor.

"He's in the cozy room," said Stina curtly. "By the way, he's only been asking for his dad."

"So why didn't you call him?" I said, leaning over to take off my boots at the shoe boundary.

The one time I had been stressed and gone past the boundary with shoes on, Stina's shrill voice had almost broken in her eagerness to reprimand me.

"I did, of course, but he didn't answer. He was probably in an important meeting."

She studied my well-polished shoes with envy in her eyes.

"By the way, it would be good if in the future you could be easier to reach. We don't have time to be calling around when the children are sick."

I ignored her and went straight into the cozy room. The walls were painted in a warm orange color and the furniture consisted of large stuffed cubes in various hues. At the back was a red sofa with giant pillows where Benjamin was lying in Linnéa's arms. Linnéa was the teacher he turned to most. He always called her Nea. She was reading from a book and looked up when Benjamin caught sight of me.

"Mommy," he said in a weak voice.

"Hi honey, how are you? Does your tummy hurt?"

"Gone, gone."

I looked at Linnéa.

"Yes, it actually seems to have passed. He had cramps at times during the morning. At lunch he felt sick and didn't eat anything, and he's just been lying here resting."

"No pancake."

"There were pancakes today that he couldn't eat," said Linnéa. "After lunchtime the cramps came back but since we called you he's been calm. Maybe he can stay, if you have a lot to do at work?"

"No, I think we'll go home and have pancakes instead, or what do you say, honey?"

"Yes! Pancake!"

The reaction was expected. He loved pancakes with blueberry jam, just as I did when I was a kid. Even if they were made of lactose-free milk and almond and coconut flour instead of wheat flour, he liked them. No lactose and no gluten, doctor's orders. Now that the cramps had passed he would probably be able to eat a little. I smiled and picked him up.

"Bye now, Benjamin," said Stina without giving me so much as a glance on my way out.

I felt peace in my body when I had him near me. His small arms around my neck. His smooth forehead against my throat. His smell.

I walked from the day care with Benjamin in my arms. From a distance I could see a man leaning against the hood of my car. It was Christer Skoog.

"What the hell are you doing here?" I said.

"Leona! Nice to see you too. I've been looking for you."

He was puffing on a cigarette that he nonchalantly tossed away, blowing the smoke out toward the sky. I unlocked the car, put Benjamin in the car seat and closed the door.

"What the hell do you mean by coming to my kid's day care! Are you stalking me? You should be fucking careful about following me or anyone from my fam—"

"Now, now, should a police officer talk that way? You don't answer when I call, so what do you think I should do? I need more information."

"You leave my family the fuck alone, do you understand that?"

I walked past him, yanked open the car door, and got in. As I drove away, I could see his provocative smile.

THIRTY-FOUR

It was nine minutes past seven, which meant that the last real estate agent who was coming to appraise our apartment was late. Peter, who was actively pushing what he thought was our impending relocation project, had contacted the agent a couple of weeks ago. I didn't get involved until it occurred to me that I could benefit from an appraisal. Now I intended to take part in selecting the real estate agent.

The appraisal was important because I needed to persuade the bank to give us a bigger loan. We had replaced the pipes, after all, and taken the opportunity to lay new floors in the apartment when the kitchen and bathroom were renovated. The apartment was in much better shape now than when we bought it, so it ought to be appraised higher.

What characters some of these real estate agents were. One of them distinguished himself by storming in and throwing himself on the couch without even pretending to look around the apartment. The only thing he had with him was a wrinkled sheet of paper on which he jotted various numbers and tables while he babbled on at high speed, explaining that he definitely knew what he was talking about because he had worked in the industry for ten years. He appraised the apartment at almost twenty percent more than the other agents, which presumably gave a hint of his craziness. Probably his tactic was to overappraise apartments to get an advantage over the other agents. I couldn't draw any other conclusion because he hadn't bothered to look around the apartment and couldn't have assumed any statistics different from the other agents where the value of similar apartments in the area was concerned. But in the present situation I was completely uninterested in his motives. I was only focused on the amount. The hard thing would be to convince Peter that we should pick this particular agent. I had told him that I didn't want to make any decisions before we met them all.

Peter poured a glass of juice and put his arms around me in the kitchen.

"Listen, if the agent who is coming now doesn't beat all the others then I think we should go with the first one who was here. She was nice, knowledgeable, and seemed to have both feet on the ground. I assume you think the same?" he said, stroking back the hair from my neck.

"I'm leaning more toward that man who was here on Tuesday," I said.

"What?"

Peter let go of me and backed away.

"The one who had worked for ten years and —"

"I know exactly who you mean but I don't know if you're joking," he said, taking a gulp of the grapefruit juice. After a grimace he poured what was left in the glass into the sink.

"He was overbearing, totally uninterested in the apartment, and completely ignored what we said to him."

"He was probably just nervous, Peter."

Excusing an idiot by saying that he was probably just nervous would drive anyone crazy. I would need to come up with some better arguments for why I thought we should hire that weirdo.

I felt a vibration in my pocket. Took out my work phone and looked at the display. Christer Skoog. I declined the call. Why was he calling me in the evening?

"He has ten years' experience, after all, and he seems driven," I said. "Besides, he appraised the apartment highest of all, which means that he must be prepared to fight to sell at that price. It would be embarrassing for him if he was mistaken and appraised the apartment a million kronor too high."

"Embarrassing? Hardly," said Peter. "He would just shrug and brag to the next seller. After he's taken home our fee, that is. No, I think that we — "

Peter was interrupted by the doorbell.

"I wanna get it, I wanna get it!"

Beatrice ran to the door. I grimaced: it was time again. Peter saw my expression.

"Put Bea to bed and I'll take care of the real estate agent," said Peter.

Relieved, I took Beatrice's hand.

"Come on honey, let's go and read a good-night story."

"No, I want to talk with the rel'tor."

"Daddy will take care of that creep. We'll go and crawl into bed together and get cozy."

"Then I want to play computer like Mommy."

Bea had picked up that I played poker at night and had started talking about it during the day. I wasn't sure whether Peter understood what she meant.

"Come on, let's go and read *The Kid's Book* instead."

She wasn't happy with that, letting out a shrill screech.

"Noooo, play computer, play computer."

I cast a glance at Peter.

"Shh, you'll wake Benjamin," I said as I took a firm hold of her hand and pulled her away from the hall.

"We'll tiptoe together."

As usual I fell asleep after a few sentences and woke up when Peter came into the room. Beatrice had fallen asleep, so I slipped out of bed.

"I think this agent has — "

"Can we talk about it tomorrow, Peter? I'm going to bed. It was a big day at work."

I went to bed. When Peter had gone to bed and fallen asleep I would get up and play. As usual.

The hours flew by. It was 3:36 a.m. the next time I looked at the clock. It wasn't possible to get comfortable in the office chair we had bought from Ikea no matter how I adjusted it. Even though I got up and stretched occasionally, my back felt like a piece of wood. I was cramping. And tired. I only had a few minutes of dozing at the desk in the scheduled breaks of the tournaments. During a couple of them I had lain down on the guest bed and slept, with my phone timer set for five minutes.

If I weren't a police officer, the obvious option would have been to ingest some strongly energizing substance. Lots of coffee helped a bit. The eyedrops I let run into the corner of my eyes at regular intervals took away the dry, gritty feeling I got from staring at the screen for hours. When the cooling fluid streamed over my eyeballs it was as if my whole head was being rinsed with clean, rippling water. Could you become addicted to eyedrops? That and the coffee, however, no longer produced as great an effect. They presumably only managed to dampen a certain tension. Now I was simply too tired. In a couple of hours the kids would rise. After that the whole machinery would start up. The very thought exhausted me.

If, in addition, I hadn't lost, I probably would have been in a better mood. The night's gambling included cash games and two slightly longer tournaments. I lost both the tournaments and most of the other games, which had resulted in a significant monetary loss. I knew that there was not much left of the money I had borrowed from our joint savings account, either. And the money from the robbery had to stay hidden until the whole plan was completed. Numbered euro bills from bank robberies could not be used in just any old way.

The currency I was playing poker in was American dollars, but I did not intend to calculate exactly how much the combined losses were in Swedish kronor.

I couldn't bear to.

Not now.

THIRTY-FIVE

I looked out the big café window on Södermalm. The rain meant Götgatan was almost empty of pedestrians who otherwise would be window-shopping. Those who hurried past struggled to keep hold of their umbrellas, which were bent back by the wind. I was not generally one to complain to others, but with Larissa I could let down my guard a little. Larissa and I had first gotten to know each other at the Police Academy.

I was overjoyed when I got into the academy. My determination about my choice of occupation had made me almost fanatical where schoolwork was concerned. All my available time I devoted to studying, to improve my knowledge on everything from the legal system to gun handling.

Larissa was my exact opposite, a party girl who took life lightly. She didn't study much and spent all her free time at the gym and the bar. A strange combination, I thought. Fitness fanatics usually didn't go out and stuff themselves with toxic substances like alcohol and cigarettes after a workout session, but Larissa did whatever she felt like.

After graduation I had done everything that was expected of me. Of an ordinary Swedish girl. I had married a nice man, had two children, and worked my way up through the ranks of the police to where I was now. Larissa had gone a different way. She worked a year or two after graduation but soon realized that the police force did not suit her. After that she changed occupations and became a fitness consultant and personal trainer. She had calmed down considerably since our schooldays.

"How are you two getting along, you and Peter?" she asked.

I sighed deeply. Whether the sigh was too deep to be credible I had a hard time deciding. I never thought all that much about our relationship. Peter was just a part of the plan.

"Peter wants to have more kids and move to a house in the suburbs," I said.

Larissa, who had recently gone through a divorce and now lived by herself in the house she and her ex-husband had shared, closed her eyes and shook her head. I took it as a sign she understood the problem. I could lay it on further.

"I shudder at the very thought," I continued. "In my mind I see only grass cutting, sealing windows, water leaks in the cellar, replacing roof tiles, painting the exterior, snow-plowing the driveway, all that sort of thing."

I looked at Larissa to see whether there was anything that suggested that the reality of living in a house was any different. She said nothing. That was answer enough. But my reluctance was not only connected to the work and maintenance that owning a house requires.

I was in fifth grade and had gone home with my classmate Sanna after school. Just inside the door, I was already astonished at how messy it was in her house. Shoes lay jumbled, and jackets were hanging in disarray. Not in rows and on hangers like at our house. Their home had no top floor, either.

And no cellar.

They lived in an apartment. It seemed good. When I grew up I didn't intend to live anywhere with a cellar. I would live high up.

Sanna's home had a strange atmosphere. Her family was big, but no one seemed to have to think about what they said; everything just bubbled out of them. At home I was always reprimanded when I talked too much. Here I couldn't think of anything to say. Mostly I just sat quietly, observing the others. Sanna's parents laughed a lot and often touched each other. Hugged. Once her mother patted me on the cheek and I jerked back.

"Oh, sorry, Leona," she said.

She put her head at an angle and rested her eyes on me. It was strange. I couldn't interpret her look. I had never seen that expression before. Was I expected to say something? Do something?

I went home with Sanna every now and then, as often as Mother allowed. I saw it as practice. When I didn't know what to do, or how I should behave, I imitated Sanna. I did exactly what she did. Because Sanna never made mistakes. Her mother and father never scolded her.

Sanna didn't understand how significant she was to me. From her I learned everything important.

How to behave.

How to be.

How to fit in.

"You don't want to have any more kids?" said Larissa.

I sat quietly. Genuine feelings always arose when I thought about the children. I wanted to be a good mother, but I couldn't find the right words to describe the darkness I saw before me when I thought about continuing to live that life. It simply didn't work anymore. I looked out toward the street. The water ran in furrows along the café window. It struck me that the weather in many ways symbolized my existence. Gloomy. Gray. I fixed my gaze on a man on the other side of the street, who in the rain was trying to wrest his bicycle loose from a row of bikes that were lying on the sidewalk.

Now was exactly the right time to go somewhere. Get away for a while. Just for a few days. For several months I had planned the trip. I would go away and prepare my move out of the country and the arrival of my new life.

Two years ago we had been there on vacation. Malta. One of Peter's colleagues had recommended it, and until then I didn't even know where it was. I'd had to look for it on the map: a tiny, tiny dot in the middle of the Mediterranean. Europe's southernmost nation, but otherwise not much to look at. I'd known nothing about the country but had thought a vacation there would be as good as any. On my way home after the trip I'd known it wasn't the last time I'd go there.

What I knew now was that Malta was a mecca for gaming companies. Even though there are only four hundred thousand inhabitants in the whole country, there are numerous casinos. Because Swedish Games has a monopoly in Sweden, several Swedish gaming companies had established themselves on Malta. During our first visit I had already started gradually testing online poker and if I hadn't been there with my family I probably would have tried playing live at a casino too.

I had quickly taken a liking to this lovely little cliff in the Mediterranean. I would go there and live. Find myself.

"I'm going abroad for a few days. Without Peter and the kids," I said, continuing to look out the window.

The man with the bicycle was wearing a rain cape and apparently suit pants underneath. He kept looking at his watch as he yanked and tore at the bicycles to get his loose.

"Oh my God, that sounds great. I'll come with you!"

The plan to prepare my flight out of the country hadn't included a travel companion.

"Lie on the beach, have drinks at outdoor bars, and nice dinners at restaurants on warm evenings under an open sky," she continued.

The man outside had managed to get two bikes loose and had started tugging at a third that was on top of the one that seemed to be his.

"But can you really take time off?" I said, hoping she had only temporarily forgotten that she had a job to take care of.

I had requested leave back in March when the vacation applications for the whole year were supposed to be turned in. I had asked for two days, so that I could go from Thursday to Sunday. The leave was already granted and if Claes were to protest about it now he would be forced to order me to recall the vacation and presumably work overtime, which would cost too much. Overtime was a sensitive subject for management. Those who gave their personnel too much overtime were considered unable to manage their personnel planning and, as a result, their managerial role. And if you couldn't manage your role, there was always someone else who would manage it better. The organization was packed with supervisors. For once I could be happy that the vacation planning was done so early. If Claes complained, I'd point out that we had those excellent workers he'd arranged, Minna and Sam, who could hold down the fort while I was gone. I wasn't particularly worried about leaving the investigation. I knew what information would conceivably come in. Preparing for my arrival in Malta was a must.

"Oh, I can arrange the time off. I'm self-employed, you know. I mostly have workout sessions with clients at the moment. I'll just have to reschedule a few of them."

I thought about it. It might be good to have Larissa along anyway. I had told Peter I needed to get away from home for a while and that I would be traveling with a colleague. Now I could say that the colleague had conflicts and that Larissa would go along instead. When I got home I could show him pictures of the two of us. Larissa would presumably want to lie on the beach all day anyway. Then I could take care of my business.

"A nice weekend at a hotel somewhere on the Mediterranean. Spain. Barcelona maybe?"

"I've already booked it," I said. "Malta. I'm going this Thursday."

"Malta? I see…Okay, whatever. I'll book this evening, there's always a leftover seat. At least one good drunken night and a lot of chitchat. Maybe I'll be courted by some Stavros."

I smiled at her enthusiasm and impulsiveness. For Larissa, anything was possible.

"Stavros is a Greek name."

"Oh, you know what I mean," she said, waving one hand. "Marvelous!"

I looked out the window. The man was still there. The rain was pouring down now. After another quick look at his watch he abandoned the bicycle and jogged away.

It really was the right time to go.

THIRTY-SIX

I put the car in reverse to get out of the hospital parking lot. My thoughts were whirling. The meeting with Dr. Elerud had dragged on, and the news we'd received did not make life any simpler. I couldn't bear to talk to Peter about what had been said.

"Shall I drive you to work or are you done for the day?" I said.

"Work."

Peter's tone was short. He too seemed affected by the meeting with the doctor. Benjamin's intestine was more inflamed than they had previously thought and it wasn't possible to surgically remove more of it. He would most likely need a bowel transplant, which was an extremely complicated operation. Not to mention risky. But a life with tube feeding could be the only alternative if it wasn't done.

"Why can't they do it at Sahlgrenska Hospital in Gothenburg like the last operation?"

"The operation takes fifteen hours and there is a risk of blood poisoning. Weren't you listening?" said Peter. "She said that when they started doing the operation in the nineties in England patients died on the operating table."

"Strange telling that to parents of a sick child," I said, pressing down on the accelerator to cross before the light changed.

"That was a long time ago."

"Too bad the local council won't pay for the operation, or at least part of it. That along with travel and lodging in Oxford for a whole family will cost a fortune," I said.

"We have to be happy it's possible to operate."

"Yes, but can we be sure he'll really get better? What if…"

Peter looked at me. "Leona, you know we can't go on like this. If there's a chance for him to get better we have to take it."

I nodded. He was right. The alternative, to let Benji live in pain for the rest of his life, was too unbearable to imagine.

"We do have the money," said Peter. "Think about the families that can't afford it. What a frustrating situation to have a sick child and not be able to pay for health care. How much do we have in the savings account?"

Peter looked at me.

"Uh…It's been a while since I looked…I don't really know…"

I knew exactly. Three hundred and twenty-three kronor.

"Considering how many years we've saved we should be well on our way," said Peter.

"Hmm."

I was calm. As soon as I had won back the money I would put it in the savings account again and we would have enough for the operation.

"Thanks for the ride, darling."

Peter got out of the car. He leaned over and looked at me through the half-open car door.

"Don't worry," he said. "He's going to get healthy if we just have the operation. We have our savings."

THIRTY-SEVEN

"Look, look, Mommy on TV, Mommy on TV!"

Beatrice laughed loudly and ran closer to the TV. She and Peter had turned it on to get a glimpse of me.

"Yes, look, there I am. How do you think I look?"

"You look weird, Mommy."

I smiled.

"You can be a bit weird yourself," I said, rubbing a pillow on her stomach so that she started laughing out loud. "Now you've seen me, run off and start brushing your teeth, then Daddy will come and help you."

"But I want to see, Mommy."

"We've already talked about this, Bea. It's way too scary for kids. You'll have nightmares. Off you go now."

She moved toward the bathroom with her arms hard around the pillow.

I had managed to back out of my promise to be at the *Sweden's Most Wanted* studio for the broadcast. Blamed it on too much work. Despite my opinions about *Sweden's Most Wanted* I had to admit that the reporting was entertaining. With their reenactment, they managed to make the robbery resemble an action film with elements of horror.

Presumably tips would pour in about everything under the sun, most of them completely unusable. There was always a gang of wackos who called in and gave totally irrelevant tips. But suddenly, in the middle of the tips, someone might turn up who had information of substance. I had asked Anette to turn all tips directly over to me when they came in. The fact that the *Most Wanted* editors knew about them didn't matter, because they had no idea of the content of the investigation in general, but I didn't want others on the squad snooping. Least of all Minna and Sam.

"Mommy, why did the girl do that?"

Without Peter and me noticing, Bea had come back from the bathroom and was standing in the doorway with the toothbrush in her hand.

"Oh honey...Peter, please, will you help her?" I said.

Peter got up quickly.

"Come on, I'll help you finish brushing."

"But where is she?" said Bea on her way back to the bathroom.

"Mommy doesn't know yet," said Peter. "She's the one who's trying to find out."

When I thought the feature about the robbery was over, they stayed with the camera outside the crime scene in Old Town. A reporter was speaking to an elderly man who was standing beside her. The man was wearing a checked cap and supported himself with a cane. I had never seen him before but realized immediately who he was — the man who had touched the girl during the robbery. He was recorded as a witness in the investigation. I had read the interview with him, but I hadn't seen what he looked like. It was a very emotional interview. The man had no new facts to add to the investigation, but said several times that the incident had upset him. It wasn't particularly surprising that TV3 had chosen him for an interview.

"I had read about the first robbery at the bank at Öster-malmstorg and thought it was strange that no one could do anything for that little girl, but when I stood there in Forex and saw her...then I understood why." He shook his head. "It was frightfully horrid…gruesome. The little girl was so fragile. The voice on the tape forbade us to touch her or contact anyone outside…Otherwise…"

He fell silent. The reporter held the microphone by his mouth. Waited, hoping for more details. When the old man did not continue the reporter said, "What would have happened if any of you had helped her?"

The man took a deep breath.

"They would not let her live, to put it simply. The voice said that he could see everything that was happening in the room, so everyone did as the voice said. I wanted to take hold of her and keep her there but…I simply didn't dare. For the girl's safety."

"How is it that you dared to go up to her anyway?"

"I just wanted to try to talk with her a little. Maybe get something out of her that might help the police later…but she didn't answer."

"You touched her?" said the reporter.

"I hoped that she would talk with me, but she ran away. Since then I've…"

The man fell silent again. The reporter waited. I was astonished that they had set aside so much time for this story. The reporter didn't speak. She let him work through his emotions, waiting.

"…Since then I've been worried that my actions may have made it worse for the girl. I hope that she is still alive. I wouldn't forgive myself otherwise…"

His eyes filled with tears. The reporter turned straight to the camera.

"A child's life is in danger. If you know anything about the girl, or have any information about the robbery, it may be important. Call *Sweden's Most Wanted* at 08 702 00 90."

They nailed it. The broadcast presumably went straight into the hearts of Swedes. A poor little girl-child who was being treated badly. It wasn't hard to imagine people's fantasies about what such a small child might have been subjected to.

"I don't get what makes people tick," said Peter, throwing the pillow back on the couch that Bea had taken with her to the bathroom. "This is just a child. Some people have no boundaries at all."

He left to look after Bea.

"Hope you get hold of those sick people soon," he called on his way. "Lock them up and throw away the key."

THIRTY-EIGHT

"You did so well on *Most Wanted* yesterday, Leona," Anette called as I walked past in the corridor in the morning.

I went into my office, set the pile of incoming tips on the desk and took a deep breath. Needed caffeine. At least one cup. I took off my jacket and went into the break room to get some coffee.

"Leona! As seen on TV!"

Julle, one of our local crime scene investigators, gave me a thumbs-up from one of the armchairs. He and his constant companion, Bubble, had the habit of hanging around in our break room when they had extra time, of which they seemed to have a fair amount. Now they were sitting on our sofas making comments as people walked past.

"Well now, if it isn't my favorite technician," I answered sarcastically. "In need of another cup of coffee?"

"Equally attractive and sarcastic," Julle continued with a smile. "It's more than you can say about that half-baked program host they have on *Most Wanted*."

"Were you thinking about inviting us in for coffee in your office?"

Bubble was looking at the two cups of coffee I had taken from the machine.

"You wish! Unlike you, I take responsibility for my work, which requires serious concentration. For that I need to get high on a double dose of caffeine."

"Sure, it probably takes a lot of concentration to turn over all the papers on your desk. Don't forget to turn them back over later."

The two of them looked at each other and laughed loudly. It had been many years since I had thought that Julle and Bubble, or Jacob Nordlund and Bengt Sandström as their real names were, added anything humorous to life at the agency. To begin with it had been amusing to hear their drivel, making fun of everything and everyone. These days I found them irritating.

"Don't you ever deserve a pastry down there at your squad — is that why you always come up here and mooch?"

"We work during the day, you see, Leona. We don't have time for coffee breaks down there. How's work going for you? I heard you're investigating the girl robbery and that you have Nina Wallin as preliminary investigation leader. Congratulations! You'd have to search hard for a more zealous prelim leader."

Julle laughed loudly at Bubble's commentary and added to it as usual.

"There won't be any reclining in your chair with your footsies on the desk for you, Leo. Now you'll have to toil for your daily bread."

I went into my office and quickly skimmed through the bundle of tips from *Most Wanted*. Most were total trash. Either whoever had turned in the tips was completely incoherent or else the police interns transcribing them had limited knowledge about how you put an oral statement down on paper. One tip, however, seemed interesting and suited my needs. There was a witness who claimed to have seen a man running from the scene at the time of the crime at SEB. I put that tip on my desk and continued browsing. Another witness described standing on the other side of the street and seeing a child with bare legs walking along the sidewalk on Nybrogatan on her way from SEB. A delivery van had come along the street between them and when it drove past the girl was gone. The witness had crossed the street to look, but hadn't seen the girl anywhere. She thought that she must have seen wrong, until she heard the news on P3 a few hours later. I set the tip aside and continued browsing.

A witness by the name of Madeleine Lundby, a manicurist at a salon on Scheelegatan, a block from the police building, remembered a strange man who came in and bought fake blood early the same morning as the robbery at Forex. The man had spoken with a Finnish accent and had said to Madeleine that the blood was for his children who were going to a Halloween party. According to Madeleine, everyone who bought blood also got a cheap Halloween mask along with it. She had thought it was strange that the man only wanted the blood and didn't take the mask, and that he'd bought three bottles. According to Madeleine one bottle is enough to cover a grown man from head to toe. Madeleine was not sure it had anything to do with the robbery but she wanted to contact the police to be on the safe side.

I stared at the piece of paper. It was inconceivable that Ronni had managed to fuck up that one simple thing. How could he be so stupid that he hadn't taken the mask? Not to mention buying three whole bottles at once. I felt my own blood pulsing in my veins. I tore the tip into pieces and went directly out to the document shredder. While I pressed the tip down I reeled off a string of words in my head, swearing to myself that I would never work with criminals again.

Never.

They were simply unable to commit crimes.

In yet another tip, a man who had driven past in his car saw another car stop a block or two away and let out a girl who had been "strangely dressed." He hadn't thought about it until he saw it on the news. It was fine to contact him at any time of day if that was needed, he said.

"Thanks but that won't be necessary," I said out loud to myself, putting the tip in the top drawer of the desk.

"What isn't necessary?" asked Claes who was suddenly standing in the doorway, looking at me.

"What? Uh, nothing in particular, I'm just babbling to myself as usual."

"Nice appearance on *Most Wanted* yesterday, by the way. They should have you in the studio, damn it, instead of those old bores they have. You're much more photogenic."

He winked.

"Thanks. Don't forget that I've now represented the agency in the media and hopefully increased our credibility. That should make my coin purse jingle at the next salary negotiation," I said.

He laughed and started to head back toward his office. After a few steps he turned and said, "I want you to set up a meeting where you account for the incoming tips from *Most Wanted*. I also want to be updated on the case as such." He took out his phone. "Three o'clock on Thursday. Then you'll have plenty of time. Be sure to make some progress."

I understood what this was about. Claes wanted to be able to tell the head of investigations and the county police chief that he had the situation under control. I would check further on the tip that concerned the man seen running from the scene. He needed to be brought in.

I took the rest of the tips to Minna and Sam.

"Check through this bundle. These are tips from *Most Wanted* yesterday. Concentrate on what might concern the girl."

None of the tips would give any lead as to where the girl was, but I needed to keep them busy.

"On Thursday at three o'clock we'll have a meeting in the conference room. I'll update Claes and the head of investigations about what has emerged in the case. Have you found anything interesting?"

They looked at each other as if they both wanted the other to say something. Did they know something they hadn't told me?

"What?" I said.

"Not yet," Sam answered.

"Okay, keep working then. I know you're doing what you can."

I could afford a little praise, since they had been so obliging and not managed to produce any evidence at all. I was starting to realize the advantage of working with two inexperienced investigators.

I dialed the number of the person who claimed to have seen a man running from the scene. It was best that it was me who took his information and no one else.

A stressed voice answered on the other end.

"Sandström."

"Kent Sandström?" I said.

"Yes?"

"Leona Lindberg. I'm calling from the city police in regard to the robbery at SEB at Östermalmstorg. I have received information that you were in the vicinity when it happened."

"That's correct."

"I see that you live in Uppsala. Do you know the streets in Stockholm well?"

"No, not really. But I wonder if the street isn't called —"

"I'd like you to come in here as soon as possible. We'll do the interview here at the station so you can show us on a map. It's important that it's right."

"I can't come now. I've got an important meeting in ten minutes."

"Kent, this is a police investigation that concerns a serious crime with a child involved."

"Yes, I realize that, but—"

"Where are you?"

"At Sveavägen 147. I'm only in Stockholm for today, for this meeting."

"Okay. I'll come there."

People were so troublesome. He sounded like a typical businessman in a suit who thought that his meeting with other businessmen in suits was more important than anything else. That really provoked me. If I had the option, I would have used coercive measures against him. Sent a marked car with blue lights and sirens. Made sure that four uniformed, muscular, male officers thundered in with guns drawn, and dragged Kent Sandström out of his "important" meeting.

It was a flashy office I stepped into at Sveavägen 147. The floor was made of large white tiles so well polished you could see your reflection in them, and from the ceiling hung what must have been the biggest crystal chandelier in the city. Flashing prisms hung in twisted lines toward the floor. The light from it made an impressive formation on the shiny surface. Sound was dampened by large white curtains that hung from the high ceiling down to the floor by the windows. The whole place resembled a grand hotel lobby. I went straight to the reception area on the other side of the entrance.

"I'm here to see Kent Sandström."

The older, well-dressed woman behind the counter did not respond. She looked at me with an expressionless face and let out a deep sigh before she began tapping on her computer. After a moment or two she stopped and said in a monotone, "There's no such person here."

"I just spoke with him."

"We have no such person here."

The woman, whose nametag read Siri von Platen, didn't look up at me.

"Would you please look again?" I said. "He is supposed to be here today."

"You do hear what I'm saying?" Siri raised her voice. "We have no such person here. You'll have to go somewhere else."

"I'm not going anywhere until you've seen about getting Kenny."

It felt good to say Kenny. As if we were good friends.

"Are you having a hard time understanding?" said Siri, raising her voice even more. "*There is no such person here!*"

It was obvious that Mrs. Siri von Platen wasn't in the best mood today. I thought I had given her enough elbow room. Now my irritation had been transformed. Not to fury, but to an amused calm. I waited, with enjoyment, for the familiar phrase to come. It probably wouldn't take long.

"Now you need to get out of here!"

Siri truly had the capacity to look terrifying when she wrinkled her whole face up into a raisin and fixed her small eyes on me. I leaned over.

"No. Get Kenny!"

I deliberately expressed myself like a defiant teenager. Siri looked around. She seemed to be searching for someone to come to her rescue. When there was no one there she pushed a button on the side of the counter that made the screen of glass between us slowly slide down. I calmly put my hand on the counter under the screen. Siri let go of the button.

"What are you doing? Remove your hand!"

I smiled. Waited for the phrase to come. Come on now, say it!

"*Remove your hand, I said!*" Siri roared with the screen half-closed.

"No," I said calmly.

"Remove it *now*, or I'll call the police!"

Ha! There it was. Now it was Christmas Eve. With my other hand I pulled the badge I had around my neck from under my jacket. I pressed it hard on the glass between us and smiled.

"That won't be necessary. I'm already here."

I would have paid a lot for a framed photo of Siri von Platen's face. The raisin face with the narrow squint was transformed into an oblong horse face with wide-open, globular eyes. Siri stared at the badge. She didn't make a sound.

"Raise the window," I ordered.

I loved how the whole process was reversed. Now I was the one in control. Without a sound and with her eyes still fixed on my badge, Siri pressed the button so the screen went up.

"So, now you can start tapping on your little keyboard again and find my buddy Kenny."

Now we had become buddies too, Kent Sandström and I. Funny how different situations can bring people closer together.

Siri began to search nervously. Tapped on the keyboard, rooted in binders and lists. I took out my phone. This seemed to be taking a while. Better that I called him myself.

"Kent. Leona here from the police. I'm in reception and waiting for you. I see...What? Okay. I'll go there."

I turned to Siri von Platen.

"Well, it looks like you'll be rid of me now. But I think you need to start thinking about how you conduct yourself. This kind of behavior is unacceptable for a receptionist. If you're going to sit behind that window anyway, why not do it with a little dignity, Mrs. von Platen?"

She nodded slowly. I started to walk away, making my way to the entry next door. Kent had obviously said the wrong street number. I stood outside and waited. He came out and shook my hand. He didn't look as formal as I had imagined, but was instead dressed casually in jeans, a jacket, and sneakers.

"Is there a room inside where we can sit?" I said.

"No, I'm only here on a visit."

"Okay, my car is over here. We can talk there," I said.

We got in. I checked his identity and noted the time.

"Okay, here is a map of the area. The bank is here. Here you see a square, Östermalmstorg. There is a subway entrance here." I pointed at the map.

"Yes, okay, then I know where we are. I was walking here when I saw a man come running in that direction with a bag in his hand."

"What type of bag was it?"

"A backpack. Small and colorful. I noticed him simply because he had it in his hand. It looked funny somehow. I thought that if he was in a hurry and had to run it would be easier to put the pack on his back. I got a feeling that there was something fragile in it."

"Describe the backpack in more detail."

"It was pink and red and had something on the front. A cartoon animal I think."

"What did the man look like?"

"Dark clothing. I guess he looked like most people do. He jumped into a car approximately here."

Kent indicated on the map. It was two blocks from the bank.

"What kind of car was it?"

"Golf, I think. Dark."

"Do you remember any of the license plate number?"

"Unfortunately no."

"Can you describe the man's appearance a little more. Physique? Height?"

"Normal, perhaps my height, about 183 centimeters, though it's hard to say because he was running on the other side of the street."

"Hair?"

"Dark, cut short."

"Do you think you would recognize him if you saw him again?"

"I didn't really see him from the front."

"Was there anything else you noticed? Was he alone?"

"As far as I could see. He put the bag on the passenger seat and took off quickly. Turned right at the intersection."

"Okay, Kent. I won't keep you any longer. Here's my card if you think of anything else. Otherwise, thanks for your help."

"No problem."

Kent left the car. I was satisfied. He had submitted information about a possible perpetrator. I just needed one more witness that pointed in the same direction.

I reached for my phone, which was vibrating so much it was about to fall from the dashboard. It was Christer Skoog. Damn it. I didn't have any more information for him right now. I let it buzz while I opened my laptop and browsed through all the witness interviews. There were still a few who had been questioned very briefly, among others a young woman, Alexandra Nilsson. I entered the number.

"Alexandra, I'm calling you with reference to the bank robbery at Östermalmstorg. I would like you to tell me what you saw. Do you have time?"

"I'm on the subway. On my way to school."

"That's fine. We'll do it on the phone."

Good, the more unfocused Alexandra was, the better.

"Well, I didn't see that much. Just a guy on the street with a bag, like. I guess it was a man, you know."

"What did he look like?"

"Tall. Dark hair."

"How tall, approximately?"

"Pretty tall."

"Could he have been over 180, around 183?"

"Yes, about that."

"You said that he had dark hair. Was it cut short?"

"Mmm."

This was going well. Alexandra's testimony needed to be as close to Kenny's as possible. I needed two independent testimonies that pointed to the same person. With a few more leading questions to Alexandra, I would hopefully achieve that.

"Do you remember whether he had dark clothing on?"

"I think so."

"The bag he was carrying, was it small or what?"

"I don't really know. Pretty small, I think. Dark blue or black, I think."

Damn it. Kent had said it was colorful.

"Are you sure about the colors?"

"Not completely, but it was some dark color."

"Alexandra, it's extremely important that this is right, so we don't accuse the wrong person. The color of the bag is essential information for us. Are you completely sure that it was dark?"

There was silence on the line a couple of seconds.

"Well…I guess I'm not a hundred percent…"

"Were there any bright colors on it?"

"I don't really remember…"

"Could it have been red or pink?"

"Maybe in some small place."

"But you saw something dark on it too?"

"Yes."

"Dark, red, and pink then?"

"Yes, it was probably something like that…"

I read out loud while I wrote. It was important to fix the colors in Alexandra's memory.

"'Alexandra describes the bag as dark, red, and pink,'" I repeated.

She did not contradict from her end. Good.

"How did he leave the place?"

"He was walking."

"Slowly or fast?"

"Pretty fast I think."

"Did you see his legs or was there anything that blocked your view?"

"There were a few parked cars."

"So you actually only saw his upper body?"

"Mmm."

"Could he have been jogging?"

"I think he was going pretty fast. He may have been running a little."

"Is there anything else that you remember in particular, Alexandra?"

"Not that I can think of…But my friend Angelica was there and she saw —"

"I'll read my notes here for you, Alexandra. Listen and speak up if something is not correct. You have seen a man with normal physique, short-cut dark hair and about 183 centimeters tall come walking on Nybrogatan carrying a small bag. The bag was dark, pink, and red. He left the scene running a little. Does that tally?"

"I'm not quite sure about that part with the bag but —"

"Okay, I'll change it then and write that the bag was *probably* dark, pink, and red. Is that okay?"

"Yes, that's fine."

"Thanks so much for your testimony, Alexandra. You've given us some valuable information."

I looked down at the interview notes. The interview was completely miserable from an investigative viewpoint. Totally incomplete, with many obvious questions I had chosen not to ask. The questions I did ask were leading and besides that I had planted things in Alexandra's memory that she hadn't mentioned on her own. It violated all ethics and reasonable interview methods, but what could I do?

Now that both Kent and Alexandra had submitted similar testimonies I only needed to ask Minna and Sam to find a man, preferably living in the area, who tallied with the descriptions and who had some prior criminal offenses. That would not be hard.

A man.

Normal build.

Middle-aged.

Dark-haired.

Short hair.

Dark clothes.

A pleasing description.

THIRTY-NINE

There at the top of the stairs it was as if everything from home disappeared from my thoughts.

House.

Children.

Marriage.

Work.

Everything was blown away by the mild Mediterranean breeze. I stood there for a moment, soaking up the atmosphere. I was astonished at the landscape. The warm, glowing light of the afternoon sun glistening on the roof of the arrivals hall. The swaying palms. The humid air. It was heaven.

"Come on, you're blocking the line."

Larissa called from down on the ground. I started down the narrow stairs. Larissa had managed to find a ticket even though she booked so close to the departure date. Claes hadn't been happy to see me go, but said nothing, as I'd told him Minna and Sam were carefully instructed in which investigative measures were to be prioritized. Personally, I felt calm. I was in control of the investigation. Minna and Sam would only do what I told them to do, and I would be back on Monday.

Peter, who always thought I worked too much, was encouraging and thought it would do me good to think about something else for a weekend.

The hotel was in a beautiful location, with an amazing view of Spinola Bay, dense with boats and restaurants. I set down my bags in the room and went straight out onto the balcony. Warm, pale cliffs against the turquoise blue sea.

"God, this is wonderful. A paradise."

Larissa came out onto the balcony with cigarettes and a lighter in her hand. She had already changed into a thin skirt, chemise, and flip-flops. Silently we looked out over the sea.

"Wow, what kind of building is that?"

Larissa pointed out toward a long pier. Far out on it, framed by shoreline cliffs behind it, was a magnificent white building with stately pillars along the front side. On the roof was a large neon sign that said CASINO.

"We have to go there tonight, Leona! We'll dress up, go out and have a good dinner with three courses and good wine and then go to the casino and gamble away all our money."

I laughed. I knew she was joking. Larissa would never set foot in a casino. Despite her very liberal attitude to most things she despised all forms of gambling. That was why I hadn't told her about my poker playing. She was of the opinion that anyone who gambled became addicted sooner or later. Even if it was tempting, I didn't intend to gamble while we were here. I had other things to do.

Larissa's enthusiasm was contagious. We changed and didn't have to search long before we found a nice restaurant.

"Table for two?"

The waiter showed us in. I had put on a black dress. I wore skirts occasionally but I seldom wore a dress. I felt much too dressed up in one at home. Here everyone was dressed up. Tight-fitting dresses and high heels stood in line behind us. The women wore beautiful jewelry and elegant hairstyles, the men, jackets.

It was as if the waiter knew exactly what we needed. We got a table for two with a view of the sea. The restaurant was in Porto-maso Bay, where multimillion-dollar yachts were moored.

"How can people afford it?"

Larissa looked out over the bay.

"Oh well. If we start saving now maybe we can afford to buy one of those in a few years."

I pointed at a water scooter that was hauled up on the white yacht *Sea Pearl*.

"Just think, that's only a little toy they bring with them when they go out and cruise. Sick," said Larissa.

"But there are so many problems with having that much money. Imagine not knowing who your real friends are."

"Hmm...And what to do with all that money. Invest, save, give it away?" Larissa continued.

"All those options would only confuse you, and you have enough problems as it is."

"Give me the ordinary person's life. There you know what you have and don't need to worry."

We laughed heartily at our own sarcasm.

"Let's order a good, expensive wine to get us going," said Larissa.

I knew I couldn't afford an expensive wine, but I ignored that.

This evening I was free.

The locally produced Maltese wine tasted rich and fruity, which was the most important thing. After some consideration Larissa decided to try the national dish, rabbit. It was a disappointment. Dinner was no taste sensation. Considering that we were at a nicer restaurant, that was a bit surprising. We decided that the Maltese were not star chefs. With that discovery, our drinks acquired more significance. We moved to the high bar stools and switched to cocktails. The young bartender made it a sport, getting us to try the best drinks he could make. Their taste was almost orgasmic. The bartender seemed to enjoy studying our reactions as we imbibed one colorful drink after another. The level of maturity in our behavior might have been debatable, but who cared about such things when you were on an exotic Mediterranean island?

Presumably we'd been sitting in the bar a little too long, because we were both seriously intoxicated. As Larissa's and the bartender's conversations became longer and more intimate, I started to feel bored.

"Shall we get a move on, Larissa?"

It was the third time I had asked.

"Noooo, let's stay a little while longer, just a liiittle more."

Larissa showed a gap between her thumb and index finger to indicate how short a time we would stay. What time scale or calculation she was referring to was unclear, but she seemed to have no intention of leaving either the bartender or the drinks.

"You stay here, you're in good company."

I nodded to the bartender and winked at Larissa.

"I'll take a little walk and look around a bit, then see you in the room later."

Larissa barely seemed to hear what I said. She tossed her hair and leaned over the bar toward the bartender.

My high-heeled shoes, which I had only worn once at a friend's wedding the previous summer, were starting to feel comfortable. Maybe the drinks had dampened the pain. With light feet I danced past the large illuminated entry gate out toward the pier. On the left side was the luxury hotel—Westin Dragonara Resort—with large illuminated balconies and roof arches facing out toward the walkway and the bay.

Stray cats occupied the wall on either side of the single-lane road leading to the pier. They were lying there like majestic lions, peering at me as I went past.

A car drove around me, honking. But no drooling men in the world could put me in a bad mood now. I walked farther on steady heels, past the elegant hotel, toward Dragonara Casino. I was a good way out on the pier when I saw a platform out on the water. I went there, looked out at the sea, then in toward land. The buildings were lit up, glowing warmly against the pale stones along the coastline. The lights, from small local restaurants mixed with luxury bars and nightclubs, created glistening shadows at the water's edge. The sea was dark. Almost black. There was something frightening about it, but I still felt such freedom. I closed my eyes, drawing the aroma of sea and salt in my nostrils and listening to the rhythmic rippling sound of the waves as they swept in toward the cliffs. When the wind took hold of my pulled-back hair I undid it and let it flow down.

What liberation.

I continued on in the direction of the casino. Walking firmly, feeling more decisive with every step I took up the magnificent stone stairway to the entrance.

Now is when it would happen.

I would win.

FORTY

Olivia had always dreamed about other countries. Getting to take a long boat ride over the sea. Going to visit Grandma. Mommy always said that Grandma was nice. That she wished Daddy was more like her. Olivia did not remember ever meeting Grandma, but that didn't matter. In Mommy's photo album there were many pictures of her and Olivia. She looked nice, a round little old lady. Olivia remembered a picture where Grandma was kneeling and the two of them were hugging. It looked so cozy. In another, Olivia was standing outside a big entryway holding Grandma's hand. Mommy said that the photo was taken outside Grandma's house.

Daddy was not at the apartment so Olivia could stand and look out the window. She had been standing there for an hour. She knew that because the big hand on the wall had gone around one whole time.

The entrance on the other side of the street looked just as she remembered it from the picture. The one that Grandma lived in. It was big and rounded off on top. If Grandma would only come out of that entrance. Then Olivia would run there as fast as she could. She would throw her arms around her neck and squeeze, just like in the picture. Grandma would probably be happy if Olivia came to visit, and she would certainly give her something to eat. Maybe bread rolls. Oh, if she only got a roll. It was probably warm at Grandma's too. Otherwise she would borrow a cozy bathrobe or a warm blanket.

But Grandma did not come out. Only three people had come out of the entrance during the whole time Olivia stood watching. Perhaps she could go over there herself and knock on the door?

It was getting darker. Olivia had to turn off the light in the ceiling to be able to see out. What if she missed Grandma? She better go over there before it became completely dark.

Daddy had locked the door with a long key but Olivia knew where there was one like it. It was hanging on a hook high up in the wardrobe in the hall. She went into the kitchen and took hold of the back of one of the chairs by the table. She pulled at it to get it away from the table. It was heavy. One leg was stuck against the chair next to it so she had to pull as hard as she could to get it loose. When it came loose it came out so quickly that she almost fell backward. She dragged it along the kitchen floor, across the threshold, and out into the hall. It made a lot of noise but Daddy wasn't home so it didn't matter. She opened the wardrobe and placed the chair as close as she could. Her knees hurt when she climbed up on it but it worked anyway. She could probably get a bandage from Grandma later. She had to stand on tiptoe on the chair to get the key down from the hook. Then she was in such a hurry that she almost fell off the chair.

Daddy had said she was not allowed to go anywhere, but he probably wouldn't be angry when he found out she was with Grandma. Grandma was, after all, Daddy's mother. Maybe she should write a note to Daddy. She looked in the kitchen for a pen. There was a pile of newspapers and envelopes on the kitchen counter. She took a white envelope and started to write.

I gone to grammas.

She put on her shoes, and then she set the long key in the lock highest up and turned it. Two turns, as she had seen Daddy do. Then the lock below. It echoed in the stairwell outside when she carefully opened the door. She tiptoed down the stone stairs. There were many steps, but she didn't dare take the elevator. What if she pushed the wrong button?

The stairwell was scary. The slightest sound echoed loudly. Her knees hurt from walking down the stairs, but she had to hurry. What if Grandma went out now? While she was on her way? She slipped as quickly as possible down the hard, high stairs.

Far down below she heard the entry door close. She stopped. Listened. No one said anything. She heard heavy steps on the stairs, making their way upward. Thump, thump, thump. She didn't dare move. Stood completely stock-still. It was too far to run up again.

Suddenly the steps stopped. Keys rattled. A door was unlocked and opened. The door closed again and was locked from inside. Olivia continued. Now she had to run before any more people came. Before Daddy came. She ran down and opened the entry door. The cold struck her. She wished she had brought her jacket but it was impossible to go back. She started running between the parked cars and out onto the street to make her way over to the other side.

Just as she was close to the white lines she saw two adults approaching on foot. She met the man's gaze. Daddy! She almost froze to ice there in the middle of the street. She stopped. Did not know where she should go. Should she turn back? No, Daddy looked angry. He let go of the bag he was holding and started running toward her. She turned away from him and continued running across the street. Between the cars that were parked on the other side. Up onto the sidewalk. Toward the short little stairs near the turning area outside Grandma's building. A few more steps and she was at the stairs. She turned around. Daddy could be seen right behind a car driving past on the street. He shouted her name. Came running toward her. She had to hurry. Just four steps, then she would run as hard as she could to Grandma's doorway. She took hold of the cold iron railing. One step down. She turned around. Daddy was close now. She had to run faster. Three more steps left. She got ready. Jumped.

FORTY-ONE

"Here is terrace," said the real estate agent in broken English, pressing on the remote control she had taken from a holder on the wall.

The apartment was somewhat larger than the one I had just looked at on Portomaso Bay in St. Julian's on Malta. This one was in Sliema, a stone's throw away. According to the agent it should have a fine view of the capital, Valletta.

As the agent held down a button, the curtains along the panorama windows glided slowly to the sides. The whole room was lit up by daylight. The stone tiles of the terrace and the marbled frame around the pool shone like shimmering silver. The water in the pool, along with the sea and sky, were shades of blue clearer than I'd ever seen in a Swedish summer. On the other side of the bay Valletta's old churches and fortresses could be seen. I gasped for air. I had never seen anything like it. The night's poker playing at Dragonara Casino, which hadn't gone as I'd imagined, was completely blown away.

I was high.

This beat everything.

The agent stood in the far corner smiling at me. When I couldn't think of anything reasonable to say she went over and slid one of the big windows to the side. The next one followed along. And the next.

"You can slide open the whole row if you want it completely open here," she said, taking a step out onto the sun-drenched terrace.

I followed her.

"Isn't this great?" she said. "There's a remote control for the awning too if you want shade."

I didn't talk much with the agent. My words were unnecessary. She understood. We made a quick round through the two bedrooms, two bathrooms, and kitchen, and then sat down on the light-gray sofas. She talked about prices and closing dates. I was thinking about other things. About the life I could live in this apartment. Far away from any life I had ever lived. Far from the apartment on Södermalm. Far from the single-family houses in the suburbs. Far from my childhood home with its cold cellar. This would be mine.

When we left the apartment I turned around, looked out the windows one last time and fixed an image I'd make sure I'd see again.

FORTY-TWO

"She's awake, Ronni!"

Olivia looked up at a blond head of hair, hovering above her. She was in bed. Her eye felt strange. It would only open halfway. Her eyelids were heavy. She tried to raise her head but it was stuck. The mattress spun. She felt sick.

"Ronni!" the blond hair called again.

Olivia looked around. Now she remembered. She recognized the room. Not at home with Mommy. Not with Grandma either. She was back. Now she heard Daddy's steps approaching the door. She closed her eyes again.

"She just looked up, I saw it," said the blond hair.

Daddy came up to the mattress. He leaned down over her. She could smell his breath. Beer. Smoke.

"Olivia!"

He took hold of her shoulder through the blanket. Not hard, but it still hurt. She looked up. Right into Daddy's eyes. His eyes were glazed. He stood up again. Olivia's vision was too blurry to make out whether he had a frown on his forehead as he usually did when he was angry.

"What is this, Olivia?" said Daddy, throwing something down.

She had to strain her eyes to keep them open. Her head ached. She tried to see what Daddy had thrown on the covers. It was the envelope. The one she had written on. Had she destroyed an important piece of paper?

"Grandma? What were you thinking? Grandma lives in Östersund, Olivia. That's six hundred kilometers from here, damn it. Were you planning on running there or what?"

Olivia reached up to take away something that was chafing against one of her eyes.

"Jumping on the stairs like that, of course you're going to fall down and hit your head. Obviously!"

Daddy sighed and mumbled something about there only being problems with her. She felt her forehead with her fingers. There was some kind of bump.

"But now, Olivia, you see what happens when you don't do as I say. And leave the bandage alone; it was hell to get hold of."

He took her hand and pulled it away from her forehead. Olivia tried to say sorry but she had no voice. She could only make a hissing sound.

"Shouldn't we take her to the hospital anyway, Ronni?" said the blond hair.

"Shut up! You can leave if you're going to be that way."

"I haven't been paid."

"You haven't done anything either, damn it."

Olivia tried to say that she felt sick but she didn't have time. She felt her stomach churning. She leaned to the side and vomited on the mattress and down on the floor.

"No, damn it. Get a bucket," Daddy shouted.

The blond hair ran out of the room. Her heels tapped on the floor. Olivia's head was pounding, and she was cold but still sweaty. There was a large pool on the mattress.

The blond hair came back with a bucket and paper towels. Daddy started cleaning off the mattress and floor.

"Maybe she has a concussion?" said the blond hair.

"Oh, knock it off," said Daddy. "Are you a doctor now? No one ever died from a few scrapes and a bump on the head."

"I can't cope with this. Is there going to be anything, Ronni? Otherwise I'm splitting," said the blond hair.

"Well, that was a lot of fucking talk. Leave then!"

Without looking at him she stomped out into the hall and slammed the outside door.

"You manage to scare away everyone, Olivia," said Daddy while he wiped the floor. "Damn it!

FORTY-THREE

I stared out the window on the airport bus from Skavsta. I had thought it was gray and gloomy when I left, but that was nothing compared to now. Malta and Sweden were like comparing full color and gray scale. I was amazed that the end of September did not mean warm autumn colors with red, yellow, and green leaves as in past years.

The days on Malta had passed quickly, yet I had managed to do what I'd planned. Larissa had stayed with the bartender the first night and after that they had been inseparable. Saturday morning they went out on his boat. Larissa told me how they lay on the deck in the sun while the boat bobbed in the turquoise-colored water in one of Malta's bays. He had taken her to the other side of the island and the bathing beach on Golden Bay, where they made out. I had explored the island, looked at apartments during the day, and spent the evenings and nights at Dragonara Casino.

I had won.

I really had.

But, in total, the nights at the casino had brought me down to a minus sum. At one point I had been so sure of winning that I managed to persuade a man to loan me some money, when I had already gambled away what I had with me. If you don't have any money for the stake, you have no way of winning back what you've lost either, which I needed to do. I couldn't see any other way out. The man demanded to see my business card and because I was too drunk to think about it I handed it over. It amused him that I was a police officer and that I hadn't told anyone that I played. Now he had a proper hold on me if I didn't pay him back. I would deposit the money in his account in the Bank of Valletta. The losses were a defeat, but I avoided thinking about it.

The thing that had made the strongest impression on me during the trip was the view from the apartment. The image was etched on my retinas. The sky. The blue sea. The buildings far below. The feeling of being dizzyingly high above the ground gave me strength. Power.

With that in mind I stared at the gray, wet landscape outside the airport bus until I fell asleep.

FORTY-FOUR

"Hello, I'm home!"

I tried to sound as cheerful and happy as I could. I took off my autumn jacket and shoes. The children shouted and came running out into the hall. I leaned down and hugged them both. I had missed them. Peter didn't come to the door.

"Where's Daddy?" I said.

"In the kitchen," said Beatrice.

I left my suitcase in the hall and went out into the kitchen. He was standing with his back turned, doing the dishes.

"Hi darling," I said.

He turned around, wiping his hands on the tea towel.

"Mommy, do you know what I did at day care?" Beatrice called.

"Honey, you can tell her later," said Peter. "I want you to take Benjamin and play in your room for a while. I need to talk with Mommy."

Without protest Bea took her brother's hand and guided him away. I looked at Peter.

"Has something happened?"

"Do you remember when I asked you how much money we had in our joint savings account?"

"Yes..."

I understood at once where this was headed. It was crucial to keep a cool head. I went over to the kitchen cabinet and took out a glass. Opened the refrigerator.

"You said you didn't know how much was there," Peter continued.

"What's this?" I said, taking out a plastic container with something in it.

"I checked today," said Peter.

I cracked open the lid. A pungent, rancid odor came out of it. I recoiled, grimaced, and closed the lid quickly.

"Jeesh, what's in this?"

I looked at Peter. I needed time to think.

"Do you hear me, Leona?"

I quickly opened the cabinet under the counter and threw the whole container as it was right into the garbage. It landed with a thud far down in the can.

"That wasn't really necessary," said Peter. "It was Tupperware. We got it from your mother."

"I can't stand moldy old food."

"Leona, I've checked the bank account."

I was just about to pour juice in the glass but stopped. I sighed deeply and turned slowly toward Peter.

"I didn't want to tell you because I was afraid you would say no."

Peter looked with raised eyebrows at me. As if he had expected a different response.

"Larissa was in financial straits after the separation and needed to borrow money," I said.

"What?"

I didn't know what Peter had expected, but it obviously wasn't this.

"She wouldn't have been able to stay in the house if she didn't buy him out. Without the money she would have been thrown out onto the street."

Peter stared at me with wide open eyes. He didn't say anything.

"She was in trouble, Peter. I had to loan her the money."

It was true that Larissa was divorced, but the house she lived in was completely hers, because her deceased mother had left it to Larissa in her will. Hopefully I hadn't mentioned that to Peter before.

"But what the hell, Leona, 450,000 kronor?"

"That was what she needed so that she could keep living there. What could I do?"

"Suggest that she sell the house and move into an apartment of course, just like all the rest of us who can't afford to live in a big fucking fancy house. Now *we* can't buy any of the houses we've looked at."

"But were those houses really anything to have anyway, Peter?"

Peter took a breath as if he was about to burst out shouting. He stopped himself, stared at me, and shook his head. Didn't seem to know what he should say. He sat down at the kitchen table and said calmly, "When is she going to pay it back?"

"We'll just have to make a repayment plan."

"But my God, haven't you even talked about when she should pay it back? Are you out of your mind? For that sort of thing you should have signed a contract."

"She has her own business, alongside her job, and brings in quite a bit. It will all work out."

I could hear how lame that sounded. But it would have to sound the way it did. I didn't have the energy to bother sounding credible. I knew it wouldn't be long until I could put the money back in the account.

Peter stood up.

"This is completely insane. I don't get that you could loan out 450,000 kronor without asking me."

"So what would you have said if I'd asked?"

"*No*, of course! No sane person lends that much money."

"Have you thought that perhaps there are people who still stand up for others when they're having a hard time?"

"Oh, what a pity it would be if poor Larissa couldn't afford to live by herself in a big, luxurious house but instead had to move to an ordinary apartment like everyone else."

"This was after their separation, Peter. She was completely mentally run down. The guy was unfaithful with a woman ten years younger. He wanted to marry her and have kids with her. She couldn't bear to pick up all the pieces right then."

As usual I had no problem filling out the lies with details.

"There's more money, too," said Peter.

I looked at him with raised eyebrows.

"There's more. Why are you lying to me? What the hell is this with the gaming companies?"

I remained silent. I knew that money had been withdrawn from the account by various gaming companies and I hadn't bothered to try to camouflage it. It was careless of me. A mistake. But Peter had been uninterested all these years in our finances, and had always let me take care of it, so I'd thought he wouldn't check.

I sighed. Looked down at the table.

"I gamble a little."

"What do you mean, gamble a little?"

"I've played a little poker. Borrowed a little from the account."

"Poker? But what the…How much, then?"

"I've won, too. Quite a bit actually."

Peter stared at me without making a sound. Obviously I wouldn't get out of this without giving him a better explanation. It didn't seem as if I had any choice this time other than to play the victim. I sat down, looked at the table, and let out a deep sigh.

"Peter, I think I'm a gambling addict."

FORTY-FIVE

A nature reserve without a single person in the vicinity was exactly what I needed to divert my mind. The Monday after the Malta trip had been stressful at work. Minna and Sam had a thousand questions, the phone rang constantly, and Claes pressured me for information about the results of the investigation. It was the usual. As soon as you were back after a vacation, just when you'd had time to start thinking about your life choices, you were thrown back into the demands of the everyday. You worked in order not to have time for those thoughts.

Now it was Tuesday. First thing in the morning I turned off my phone and drove out to Hellasgården in the Nacka reserve. I parked the car and took the path down toward the glassy water. I sat down on a wooden bench and took a few deep breaths, refreshing my lungs with oxygen. I devoted time to reflecting on the direction in which my life was headed. Claes had started questioning why I was not making any progress in the investigation. Soon the managers above him would be hassling me too.

I needed to show them some results.

Arrest someone.

Anyone at all.

I sighed. The strength I'd gained from the stay on Malta had, in just a day or two, shifted to a heavy feeling of hopelessness.

I slid down on the bench, leaning back and looking up at the clear autumn sky. Scattered swallows fluttered around as if they didn't know where they were going. For a second I felt just like that. Wandering throughout my existence, lacking focus. I got up quickly.

I didn't allow myself to doubt.

Refused to create obstacles for myself.

This time, as always, I would take control.

I needed to do something about my financial situation. After my conversation with Peter the mood had been funereal. He had barely said a word to me after I told him about the poker. But it would work out. I had the money from the two robberies.

Soon to be three.

A third and final robbery was planned.

With three robberies I could be sure of being completely free. I would also be able to afford any unforeseen expenses. But it would take a while before I could use the money. Laundering the numbered euro bills wouldn't be a problem, but none of that could happen now. It was much too risky. In the meantime, I somehow needed to arrange some money. It was a big problem, but the thought that I would soon leave Sweden kept me afloat. Gave me strength. I would disappear into the world all by myself. Without anything around to disturb me. Start up a new life where no one knew who I was. There I would be myself. Be true.

I closed my eyes. I could see myself on the terrace of that apartment. There I would stand and look out over the sea. Feel the strong sun bear down on my skin. Let the wind take hold of my hair and my thin white clothing.

There I would gain a new outlook.

Perspective.

I couldn't help thinking about the children. Leaving them would carve a hole in me. My feelings for the children were deep. I could feel the tears coming just thinking about them. I tried to force away these thoughts. These emotions. Impossible. It was strange — my whole life I'd wished I could feel emotions and the only ones I had, the ones for the children, I now wanted to be rid of. Without feelings it would be easier for me to leave them. I knew that they would be fine without me.

I had great respect for Peter's abilities to satisfy the children's needs. He was the kind of dad every kid wanted. He played with them. Joked with them. Consoled them. Took time to explain to them how the world worked. Peter wanted all the things that most adults strive for and that life, presumably, would also be best for the children. Stability. A good job. A house in the suburbs. A nice car. Decorative objects on the bookshelf. Family dinners. Activities. A trip abroad for a week, all-inclusive, in the Canary Islands. Security. Routines. He wanted all of that. His boss demanded a lot of him at work, which meant that sometimes he couldn't pick up the kids at day care, but that was probably the only thing. Otherwise I couldn't find any fault in his parenting. Before, I would have envied that, tried to emulate it. But the kids saw through it. Especially Bea. Sometimes she looked at me as if I was someone she didn't know and continued clinging to Peter.

I had given up. There was no point in pretending any longer. The children seemed to have a kind of built-in radar for what was genuine. My feelings for them had always been genuine, but my parenting abilities had never been adequate. I simply had to accept that I would never be able to give them what they needed. I had told myself this so many times, but still it was so hard. Now it was time.

I felt the tears coming. While I looked out over the landscape I let them run along my cheeks and fall on my jacket. The colors of the autumn leaves were reflected in the water. Shades of red, yellow, green, and brown floated all the way up toward the sky. I said it yet again to myself.

The children's needs were more important than mine.

They had not chosen me.

They deserved better.

I must let go of them.

FORTY-SIX

I was not back from Hellasgården and at work again until twelve-thirty. I was hardly in the corridor before I heard Anette call.

"Leona, Leona, I've been trying to reach you everywhere. Your husband called from Astrid Lindgren Children's Hospital. He's gone to the emergency room with Benjamin."

I dropped everything, running back to the garage as I called Peter. His phone was turned off. Damn! There had to be an end to this. I had to see about getting the money together for the operation. Peter had been forced to ask his company for an advance on his salary, but it wasn't enough.

Typically, I ended up in the middle of the lunch hour rush. I tossed the rotating beacon light onto the roof of my unmarked car. Got irritated at people who refused to move even though they saw there was an emergency vehicle behind them.

"Move, damn it!" I yelled.

My hands were sticky on the steering wheel. At the same time, I felt cold whenever I thought about how badly everything could end. Benjamin was a brave little guy but this intestinal disease wasn't child's play. I couldn't bear to see him tormented.

I threw myself out of the car and ran into the hospital.

"Benjamin Lindberg, supposed to have come in an hour or so ago. Where is he? I'm his mother."

I felt how my voice failed me as I said the word. Mother. Yes, I was his mother.

I almost ran along the corridor up to the elevators, pressing the elevator button five times in a row, as if it would come faster that way. I was having a hard time standing still. I paced in a figure eight while I waited. An older man in a dark gray coat and suit pants came and stood beside me, standing calmly and quietly. Provocatively so. I pushed my way into the elevator when the doors opened and counted every floor on the way up. Out of the corner of my eye I noticed the man looking at me. How could they have such slow elevators in a hospital? I took a big step out when the doors opened and almost ran into a doctor and a little girl pulling a drip stand. I looked in both directions. At the far end of the corridor I saw Peter sitting on a bench, leaning forward with his head in his hands. I ran up to him.

"What's happening, where is he?"

"Shh! He's sleeping. It's okay."

"Where is he? I want to see him."

"He's had a terrible morning but the doctors say he's out of danger now. He started to cramp and poop blood at day care. They couldn't get hold of you. Where the hell have you been?"

I had a hard time standing still. Paced up and down the corridor.

"We have to see about getting the money and having the operation done," Peter continued. "I don't have the energy for this anymore."

"Can't you get another advance from your job if you ask for it?" I said.

"Why is it up to me to get the money?"

The phone vibrated in my pocket. I took it out.

"Perfect, now you're answering the phone. You're not even allowed to have it on in here," Peter hissed, getting up.

The caller was Christer Skoog. He was starting to get really irritating. I declined the call and looked at Peter.

"What am I supposed to do, conjure up the money?" I said.

"You could conjure it away with no problem. If you hadn't loaned out and gambled away all of our goddamn savings, then..."

Peter stopped. He clenched his fists, turned and walked a couple of steps away, then turned back.

"Don't you think it's about time to ask your affluent family?" he said.

"That won't work. You know that."

"So because you're too damned proud to ask them for help, our son has stomach cramps and is pooping blood. When are you going to wake up and realize that this is serious, Leona?"

"Shh, you'll wake up everything and everyone."

"I'm not putting up with this," he said. "You can stay until he wakes up and talk with the doctor. Maybe she can knock some sense into you."

Peter started down the corridor.

"Peter, let's talk about this later."

"There's nothing more to talk about until you've talked with your parents."

He disappeared. I collapsed on the bench. He was right. I had no choice. No alternatives remained.

I carefully opened the door to the room where Benjamin was and peeked in. His little body was lying on its side with the hospital blanket over it. The room had framed drawings on the walls and patterned curtains with images of cakes on them. I went in slowly, without making a sound. I didn't dare get too close, only observing him from a distance. The finest thing I had was in front of me. Pale. Thin. The blanket moved with his small breaths.

There was a small cannula in his hand. He hated syringes. He must have cried himself senseless when he realized they were going to stick him. Under his arm he had his favorite teddy bear. Peter had remembered to bring it. My eyes filled with tears that then slid down around my jaw. However much I wanted to, I couldn't deny that Peter was right. I was to blame for this. If it weren't for me, Benji would have had surgery and wouldn't be lying in front of me right now. The children that I loved had to suffer for my choices. I was not good for them.

They would be better off without me.

FORTY-SEVEN

I had to pull with both hands to get the handle down on the metal door to the club. I'd had time to think. Asking my parents for money was something I wanted to avoid at all costs. I didn't want to borrow from anyone else, either. It always caused problems. But I was desperate for money. On Malta I had introduced myself to the world of live poker, and even though I'd lost quite a bit there, I saw certain advantages in supplementing my online gambling with playing live now and then. No one needed to know it was me. I adjusted my outfit.

Wig.

Dark-red lipstick.

High heels.

Tight jeans.

Leather jacket.

Inside the metal door a narrow stairway ran straight down to the floor below. The red wall-to-wall carpeting along the middle of the stairway had turned dark from people's dirty shoes. Yellow LED lights down by the floor lit up the steps.

This was not my first time. I had been here on the job on several occasions, but the last two times it was to play.

I was calm. Told myself that it would work out. It was crucial that I was attentive to the other players and stuck firmly to my principles in the game. Playing tight had never been more important than now. Waiting for a really good hand and then playing aggressively. That should work.

The place smelled both of tobacco and the sweet smell of marijuana. On the one podium a young blond woman stood in only her underwear and high-heeled shoes. She was moving lethargically to the music with her back against a chrome metal pole. I went through the room and down a narrow corridor. The bass from the music made the floor vibrate. A tattooed man with a bare upper body and piercings in his nipples forced his way past. I kept going. Opened the door to the poker room. The others were already seated. All men, as usual. Six of them. They looked me up and down.

"A chick?" said a young guy with slicked-back hair I'd never seen before.

"Yes, a chick," said Marx, whom I had played with previously. "You got a problem with that?"

The guy didn't answer. Drew his hand through his pageboy-length hair, which glistened with wax. He was surely no more than twenty-three years old.

"What the hell, Marx, are you bringing little brats in here?" I said.

"Sit down," said Marx. "The guy has cash, that's the most important thing."

I went slowly over to the empty chair. Sat down.

"We're running one tournament this evening, that's all," said Marx. "The stakes are high. Fuck anyone who freaks out. This will be a calm, clean game, then we'll split, okay?"

Everyone nodded. Except the brat.

"What?" said Marx, looking at him.

The brat shrugged.

"If you're having doubts, you can leave now," said Marx, looking at him. "I won't put up with any fucking hassle."

"I understand," said the brat.

"Okay, let's go."

Everyone took out their money. Thousand-kronor bills in bundles were placed on the table and counted carefully. Marx dealt the cards. I folded. Then folded the next hand. And the next. Where were all the good cards? Even though I was impatient I managed to resist the temptation to play with semi-good cards. But I couldn't wait too long. If I did, I risked being eaten up by blinds. I didn't bat an eyelash. Read off the others' play.

I didn't know where Marx had found the brat. The guy bluffed wildly. Played like a beginner. Maybe it was a tactic. When all the players had counted him as a bad player, he could strike with full force.

At regular intervals a half-naked waitress came in and took orders. The brat ordered one drink after another. Marx and I looked at each other. The others were playing well. Really well. I kept to my strategy. Tossed one hand after another. But now my stack was starting to dwindle. A couple more rounds and I would be out of the game. I had to get into the game now. I bit the bullet. Crossed my fingers for better cards.

Yes! King of spades, ace of spades. It was time. Now it was crucial to bet without scaring off the other players. Two players dropped out immediately. I bet more. Another two players went, but the brat and Marx were still hanging in there. Now it would happen. I went all in. It had to work. The last card was dealt. Marx showed his cards. He was out. The brat and I were left. He showed his cards. I looked.

Stared.

I didn't want to see.

How could I have let this happen? I stared in front of me. Quick images rushed past in my head. The hospital. Benji in the hospital bed. So innocent, so fragile. I ran out of steam for a moment.

The brat smiled wryly to everyone and scraped together the pile of money from the middle of the table.

"It was nice playing with all of you. How often do you play?"

No one answered. The others got up and started heading for the door. I remained seated with my eyes fixed on the table in front of me. When everyone had left, Marx came over. Sat down on the chair beside me and put his hand on my shoulder.

"You really needed to win, huh?"

I nodded slowly. Marx pulled the chair closer and whispered in my ear.

"If it's really bad you can probably ask the guy. I've heard that he..."

I looked at Marx. The thought hadn't struck me before. It was actually a way out.

"I'll put in a good word for you," said Marx. "So you can bring up the total. Five figures isn't impossible."

I smiled. It wasn't perfect in any way, but now it was about survival. I got up. Left the room. Looked toward the bar. There stood the brat with a glass in his hand, talking with a young blonde. While I went and ordered a drink a little farther away, Marx went up to him. I stayed where I was. Waiting. I didn't need to wait long before the brat came over.

"Well played!"

I didn't reply.

"Marx says you're really good."

"True," I answered without looking at him.

There was no point in playing hard to get. We both knew what this was about. I looked him up and down.

"But you can hardly afford it. You dress like a rich kid but probably you're just a wannabe."

I knew, of course, that he had money. Besides the fact that Marx said so, the guy had just won a tournament with five-figure amounts in the pot. But now it was about getting him to spend that money on me and not on any of the young girls. Accusing a brat like him of not having money had touched a nerve. I didn't realize how sensitive he was until I saw his reaction. He clenched his jaw and squeezed the glass so hard he had to set it down on the bar, so it wouldn't slide out of his hand.

"What the hell do you mean, bitch?"

I smiled.

"Try me," he answered. "How much do you want?"

Would it really be this easy?

"Thirty-five for a whole night, fifteen for an hour."

He looked me up and down.

"No problem with a whole night, but an hour is enough for me," he answered.

"That is, over and above the hotel room and taxi, which of course you'll pay for," I said.

I looked at the clock, then I took the last gulp of my drink and headed to the exit. The brat followed.

On the way up in the elevator at Elite Eden Park Hotel at Sture-plan I thought about how unexciting it was. Like a one-night stand. The guy was young and good-looking. Handsome, if you like that type. That such a guy would pay for sex seemed tragic, but it probably had more to do with the excitement, power, and pure boredom that came from being able to take whatever you wanted.

He was barely inside the door before he starting tapping white powder on the glass top of the coffee table.

"Do you want some?" he said.

I went into the bathroom. Undressed. If I had any luck this would be over within a few minutes and I could leave.

Wearing my black g-string and bra, I came out of the bathroom. I looked into the room. The brat was lying in a strange position on the couch. One leg up on the cushion, the other on the floor. His back arched to the side. His head hung. I ran over. Took hold of his head. Slapped him on the cheek.

"Hey!"

No reaction. I felt his neck. He had a pulse and was breathing, but he was completely gone. I let him lie there. Typical of kids to carry on with things they had no control over. I laid him on his side on the couch and went into the bathroom again, quickly pulling on my clothes. When I came out he hadn't moved from the spot. I went over to him. Put my hand in front of his mouth and nose. Puffs of breath warmed the skin on my hand. He was okay.

I found fifteen thousand kronor in his wallet in the inside pocket of his jacket. I stuffed the money into my handbag and left the room.

FORTY-EIGHT

"Okay, so you're saying that Leona doesn't tell you what's happening in the investigation and that she mostly sits in her office with the door closed when she's not out on a job?"

Claes was speaking as loud and clear as usual, but I couldn't make out Minna's answer. Claes's voice was stronger and penetrated the wall more easily where I stood listening, next to the binders and other office supplies.

I had walked past Claes's office and seen Minna sitting in one of the chairs in front of him. Claes had a worried look, so I'd slipped into the storeroom adjacent to his office. From there you could partly hear what was being said. Claes's voice was clear. Minna's was harder to make out.

"And?" said Claes. "That's how we work here. Everyone doesn't need to know everything. Leona is responsible for the case and I'm sure she'll tell you what you need to know to do the investigative tasks she requires."

Still nothing audible from Minna. Even though I was standing really close to the wall.

From Claes's responses I gathered that Minna thought I was closing them out of the investigation, which she had quite correctly understood. On the other hand I hadn't expected her to go and discuss that with Claes. I had heard a lot of bullshit between colleagues over the years. More often than not it never reached the boss, but this latest batch of police officers seemed more inclined to criticize both their colleagues and bosses. I should've been more careful. Minna Nordin, the newly hatched police constable, had apparently asked to speak with her boss privately and was now sitting across from him, criticizing my work.

While I stood there and cursed myself for not having foreseen this, my phone rang in my pocket. I swore, because the sound was on. Usually I had the phone on silent because I hated ring tones.

"But wait now, stop, stop, stop!" said Claes in a loud voice from the adjacent room.

For a moment I thought he had heard the ring tone and realized that someone was in the room next door.

"Are you eavesdropping on your colleagues' phone calls?" he continued in a loud voice.

I realized that it wasn't me he was talking to but Minna. I managed to get the phone out of my pocket after two rings and declined the call.

There was silence from Minna. I turned off the sound and checked the missed calls. Christer Skoog's name showed up on the display.

"You should be damned well aware of the fact that Leona is one of our best investigators," said Claes. "That she is sitting in her office with the door closed means that she is up to her ears in work. If she seems absent it means that she is concentrating on work, which you and Sam should be doing too."

I was pleased that Claes had come to my defense and that he wasn't listening to the attacks Minna was evidently making. He continued.

"That you're eavesdropping on phone calls and come running to the boss with incomprehensible and poorly founded assertions about your own colleague says more about you than about her. Your task is to do exactly what Leona tells you to. Do you have any problems with that?"

"Sorry…just wanted…to tell…"

"Thanks, but I'm not interested in a lot of bullshit behind people's backs. We don't work that way here. If you have a problem, bring it up directly with Leona. I don't have time for that sort of thing."

Complete silence from Minna. Hopefully Claes had made it clear to her that she had no business bringing gossip to the boss. There was some clatter in the office. I heard the door open and close. I remained standing. Waited awhile before I went out.

"Kenneth, you asked before if I had an investigation I needed extra insight into."

It was Claes. He must have called Kenneth Fransén, the head of investigations.

"The girl robbery. My investigator Leona is running it well, but it would be interesting to bring in someone who can look at it with, shall we say, fresh eyes."

Even though Claes had scolded Minna, she had evidently sown a seed of doubt in his mind. I had known from the start that there would be problems having Minna and Sam on my heels. I needed to be more vigilant.

FORTY-NINE

It was two-thirty when I dialed the number of the city prosecutor's office. With luck, I would get hold of Nina. I had managed to find a person in the register who lived only a few blocks from SEB and who had previously been involved in a couple of armored transport robberies. A perfect suspect. I needed Nina's permission to bring him in for questioning.

"Nina Wallin."

She sounded stressed. Now it was important to be quick, as always when speaking with the prosecutors. Convey what you wanted as briefly and concisely as possible. Being prepared before the call was the only way to maintain any sort of respect for the Police Department from the prosecutors, who usually thought that police were uneducated nitwits.

"Nina, it's Leona Lindberg. City police."

"Yep."

You would have to search for days for a shorter reply.

"I'm calling about the girl robbery. Do you have time?"

"Not really. What?"

"I have two independent witnesses, Alexandra Nilsson and Kent Sandström, who saw a man leave the scene running and carrying a small, colorful bag. The man is probably involved in the robbery."

Not a word from Nina.

"He is identified as one Steven Mellström, born in 1974.

Matches the description. Drives a dark blue Audi. Previously convicted of complicity in robbery of two armored transports."

The description the witnesses had given also fit every other middle-aged man in Stockholm, but along with the rest Nina should at least agree that he should be questioned. I didn't even intend to ask her to put out an arrest warrant — it would be enough if he was brought in for questioning.

"He lives at Banérgatan 41. He has two children, but no seven-year-old girl. Both seem to live with their mother. Do you want to bring him in for questioning?"

"Yes."

"Good. House search too?"

"Yes."

This was going unusually smoothly — a house search and bringing him in for questioning without previous summons. I heard quick tapping on the keyboard and I could not decide whether Nina was entering the order in the computer system or if she was simply working on something else while we were talking. I got the feeling that I could have asked Nina to have Steven Mellström arrested, indicted, and convicted, too, and gotten a positive response without her really thinking about what she was saying. But I didn't intend to point that out. It was up to her to make the decisions.

"Okay, thanks. That was all I wanted," I said. "We'll have to be in touch later…"

"Sorry, what did we decide on?" said Nina.

The keys fell silent.

"You just decided on a pickup and house search for Steven Mellström at Banérgatan 41, who was seen by two independent witnesses leaving the area running at the time of the robbery."

"I see, okay."

Nina continued tapping.

"Yep, then that's done," said Nina.

I went straight out and ordered Minna and Sam to carry out a house search and pick up Steven Mellström.

FIFTY

The next morning Minna and Sam were standing in the doorway, glaring into my office. It was quarter past eight.

"We've brought in Mellström. He was physically calm but babbled a lot on the way in. Said that we had made a big mistake. He hasn't done anything and doesn't know anything about anything. Yes, the usual," said Minna. "But listen, there was another thing we wanted to tell you about the crime scene…"

"Has he said anything about wanting to have a lawyer?"

"No, and we didn't ask. We thought that you would do that part with him yourself."

I grabbed my papers and started leaving the room. Minna and Sam remained standing in the doorway. As usual there was no action in them.

"And the house search?" I said.

Minna shook her head.

"Produced nothing. But listen, there was something we saw last week when we visited the crime—"

I squeezed past and walked quickly toward the interview room. I had neither the time nor the energy to listen to more.

I had asked Minna and Sam to bring Steven Mellström to the newly constructed video room. Not because I wanted to record the interview, but rather because I wanted to be able to see and read him from the adjacent observation room before the questioning started.

I could see him moving around the room, pacing heatedly back and forth. Biting his nails. This was not the right moment to go in. I turned and went toward the break room, grabbing a cappuccino from the machine. The taste was harsh and bitter, but it was still drinkable. The *Aftonbladet* from the previous day was tossed over the seat on the sofa. Just like before, the front page was adorned with news that concerned the girl robbery. GIRL MAY BE DAUGHTER OF BILLIONAIRE it said in black block letters. Once again I was astonished at the inventiveness of the newspapers. The phone rang.

"Tina Nord from *Expressen*. Is it correct that you have a suspect in the girl robbery?"

Where did they get their information from?

"I don't have time to talk. I'm in the middle of a questioning."

"Does it concern the girl robbery?"

I hung up. I hadn't even told Mellström about our suspicions yet, and still the newspapers knew.

I went into the observation room again. Looked at the monitor. He was standing still now, leaning his back against one wall of the room. It was time. I opened the door and went in. Without a sound I sat down on the office chair. The interview room had recently been equipped with softer chairs, which were much more comfortable when the interviews dragged on. I changed the settings on the chair, to get it into a good position. Without looking at him I said, "Please sit down."

"No, I'll stand."

"No." I said firmly, looking up from the papers right at him. "Please sit."

I nodded at the chair on the other side of the table.

"I'll stand," he answered, looking at me.

I got up. I took the papers and left the room. Closed and locked the door from outside. Mellström would quickly understand who made the decisions in the interview room. I had stopped arguing with interview subjects long ago. I didn't have the energy. To start yelling and shouting at them, as some of my colleagues did, only had a negative effect. Today, as well, I had a pounding headache that refused to go away, even though I had taken two painkillers. Mellström was innocent, and for that reason I could naturally expect some challenge from him about why he'd been brought in.

Too bad I'd already had a coffee. What could I do now while Mellström calmed down? I didn't have the energy for anything other than taking a little walk in the corridor.

"It should be working again now," said a young guy to Anette, closing a cover on the photocopier farther down the corridor.

"That's great," said Anette. "Thanks for coming so quickly."

Claes's office was empty. Too bad, otherwise I would have taken the opportunity to elevate myself a little by telling him I'd brought in a suspect. I checked my mailbox. Only a couple of analyses from the forensics lab on narcotics tests showing positive on a number of different substances. It concerned two suspects in a gold robbery that had been put on hold in favor of the girl robbery. I'd already figured out that the men were under the influence when they carried out the robbery. I was surprised that they had so much poison in their bodies. How much could you take and still manage to have enough acuity to rob a goldsmith's shop? Not that much, evidently, because they were caught, with a lot of fanfare. It was typical of criminals not to understand their own limitations.

I went back to the observation room and looked at Steven Mellström. He was sitting on the chair. Good. Time for a new attempt. I opened the door and went in. Without a word I sat down.

"I assume that you know how this works, because I've seen that this is not the first time you've visited us."

"What the hell? Are you going to start dredging up a lot of old shit now that I didn't do either? I haven't done anything, get it? What kind of fucking…"

I knew that the comment was unnecessary. That he had "visited" the police before sounded sarcastic, and I could have spared both him and myself by not saying it.

"What the hell do you want, anyway?"

He was staring at me. I calmly held his gaze without saying anything. A good ten seconds passed. As soon as he looked away I would start talking. He looked down. I said calmly but firmly, "Okay, Steven, that was clumsily worded. But you know how this works. I ask the questions and you answer. Listen carefully, because this is serious. You are suspected on probable cause of a robbery at SEB, Östermalmstorg, on the second of September this year at 10:37 a.m."

"What the hell are you saying? Bank robbery! What is this?"

His reaction was expected. It was a common reaction among both the innocent and the guilty. The whole interview was a torment, both for me and for him. For him, because he was innocent, and for me because I couldn't bear to hear him talk. But it was necessary so that I could show I was making progress in the investigation.

"If you want I can leave so you can let off steam. I can come back in two hours when you've calmed down."

"But what the hell!"

I saw that he really was trying to control himself. He should be happy that he hadn't already been arrested. There were also a number of possible charges that it might have been relevant to inform him of, but because in the present situation I couldn't be expected to know exactly in what way he was involved in the crime I simply told him robbery.

"As you know you have the right to have a lawyer at the interview."

I paused to await an answer. He sat with his head in his hands.

"I want a new one. The last one was so fucking lousy."

"I see, who?"

"It was that bastard who's always in the papers, what's his name now…"

"No, I mean, who do you want now?"

"I don't want one of those publicity-hungry lawyers who think they're — "

"Do you want a lawyer or not?"

I had no patience left, and I couldn't put up with much drivel.

"Oh, hell, I don't have anything to defend myself against. I haven't done anything."

"Lawyer not wanted."

I repeated it loudly so that it would be clear to him that he had just chosen not to have an attorney present. Then there was less risk later that he would babble that the police refused him a lawyer. This would be simpler than I thought.

"Okay, Steven. Both you and I know that this interview must be held, and I can't bear to put up with a lot of crap today, so instead I'll get right to the point. I will ask direct questions. You'll answer the questions I ask clearly and won't mention irrelevant matters that don't belong here, okay?"

He sighed.

"What were you doing on the second of September of this year?"

"The hell if I know."

"It was just over a month ago. You must remember."

"I was probably at work."

"Where do you work?"

"Various jobs here and there."

"What kind of odd job did you have on that particular day?"

He shrugged. I didn't intend to press him. The fuzzier he was, the better.

"What were you doing on the seventeenth of September? Just over two weeks ago."

Steven shrugged again. I had nothing that showed that he had been in the vicinity when the robbery at Forex in Old Town took place, but I really wanted to know what he was doing. Maybe he had no alibi.

"You don't want to say?"

He didn't seem to have any desire to talk, which was positive. The possibility of persuading the prosecutor to have him arrested was greater if he didn't come up with a credible story about where he might have been.

"I can't bear to haggle with you. So you have nothing more to say?"

"Nothing except that I haven't robbed any bank."

"I'm going to report to the prosecutor what you've said, or rather what you haven't said, then she will decide whether you stay here with us or not."

I went out and called the prosecutor. Nina answered before the first ring ended.

"Leona! Excuse me for being so abrupt last time."

I appreciated the apology.

"Mellström has been picked up," I said. "I just questioned him. He denies it, but refused to say anything else."

"The house search?"

"Produced nothing. Not that we expected to find a lot of bills lined up on the kitchen table, but, well, nothing."

"No bag, either?"

"The apartment was pretty empty. Hardly any furniture, just a lot of dirty laundry."

"What do we actually have on him?" said Nina.

"Two independent witnesses."

"Have they pointed him out in a lineup?"

"No, but they described him in detail. He is known to us, too. He's been in prison for armed transport robbery before. He also refuses to say what he was doing on the days when the crimes occurred."

"Okay. Arrest him. But be sure to produce something. I need more to go on for the arrest proceedings. You have three days."

"By the way, I didn't get an answer to that email—are you coming to the meeting this afternoon when I summarize the case for Claes and Fransén?"

"Claes was in touch with me, too. I thought he would have told you that I was coming."

I see, Claes had contacted Nina directly, without mentioning it to me? I probably had to be prepared for a few surprises at the meeting. I walked past Claes's office on my way back to the interview room. It was still empty but he came walking up from farther down the corridor.

"Leona! Some tipster called me and said he had important information about the girl robbery that the investigators had missed. The switchboard must have mistakenly transferred him to me. He didn't say who he was but he wanted you to call. Maintained that you knew what it was about."

Claes looked questioningly at me. I nodded. I knew. Christer Skoog was really starting to get on my nerves. It was hardly a mistake by the switchboard. He evidently did not balk at calling my boss.

"Have you been in contact with Nina about the meeting this afternoon?"

"I sent an email to her and Fransén about the meeting time. I didn't know whether you had done that. Both have said that they're coming."

I watched him. From what Nina had said, I had the impression that Claes had contacted her by phone. I wondered what they might have talked about besides the meeting time tomorrow. But maybe he was telling the truth. I couldn't be certain.

FIFTY-ONE

I closed the door to the conference room and sat down at the short end of the oval meeting table. I hoped, as usual, that this would be the last time I would have to reel off a lot of facts for colleagues who could barely stand to listen. It was just a big show designed to impress others. I had to sound professional to make a good impression on the managers, who in turn would convey what I had said upward and make a good impression on their own managers. That's how it worked. Professional life.

So tiresome.

Meaningless.

The only thing that kept me going was that I knew it was not forever.

I had never been particularly fond of the head of investigations. Claes looked at me with a gaze that I interpreted as admiration. It was obvious that he had his eye on me in more ways than one. Minna and Sam sat goggle-eyed as usual. Nina stood out as the only sensible one.

Claes had called the meeting, so the only thing to do was get started.

"As you all know, a second robbery has been committed. Because we are in need of the general public's assistance we have chosen to appear on *Sweden's Most Wanted*. Minna, Sam, and I will report the results of that in just a moment. The first robbery occurred, as you know, at SEB at Östermalmstorg. The girl herself carried the money out in a backpack and left the scene on foot. Exactly what route she took is still unclear."

I rattled off everything at a furious speed. It was probably obvious that I wanted to conclude the meeting as soon as possible.

"The dogs have not picked up any traces and we don't have any witnesses who may have seen her on her way from the scene. She was evidently wearing a black rain cape, which may be the reason that no one noticed her. Forensics has not been able to find any usable traces inside the bank."

Strangely enough, everyone seemed to be listening attentively to what I was saying. I slowed down a little.

"The girl's identity can't be established from the surveillance video from inside the bank. On the recording that the girl played, it supposedly said that she was seven years old. Otherwise we still know nothing about her. A man with a Finnish accent is said to have recited the message and a witness has also said that there was another person's voice on the recording."

Claes raised a finger. I nodded at him.

"Do you mean that no one saw the girl leave either crime scene?"

"I'm afraid so."

"But my God, both robberies happened in the morning. Östermalm and Old Town are not exactly deserted at that time of day. And how did she get there? She can't have just flown in."

Claes sounded irritated. He probably didn't want to appear incompetent in front of the head of investigations.

"No, but unfortunately we haven't found anyone who noticed her."

"*Most Wanted*, then. Have any witnesses called?"

"Not about that, even though I specifically reached out for observations concerning the girl."

He was being persistent. The people who had seen the girl and called *Most Wanted* had not been interviewed and I had no interest in interviewing them, either. If it were to come out later that I had missed their testimony I could say that some of the information from *Most Wanted* had failed to reach me. It had been sent by fax, and everyone was aware that the fax machines broke down constantly, that papers fell down and ended up on the floor, or that other people accidentally took pages that didn't belong to them. So that would presumably be accepted as an explanation.

I watched Minna and Sam, who suddenly started to look meaningfully at each other. What was going on between them? I turned to Minna.

"Was there something the two of you wanted to add?"

Minna cleared her throat.

"Hmm... We may have found the escape route," she said.

I raised my eyebrows. The head of investigations and Claes turned to her inquiringly.

"We found a storm drain about twenty meters from the entrance to SEB."

"A storm drain?" said Claes, looking at me.

"Yes, a storm drain for rainwater runoff," Minna continued. "They're all over the streets but the one that was closest to the bank didn't have a cover. No grate, that is. It's hidden between the parking spaces and extremely small so you almost don't see it when there are cars there. I didn't see that there was a hole down into the ground until I was standing right alongside it and leaned over."

"But what the hell? Did you know about this, Leona?"

Claes looked at me with wide-open eyes.

"I tried to tell you a few days ago, Leona, but you said you didn't have time," said Minna.

I was mute. How the hell had Ronni managed this? We had exchanged the original grate, which was iron, for an aluminum one, so the girl would be able to lift it and climb down. Ronni should have put the original cover back during the night when he picked up the girl with the car. I clenched my fists under the table. Cooperating with that man was truly one big fucking challenge.

Missing such a significant piece of information made it seem like I didn't have control over either the investigation or the colleagues who were working for me. I looked at the head of investigations. He was sitting with his brow furrowed and one hand on his jaw.

"I called and told Nina anyway," Minna continued.

Everyone's eyes now moved to the prosecutor, who was starting to squirm.

"I naturally assumed that this was information all of you knew about and were working on. I was surprised I didn't get the information from you, Leona."

Dead silence. Claes got up quickly.

"What the hell is going on?" He raised his voice significantly. Considering that the head of investigations was at the meeting, Claes was obviously feeling obliged to show his muscles. I could expect a real scolding. Probably more than that. Perhaps Claes would transfer me, to maintain his own reputation. I took a deep breath and awaited the outburst.

"This may be a breakthrough in the investigation," said Claes.

Minna nodded and smiled. Sam looked content. Claes continued to look at Minna.

"Do you mean that the two of you have known about this without making sure that Leona got that information?"

Minna's smile froze.

"How long have you known?" he continued.

"Since last Friday," said Minna quietly. "We worked in the field over the weekend, so we were off during the week…We haven't had time to check further on it…"

"Last Friday! That's six days ago, damn it!" Claes shouted. "Are you completely out of your minds? That sort of thing has to be checked immediately. Where does the drain lead to? Is there a similar one outside Forex? Have you sent Forensics there?"

Minna looked down at the table. Claes just stared at her.

"And…? Where the hell does it lead?"

Minna's voice was faint now. She seemed to have a hard time getting out the words.

"I shone a light down into the drain. There didn't appear to be any passageways down there. No visible traces either. We called the city of Stockholm and asked them to order a new cover so that no one would be injured. We thought that because several weeks had passed since the robbery, perhaps there was no point in sending Forensics. Outside Forex there is no such drain. But I did try to tell Leona, so that she could decide what she wanted to do."

Claes did not seem to know what to do with himself. He pursed his lips. He looked out the window and said calmly, "The two of you can leave the room. You are removed from the girl robbery."

Minna and Sam didn't say a word, but got up slowly and moved toward the door. They knew Claes well enough to understand there was no point in talking back.

"Be sure to write a clear memo about the drain and what you found, now!" he called after them before the door was closed.

"Where did you get hold of those two, Claes?" the head of investigations asked.

"They're new," Claes hissed back. "If I remember rightly, it was you who wanted me to take care of them because you didn't have any other assignments for them."

Claes was on the warpath, obviously. I was mostly dumbfounded that I'd escaped a dressing down. I had earned one. Minna had said to me that she had something she wanted to tell me, but I couldn't be bothered to listen. None of that mattered now. Everything had worked out, and I was also rid of my persistent puppets.

I had counted on someone sooner or later detecting the flight path. I just didn't like having surprises presented to me in front of my managers.

Now I saw an opportunity to end the meeting as soon as possible.

"As I'm sure you understand, I have a number of important things to work on, and with this new information, I think we'll have to conclude this meeting," I said.

Everyone nodded in understanding and started gathering their papers.

"Claes, I'll go down in the drain right away myself and see how it looks. It's been over a month, with bad weather. Probably we can't expect all that much."

Claes nodded. I turned to the others.

"I'm sorry it was such a short meeting."

"No problem, Leona," said the head of investigations, patting me on the shoulder. "It's good that there's something to go on in the investigation. Claes and I have talked about perhaps arranging a little help from outside too, so…"

"That won't be necessary," I said quickly.

The head of investigations shot a glance at Claes that I could not really interpret. I started walking quickly toward my office, brooding about Nina. Minna had apparently contacted Nina without Nina having called me, even though she was doubtful about why I wasn't the one telling her about the drain. Had Nina started to suspect something?

"Leona!"

Nina came running after me in the corridor.

"I have to ask. Someone left a message for me earlier today that there was something about the girl robbery that hadn't come out, that I should know about. I don't know where the message came from; I got it through the switchboard. They said it was a man who called."

Damn, Christer Skoog. He was apparently tired of me avoiding him.

"I see," I said.

"I just thought it was strange. Thought in case you knew something."

"No. Nothing…"

"Another thing. Where are we on the question of Mellström, now, since the escape route seems to be the drain? Wasn't he seen running from there?"

"Can we talk about that this evening? I have to go out to the drain," I said, trying to sound stressed.

"This evening? Then you'll have to discuss it with the after-hours prosecutor because I'm going home in a couple of hours."

I had no desire to talk with an after-hours prosecutor who was not familiar with the case. He or she would probably decide that Mellström should be released immediately.

"What are you doing tonight?" I asked. "Do you want to get a bite to eat and talk a little more about this? I haven't examined the drain properly yet and don't know with certainty whether it really is the escape route. After all, Mellström still hasn't said where he was at the time of the crime. He may have taken the bag from the girl and run away. The decision on whether he should be released can perhaps be made early tomorrow when we know more about the drain, don't you think?"

Nina seemed doubtful. The prosecutors hated to have people locked up a single minute longer than they had to. Personally I had no problem letting that man stay in jail. Even if he was innocent of these particular crimes he was definitely not a model citizen. Having time to think about his old sins could only do him good.

"Okay, we'll have dinner and talk about it," said Nina before we parted.

I went into my office and closed the door, thinking about what had just happened. Christer Skoog contacting Nina worried me the most. He was apparently prepared to tell her what he knew about me. At the beginning, when Nina had been randomly selected as the preliminary investigation leader, I had realized that sooner or later she would be a problem. Nina had kept a low profile so far and let me run the investigation in peace, but if, because of Christer, she started having suspicions, she would undoubtedly look more carefully at the case. Nina was too smart to be fooled. I had no choice other than to tell her. Now it had become more urgent — I needed to do it before Christer made contact with her again. It would have to happen tonight at dinner.

I took out my phone and quickly entered Ronni's number.

"What the hell, Ronni! The storm drain cover."

"Leona, is that you?"

"Shut up, you heard what I said."

That man brought out my worst mood.

He sighed. "It didn't work. Some teenagers were hanging around there when I went to pick up Olivia. I was happy that I got her out at all. I made it just before they saw me."

"Are you completely...It's been over a fucking month. Why didn't you get back there right after and put on the cover?"

"Lucky it was you who discovered it anyway," said Ronni.

"It wasn't me, damn it, Ronni! It was my colleagues. I just heard about it at a meeting with the head of investigations."

"Oh, damn it. Oh, man."

"Oh, man? Don't you get that there are going to be problems with the next robbery? You're going to have to find a drain several blocks from the crime scene. A fucking unnecessary risk, Ronni."

I hung up. I couldn't stand any more of his dense comments and was happy that he wasn't standing in front of me right now. I tore open the door and stomped out to the break room. After two double espressos, though, I came to my senses and realized that I had no one to blame but myself. I had chosen to collaborate with a hoodlum, who presumably had never been playing with a full deck. If I'd had the opportunity I would have chosen someone else. Now I needed to get the whole plan completed as soon as possible, before the guy messed anything else up. Just one robbery to go. I would need to change the plans a little.

FIFTY-TWO

You could see immediately which drain grate had recently been replaced by the city of Stockholm. The stone, gravel, leaves, cigarette butts. and other trash that was usually on the street was gone. The grate was also a different shade from the others in the area. I swore to myself as I looked down into the drain and thought it was Ronni's fault that I was being forced to crawl down into this disgusting pit.

I had asked a colleague to come along and stand up on the street while I went down, mostly so that there would be someone to witness that I really had checked the drain and not found anything. There were parked cars, and I had to stoop down under the bumper of one to get down. As I had already known, the drain was cramped and not easily accessible for a grown person. Because it had rained the past few days it was also wet and damp. On my way down I heard running water coming from other connected drains.

With each step down the bent ladder rungs, a strong smell I recognized came through. Stale, damp, mold. I did not like cellar spaces. I felt nauseated. I wanted to get this over with quickly. I had brought along a headlamp to be able to see. The other officer was lying on the ground above, shining a light down around the walls. I looked carefully every time he shone the light down. It was obviously important for the investigation to examine the drain. Now no one would doubt that it had been done.

I stepped down into the water at the bottom of the drain. On the wall there actually was something. I looked more closely. My colleague seemed to notice that something had caught my attention and shone his flashlight against the stone wall.

"Found something?" he called.

"Seems to be some type of moss."

Did moss even grow in a place like this? I didn't know for sure. Even though it was damp and discolored, I could see what it was. A piece of the teddy bear's fur. The teddy bear that the kid had insisted on having with her. I had suspected there would be problems with it, but according to Ronni the girl became completely panic-stricken when he said she couldn't take it with her. I released the tuft down into the water and watched it wash away with the rain.

There were no other traces, but I stayed down there for a while so it would appear that I had investigated the drain thoroughly. When enough time had passed I started climbing up.

"Nothing?" said the colleague.

"Nil. It's so wet down there, and considering how much it's rained the past month, there's no point in sending Forensics. There are no other passages that lead anywhere down there either. Nothing suggests that this really was the escape route. It's probably just as I suspected the whole time, that the girl was picked up in a car after the robbery."

We pushed the grate back in place together.

"Would you mind telling Claes that we've been here and investigated without result?" I said. "It's important that he knows that there are no underground passages, and that we can rule out the drain as an escape route."

FIFTY-THREE

I was satisfied with the table I had reserved at the Scandic Anglais restaurant by Humlegården, just near Stureplan. I had chosen the place with care. The meeting with Nina was the most important one of all. The table was slightly secluded, at one end of the restaurant, but maintained a pleasant sense of being around people. The decor provided a warm and pleasant atmosphere, with fabrics in earth tones and wine colors along with dark-brown furniture. It struck me how seldom I went out to eat these days.

I looked at Nina, who was sitting across from me. She was wearing the same clothes as at the meeting earlier in the day. A nicely cut granite-colored jacket, a white blouse, and a knee-length, close-fitting gray skirt. That, together with her dark, straight hair, meant she radiated style and elegance. The prosecutors were always nicely dressed. In contrast to the police officers, they had a sense of style. Possibly it was because they spent virtually every day in court, but that was not the whole reason. Few police officers had any taste whatsoever where clothes were concerned. For them, functionality was the most important requirement. That style and functionality could often be combined was not something most cops cared about.

Nina had already had two glasses from the bottle of wine we were sharing, which made her a little more open and talkative than usual. Even though I had gone over it with myself a number of times, I hadn't come up with any strategic way to tell her. All I knew was that I had to get it out now. Christer Skoog had been sending a message to me through the information he'd left for Nina earlier today. He knew that Nina would tell me she had received a message from someone who knew something about the case. I had to tell her before he got hold of her again. How it would go, I didn't know. I simply had to take it as it came. Before the evening was over Nina would know everything.

Almost everything, anyway.

I took a gulp of wine. Nina was talking about her newborn nephew, whom she'd been to see. I didn't hear the details. I was looking at her without seeing her, thinking of other things. I smiled when she laughed and nodded at the right places, but I didn't take in what she was saying. I was more bothered by the situation than I had expected. The thought of how Nina would react had taken over my mind. I had previously imagined there was only a slight risk she'd strike back and report me. Now I wasn't sure how I'd arrived at that conclusion. Instead, it became obvious to me that a total catastrophe was more likely. Nina could gain a lot by reporting me. In purely career terms it would be a giant step for her. She would be noticed as a very capable prosecutor, and in addition to the general acknowledgment from managers, colleagues, and others for being loyal to the legal system, it was also likely she would get a management position in the future. My career and my personal life would, naturally, be over. Without a doubt I would have a divorce to look forward to, and a number of years in prison. Not seeing the children would be a nightmare, but subjecting them to the prison environment simply because I longed for them to visit me would be cruel. Afterward I'd be unrecognizable. No one stays the same after a long sentence. People around me would naturally be shocked that a police officer could do something like this. It wouldn't matter what explanations I had.

I would be guilty.

In the eyes of everyone.

This moment was decisive for my future.

Nina had fallen silent and was looking at me with raised eyebrows. Had she asked a question that I ought to have understood and answered?

"Sorry," I said. "What did you say?"

"What's going on with you?" she said. "Has something happened?"

I took a breath. It was now or never.

"Nina, I have something to tell you."

Nina looked at me. She appeared to hear from my tone of voice that it was important. How should I continue? Should I say that I had done it all because I needed money for Benjamin's operation? That I had forced someone else's child to commit crimes so that my own child could get well? Or should I say that I was a gambling addict and had gambled away all the money and put my family in debt? No, I couldn't take the easy way out. I refused to tell a tale that I was a failed gaming abuser or a desperate mother with a sick child. Should I simply tell it the way it was? That the Leona that most people knew was not me. That since I was little I had mechanically imitated other people to learn to fit in. Be accepted. That I couldn't handle it anymore.

Family life.

Coworkers.

The police corridors.

The criminals.

The nine-to-five.

Explain that the everyday physical and social existence had mentally chained me, worse than when I was locked in the cellar as a child. Get her to understand that I could no longer repress what was me. That I had no choice other than to break free from everything to be able to live, for real.

No, that would presumably sound insane to the ears of a normal person. No one would understand it. Women don't do that. Only men can commit crimes for that reason. For power. Money. For the freedom to leave everything.

"I wonder if I can tell you something in confidence," I said.

Nina looked right at me.

"How long have we known each other, Leona?" she said.

"You don't understand," I said. "This is information that not just anyone can handle. I haven't been able to confide this to anyone."

Nina reached across the table and took my hand. Perhaps she thought I had a fatal illness. In that moment it almost felt that way.

"I give you my word. I can't do more than that," she said, squeezing my hand.

I took a deep breath. My palms were sweaty. I wondered if she noticed. I swallowed and looked down at the table. My thoughts flickered. Where should I begin?

"Nina, what I'm about to say is going to be shocking to you. I hope that, before you judge me, you will listen carefully. Whatever happens after this…"

I fell silent. Looked around.

"I want to say that it has been very meaningful for me to work with you. You are one of the best prosecutors and you are hopefully sufficiently open-minded to be able to handle this."

I wasn't getting to the point. I looked at Nina, who was looking at me with her eyes wide open. Analyzing, trying to read what I would say next. I breathed in. It was sink or swim.

"I'm the one behind the girl robberies."

Now it was said! There was no going back...or? It felt strangely surreal. Had I said the words or simply thought them? I wasn't sure.

Nina looked at me.

I looked at her.

I tried to read her.

She was trying to read me.

Everything around us stood still. Nina frowned with her eyes fixed on me.

"I don't understand..."

Nina forced me to be explicit. There was no point in trying to soften it. The shock would be what it would be.

"It was me the whole time, Nina. I staged the robberies at SEB and Forex with the girl, the money, everything."

Nina slowly withdrew her hand. She looked at me with suspicion in her eyes.

"I don't believe my ears."

I had to convince her. The quicker she understood the shorter the stage of shock would be.

"The seven-year-old girl is the daughter of a criminal who was convicted in an old case you and I handled several years ago. You probably remember the arson at..."

"Sockenplan?" said Nina with eyes wide open.

I nodded.

"But what...Are you out of your mind?"

Nina raised her voice. I had been too preoccupied by the situation to notice that the restaurant, which had been rather empty before, was now full of people. I put a finger in front of my mouth to dampen Nina's outburst.

"But my God. What...? Have you been threatened or something? Why have you..."

Nina could not seem to get the words out. I answered by slowly shaking my head. I could understand Nina's reaction. Without more information that was presumably the only reasonable explanation for why someone would do something like this, that they would do it under coercion. Nina continued.

"We are friends but…this is not something you can just toss out over dinner. This is about your whole life, Leona."

I didn't say anything. It was best to let the whole thing sink in for a few seconds. This was a lot for Nina to handle. She fixed her gaze on the side of the table.

"And not just yours. Now this is about my life too," she continued.

I knew that it would not take long before Nina realized that I had forced her to confront a major moral dilemma.

"Don't you understand what a fix you've put me in? I have to report you, you know that. You get that, right? It doesn't matter that I gave you my word. This is bigger than what I might want. I have no choice."

That was exactly the perspective on life I had turned against. I had been there myself. Struggling to fit in, believing I had no choice other than to go with the flow and live my life like other people. That it would be best that way. And simplest. Whatever people said, it was easy for most people to live like everyone else. If they didn't have the will or the drive to do something else and truly struggle for it, they ended up in an expensive suburban house, spending the vast majority of their waking time at work, to chase money to buy more things for their expensive house and car, with not enough time to spend with the family, and living in a semi-lousy relationship. For me, on the other hand, that hadn't been an easy path. I had to strive harder than others for all that. It had been a daily struggle. And to what end?

Nina didn't have the same starting point as me. I was different. She was like the majority. But perhaps, perhaps I could get her to see that that life did not suit her either.

"You always have a choice though, Nina, don't you? Isn't that what we always say to the criminals?"

"Yes, exactly. And by that we mean you always have a choice to do the right thing."

"Do you really see life as being that black and white, Nina? Where everything is either right or wrong? So what is the right thing? Is it right to live the kind of life you and I are living? Sitting at the office ten or eleven hours a day. Stressing our asses off every day, every week, every year. For what? To either hit the wall before retirement and take disability, or retire at age sixty-five completely worn out and bitter, with a pension that you can barely live on. You can afford to mess around in your garden at home, and that's it! And if you have money for more, then you don't have the energy because you've worked so hard over the years. Is that a life you want to live? Is *that* the right choice?"

Nina was silent. We had talked many times about the workload and the profession, about life and dreams. I knew that Nina also had thoughts about whether it really was worth living this way.

"So what is the alternative? You've injured a child, Leona. That's crazy. Where is the girl?"

"Don't worry about her. She is well taken care of. Doing well. A very capable little girl."

"Capable? No, I don't understand what's happening. Tell me this is a joke. That they've started showing *Candid Camera* on TV3 again and now they're fooling ordinary people. That I'm just one of the many dumb prosecutors who will get flowers and a good laugh in a few minutes. Leona! Tell me this is one big joke."

"Three and a half million euros is not something you joke about."

Nina's mouth dropped open. I continued.

"SEB told the police who were first on the scene that the take was 1.2 million kronor, but that was a misunderstanding. The police officer who took the information wrote the total in kronor, but it was euros."

Nina continued staring at me without saying anything.

"At Forex it was one and a half million euros."

I looked at Nina. I couldn't interpret her expression.

"One and a half million euros is yours, if you're part of this, Nina."

"You're out of your mind, damn it!"

She got up. I took hold of her arm.

"Nina, sit down. Listen to what I have to say. You can report me or do what you want, but please, listen first. Then the choice is yours."

Nina stopped. I wasn't sure whether she would hit me or sit down again. I looked her right in the eyes. She sat down slowly.

"You have to understand," I said. "I'm not an idiot. I've thought this through, Nina. We've worked with serious crimes for many years. Seen all the mistakes clumsy crooks have made. If there's anyone who should be involved in this it's us. We're the experts. We know how the legal system works and we know how police work. We know everything about the evidence, how prosecutors and defense attorneys think, and how courts function. Besides, we're women. You're aware of the statistics and know exactly how small the risk is that we would be even suspected, much less indicted, and even if against expectations we were to be indicted the risk is slight that we would be convicted. Women seldom commit these kinds of crimes."

Nina listened attentively.

"Everything has gone according to plan so far," I continued. "No one at the bank was injured, either. Okay, people were scared, that's unavoidable, but nothing more. The only thing I was worried about was which prosecutor would be assigned as preliminary investigation leader. When I heard that it was you I realized immediately that I couldn't fool you and naturally wouldn't want to either. I only needed to find the right occasion to tell you. And now I see the possibilities for both of us to be able to change our lives. If we just cooperate."

Nina remained seated. She took two large gulps of wine and shook her head.

"I should have known this about you, Leona. You're not like the other cops."

"Do you mean that in a positive way?"

Nina stared vacantly ahead of her.

"Life has probably never been black and white and simple, even if we've wanted to imagine that it was, don't you think, Nina?"

She seemed completely lost in her own thoughts. Was I saying the wrong things?

"You're forcing me to make a major life decision," said Nina quietly.

"Good," I said.

"Good? I have to determine my whole future here and now. I can't go home and think, that would just seem strange. If I'm going to report you, I have to do it now. If I don't do it and instead latch onto your sick ideas then I risk prison for both you and me. Then all we'll be able to do is dream about having a chance to return to the existence we have now, which you seem to despise so intensely."

I shrugged.

"Sometimes others make choices for you, Nina. You know how hard it is to take yourself out of your own existence and usual patterns despite the fact that you're not even comfortable with them. Maybe this is the push you need to get out of the rat race."

I was on my way to turning her around, I sensed it.

"See it as me giving you a chance, a possibility to change. We've talked about this before. But talking won't do. Don't you owe it to yourself to do something?"

I paused. Wanted to be certain that she was taking in what I was saying.

"Nina, think about the possibilities. What you could do with that money. You could do all the things you've only dreamed about. If you still want to work, you could go down to part time. You don't have any small children either. Travel, find a man abroad, move to another country for a few years. Come back and start working again doing something you like. None of that would be impossible to achieve. The possibility is right in front of you, Nina."

Nina sighed. I thought I could detect something dreamy in her eyes. I smiled at her.

"You have to risk something to get something, don't you?"

She shook her head.

"This is completely sick."

"Or else this is the best thing that has happened to you. Happened to both of us."

I hadn't convinced Nina, I saw that. I would have to use more weapons.

"There's another thing, too."

Nina only stared at me, as if she expected yet another shock. A bomb that would strike her even harder than the last one.

"It's Benjamin. I need the money for his operation. The county refuses to pick up the tab. They maintain that the chances for a good result are too uncertain. I really need the money."

"But can't you borrow it? The bank, your parents, friends, I have a little…"

"That won't work, Nina. I've already done that. Put me and my family in debt. I've thought of everything," I said.

My patience was starting to run out. Didn't she understand that everything had already begun? It was too late to start finding new solutions. But it was evident that what I had said was not enough to convince her. I needed to pile it on a little more. I leaned forward. Almost whispered.

"Nina, I'm in serious trouble and need your help, do you understand? From what I remember I stood up for you once when you needed it, even though it involved breaking the law."

Nina leaned back and crossed her arms.

"I wondered just how long it would take before that would come back and bite me."

We sat in silence.

"I stood up for you, Nina. Now it's your turn. Friends stand up for each other."

"But damn it, you're a police officer, Leona. And no real friend puts someone in this kind of difficulty. You've gone way too far over the line."

Nina got up quickly, grabbed hold of her coat and handbag, and moved quickly toward the exit. I pushed back my chair and ran after her. I ran between the tables. Nina was already at the exit. I ran into the waiter, who looked at me with surprise. I pulled the badge out of my pocket.

"I'm a police officer," I called on my way past him. "I'll come right back in and pay."

Nina had run out onto the sidewalk, moving toward Sturega-tan. I caught up with her. I took a hard and unrelenting hold on her upper arm.

"Stop, damn it, Nina! We're not done."

"I don't want to be part of your awful criminal plans, Leona, don't you understand?" she sputtered, trying to tear herself loose from my grip.

"Calm down, you're behaving like a five-year-old," I hissed, letting go of her arm. "None of this goes away just because you run off."

She looked around as if she hoped someone would come and rescue her. I sighed.

"I would really like us to do this together, as friends. But you give me no choice, Nina."

She stared at me as if she sensed that I would bring up more difficult news.

"You're already involved in this, whether you want to be or not. Do you think I would take the risk that you would report me? Nina, you're not going to be able to. If you try, you'll go in yourself. I'll say that you and I planned all this together. We are both already linked to the girl through Ronni, who was convicted after our arson investigation seven years ago. People have seen you and me have lunch. We've had all the time in the world to plan this together."

Nina stood silently with hunched shoulders. She moved her eyes from me to stare vacantly down at the sidewalk.

"I didn't want to have to resort to these methods, Nina, but you give me no choice."

No answer. It was time to finish up. I had said all I wanted. Perhaps I should give Nina the tiniest feeling that she still had a choice, so that she would not feel completely run over. A false feeling, but still...

"Nina, if you decide to report me then you can just as well do it in the morning. You lose nothing by thinking about it over-night. We'll talk more tomorrow."

She didn't answer. With her head lowered and with her coat and bag in her hands she turned and started stiffly walking away from me toward Stureplan.

I let her go.

FIFTY-FOUR

I had expected it to be completely dark when I quietly unlocked the front door. A faint glow from inside the apartment made the hall look spooky. Shadows spread out from the doorframes. It was strange that there were any lights on at all. Had I forgotten to turn them off?

The wig chafed on one ear and the high-heeled ankle boots pressed all the weight down against my toes. Even though I had mostly been sitting at the poker table, my feet felt as if I had spent the whole night on the dance floor.

The brat hadn't been there tonight. I had hoped he would be interested in an hour's pleasure for the same amount as before. I had basically taken the money without giving him anything in return, but because he had passed out I assumed he didn't know how the night ended. But he was impossible to get hold of, so instead I went home with another man. Considerably older.

With a beer belly.

And greasy hair.

He smelled of snuff, beer, and smoke. Focusing on the money, I steeled myself and went with him in a taxi to Hjorthagen. I accompanied him to an apartment which, considering the state it was in, had probably not been cleaned in the past year. When he pulled a suitcase out of the closet with instruments that resembled something I'd seen at the gynecologist I left the apartment after a few well-chosen words. With that, my career as a prostitute came to an abrupt end. I was disappointed, in a way, because

I needed the money, but realized my own efforts would be too great compared to the returns.

I locked the security door behind me and wriggled out of the ankle boots as I pulled the leather jacket over my shoulders. Put the wig back in the suitcase. Pulled my fingers through my hair and scratched my scalp. Wearing the wig on top of my own thick hair was like having a warm, scratchy cap on my head. Even though the pads of my feet were burning I walked on tiptoe. Slowly. I knew where the floor creaked. It must be the light under the cupboard by the counter in the kitchen that I'd forgotten to turn off...

"Where have you been?"

Peter was sitting at the kitchen table in his bathrobe. His voice was deep, as if he hadn't talked in a long time. A half-empty glass of milk was in front of him.

"Are you awake?"

That was unusual. Peter usually never woke up at night if he wasn't sick. He didn't wake up even when the children were crying.

"Where have you been, I said?"

"Working."

"Dressed like that?"

Peter looked me up and down. Tight-fitting jeans and a T-shirt were not unusual clothes for me to work in, but he apparently noticed that it was not the usual jeans and that the top was a tad low-cut. Besides that I had smoky eye makeup and dark red lips.

"Yes. We're working on a procuring case where we have to do surveillance on two possible pimps."

I recovered quickly. The lies came naturally to me, as usual. I sneaked a glance at his reaction while I took a glass out of the cupboard and turned on the tap.

"Since when have you started working in the field? And in surveillance?"

"Shh, you'll wake up the kids. I hadn't realized that it would be so late."

A semi-smooth transition, perhaps. Create a diversion by starting to talk about the children and the time instead. I reduced the force on the tap and held the water glass under the stream.

"Late? Early, you mean. It's four-thirty. It never occurred to you to call?"

"I didn't want to wake you and the kids."

I took a few gulps, feeling the chill from the ice-cold water reach my head.

"Thanks for that. I haven't slept a wink."

Peter got up. He poured the milk out in the sink and walked toward the bedroom.

My evening had not gone as planned. Poker seldom went well anymore and now I had no plan for how I would get the money together to at least keep the family rolling while waiting for the robbery money.

Peter went to bed. I didn't spend any time wondering whether he bought my lie. I was tired. Went into the bathroom. With the water rippling on my face I not only rinsed the makeup away. Something else went with it. I wasn't sure what.

I sank down on the bed with an uncomfortable feeling in my body.

FIFTY-FIVE

"Damn, how nice of you to call, Leona. It's been a long time since I've seen anybody from before."

I had arranged a meeting with Jakob Isaksson in his workshop, a cellar at Odenplan. "Issy" was a computer nerd who had been fired from the agency two years ago because of data intrusion. We had got to know each other at an IT seminar a year or so prior. Issy would hopefully be able to help me get authorization to invisibly surf around in our computer system. He was standing outside on the street, smoking.

"For a data nerd who works in a cellar you really keep yourself in shape, Issy," I said, giving him a hug.

He laughed and blew the smoke out before he dropped the cigarette and crushed it against the asphalt with a blinding white Adidas sneaker.

"Do you ever miss the police?" I asked him on our way down the stairs to the cellar space.

"I'm doing so much better now. If you only knew. I work when I want to and take the jobs that seem fun. There's nothing wrong with being a self-taught hacker. You get a lot of interesting, exciting jobs."

The cellar passages he guided me through were endless and seemed to get narrower and narrower. With a rattling key ring in his hand he unlocked door after door.

"A lot goes on behind the scenes, you know. These days I have the Defense Forces and Secret Service as clients."

"Really, they don't care that you were fired for that intrusion?"

He unlocked yet another steel door and let me go in first. Red wall-to-wall carpet brightened up the room, which had white-painted stone walls. At one end was a white couch with big pillows in front of a gigantic LCD screen hanging up on the stone wall. The other end was filled with large computer screens. Issy went over to a coffee machine that looked like a miniature spaceship and placed a gold-colored coffee capsule in it.

"It's more like they see it as an advantage. They know I can hack my way in almost anywhere, even with them. If you can't beat 'em, hire 'em, maybe they're thinking."

He pointed to the couch. I sat down. After the little spaceship stopped whistling he came over with a cup of coffee for me and sat down in the armchair opposite. He leaned over with his elbows on his knees. Looked at me.

"So you have problems, Leona?"

I laughed, trying to downplay it.

"Why do you think that?"

"Most of the people who come to me do. I hope you haven't gotten yourself too tangled up."

"No, no danger of that."

I tried to sound cheerful. Didn't like that he was looking at me with sympathy in his eyes. There was no reason to feel sorry for me.

"I need to be invisible. Can you help me?"

"Within the county or all of Sweden?"

"Just the county. Is it possible?"

"There are two alternatives. I'll explain…"

"As if I were a three-year-old, please," I said. "Hacker talk is not my strong suit."

Issy smiled. He was about to continue but stopped.

"This must be the only time you don't know what to say, Issy. When you're going to explain something to a mere mortal," I said.

To my delight he was modest enough not to take advantage of my ignorance.

"One alternative is that I give you authorization from within your squad. Then you can make yourself invisible so that nothing is logged on your ID. But keep in mind that you're going to leave traces after yourself that show which squad you're surfing from and which computer you used."

"So it could be anyone at all at Violent Crimes surfing around?"

"Exactly. But because someone can see which computer you used, you would have to use someone else's computer, like someone who was off for the day, so as not to point to anyone in particular if queries were made."

"The computers in the interview rooms?" I said.

"Same thing."

"What's the other option?"

"That you surf from an outside computer, for example from one of my computers. The good thing about that is that no one will be able to attribute it to you. The snag is that then the computer system is not going to look the way you're accustomed to. The graphics are different and menus and texts may be hidden and hard to find if you don't know where to look."

I thought quickly. Doing it from inside the squad was risky, of course. It would be hard to find a time of day when no one was there. If I did it from outside I would be forced to get help from Issy, which wasn't good at all. He would be sitting alongside me and would see everything I saw. Even if Issy was a nice guy, I didn't trust him.

"I'll do it from inside," I said. "I want to take up as little of your time as possible. It'll have to be during the evening."

"There's another problem, too. I have to open and close your authorization manually, because it's not good to leave the portal open. Sooner or later someone is going to check. Right now I'm doing a job for Defense, so I can only set it up for you between eleven-thirty and twelve-thirty, during the day when I have lunch. You'll have an hour. If you want we can do it tomorrow, okay?"

I had hoped to be able to do it in peace and quiet when my colleagues had left for the day. But by eleven-thirty some had probably already left for lunch anyway.

"I'll have to adapt. How much do you want for this?"

Issy looked at me up and down with a sly smile.

"Forget it, Issy," I said, laughing. "We're talking cold cash."

"I'll do it for old times' sake."

"You're an angel. How will I know when it's free to go in?"

"I'll send you a text from an unknown sender when it's arranged and another one three minutes before I cancel so you get out in time."

I gave him a kiss on the cheek before I started walking toward the door. At the door I thought of something.

"Listen, by the way, how do I know that I really am invisible?"

"Leona, don't you trust me?"

"Every rose has its thorns, Issy. There may be some error along the way."

"Test by going into an access-protected investigation first. If you get in then you know there's a green light. Keep in mind, you're not really invisible. Someone will see that someone is doing what you're doing, but they won't see who. So choose carefully which cases you go into."

I left Issy. It struck me that a few years ago it would have been inconceivable for me to do what I was going to do tomorrow. I was fascinated by my capacity to adapt to new circumstances. It was a good quality. I hadn't thought about it before.

FIFTY-SIX

After the visit with Issy I took the car to Birkastan. To Nina's place. Along Sankt Eriksgatan the newly fallen snow lay in narrow, black furrows along with gravel, lead, and oil. I could smell the exhaust fumes even though I was inside the car. I rubbed my nose to get rid of the odor.

Nina hadn't reported me yesterday, which hopefully meant that she had no intention of doing so today, either. But I couldn't be sure.

I got takeaway from the Thai restaurant around the corner and went in through Nina's entry. I had never liked rickety elevators with grates, so I took the three flights of stairs up to the apartment. The spiral staircase was broad. The man I met on the stairs could pass on the inside easily, with no risk of tripping on the stairs.

I didn't know what the meeting with Nina would be like. Took a deep breath and rang the bell. She answered with a resolute expression. She held open the door and showed me in. I couldn't remember ever having seen her in a pair of worn jeans and a hoodie before. Without the tailored jackets, high-heeled shoes, and glasses, she looked vulnerable, somehow. I handed over the bag of Thai food.

"I heard that you weren't at work today so I thought I'd come over with a bit of food."

Nina took the bag into the kitchen without saying a word. I hung up my jacket on the coatrack in the hall and put my shoes next to Nina's.

"What great shoes!" I said, picking up a dark-brown, low-heeled ankle boot. "I need something like that."

When I put my foot down I noticed that it was a little large, but really comfortable. I looked at the bottom of the shoe and noted that Nina was a size seven. One size bigger than me. I went into the kitchen.

Nina took out two cream-colored placemats while I removed two square plates from the kitchen cabinet. As soon as Nina set the placemats down on the table, I placed a plate on top.

"We're a good team, Nina," I said.

The atmosphere had to lighten a little. I regretted not bringing some wine. Nina seemed to need it.

I sat down, opened both boxes of food, and started scooping up chicken with red curry sauce. Nina sat down after lighting three block candles that stood on a designer concrete plate with black and gray stones around it.

"Leona, I've been thinking about what you told me yesterday. Or to be more exact, I didn't sleep a damned wink last night because of it. I would have preferred never finding out."

I didn't answer. I intended to let her talk.

"I can't understand why you've done this, Leona. How does a police officer even come up with the thought of doing something like this? And why have you dragged me into it?"

If I could have completely trusted Nina, I would have told her everything. We had known each other a long time, but I didn't trust anyone. Nina could hurt me seriously. I couldn't afford any digressions. I needed to keep a tight rein on her. Get her to understand that everything had to happen on my terms.

"The less you know, the better for you, Nina. I had no choice other than to tell you. You're a skilled prosecutor with full insight

into the investigation, it was just a matter of time before you discovered it yourself."

My flattery didn't seem to have much effect. She shook her
head.

"I felt that there was something shady about this investigation right from the start. That it was not some ordinary clumsy
robber who had committed it. But I could never suspect...and
least of all you."

"Nina, knock it off. That's enough!" I said, getting up.

I took my water glass from the table and turned the tap to the
coldest setting. I poured a glass and turned around.

"There's no time to sit and think about this now. Everything
is already planned. If it feels easier for you morally you can tell
yourself that you have no choice, which is true if you add in the
fact that you're choosing not to sit in prison for many years in the
future."

I gulped down the whole glass of water.

"The end is what's remaining," I said. "You won't have anything to do with the robberies themselves."

Nina was sitting pretty. I was almost angry that she didn't see
that herself. It was the rest of us who were doing the heavy lifting.

"The plan is that I do a poor investigation so that no suspect
is found, which means that you are going to close down the case
on the basis of 'no result.' If we are still forced to produce a suspect for a main proceeding we will have a defendant that we both
know is innocent. Then you can make sure to submit really thin
evidence during the proceeding. The defendant's defense attorney will drive through the case like a bulldozer when he or she
notices that you have nothing to go on. The indictment will be
dismissed and everyone will be happy and content."

Nina sat quietly.

"I'm offering you one and a half million euros to keep quiet. It's not all that difficult, is it? You'll never get another opportunity to get rich like this, Nina. We can sit here and talk back and forth all night, but there is nothing you can do about it, provided that you don't want both of us to get long prison sentences. I don't need to explain to you what the consequences could conceivably be for three robberies plus the kidnapping of the little girl."

"*Three* robberies?"

Nina almost screamed. I nodded slowly.

"You're out of your fucking mind, Leona!"

She got up and quickly started heading for the hall. I ran over and took hold of her. I pulled her back to the kitchen and pressed her down on the chair again.

"*Sit!*" I shouted and held hard on to her shoulders. "*It's too late, do you understand, Nina? You no longer have any choice!*"

She became rigid. Made no resistance. Didn't say a word. Looked at me terrified, with big eyes, as if I was going to hit her.

I wanted to scream that now it was even more important that the third robbery went according to plan. Now that I was being forced to share the money with her. Bringing in money in other ways hadn't worked. The only thing that worked was the robberies, and now the third robbery was needed more than ever. Threatening Nina into silence would not have sufficed. I had needed to offer her a large sum of money. In that way she would see herself as an accomplice, and not merely as a victim. Someone who was involved wouldn't report.

I was getting tired of Nina. I didn't intend to let anyone or anything destroy my chance of reaching peace. Freedom. Least of all Nina, who had come into the picture so late. I had to continue until all three robberies were done. There was no other way.

I saw her eyes fill with tears. Nina, the hard-boiled prosecutor who didn't back down for anything, was sitting in front of me, crying. I let go of her. Calmed myself. Backed up and sat down on the chair next to her. Gave her a napkin from the holder on the table. She didn't take it. She just sat there, staring straight ahead.

"Nina, I'm going to protect you as much as possible. Everything will soon be over. Don't make this worse than it is now. No one has actually been injured."

Nina stared with red eyes straight ahead. Then she said quietly, "Where is the girl?"

"She's staying in an apartment with Ronni. She's in no danger. She's a timid little girl who barely says anything. You know Ronni from before."

She gave me a quick look.

"I'm keeping an eye on Ronni," I said. "Where this kind of money is concerned the meanest men get submissive, believe me. He does as I say. He's aware that his previous criminal career has not been particularly successful and has the sense to understand that I know what I'm doing."

"The girl was completely covered with blood and had bruises," said Nina.

She picked up the napkin. Blew her nose. Dried her cheeks.

"The blood was bought cheaply at Buttericks, along with a blond wig. The bruises she had from before. You know how kids are, they fall down and hurt themselves."

"Where is her mother?"

"She lives in Finland. She thinks that Ronni took the girl to Sweden to see her grandmother. That's why the girl hasn't been reported as missing. Once he's got his five hundred thousand euros he'll go back to Finland with the girl. That's the deal, anyway. I would be very surprised if he doesn't follow through. He hasn't exactly been a model father, and he mostly just seems to think the girl is a nuisance. Probably he wants to be rid of her as soon as possible. I have to use your bathroom."

I left the table and went into the bathroom. Wanted to get away from Nina's interrogation. Didn't intend to give her any more information.

In the bathroom I opened her medicine cabinet. Among skin care products and nail accessories I found what I was looking for. The wood-colored hairbrush with a black handle was full of hair strands. I found a pair of small tweezers among the nail accessories and carefully pulled a few strands of hair out of the brush. From my pocket I took out a small redline bag and placed the strands in it. I had been collecting the DNA of various people for some time. Carried it with me in my pocket wherever I went. I had faith in my plan, but I wasn't so naive that I didn't understand that things could go wrong. When you had to deal with people, unexpected things often came up. The bags were the smallest at work and on the writable part I made careful notations to keep track of whom the samples came from. I had no pen with me, so Nina's bag had to stay in my pocket without labeling. I flushed the toilet and turned on the tap as if I was washing my hands.

"That pad Thai was really good," I said to Nina when I came out. "Thai restaurants have been opening all around town recently, but yours is definitely one of the better ones."

I needed to talk about something easily digestible. Normally our work involved traumatic events that neither of us had any problem relating to, but this was completely different. I started walking toward the hall.

"And that business with the drain?" said Nina, coming after me.

I repeated what Nina already knew. That it was true what Minna said at the meeting, that there was a storm drain approximately twenty meters from the bank, suitably located on Nybrogatan below the curb between two parking spaces. A perfect place for a little girl to slip down into without anyone noticing her between the cars. I explained how the girl had climbed down on the ladder to the bottom of the drain and crouched there until Ronni had picked her up.

"It's not as complicated as you might think, Nina. The only thing that went a little wrong was that there were people around when Ronni was supposed to pick up the girl after the first robbery, so he didn't have time to put back the drain grate. Otherwise everything is running like clockwork. Ronni's done everything he's been told to."

The collaboration with Ronni had not been completely painless but Nina didn't need to know everything. He had, after all, managed to get the girl to commit the two robberies correctly according to my instructions. He had missed a few minor details that made me really irritated, but the fact was that he'd managed the girl, and most of his responsibilities, above expectation.

I had put on my shoes and jacket. Picked up my bag as I went toward the door.

"Where's the money?" Nina asked.

"It's in a secure place until you've closed down the investigation or until a verdict is announced. Ronni will get his share right after the third robbery is committed so that he can return to Finland with the girl."

I didn't intend to tell either Ronni or Nina where I had hidden the money. I went slowly up to Nina and said in a calm voice, "I have to go now, Nina. I promise you, you have nothing to worry about if you do what I've said. Just continue as usual. As if you don't know anything about this. I'll take care of the rest. The most important thing is that we can rely on each other. I stood by your side and risked my entire career when you were in difficulty once. Now it's your turn to do the same for me. In a few weeks all of this will be over."

I wasn't sure whether Nina was listening to what I said. She stared at the floor in front of her.

"Nina, forgive me for taking hold of you like that."

I reached out both my hands and she took them slowly, looking at me. And what I thought I saw in Nina's eyes I would never forget.

Collusion.

Calm.

I was one step closer.

FIFTY-SEVEN

It was 11:24 a.m. The text from Issy had just arrived. I took a pile of papers with me and made a round of the corridors at the squad. Two of the pictures that had been leaning against the wall just outside my office for a couple of weeks had now been hung up. The dark motifs were hard to interpret. If they'd had more color they possibly would have lightened up our formal office environment. But I didn't care about the motifs — I was just pleased that they'd managed to hang the pictures straight.

One, two, three, four offices in a row were vacant. A number of my colleagues always had lunch early.

"Are you looking for somewhere to sit, Leona?"

Gunnel, one of my oldest colleagues, had seen me strolling around in the corridor.

"No, I just..."

"Don't say he's thrown you out too. I'm starting to get really tired of all this moving. I've only been in this office a week but apparently I have to move again next week. To where I don't know."

Gunnel was standing in the doorway to her office, holding the doorframe as if she was going to refuse to move a millimeter.

"I'm still in my office for the time being," I said.

"Be happy as long as it lasts. This squad is sick. We were supposed to get peace and quiet when we moved to this floor. What happened to that?"

Gunnel inhaled and exhaled as she talked.

"It's like I've always said. However much they build it's always too cramped in this building. Did you hear that maybe they're going to close the firing range too?"

I looked at her with raised eyebrows.

"You know, soon we won't be a police station any longer," she continued. "Just a lot of pen pushers. Possibly we'll shoot with Defense in their headquarters up by the stadium. That's what Claes said. It'll be running around with a lot of little boys dressed in green from here on in."

I had a hard time seeing Gunnel on a firing range at all, much less with soldiers. I continued down the corridor. Chose the last office at the far end.

I sat down. The office chair was set for someone half reclining at the desk. Extremely ungainly, but I didn't think it was time to start readjusting it. I put my ID into the computer and logged in with the code Issy had texted. It took a while to log in, as usual. Many people before me had complained about the agency's computers. This one was unusually slow.

A worrying thought that I couldn't trust Issy had taken firm hold in my mind.

I pushed it away.

Every time it appeared.

Now! Now I was in the investigation program. Because I didn't have the reference number, I had to search for the politicians' names. That alone could get me fired if anyone found out it was me. It was tempting to check them in the crime registry, too, once I was in, but now was not the time to get greedy. I would quickly take the info I needed, log out, and leave.

There it was. Access protected, just as I'd thought. I closed my eyes and double-clicked. When I looked up, the investigation appeared on the screen. I scrolled through all the documents in the case. I wanted to give Christer Skoog as little information as possible. Preferably the sort of thing you might imagine he had already found out from some other source, but at the same time something he would be content with, which wouldn't be just anything.

I read an interrogation report for the minister for finance.

Olander denies the crime. He has not done the things he is accused of and does not know anything about betting between other politicians concerning prostitution. He does not know any woman by the name of Dina, either.

I scrolled down to the end of the interrogation, where the suspect is usually confronted with evidence that has emerged in the investigation.

To the question of whether it is true that Olander has a birthmark on his left groin, Olander answers in the affirmative.

"Leona, have you had to change offices now too?"

I was startled. I hadn't heard anyone approaching in the corridor. Anette stood in the doorway with a watering can in her hand.

"Uh…No, my computer crashed, so I've just been sitting here awhile."

I quickly minimized the case from the screen.

"How tiring it is to have computers that never work the way they're supposed to. Good thing we'll be getting new ones soon. I'm just going to water Agneta's plants. Apparently she's on sick leave now. The flu again, it sounds like. I thought you could only get that once every year, but the doctors told her you can get it several times if you're unlucky."

Anette went around behind me over to the window.

"These really needed water. Dry as dust. What a lovely wax plant she has. Look how it's blooming."

"We're lucky to have you here on the squad, Anette, otherwise it would be more than just flowers that died."

Anette laughed.

"You're sweet, Leona. Don't work yourself to death now. You have to have lunch too."

Anette continued to the next office. I continued reading.

To the question of whether Olander has any idea how Dina can know that he has a birthmark on his left groin Olander answers that he does not know. She may have seen the birthmark when he was swimming at the beach during summer.

To the question of what kind of swimsuit Olander generally wears, he answers that he has two pairs of swimming shorts.

To the question of whether Olander in recent years has used smaller-style swimsuits such as Speedos, Olander answers that he does not go around in just anything at the beach.

To the question of whether Olander often sunbathes and swims at the beach without a swimsuit Olander answers in the negative.

To the question of whether Olander would please show his birthmark Olander answers that he does not intend to do that and that it would be offensive. The interrogator explains that in that case the prosecutor will be forced to make a decision on fingerprinting and that Olander will then be forced to undress completely, roll his fingers and palms in ink, be photographed, and show all scars, piercings, and tattoos on his body. Olander answers that in that case the prosecutor will need to make the decision, and that he would never sink so low as to mar his body with tattoos or piercings.

A birthmark. Interesting. As far as I knew this hadn't emerged in the media. This would be a candy store for Christer. I quickly jotted down some personal information and contact details for the prostitute, logged out, and then left the office before I phoned.

"Christer, Leona here. Are you aware that Minister for Finance Olander has a birthmark on his groin?"

"No."

"The prostitute described it extensively. There is even a sketch where she has revealed the shape, color, and exact location. Olander refused to show the birthmark to the investigator during the interview because he thought it was an offensive question. The prosecutor was bold enough to order fingerprinting of the minister for finance."

I saw the picture in my mind. The finance minister without clothes and a colleague checking off every birthmark and scar on his body, photographing him with the civic registration number tag over his chest from in front and in profile, and then taking his fingerprints. The digital fingerprint scanner malfunctioned time and again and it was not unusual that you were forced to use ink instead and first roll the suspect's fingers and finally whole palms a number of times before there was an impression that could be read. Not exactly like on *CSI*.

Christer sounded impressed.

"The birthmark tallies ridiculously well with what the woman drew," I said.

"I'll be damned. Did you make a printout?"

"No, but I have the most recent address for the woman, which appears to be correct."

I couldn't risk confidential documents going straight to the presses at *Aftonbladet*, so I deliberately hadn't printed anything out.

"The address is Nybohovsbacken 77. The apartment is under the name Ida Svensson. Reportedly she is a prostitute too. I have to go. Now you have the information."

Christer Skoog seemed content for the moment.

FIFTY-EIGHT

Only a milk carton, salt, and pepper were on the kitchen table, besides the tableware. The food was still in the pans on the stove. It wasn't ideal for a family with two children to have such a small table but a larger one would have taken up too much of the kitchen. I agreed with Peter that the apartment was too small for us, but avoided talking about it.

I had made spaghetti with meat sauce. The kids loved it. There was some part of me that still enjoyed making it happen. Family life. Not because I was happy living that way, but because I was satisfied knowing that I succeeded in pretending. There I had a long list of credits.

"Sit up properly when you eat," I said to Beatrice, who was reclining in her chair.

"I'll cut the spaghetti for you, Bea," said Peter.

He reached across the table with knife and fork in his hands. Halfway to her plate his arm bumped against the milk carton and knocked it over. Milk spilled all over his plate, the tabletop, and his recently dry-cleaned suit pants, and the carton fell to the floor.

"Damn it!"

He got up quickly. Milk was running down one pant leg.

"Daddy, you said damn."

"I'm getting sick of this! We have to move to a sensible house that has room for real furniture."

"Daddy, you swore," Beatrice cried.

"Quiet now, Bea. Eat instead," I said, tearing a paper towel from the roll.

When Beatrice was born, Peter had already started saying that we needed to move to a bigger place. For him that meant moving to a house. He finally agreed to the compromise of building a wall in one bedroom. "An extremely small four-room," as a few prospective buyers called the apartment at the showing, had become an even smaller five-room. The kids each had their own little room, plus we had a small study with a bed and a desk. Then there was our bedroom, the living room and the kitchen. It worked.

He got a rag and started wiping the floor.

"Daddy, Daddy, when are we going to move?"

"As soon as possible. How is Larissa doing with paying back the money?"

Peter looked up at me while he wrung out the rag in the sink.

"She hasn't been able to pay that much yet."

"How much?"

"It's coming," I said.

"How much, Leona?"

I didn't see the point in starting to argue about it now. Peter was an emotional person. He overreacted to trifles.

"Can we maybe talk about it later, darling?"

I looked meaningfully at Peter and hoped that he would spare the children from our discussions.

"She hasn't paid anything, right?"

I set down my silverware, heaved a demonstrative sigh, and looked at Peter.

"I'll talk with her."

"Maybe it's better if I call her and explain the situation. So she understands how living this way is affecting our family."

"That won't be necessary. I'll take care of it."

Peter didn't look satisfied but seemed to calm down a little.

The question was how long he would accept my explanations.

Taking out money from the robberies now was inconceivable. It was much too risky.

It would take time.

FIFTY-NINE

The reflection of the sun forced me to lower the sunshade in the car as I passed Hornstull on my way back to work after lunch outside the office. Up on Västerbron I looked out over Riddarfjärden toward Norr Mälarstrand. The sun displayed the city from its very best side. You could almost be led to believe that Stockholm was a cozy, pleasant city to live in.

I didn't let myself be fooled.

I knew better.

I felt a vibration in my pocket. With my right hand I wriggled out the phone as I drove across the bridge above Rålambshovsparken.

It was Nina.

"Nina, how nice. I was just thinking about calling you about Steven Mellström."

I knew there wasn't much more we could do. Mellström may have been an idiot but it wasn't possible to get it to look like he was involved in the robbery any longer.

"It's too thin," said Nina. "Release him. The time is 12:48 p.m."

I memorized the time.

"Report to me the time for completion later," said Nina.

"It's better if he's out before the next robbery anyway," I mumbled.

"Leona, I've received a strange message again," Nina whispered into the phone.

"Who did it come from?" I said.

I realized of course who it was, but I wanted to gain time.

"Some man who calls himself 'C.' He wants to see me this evening at seven o'clock. Claims to have important information about the robberies."

Christer Skoog didn't know that Nina already knew that I was behind the robberies. That she would find this out again meant no additional damage, but it wasn't a good idea for her to become aware that a journalist knew what I was up to. It bothered me that Christer had started to take his own initiatives and had contacted Nina like this.

"I'll take care of it."

"Do you know what it's about? Who is he?"

"Uh, just a persistent journalist who is after me about the case, but it's fine."

"What! A journalist?"

Why had I said anything? Now Nina would hardly give up before she found out everything.

"What does he want?"

"I'll take care of it. Nina, I have to go. I'll be in touch later."

After we hung up I immediately called Christer Skoog.

"Leona, I've called you a dozen times," he said.

"What the hell do you mean by contacting Nina Wallin?"

It was best to start off hard. Christer was silent on the other end.

"You refuse to answer my calls. I need to know more."

"Calm down. It takes time to get this sort of sensitive information."

"Damn it, I don't have time to sit and wait while you twiddle your thumbs, Leona, do you understand? I have to have something before my deadline runs out at three o'clock tonight. You'll have to see about getting more info. If I haven't heard from you before seven o'clock then I'll meet with Nina and tell her what I know about you. She'll probably take measures immediately and I'll publish your name and your picture on tomorrow's front page."

"Okay, okay, take it easy, I'm doing what I can."

"You'll have to see about doing more than that. I haven't got shit from you and I — "

"I gave you info about Dina."

"I can't get hold of her. Not by phone or at the address you gave me. As far as I know you may have made up her contact information."

"I'll fix it."

I hung up. The situation with Christer was starting to get out of control. He sounded as if he meant what he said. Seemed desperate. I would be forced to involve Nina. Change strategy. I called her again.

"The journalist is threatening to publish information that I'm behind the girl robberies. You'll have to go there and straighten that out. He's not listening to me."

There was silence for several seconds. Was she still there?

"What's he after?" said Nina quietly.

"He wants to get facts about the politician case. I have nothing to give him at the moment."

Nina sighed at the other end.

"I have to warn you, Leona. The politician case is a really corrupt affair, according to the rumors at the prosecutor's office. Starting to snoop around in it is not a good idea."

"I know! You'll have to solve the problem with Christer tonight. I have other things to do," I said.

That was the least Nina could do. Talking with journalists was something she did on a daily basis. Hardly any great sacrifice for her. By taking care of Christer she would be more involved, which was good. She sounded reserved, which worried me a little. But what could I expect? She had a lot to digest.

SIXTY

Christer had suggested the hotel lobby at the Amaranten on Kungsholmen. He was there in good time and was sitting at a table. In his bag he had brought the pictures of Leona, Ronni, and the little girl. He looked at the picture of Leona outside the bank. If it hadn't been that he needed classified information about the Hooker Affair he would have dug deeper for evidence against her in the girl robberies right from the start. Evidently Leona was so certain that Christer would not put his threats into action that she couldn't be bothered giving him more information. If he wasn't going to get any more from her, then he had nothing to lose by informing the prosecutor and publishing it in the paper. Leona would have to live with the consequences. It was time someone stopped her.

But Christer knew it wouldn't be easy. Accusing a police officer of anything at all was always unpleasant. Alleging that a police officer was behind these specific crimes involving a child, as well as being the detective who was investigating them, was an extremely serious accusation. Plus, there was the added element of her being a female detective. When he thought about it, it seemed so unbelievable that he started to have doubts. He quickly browsed through his papers. Wondered whether the pictures would be sufficient to convince Nina Wallin. Leona's reaction to them clearly showed that she was involved, but it wasn't enough that he knew it, he had to be able to prove it. He looked at them again. How would Nina react? Christer hadn't met her before, only spoken with her on the phone and seen her on TV. Every time she spoke, she did so with clarity and sharpness, in a calm, firm voice. She was the kind of person people listened to.

Now he saw her enter the lobby. A waiter went over and led her to his table. She wore a black coat, belted at the waist. Dark, straight hair in a strict pageboy cut, with glasses, lightly madeup eyes, and shiny, natural-colored lips. Simple and tasteful. Christer stood up.

"Nina, nice to meet you. Christer Skoog."

He extended his hand. She took it firmly. Didn't say anything, but nodded curtly. The waiter hung her coat on the hanger behind her, pulled the chair out for her and lingered a little too long before he retrieved the menu. Nina undeniably had a special aura around her. Looked better in reality than on TV. The waiter turned to her.

"Something to drink before dinner?"

"Mineral water. I'm not staying to eat."

Her abrupt manner made Christer nervous.

"A latte for me, thanks," said Christer.

Nina moved her purse from by the chair to her lap. Picked up her phone, looked at the display, and quickly set it down again before she put her purse back on the floor.

"I assume that you're going to tell me who you are and why I'm here?"

"I'm a journalist and I have important information to tell you about the bank robbery at SEB, for which you are the preliminary investigation leader. Probably also about the robbery at Forex."

Nina's expression did not change. This wasn't going to be easy. He took out the folder and placed the pictures on the table in front of her. Waited for her to say something.

"What is this?" she asked.

"The pictures show that Leona Lindberg, the officer who is investigating the girl robberies, is involved."

Nina raised her eyebrows. Looked at him as if he spoke a language she didn't understand. His mouth felt dry. He cleared his throat. He pointed at the photograph where all three were sitting in the car.

"That's Leona, as you can see. Sitting beside her is Ronni Palm, whom you perhaps remember from the arson at Sockenplan a number of years ago. I covered that incident and also had contact with Leona then."

Nina leaned forward. Picked up the photograph and held it in her hand.

"You ran the preliminary investigation, if you recall. Ronni got four years in prison."

Christer tried to be calm, factual, and clear. Nina still said nothing but instead twisted and turned the photograph against the light.

"Ronni's daughter is sitting in the backseat. She's the little girl who carried out the robbery of SEB on Nybrogatan and Forex in Old Town."

Nina looked up at him without batting an eyelash.

"Where did these pictures come from?"

"An associate at *Aftonbladet* was writing a major story about citizens who have been released from prison. He looked up a number of convicted criminals who had served longer sentences and had pictures taken of them in everyday environments. He knew that I had written about Ronni before and showed me the picture. I reacted immediately to Leona. Thought it was strange that those two were sitting in the same car."

Nina set down the picture and looked at the others.

"I went down to our photo archive and searched for more pictures of Leona through facial recognition, if you know what that is?"

Nina nodded slowly. Christer was uncertain if she really knew.

"It's where the computer searches and matches images that show the same faces. Several images came up. No others together with Ronni, but the picture where she is walking on Nybrogatan and the one when she is on her way into SEB I thought were very interesting."

Nina pushed away the pictures on the table and leaned back in her chair.

"Do you have anything else?"

She took a lip balm out of her purse and started applying it to her lips while she looked at him questioningly.

"So these pictures don't say anything to you?" asked Christer.

"How do you know this is the same girl as in the robberies?"

"She matches the descriptions from witnesses."

"But dear, it's not possible to identify the girl based on that grainy image. Besides, she appears to be dark-haired. The girl at the bank was blond. We can't say for sure either if it's Ronni because the picture is so dark. If you don't have anything else I think we're done here."

Nina took a gulp of mineral water and leaned down for her purse. Christer sighed and shook his head.

"As usual within the legal system," he mumbled while he put the folder into his bag.

Nina stopped and looked at him. "Excuse me, what did you say?"

"This is not the first time I've pointed out strange circumstances involving police officers or others within the legal system. But you always have each other's backs, don't you?"

Nina dropped the purse on the floor.

"What differs between our jobs is that within the legal system we don't sit around guessing or making our own little assumptions about various events. We gather evidence that we then make use of in court. If you're going to accuse someone of a crime, you need something that shows a connection between that person and the specific crime. Not fuzzy suppositions, but concrete evidence that shows that things are a certain way. What you have produced is nothing in the vicinity of what would be required to indict someone of a crime. There is not a prosecutor who would want to touch that."

She was a good speaker. Clear and definite. She was probably right, besides, but he didn't intend to give in.

"Don't you think it's the least bit strange that a police officer like Leona is in the same car as a criminal whom she put away a number of years earlier? That she goes into the very bank on Nybrogatan where a robbery is committed a couple of months later by a girl who resembles the girl who is sitting with her and Ronni in the picture? Is that just coincidence, or what?"

"You haven't been able to show any connection," said Nina. "Simply because a person is sitting in a car with an ex-convict doesn't mean that the person is guilty of a lot of crimes. We have no idea why she is sitting there with Ronni, if that even is him. Leona is a police officer and she also works with informants. It may very well be the case that she is Ronni's handler, we don't know. The fact that she has had contact with him previously is an indication that that might be the case. Information about informants can absolutely not come out in the press. You do understand what that might mean for the informant. Direct mortal danger."

Christer had to admit that in his eagerness to get information about the Hooker Affair out of Leona the thought hadn't occurred to him before.

"I've shown the pictures to Leona. Her reaction was strong. She gave no hint that Ronni might be her informant."

Nina smiled and shook her head.

"Do you think she would tell that to a journalist? This is the sort of thing police officers don't even talk about with each other. Presumably she would do everything she could so that you would refrain from publishing that picture. Under no circumstances does a handler expose her informant."

Christer could not think of anything to say.

"I was thinking about publishing this tomor — "

Nina snorted. "You would risk lives by doing that. Do you want that on your conscience? If you're wrong you're risking your whole reputation as a journalist based on what are only loose suppositions on your part. Explained briefly, you're going to open up a nasty can of worms and be the one who loses most. As a prosecutor with many years of experience, I'm telling you that you have too little to go on to accuse a police officer of such a serious crime. Do as you wish, but keep in mind that I warned you."

Christer sighed. She was right. Too much was at stake. He put the pictures into his bag.

"Maybe I don't have enough evidence, but I still think it's strange that you, as preliminary investigation leader, are not more interested in this."

"Christer, I think you're completely wrong but simply to show my good faith, I will look more closely at it. If I do, though, you will not move a finger for the time being. If you release the information on your own initiative without any evidence, I'm going to do everything to thwart you. You do not risk people's lives or accuse someone for no reason. Do you agree?"

Christer understood that he didn't have much choice. He nodded. Nina put on her coat, tied the belt around her waist, and left the lobby.

Christer remained sitting with his half-finished latte. Realized that it was much too risky to release any information in this situation. But he could still use the pictures to demand information from Leona. If it was as Nina said, Leona would clearly be prepared to do everything to protect that hoodlum Ronni.

SIXTY-ONE

During the drive to my parents I repeated some phrases in my head. I would swallow whatever they said. Not let myself be provoked.

Not argue.

Not get upset.

Simply tolerate the fact that they had never accepted me and presumably never would.

I needed money, so I would ask for it, say thank you, and leave the house. The swearing I could save for later.

I drove into the driveway. The windows looked dark. Strange. They should be home at this time of day. I walked up the steps and rang the bell.

"Leona, what a surprise. How are you doing?"

She was right. It was unexpected. I went inside. Took off my jacket. Mother looked at me.

"Is something wrong? Come in and sit down. I'll put some coffee on."

She went ahead into the kitchen. Even though I had grown up here I always felt like a stranger in this house.

"Where's Dad?"

"He hasn't come home from his round of golf yet. He's playing with the usual gang."

She cut three pieces from a sponge cake and set them out on a plate.

"I baked yesterday; it turned out really well. Take a piece while the coffee is brewing."

Mother had always been good at baking. I took a piece, which fell apart on its way to my mouth. A few crumbs ended up on the table. Mother got up immediately and went to get a rag, wiped the table in front of me, and sat down opposite.

"Let's hear it now."

"It's Benjamin. He's gotten worse. Needs to have surgery."

"Poor little guy. How is he doing?"

"He's at home now, but he's been going back and forth to the hospital for a while. The bowel disease means that he can't assimilate nutrients from his food. Before they removed a part of his intestine that was diseased, but it's not possible to remove any more. He needs a bowel transplant."

"Poor little guy," she said again.

"It's a complicated transplant that can't be done at Sahlgrenska in Gothenburg where we did the previous operation. It has to be done in England."

"Then of course you need someone to take care of Beatrice while you're away. Of course we'll do that."

"The problem is that the county won't pay the costs. They think that the operation is too expensive and the results too uncertain. There is evidently a major risk of complications with this kind of bowel operation. Rejection of the transplanted organ is just one of many things that can go wrong."

Mother listened with a worried expression.

"We feel that we have to do the operation anyway. We can't let him be in the kind of pain he's in now. Soon he won't be able to sleep a single whole night."

At this point she should've understood why I had come. She nodded slowly. It was time to ask the question.

"So this means that we have to pay for all the expenses

ourselves. Travel, lodging, the operation — everything. We have some money, but not enough to cover it."

I stopped. Perhaps she would offer. She looked down. Didn't say anything. I continued.

"So I would need to...borrow."

"I see...I see...I don't know. Your father isn't at home...I would have to talk with him."

It drove me crazy that she couldn't make a single decision without asking him. Good Lord, her grandchild needs medical care, why not just lend me the money? I took a deep breath.

"How much are we talking about?" she asked.

"The whole operation costs sixty thousand pounds. We have half in savings but we would need to borrow the rest, about three hundred thousand kronor."

That was not true. We no longer had any money at all, but because it was humiliating enough to even have to ask for a loan and I wanted to avoid any comments that we ought to have savings, I only asked for half. If I could borrow three hundred thousand kronor, I could probably double the money myself.

"You'll get the money back. We can draw up a payment plan if you want."

"You should have a bigger buffer, you and Peter. As a family you need that to manage unforeseen incidents like this."

I sucked it up. I wanted to scream that it was her fucking duty as a mother and grandmother to help out when her children and grandchildren had problems.

"I've always said that you should've gotten a sensible education and a better-paying job, like your brothers."

Now I had to get away from there before I said something that meant I definitely would not get to borrow any money. I got up and headed toward the hall.

"I have to leave. Could you please talk with Father and let me know as soon as possible?"

"Are you in such a hurry? The coffee isn't even ready."

"I have to get back to work before I pick up the kids."

I got in the car. Satisfied at having managed to avoid a conflict with Mother. But I regretted that I hadn't asked for more money when I was asking anyway. For them, three hundred thousand or six hundred thousand hardly made any difference. They didn't do anything with their money anyway. Sat on their savings, as if they could take the money with them to the afterlife. But I would have to see about solving this another way. Doubling the money myself would probably work out. I only needed to concentrate properly and play the way I knew worked. If I only made sure to stick to my own rules and not take any risks, it would be okay.

I had it in me.

I knew that.

SIXTY-TWO

Christer Skoog rang the doorbell of the apartment for the third time, at the address Leona had given him. Just like the day before yesterday when he had visited, no one was there to answer. Besides the bell not a sound was heard from the other side of the door.

The information Leona had provided about what the prostitute had said during interrogation was extremely interesting. Christer wanted her to expand on it now. Perhaps draw the birthmark again so that he could publish it in the newspaper. Hopefully she had more to tell, too. People would be shocked, especially the minister's wife. The prostitute would get vindication and Christer himself would get a scoop. Most importantly, the finance minister would get to feel what it's like to have everyone against you. Christer felt sick just thinking about all the years of anxiety that the finance minister had caused him. Christer could not tolerate that a bully who had grown up to become a person who bargained and paid for sex from prostitutes had succeeded in getting a ministerial position in Sweden. Or the oily, well-polished smile he put on as soon as a camera was focused on him, either.

Christer rang the doorbell again. Persistently pushed the button. A young, pale woman dressed only in a large T-shirt tore open the door.

"What the hell is this? Knock it off!" she screamed.

He couldn't help but sympathize. When the door was opened the sharp sound of the doorbell ricocheted off the concrete walls in the stairwell. He smiled broadly in the hope that she would overlook the noise he had caused.

"Hi, my name is Christer. I'm looking for Dina."

She looked him up and down as if she were searching for something in his appearance that revealed what type of man he was.

"Wait."

She closed the door. He could hear her going farther into the apartment. Her steps revealed that she was not completely sober. Christer looked around on the stairwell landing. Hoped that he wouldn't have to spend too much time there. His gaze landed on a door that was decorated on the outside with a dozen taped-up pieces of fabric with words on them. The door was ajar. Strange that he hadn't heard when it opened, he thought. In the darkness inside the apartment stood an elderly, gray-haired woman with upswept hair. Dressed in some kind of white nightgown. She stood completely still. Squinted at him and hissed.

"A pox on those like you. You are emissaries of the devil. Hell is where you belong."

Christer stared at her. When he took a step closer she slammed the door. He went over. Saw that the white pieces of fabric were decorated with embroidered Bible quotations. While he stood looking at them he heard steps from inside Dina's door again. The same woman opened it.

"She's out."

"Did it take five minutes to figure that out?"

The woman seemed totally uninterested in even trying to think up a lie about where Dina was. Christer came slowly closer. A taped-up piece of fabric on the old lady's door fell onto the floor. The young woman started laughing hysterically.

"She's mental, that old woman. She's taped up pieces of cloth the whole fucking night and now it's all falling down."

She continued laughing. Christer tried to peek into the apartment but the darkness meant that he could only see a few jackets hanging close to the door. How would he get hold of Dina? He realized if she was in there his only chance was now, when the door was half open. He made a run, pushed it open, shoved aside the woman and stormed into the apartment.

"Dina! I know you're here. I just want to talk with you."

In the apartment he was slowed by newspapers, clothes, and shoes that were strewn everywhere. The apartment stank of smoke and booze. He opened every door along the hall. One of these rooms was the bathroom which, judging by the smell, had not been cleaned for weeks.

"What the hell?" screamed the woman from the hall. "I'm calling the cops. Dina! Watch out, a crazy john is coming!"

In the kitchen with a big knife in one hand and a cigarette in the other stood Dina, in a combat-ready stance, dressed only in a bra and underpants. Her hair was swept up in a ponytail high on her head.

"I'll cut you, you bastard," she screamed.

"No, no, take it easy, don't worry. I just want to talk with you. It's Christer, the journalist. We talked on the phone. You were going to meet me but you called and said you couldn't come."

Dina remained in her position. Looked him skeptically up and down.

"I was worried something had happened to you when suddenly you didn't want to talk to me," he continued, to show that he was on her side.

She slowly lowered the knife.

"Damn it, you scared me. Are you out of your mind?"

Dina went over to the window. Looked frantically in all directions and then quickly pulled down the blinds.

"Does anyone know you're here?"

"No. Can I sit down?"

She nodded to the kitchen chair, then went over to the stove. "Coffee?"

When he saw the piles of dirty dishes on the counter he hesitated. She looked at him with raised eyebrows. Christer, uncomfortable seeing her disrobed body, didn't know where to fix his eyes.

"Perhaps you can put the knife down now?"

"Do you have any idea how many crazy johns I've met? Storming in here like that. You're out of your mind. I could have stuck this in you."

She put the knife in the top drawer, rinsed out a mug, and set it down, after wiping it dry with a dirty hand towel that was hanging over the handle of the oven door. Into it she poured a brown liquid that looked more like burnt tar than coffee.

"I know you told the police about the birthmark," said Christer.

She sat down. Put out her cigarette in the overfilled ashtray. "And?"

"The thing is, the prosecutor seems to have disregarded the most important piece of evidence that shows you're telling the truth. The birthmark you drew matched almost exactly with the minister's."

"I know. But what can I do about it? I've told the police everything."

"I can publish your story in *Aftonbladet*. Then you'll get a chance to tell everyone what actually happened. People don't know that."

"What's in it for me? Only more problems. I haven't exactly been getting more customers after this. The rumors spread quickly as hell on the street. Everyone knows I was the one who reported it. The johns are scared I'll report them too. Besides, I've been threatened."

"By whom?"

Dina took a sip of coffee and lit another cigarette. Didn't answer.

"You can get protection," said Christer.

"From you? Or what? You live in your own little world. No one cares about me, do you understand? In people's eyes I'm just a whore who only has herself to blame. The police don't give a damn about us."

"But if I publish this the prosecutor will be forced to reopen your case and you'll get vindication."

"Vindication?" Dina snorted. "There's no vindication for someone like me. I wanted people to understand how disgusting our politicians are, that's all. I'd be crazy to expect anything more. Up till now I've been presented as a liar in the media. A celebrity-crazed gold-digger who only wants to make trouble. No, damn it, right now I'm doing all I can to go underground. It's a matter of shutting down and moving on."

Christer had to try a different angle. This was the second time Dina had made a police report against men in the upper levels of society. Christer knew she had a strong sense of justice and wanted to raise awareness about the situation of sex workers. Maybe it would work.

"But can you live that way? Not bothering to fight for what you believe? Then you're letting those big shots win, even though they're complete bastards."

"Listen, damn it, don't talk to me about fighting for what you believe in. I've done it so many times, and I thought maybe I could change something. But it's impossible to win in my position. The only one that gets shit is me. Oh, damn it, there's no point in even talking with you. We come from different planets."

Christer felt he could no longer argue against her in a credible way. No matter how little he liked it, he knew she was right. She had taken a lot of beatings.

"I understand you, Dina, but I hate that they're free simply because of who they are. Besides, they've threatened you and God knows how many others. Apparently the prosecutor too, it seems."

Christer sighed and stood up. Put the untouched mug of coffee on the counter.

"Thanks for the coffee. Sorry about scaring you and your friend."

He started heading toward the door. Halfway out in the hall he heard Dina.

"Wait!"

She disappeared into one of the rooms and came back with a phone. Not until she raised the volume to maximum was it possible to hear the voices. Christer could hardly believe what he was hearing.

"Have you played this for the police?"

"No, I didn't know until a few days ago that it had been recorded. I have recording on quick code on my phone because I run into so many sick johns. When it starts getting nasty I hit rec. This time I must have accidentally touched the button."

"Who knows about this besides me?"

"No one."

This was all the information Christer needed. With it he could print in the newspaper that there was a recording and if nothing happened, he could publish a transcript of it. It was evidence that might be enough to convict them. Dina's name and picture would of course have been the icing on the cake. He looked at her. She seemed to have understood his thought and shook her head.

"Not a chance."

She stood with her arms crossed. He realized it was probably impossible to convince her. But the recording would be enough.

"Can I get a copy?"

"You can take it. I have a new, better phone now. I got so many threats and shit from everyone possible on that one. It has loads of messages on it that I couldn't stand to listen to."

"Messages from any of the ministers?"

"Like I said, I haven't listened to them. When you've heard enough times that you're a disgusting whore who should die in the sickest ways, you can't bear to hear that shit anymore."

Christer wasn't listening. He was exhilarated at the turn the meeting had taken but at the same time a little distressed at the misery of her living conditions. He left the apartment and walked, as if intoxicated, toward his car. This information would produce headlines. It would be major. Now it was important to do everything just right. He needed a competent, credible person who could back his story. He would contact Nina Wallin, the prosecutor. With her in his corner the facts he submitted would have real impact. Finally he would be able to put away those suits.

SIXTY-THREE

Everyone was equally confused about why Claes had summoned us to an extra squad meeting. My colleagues looked questioningly at the whiteboard in the big conference room, as though it could tell us what was going on. Someone had heard that a new working method would be presented, which was not a popular idea. That sort of thing was presented time and again. Those who'd been around a long time had seen many changes come and go. Personally I had other things to think about, and wasn't particularly amused at the idea of having to sit and listen to information about how some efficiency model would be introduced.

"Yep, now it's time again."

Rolf, one of the older officers, looked at me.

"I wonder how many millions this idea is going to cost the taxpayers?"

Rolf was right. The agency spent millions introducing new working methods. Buying expensive new computer systems, training all the personnel in the country, and then scrapping the systems when it turned out they didn't fit the operation. Then they'd have new systems and working methods developed, and then train all the personnel in the country over again. Reorganizations, where squads were reduced, followed by ones where squads were expanded; a constantly ongoing change process that never seemed to end, nor change anything for the better.

"Something new is always fun," said Sam, looking at Rolf.

He got a snort in return.

Claes stepped into the room, followed by a middle-aged man. He had dark, mid-length hair with streaks of gray. Glasses. A normal build. I used to amuse myself by guessing the background of unknown people. This man was hard to assess. He was probably not a police officer. He looked out over the room in an analytical way. A psychologist? Maybe the idea was that we'd all get counseling, like other people with mentally stressful occupations.

"I would like to introduce a person who will be working with us over the coming year. He is going to assist us in our investigations, primarily in the reconnaissance cases."

Help out with investigations? Probably not a psychologist then. I might have guessed he was a profiler, but they worked in teams, not alone. Besides which, there was only one such team in Sweden. It would be strange if Claes had managed to get that profiling team to support our squad alone. No, this must be something else.

"His name is Sören Möller. I will turn the floor directly over to you, Sören, so you can introduce yourself and tell everyone what you'll be doing."

What was this? Claes always liked to show off by giving nice-sounding introductions of visitors, thus implying that it was his doing that such capable people worked for him. This was getting stranger and stranger.

"Hi everyone, so my name is Sören Möller."

My colleagues sat quietly but seemed not to have understood that there was something peculiar about him.

"I work as a medium."

A medium! My jaw could have dropped to the ground. That was the last thing I would have imagined. Many strange things had come and gone in the agency over the years, but this probably took the cake.

"My primary area of work so far has been communicating with deceased persons and their relatives, and finding missing persons."

I looked around. Was this a joke? Everyone was silent and staring at the man. I made eye contact with Fredrik, who seemed to be trying hard to keep from laughing. Claes stood to the side, looking down at the floor.

"When you work as a medium, you get used to many people doubting your ability."

Could he read minds?

"For that reason I always keep statistics about my own work."

I see, an attempt to turn hocus-pocus into some kind of science. I looked at Claes, to read his facial expression. He seemed to have all his attention on his phone. He took a few quick steps out of the room with the phone against his ear. The man clicked on the remote control for the ceiling projector. An image with pictures of various people appeared on the screen behind him.

"Where missing persons are concerned, where the results are easiest to measure, I have worked with twenty-six different cases so far. In all these cases the family has come to me when the police had not found the person and had abandoned the search."

He clicked to the next image.

"With the help of my abilities, we have found twenty-four of them. Twenty were alive and staying away voluntarily, and four were unfortunately deceased and resulted in murder investigations. In those murder investigations four persons have been indicted and three convicted."

Impressive figures. But was that really enough to make him credible within the agency?

"Swedish police have made use of a medium to assist with a criminal investigation only once before. I'm sure you've read about your former police colleague, Tore Hedin, who in the 1950s murdered ten people, including his own parents, his ex-girlfriend, and her boss. As if it were not strange enough behavior for a policeman to kill all those people, he himself also hired the medium Olof Jönsson."

So, the medium had a little humor and self-awareness too. I couldn't help admiring his timing.

"Olof Jönsson was so close to revealing Tore's actions that Tore finally confessed to all the murders in a suicide note before he drowned himself."

They were known as the Hurva murders from 1953. My colleagues and I were very familiar with that incident.

The door opened and Claes came in again. He nodded to Sören and sat down on a chair in the very front.

Fredrik raised his hand.

"Didn't Channel 5 make an attempt to investigate some cold cases with the help of a medium on some obscure TV show a few years ago?"

"*Impressions of Murder*, yes, that's correct," Sören answered. "But contrary to what some believe, the police were not the client, and the agency's involvement in the series was minimal. When the so-called mediums found leads they were turned in to the police, who registered and processed the information just like any other tip. In a case or two a murder investigation was reopened, but otherwise it produced no great results for the police."

"So there wasn't a single murder that was solved with the help of the mediums?" I asked.

"That is correct. And that was why I said 'so-called mediums.' There are many charlatans in my trade who unfortunately ruin the reputation of the rest of us. The production company contacted me and a few of my serious colleagues, all of whom said no to the program. We thought it didn't seem serious enough. In retrospect, I'm pleased about that, but unfortunately it meant they got hold of the wrong people for the program, which has damaged the trade. Those of us who take this seriously want to work in the background. Not become celebrities on some advertising-financed reality show. Unfortunately the program has left its mark on people's general perception of mediums and our ability to actually assist a crime investigation."

"So there are no serious experiments in Sweden that suggest using a medium with crime investigations actually produces results?" I asked.

"You might say so."

"This is, in other words, yet another experiment by the agency that the taxpayers will have to pay good money for?"

I couldn't keep quiet. The presentation was good but the whole idea was absurd and illogical. Claes stood up and intervened.

"Other countries have had a greater tradition of using this working method, with varying results. In many places there have been a lot of positive ones. The agency has now decided to test it and we here at VCD are the first in the country to have the opportunity to work with Sören."

As usual it was the manager's task to make every misery seem like an amazing opportunity.

"The first investigation that Sören will work with is actually the girl robberies that you're investigating, Leona," said Claes.

I stared at him. Of course all this shit would end up on my plate. As if I didn't have enough to keep track of. Now I would have a charlatan hot on my heels as well. Everyone stared at me as if they were afraid I'd have an outburst. Fredrik rolled his eyes.

I didn't bat an eyelid.

The day continued more or less in a fog. My head ached. When my phone buzzed in my pocket I stuck my hand down and managed to accidentally hit the answer button.

"Now you damn well better not hang up, Leona. You listen now," said Christer at the other end.

Without having the energy to do otherwise I continued to hold the phone to my ear.

"You haven't given me any information, Leona; I haven't received one lousy bit. I'm getting tired of talking to your fucking voice mail. I've talked with Nina instead. Told her about you. She knows everything now and we, Nina and I, are going to put you away together. Do you get that?"

He hung up. I knew, of course, that he'd told Nina. But I had a hard time believing that Nina would be involved in putting me away. I picked up the phone and called Nina, and asked what she actually said to Christer when they met.

"It's all fine, Leona; I'll take care of him. I have it under control. I have to go, they're calling us into court. We've just been on a break."

I hung up. Had she sounded a little strange? I was uncertain. I'd have to be extremely watchful of Nina's actions.

SIXTY-FOUR

After the day's surreal introduction to the supernatural it was a relief to hurry away to day care to pick up the kids. They'd learned a new song and in the car sang loudly about blueberries, small berries, and a big fruit store.

Ringvägen was full of cars — rush hour — but the traffic flowed nicely. I reached for my phone, which was vibrating on the dashboard.

"Mother, I'm in the car on my way home with the kids, but you can talk."

"It's been a long time since we saw them. You'll have to come here and have dinner again soon."

"Hmmm..."

I didn't plan to do that. The kids continued singing in the backseat.

"You'll have to be quiet now, Grandma's on the phone."

The children fell silent after a few happy shouts to Grandma.

"I've spoken with your father and we've agreed to loan you the money."

"That's nice to hear, Mother. We're very happy about that."

"We have even decided to loan you a little more than you asked for. I've transferred 350,000 kronor to your account today. But it probably won't appear until tomorrow because you don't use the same reliable bank that your father and I do."

I ignored the dig. The money was the essential thing.

"The most important thing is that Benjamin gets the operation he needs, Leona. Just make sure it's a good doctor and surgeon. Your father wants to know what clinic it is so he can check up on them. You never know when it's outside the country like that."

My heart started to beat faster. Typical of them to assume that health care would be worse simply because it wasn't Swedish doctors at a Swedish clinic.

"We got a recommendation for them from Karolinska."

"You can never be too careful."

I knew that her prattle about it being important that Benji got a good doctor didn't mean she cared about me, or Benji. Everything was about control. They would show that they knew best, and that I ought to adapt to their wisdom. It was time to hang up.

"We'll be in touch later. The kids are tearing apart the backseat."

Mother didn't have time to say goodbye before I ended the call.

"Now you can keep singing back there as loud as you want. Why don't you teach me the song too?"

They both started hollering happily in the backseat. Beatrice sang a phrase and I tried to sing it back. Both laughed loudly when I sang the wrong words. I enjoyed hearing them laugh. By the time we got inside the door I had learned it. All of us sang while our jackets, caps, and shoes flew off.

"Daddy, Daddy, Mommy knows it now," Beatrice called, running into the living room where Peter was sitting.

It was unusual that he was home so early. He got up out of the armchair and looked right at me. He was red-eyed. His eyelids were swollen. I stopped.

"Kids, run into your rooms, I'm going to talk with Daddy."

Beatrice jumped away with Benjamin close behind.

"Has someone died?" I said.

The only time I had seen Peter cry was when his father passed away six years ago. He could get upset, but never like that.

"Leona," he said.

"Yes, what's happened?"

"I want a divorce."

SIXTY-FIVE

I spent the night on the couch in the living room. In the morning I quickly put away the sheets before the children woke up. My eyes still felt as if someone had poured gravel in them. Tried to blink it away. I didn't expend any great amount of time or energy on analyzing Peter's initiative yesterday. On an emotional level it was of minor significance to me that he wanted a divorce. I was no longer exerting myself to be the Leona he was used to. I saw no point in that. From Peter's point of view it was obvious that I'd changed. He felt I'd become a different person. Someone other than the one he had married. In a way, that was true.

I had expected that he would want a divorce. I had hoped, however, that it wouldn't come so soon.

I needed him.

For a little longer.

Claes and the medium were already seated at the round meeting table in Claes's office. I was two minutes late. Looked for a decent office chair but was forced to sit on the remaining chair at the table.

That the department had forced me to work with an outsider without informing me about who it was or what the collaboration would look like irritated me. It was the Police Department in a nutshell.

"Since I don't know how this is supposed to work I think I'll lean back and listen to your plan for how it will be structured, Claes."

I looked at Claes, who was occupied with browsing through some papers. I turned to the medium.

"Do you have authorization to use our computer system so you can do your own searches on people and read the case files? Are you going to work independently, or will we have regular meetings? What about confidentiality?"

The medium looked at Claes.

"The idea is that he will work together with you, and you have access to our registers. He has no authorization of his own. Obviously he has signed a confidentiality agreement."

"And the information that you're going to, um…see…in your visions," I said. "Will you communicate that directly to me, or what?"

Perhaps this would be simpler than I thought. No point in assuming the worst.

"In order to be able to see at all I'm going to need to follow you in your daily work," said the medium.

I looked quickly at Claes.

"I hope you've mentioned the fact that I work extremely independently."

"Leona, this is an order from above," said Claes. "A pilot project. Everyone is eager for it to have a positive outcome. It's crucial for both of you to create a functioning method of working and maintain a pleasant work environment."

"Excuse me, but I'm noticing that the two of you haven't talked this through," said the medium. "Perhaps I should come back tomorrow when you've had time to discuss the matter?"

I respected him for backing off. It wasn't his fault that management within the agency failed to form competent plans for their projects.

"Sören, I hope you understand that this has nothing to do with you," I said. "I'm used to working in a certain way and, well, this came as a big surprise. I wish that someone" — I looked at Claes — "had prepared me for it."

There had been plenty of opportunities for Claes to let me know what was happening, but instead he had chosen to bring it up at yesterday's squad meeting, when the guy was already in place.

"I think your suggestion is good," I said. "If it's okay with you, Claes and I will talk about this tomorrow and then we'll contact you on Wednesday."

Claes intervened.

"Sören, I apologize for Leona's behavior."

He turned back to me.

"This is not open for discussion, Leona. You'll have to put up with—"

"Claes, I insist," said Sören. "I think you should talk about this without me. I understand Leona's reaction. Contact me sometime tomorrow, then we'll talk further about what comes next. I'll ask Anette to show me out."

"As you wish," said Claes. "Again, I apologize."

Sören left the room. Claes closed the door behind him and turned quickly to me.

"What the hell makes you tick, Leona? You're embarrassing both me and the agency. And what's with the face? You look like you've been on a weeklong bender."

"What were you all thinking when you decided to bring a medium into my investigation? Did you think it would help conjure up a better work method? Along with all the other hocuspocus you seem to be putting your faith in? I had to pinch myself on the arm when I heard."

"I can agree with you that this is, well, a somewhat odd move by the agency, but it doesn't change the fact that he's here now."

"And whose idea was it that he should work with *my* case?"

"Don't make a big deal of this, Leona."

"It was you, wasn't it?"

"They wanted a current case without a suspect."

"Think of what will happen when the media gets wind of this. They're going to laugh at us. I can already see the headlines. 'Police Agency Can't Solve Crimes — Hires Charlatans.' The taxpayers are going to wonder what the hell they're paying for."

"The idea is that we should all keep a low profile about Sören being here. If anyone asks, we're not going to make a statement."

I could hardly keep from laughing. The whole thing was ridiculous. How naive was it to think that the press wouldn't ferret this out?

"Look at the bright side. If you solve this in cooperation with Sören and he actually manages to produce something, then you get all the glory. No outsider is going to know that we worked with a medium. You'll be seen as one of Sweden's sharpest investigators."

"And what advantage would that give me?"

"You should not underestimate glory and renown, Leona. That's what we all live for. You'll need to take Sören out for a coffee and cake or something. It's your job to make sure he's comfortable. He's going to write an evaluation of his work here and I don't want to read a word about lack of cooperation or distrust of him as a medium."

I shook my head.

"I'm serious, Leona. This is important for both you and me. I'll have to take measures if you don't resolve this."

"Is that a threat or what?"

"See it as a promise. If it turns out that you refuse to cooperate, I will have no other choice. Don't think I'd hesitate to transfer you. Now beat it and get to work."

Claes waved one hand as if fanning would make me disappear. I got up and started for the door.

"And listen, see about making yourself presentable, damn it," he called after me. "You look like a wreck."

SIXTY-SIX

Trying to get a parking space in Vasastan involved constant circling until a car finally pulled out. Then it was crucial to take the
space quickly before someone else did.

After circling around Sankt Eriksplan and searching on
Tomtebogatan and Birkagatan I finally lucked out with a spot on
Bråvallagatan, across from Nina's entrance. I'd tried to reach
her the whole day to tell her that we had an occultist breathing down our necks. Thought it was just as easy to stop by on
the way home and tell her. It was already eight o'clock, so she
should be home.

I parked and looked up at her window. There were lights on.
I opened the car door and got out. Realized I'd left my bag on the
passenger seat and leaned in again on the driver's side. Just as I
was reaching for the bag, I saw a familiar person walking up the
sidewalk on the other side of the street. I followed him with my
eyes. When his entire body was visible between the parked cars I
recognized the clumsy gait. Was it really him? The gray cap and
the collar on the dark parka concealed part of his face. I couldn't
be completely certain. Without taking my eyes off him I got back
in the car and pulled the door closed. He stopped outside Nina's
entrance and tossed the cigarette he'd been smoking. Before he
went up to the door he turned toward the street to step on the
butt. Then I saw his face clearly.

It was him.

Christer Skoog.

I turned cold. What business did he have with Nina? I knew that he didn't live in Vasastan. That he would have an acquaintance living in the same building as Nina was too unbelievable. He entered the code and disappeared into the entrance.

I stayed in the car. Tried to think clearly. Could it be true what he had said, that he and Nina...? I thought back. Nina had said that she met Christer at Hotel Amaranten as planned. She had also said that I shouldn't worry about him. That she had him under control. I picked up the phone and entered Nina's number. She answered after four rings.

"Nina, it's me. I'd like to go through a few things that have come up. I thought about stopping by, are you at home?"

"Uh...no. Mother has fallen ill so I'm at her place. I'll probably be here all evening. Was it something important?"

It was obvious that she was lying. There were lights on in her place, and now I could even see shadows of people in the apartment.

"It'll keep. Take care of your mother now and we'll deal with it later."

My thoughts were buzzing. I tried to get a handle on what had just happened. Nina had just lied that she was with her sick mother when in reality she was at home in her apartment with Christer Skoog, who had said on the phone that the two of them were going to put me away.

I placed my arms and forehead against the steering wheel. Closed my eyes. It was as if all the energy had drained out of me. My whole body became heavy. I tried to get rid of the stifling sensation in my chest by taking a few deep breaths. The sound from the cars outside had changed to a diffuse, dull rumble. All the obstacles and difficulties I had run into so far felt small compared to what I faced now. Christer was a greedy journalist who would do anything to get what he wanted. He had apparently managed to bring Nina over to his side. I'd hoped it would be possible to keep him in check by supplying him with a little information now and then. I had misjudged him. Now he'd become too great a problem for me to handle. I couldn't let that continue.

It had gone too far.

Something drastic had to be done.

Nina was a total disappointment. Even though I had been on my guard with her, I had thought she understood my message. That if I go to prison, she goes with me. But Christer Skoog had presumably given her a better offer than me. Now I was alone. Abandoned to a situation that had become harder to handle than I ever imagined.

I slowly opened my eyes and looked out over the hood of the car onto the street. People were moving as usual outside, but for me, everything had changed.

Images flickered in my head. Memories of the first robbery, which had started as a fleeting thought and transformed into a complete, definite plan. How liberating it had been to finally do something about the feeling of imprisonment that was eating me up from inside. Fighting to be true to myself. I couldn't back out now. When I saw the stressed people walking by outside the car I was once again reminded of the meaninglessness of the life I was living.

This constant struggle.

To what end?

The mental confinement of life scared me more than anything else.

I leaned back in the seat. Strengthened by the thought that there was no going back. It would be a solitary fight from here on. Presumably Nina and Christer were sitting there in the apartment forging common plans. I needed to be one step ahead. Now it was about my own survival. Those two people had to be out of my life. I could no longer afford to leave any stone unturned. They had entered the game. Perhaps they didn't understand with what high stakes they were playing.

They would soon find out.

SIXTY-SEVEN

Olivia opened her eyes. Like every time she woke up she had to look around the room for a while before she remembered where she was. A beam of sunlight shone in, forming a light triangle across the floor next to her. The desk, the Windsor chair, the wig. She was still there. In the same room she had been in for many, many days. She didn't know exactly how many.

When she moved, she found that she was still sore in some places. She slowly lifted the covers and looked down at her body. The light-blue nightgown Mommy had given her was stained. The lace hem at the bottom had come apart. She ran her fingers along one knee and felt that the scab from when she had fallen on the way to Grandma's was almost gone.

Daddy said she'd had a concussion. Olivia thought that it must have been true, because she'd felt so dizzy afterward, like her brain had been shaken. But now she only had an occasional headache.

The only thing that still hurt a lot was her foot. Daddy hadn't noticed until afterward that it had also been hurt when she fell. At first it was just a tiny, tiny cut, but then it had turned blue, and had swollen. When Daddy had found out, he'd tied a piece of cloth from his T-shirt around the foot. This time he had bandaged it so hard that it hurt. As she sat up she happened to move the blanket so that it pulled against her foot. She took a deep breath. Tried to loosen the cloth around her foot a little. She had to hold on hard with both hands to loosen the knot. Pulled as hard as she could. Grimaced as the cloth pulled tighter. Finally she got the knot untied. Carefully she unwrapped the cloth, which was wound in several layers. The bottom one was sticking a little to her skin. She pulled carefully so it would loosen but had to stop because it stung so bad. She lifted the cloth again from the other side and gasped. The skin had turned even bluer than before.

She started sobbing loudly. Couldn't help it. It looked so horrible. The sound echoed in the room. She heard steps. It was Daddy. She put the cloth back over her foot and quickly pulled the covers up to her chin.

The door opened. Daddy entered. Without saying anything he went over to the mattress and pulled down the covers. Olivia was crying loudly but that didn't matter anymore. He had already heard her anyway. He swore a little, quietly, and quickly left the room. Olivia listened to the steps. Into the living room, then the kitchen. A drawer was opened; he took something out of it. Ran water in the sink. He quickly came back with a red T-shirt, a scissors, and a water glass.

"Open wide."

In one hand he held the water glass, Olivia could not see what he had in the other. She opened her mouth between sniffles. Knew she had no choice. He put two pills in her mouth and handed her the glass.

"Drink."

She took the glass. It was hard for her to balance it when she was lying down. The pills were big in her mouth. She tried to hold her head up to be able to drink.

"Drink, I said. It won't hurt as much then."

Olivia took two big gulps. Some water ended up outside her mouth. The water was good. She took several smaller sips more, but it ran too fast. She started coughing.

"What the hell! Can't you do a single thing right?"

Daddy took the water glass and set it on the table. He cut a gash in the red T-shirt and started tearing it apart into long pieces of cloth. While Olivia coughed and cried quietly he took away the old pieces of cloth and started bandaging the foot with the new red cloth. Not as hard as before. Much gentler, more careful. On top of the foot he fastened the piece of cloth with a knot. He told Olivia not to open it again. Olivia nodded and tried hard to stop crying. Daddy reached his hand toward her face. She turned her head away. Closed her eyes. Then she felt Daddy's rough hand against her cheek. He stroked it quickly and left the room.

SIXTY-EIGHT

I was sitting in the car a couple of blocks from Christer Skoog's house in Vällingby. I'd been forced to prepare everything in a single evening. The night before I had made my way into his house, retrieved a knife from his kitchen, bought boots in the wrong size, and arranged clothing. I would have liked more time, to learn about his evening habits. My plan was far from perfect, but I couldn't wait.

I sat in Peter's and my car. Memories flooded me. Family outings in the car, to Skansen, the swimming pool, movies, other children's birthday parties... The life that I was used to, it was over. I hadn't had time to reflect on the change. But I was relieved. With every piece that came loose from my self-created sandcastle, I felt more free.

More alive.

Was I ready for what I was about to do? What was the use of asking myself that? I had no choice. I needed to defend myself. To make sure to keep my own head above the water.

I went through the steps in my head. In through the cellar door. Up the seven steps of the cellar stairs, then in through the door up to the hall, which would probably be unlocked. It had been yesterday. If it wasn't, it would take me another two minutes to get into the house. He would be sitting at the computer in the living room facing toward the window, his back to the living room door. If I hadn't managed to turn off the ceiling light he would see me in the reflection of the window as soon as I entered the living room. Then I would only have a few seconds. A couple of steps to reach him. Get him down. It was important that he wasn't able to get up. Under no circumstances could this become a wrestling match between us. Not because I was worried that I couldn't handle him, but a struggle meant a greater possibility for the police to produce evidence. I needed to get into the house and reach the living room so soundlessly that I could turn off the light without him getting up from the desk. It was also important because the big window was like an illuminated aquarium facing out toward the street. I couldn't risk anyone from outside seeing.

I tried to breathe calmly. Focus. Committing a murder was something quite different from averting one.

Murder.

The word, which I had said so many times at work, had now acquired a completely new significance. The thoughts...the thoughts about what in God's name I was doing. They were there. They came and bounced around in my head. I did everything to push them away. I no longer had any choice.

I had to do this.

Didn't I?

My heart pounded hard in my chest. I was used to the feeling of excitement, of adrenaline, but it was different now. I had to stop thinking and act instead.

I opened the car door. Got out. The shoes were one size too big but a pair of extra socks had solved the problem. With calm, deliberate steps I moved along the sidewalk. The house came closer. I disappeared into the hedge by the property line. There were still leaves on the trees. I crouched in the bushes. Peered out. Drops of water from the leaves fell down onto my clothes. The darkness and the backlight made it impossible to see what was around me. From the bushes I could see into Christer's living room. It was brightly lit. The flicker from the TV created a white glow against the walls. Where was he? I stood there for a good five minutes, waiting, until I saw him come into the living room with a bowl in his hand. I ducked instinctively when he looked right out toward where I was standing. It was just a reflex. He couldn't see me. I knew that. For one thing, I was completely clothed in dark garments, and in any case the light was reflected by the windows indoors, so it was hardly possible to see out. I had to relax. I drew the cold, damp autumn air deep down into my lungs. He sat down at the desk next to the window, opened the cover on his laptop, and started eating. Pasta. It was a good sign that he was eating at the computer. Then I could be sure that he was alone. Between bites he was writing. Besides his eating and writing at the same time he looked fairly relaxed, almost pleasant. But if there was one thing I had learned in my profession it was not to rely on appearances. His way of threatening me and pressuring me for information showed who he really was. The fact that he had gotten Nina on his side, and that together behind my back they were trying to frame me, had driven me to this. It was his life or mine. I had to defend myself. Perhaps he was even sitting there writing lies about me that he intended to publish tomorrow. Yes, he probably was. Just as well I get it over with now.

I moved quickly toward the cellar door. After a minute and a half I got the lock off. Many years working with locksmiths to get into other people's apartments made it easy for me to get in. I opened the door carefully. The muffled, murmuring sound from the TV was the only thing I could hear. I determined my location with the help of my flashlight. Step by step, one at a time. Silent, calm, and steady, even though my heart was pounding. When I took hold of the handle on the hall door I heard a scraping sound and his steps across the floor. I stopped breathing. Released the handle. Stood stock-still. Prepared. If he opened the hall door I would be forced to do it here and now.

He walked past, and into the kitchen. Pulled out the silverware drawer and took something out. Then the steps moved back toward me and again out into the living room. I heard the scraping sound of the wooden leg of the chair as he pulled it over the floor. I took a deep breath. Without a sound I pressed down the handle on the hall door. The strong light in the hall meant that I had to squint. I was in. Only a few meters from the living room. I crept forward, with my back against the wall in the narrow hall. I saw myself in the full-length mirror that was on the wall opposite. I stared at my own reflection. Didn't recognize myself. It was like looking at someone else. It was a movie with a scared protagonist who was just about to commit the crime on which the story was based. I was rigid. With wide-open eyes like a cocaine user. I looked away. Had to keep going. The doorway into the living room was only a meter or so away. Now I didn't have much time to spare. He could get up at any time and go out to the kitchen again. I was there now. By the doorway. I leaned my head out and looked into the living room. Saw him sitting with his back to me, tapping on the computer.

I took out the knife. Slowly. Soundlessly. Four short steps was all that was required. Then three quick stabs. Was I prepared?

Yes.

No.

My heart wouldn't stop pounding. I adjusted the knife in my hand. It slid out of my glove and thudded on the floor. Damn it! He stopped writing and looked over his shoulder. He had seen me. Now I had seconds left. I picked the knife up from the floor. I got hold of the switch that turned off the ceiling light and ran four steps straight toward him. A quick stab in the upper part of his back. It was hard to get the knife in. Not at all like I had imagined. He let out a moaning sound. Blood started seeping out through the blue T-shirt. I pulled out the knife. Another hard stab next to it. Out with the knife a second time. A final stab to the lung. He was lifeless. His upper body lay across the desk. I left the knife in his body and quickly closed the blinds on the window facing the street. Went back. I took off one leather glove and put two fingers on his neck. I had put on plastic gloves under the leather ones for just this purpose. No pulse. I pulled the knife out slowly. As if I was afraid of injuring an organ. His whole back had turned dark with blood. I had seen a lot of blood in my job, but I was disgusted by this. I began to feel nauseated by the smell of bodily fluids that had spread throughout the room, but I couldn't get myself to leave. I stood there, paralyzed. Observed him. Astounded by how quickly it had happened. A minute ago he'd been sitting there writing. Completely alive.

Now he was lifeless.

It was impossible to take in.

I knew that I had to finish and get out but I couldn't. My body would not obey me. To get rid of the overwhelming image of him I closed my eyes and took a few deep breaths. I wiped the knife a little carelessly on the couch. Took the plastic bag out of my pocket. Held it up. The dark strands of hair in the bag weren't visible in the darkness but I knew they were there. My hands were shaking. I tried to calm myself. Had to get this done now. The little bag was well sealed. I had to pull hard, but I couldn't really get a grip. With trembling hands I tore harder. The bag burst open, ripped along one side.

"Damn," I whispered, as if someone could hear me. I held the bag up toward the light coming from the kitchen down the hall. The strands of hair couldn't be seen. Because I couldn't make myself turn on the light in the living room I went into the kitchen with the torn bag. The hair strands were gone. Must have fallen out. Where? I had planned to place a strand of hair in the blood on the knife, and one near the chair where Christer was seated, and one more on…damn, my hands were still trembling. I clenched them. Walked steadily into the living room. Stood in the doorway, focusing my gaze on the couch to avoid seeing Christer. I switched on the light. The large fixture on the ceiling illuminated the room. Focusing on the couch, I moved in. My eyes flicked to the desk chair where Christer sat but I forced them back. Stared at the black fabric couch. Finding a brown strand of hair there would be impossible. I crouched down by the coffee table and swept my eyes across the rug. Nothing but crumbs.

A dripping sound from the desk chair made me look. Blood. It dripped from his body. Down onto the wood floor where a red pool was forming. I got up quickly. Had to get out of the house. I crumpled the redline bag into my pocket. Took the knife and went into the kitchen. Pulled out the kitchen drawer a centimeter or two. The same drawer the knife I'd taken the night before had been in. I unlocked the outside door and moved backward through the door and away from the house in the too-large boots. I walked around the block and placed the knife in a bush under some leaves not far from the house. Then I went back past the house and to the car. I looked at Christer Skoog's house.

It looked different now.

Soulless.

It was over.

SIXTY-NINE

I'd been forced to take a sleeping pill. Even so, I only slept for two hours. My body felt ten kilos heavier in the hard office chair. I had to exert myself even to pick up the pen on the table in front of me. Everything was happening in slow motion. Blinking, turning my head, taking hold of the pen. My entire existence felt surreal. When I had woken up that morning I'd been uncertain whether the events of the day before had really happened. Everything was normal. Breakfast with the children, Peter dropping them off at day care, the road to work with red lights turning to green, pedestrians crossing the street, buses following their regular route, colleagues who said good morning in the corridor, my office that looked the same as the day before — all of that was as usual. Inside, I knew. It was no dream. I could now count myself as being a part of that small group of people who had taken someone else's life. It was impossible to comprehend.

It was what it was.

Unreal.

The day didn't become any more real from the fact that now, at eight o'clock in the morning, I was in a meeting with a medium. Now was the time for us to try and somehow combine fact and nonsense into something sensible. I needed to be friendly to him and at the same time keep him at a distance from the investigation. Not because I thought he would actually come up with anything by means of his supernatural talents, but because having someone on my heels, analyzing my every movement, would complicate my work.

"I've never worked on an investigation together with someone who is not well schooled in police working methods. How do you see your role in the collaboration?" I asked.

He gave me a look that I could not decipher. Had I been slurring? I didn't know for sure. Felt numb.

"In order for me to be able to *see* anything I need to get in contact with the environment in which the crime occurred. I'm also going to want to acquaint myself with the interviews and the surveillance video from the investigation."

"You can visit the crime scene whenever it suits you," I said. "It's probably best that you work by yourself there and not have me around disturbing you."

"Well, it would be nice if..."

"I have a lot to do, because I'm also working on other investigations in parallel. It will probably be best if you can try to work as independently as possible and then come to me once you've had any visions."

It was taxing for me to talk. Partly because the sleeping pills were still working in my body and partly because I didn't know how I should speak to a medium.

"I need access to all the documents in the investigation, especially the interviews."

"No problem. I'll print them out for you."

Then he could work as he wished and I could avoid having Mr. Hocus-Pocus at my heels.

"I work outside a lot, but you can always reach me on my mobile."

I got up. The room turned black in front of my eyes. I staggered and had to sit down in the chair again.

"How are you doing?" he asked, taking me by the arm.

Shouldn't he already know what's going on with me? That I had spent the previous evening killing a journalist and was slightly affected by it all?

"Must be a little anemia," I said.

I took a gulp of water from the glass in front of me.

"Another thing, Leona. Do you know if there's a vacant office I can use?"

The eternal question of space. So the agency had not even arranged an office for him. Remarkable, since he was clearly so important.

"Claes will make sure you get a nice office."

I wanted to end the meeting. Felt dizzy. But first I needed to reassure myself.

"By the way, has Claes talked to you about the media?"

"Nothing other than that the case is extensively covered. I've studied what's been written myself."

"Not a word to anyone about the investigation. Even within the police there are many eyes and ears. Even here at the squad. If you come up with anything, it's important that I be the first to find out about it."

"Sure."

Hopefully I wouldn't have any problems with him. But I didn't like the way he looked at me. The kind of analyzing gaze you might get from a psychologist or therapist. Scrutinizing. As if the person was trying to take your whole personality into their mind. I went into the restroom, sat down on the toilet seat, and rested my head in my hands. Even though I closed my eyes and sat completely still, everything was spinning.

I needed to focus on the third and final robbery. If not for the fact that Nina would now be involved and get a share, I would have chosen to stop after two. It now wasn't possible. There wouldn't be enough money. But one more robbery felt like a gigantic mountain to climb. A mountain where boulders and mud slides had already started rolling down toward me. How would I have the energy to finish? I sat with my elbows against my knees. Rubbed both palms against my forehead while I repeated the words in my head.

Pull yourself together, Leona.

Pull yourself together.

SEVENTY

I tried to get up from the chair in the guest room but I had to sit down again. What could not happen had happened. I stared at the screen in front of me. Didn't see. Didn't hear. I was completely disconnected from my senses. Maybe time could be turned back if I just sat completely still.

I wished I could back up. Only a few miserable minutes. That would have changed everything. I would have played it differently then. Not been so dead certain. Refrained from betting everything. Not gone all in.

I was now observing my life from the outside. Certain incidents felt as if they were in slow motion. Others whirled past in high speed. Arrhythmic. The cellar, computer intrusion, the girl, Malta, uniform, Ronni, murderer, the storm drain, money, prison, realtors, hospital, politicians — all in one big mess.

I took hold of the desk with both hands. The room was spinning. I closed my eyes but it continued to whirl. I needed to get to the bathroom. Managed to get up into a standing position but my stomach ached and nausea washed over me. Fumbling with my hands against doorframes, walls, and furniture, I made my way to the bathroom. Even though the room was whirling I managed to get the entire contents of my stomach into the toilet, and then remained on my knees in front of the toilet bowl. I couldn't reach the flush handle and when I happened to look down into the toilet I vomited again from what I saw. With my last bit of strength I managed to flush two times in a row. The second time there was hardly any water but the contents passed down into the sewer. I collapsed on the bathroom floor, thinking back over the minutes that had passed. A single move had gone wrong. That was all it took. One move, to change my existence from being controllable to being chaos.

I had fallen asleep at eight o'clock, right after I put the children to bed. I had woken up at one o'clock, got up, and had then played poker for three hours.

The money I borrowed from my parents was meant to be the solution. The plan to double it had perhaps been too optimistic, but in any event I should have been able to up the total considerably. The tournament had gone well, for a long time. So long that I had to tell myself not to get overly confident and start taking risks. I hadn't taken any risks, either. Or so I thought. Still, what could not happen had happened.

I was at the bottom.

Ground zero.

I had lost that much. A total of several hundred thousand kroner. The amount was staggering. My last thought was of Benjamin, before I fell asleep on the bathroom floor.

SEVENTY-ONE

The days had started to blend together. It was now the third time within an hour I had looked at my phone to see what day it was. Monday, October 21. I was sincerely surprised and worried at my own reaction to everything that had happened. I could no longer control my senses. Now I was standing in the break room staring straight ahead. Sat down and had just started chatting with a colleague when Claes stormed into the room.

"Listen up, everyone!" said Claes. "They've just brought in a person for questioning about the murder of the journalist Christer Skoog, who was knifed to death in his home last week. Hold on to your seats. It's Nina Wallin, the prosecutor. She's in interrogation right now. They seem to think she's involved in the murder."

The murmur in the break room disappeared. Everyone was staring at Claes.

"What?" I said, standing up.

"I know. It's hard to imagine. I have no idea how she could have anything to do with it."

"That's just crazy!" I said.

That was enough. I couldn't overreact. I saw in the corner of my eye that Sören was observing me.

"I realize that this must come as a shock to you, Leona. You'll be assigned another prosecutor for the girl robberies but for the time being she remains as preliminary investigation leader. We will presumably know more when the interview with her is done later this afternoon. Until then, I want you to freeze the case. No more investigative measures until preliminary investigation leadership on the case is clear to us."

I got up and went toward my office.

"Leona!"

Sören came after me with a cup of coffee in his hand.

"Isn't there something strange about all this?"

"That's the least you could say about it. Nina, of all people. I guess you can't trust anyone."

Sören walked with me to my office. I stopped outside the door. I had no desire to let him come in and start analyzing my reactions.

"There is something very strange about the whole thing. I have a strong feeling that Nina doesn't have anything to do with it," said Sören, looking at me.

I shook my head.

"It's hard to understand. But sometimes you have to accept that anyone at all can be a criminal, even the one you least suspect."

Sören looked right at me and nodded slowly.

"Hmmm...The one you least suspect."

SEVENTY-TWO

Daddy was the only person Olivia had seen for several days. The quiet lady almost never came over and when she did Olivia was always in the bedroom. That was the way Daddy wanted it.

This was the last time, he had promised. After that she would get to go home. But how would she manage? Daddy was still giving her pills so that her foot would not hurt as much. Her head had gotten better by itself. Most of the small scrapes too. But she was so tired all the time.

She had to be strong, Daddy said. If she was good she would get good food afterward, he had promised. Waffles, her favorite. He said that every time, but there still hadn't been any.

He didn't want her to go out, either. Only he got to go out. He would leave her alone in the apartment for hours, sometimes the whole night and the whole next day. Then she got to eat a container of food that he had put in the fridge. She just had to put it in the microwave, turn the knob to two, and then wait till the food was ready. Sometimes he forgot to buy food. Or else there was only one container, which was supposed to last a whole day. Then she would be hungry for a long time. Sometimes she didn't dare say that she was hungry.

When he was home she was only allowed to stay in the bedroom, but when he was gone she sneaked out into the living room and watched TV. She tried to call home to Mommy once, but the number didn't work. It only beeped strangely on the line.

Daddy opened the door to the bedroom. Looked at Olivia and handed her a chocolate biscuit. Olivia took it slowly while she tried to decipher Daddy's mood. Sometimes she didn't know whether he was just joking with her. Whether he would laugh and say that it wasn't for her at all. But he didn't do that. He let go of the chocolate biscuit. Olivia picked it up quickly and took a bite. Small pieces of chocolate fell down on the covers. She put her hand on them so that Daddy wouldn't see. She took another big bite.

"Soon you'll get to go home to Mommy," he said and went out.

Olivia had been longing so much for Mommy but now she was mostly tired. She closed her eyes. Let the taste of chocolate spread in her mouth while she slowly fell asleep.

SEVENTY-THREE

The letters flowed together. The sleeping pills I had to take almost every night to get any rest stayed in my system and made me drowsy. I sat at the desk in the office and tried to focus on reading through a few witness interviews that Minna and Sam had held. My thoughts were carried away after every line I read. I moved my eyes to the beginning of the paragraph for a third time when the door flew open. Nina stormed in and slammed the door behind her. I stared at her. I didn't know if I had started hallucinating. Had she been released already? She threw her handbag down on the floor and threw out her arms.

"What the hell, Leona! Are you really out of your mind?"

"Shhh. Let's go somewhere else and talk."

I could hardly breathe. Nina had apparently realized I was trying to frame her. The question was why she had been released. I got up to take her out to one of the conference rooms.

"We're staying here. I don't have time to run around and I have no damned desire to dance to your fucking tune any longer."

"Nina, calm down. Have a seat."

I pointed at the visitor's chair next to the door and quickly pulled the curtain facing the corridor.

"How the hell could you do this to me?" said Nina. "Didn't you realize I'd know it was you?"

"How did you arrive at that conclusion?" I said, sitting on the office chair.

I didn't try to deny it. There was no point. But I wanted to know how she had found out it was me.

"The police who questioned me said they found my DNA on the couch at Christer's house."

So that was where the strands of hair had ended up. If they had been on the knife as intended, Nina would not likely be in front of me now.

"I had to explain that I knew Christer and that it wasn't strange that my DNA was there because I had been at his house, which isn't true."

"No, because the two of you evidently always meet at your place," I said.

Nina stared at me in surprise.

"Perhaps you should have thought a little further before you went behind my back," I continued.

She didn't answer. Presumably she was playing dumb to gain time.

"Knock it off, Nina," I said. "You lied right to my face that you were at home with your sick mother when really you were at home in your apartment making plans with Christer. I saw you."

Nina stood silently. She took off her coat and hung it over the visitor's chair.

"Listen carefully now, Leona. Christer and I were in contact because he was doing everything he could to get a prosecutor to reopen the Hooker Affair. He said he had confidence in me after our conversation about your involvement in the girl robberies. He called and threatened to release information about you if I didn't help him. I didn't want to be seen with him in public again so I said that he had to come to my place if we were going to talk. That was all. I was doing everything to calm him down and get him to lie low."

I didn't say anything. I was skeptical of her explanation. Why hadn't she told me this?

"When you called he had just arrived. I couldn't let you come up, couldn't even say that it was you calling. He didn't know that we were cooperating. Besides, he hated you. Probably me too. He maintained that we didn't care that politicians exploited women and said that everyone in the legal system has each other's back."

"What could have been so important that you invited him to your place?"

"He said that he had gotten hold of a recording from the prostitute. A recording that could convict the finance minister. It seemed undeniably interesting."

"But why the hell didn't you call me afterward?"

"I didn't know it was such a big deal to you that we had met. I did say to you that I would take care of him. Didn't think any more about it. Of course I had no idea that you planned to go to his house and kill him. That's completely sick!"

"I had no choice, Nina," I said. "Christer called me and said that the two of you together were going to put me in prison."

Nina was silent. It seemed she'd just realized the way in which everything connected.

"Seriously, Leona, do you think I would put myself in that situation? Collaborate with a journalist I don't even know? It would be the same as turning both you and me over to the police."

I studied Nina carefully. Of course it would be incredibly stupid of her to do that, but stranger things had happened in my world. You couldn't trust anyone. I didn't say anything. She didn't speak either.

I realized that there was a possibility she was telling the truth.

But I didn't want to think that.

Couldn't think that.

I could see that my deficient capacity to feel emotions had helped me to commit murder. But could I come to terms with the knowledge that I had murdered for no reason?

"When you lied to me on the phone like that and Christer had said right before that the two of you were going to put me in prison...what was I supposed to think?"

"This is incomprehensible, Leona. You tried to put me in jail for a murder you committed yourself. You killed Christer. It's insane!"

"Quiet! Don't you know that this is a police station?"

Now I was getting tired of Nina's harping. We had to accept what had happened and own up to the fact we were both involved in it.

Nina became quieter. She said in a subdued voice, "Yeah, thanks. It's easy to forget where I am now that I know what certain police officers are capable of..."

She was interrupted by three knocks on the door. We looked quickly at each other. Nina was sitting with her back to the door and didn't turn around to see who it was. Instead, she put her hand to her forehead and shook her head as though, after all this, it might be the devil himself.

The handle was pressed down and Sören Möller stuck his head in.

"Am I disturbing you?" he said, looking cheerfully at me.

He had a talent for showing up when you least wanted him.

"Uh, yes, actually," I said.

He looked at Nina.

"Nina Wallin?"

With warmth in his eyes he took a few steps toward Nina and extended his hand.

"Nice to meet you. Sören Möller. I'm helping Leona with the case."

Nina slowly took his hand and stared at him without saying a word.

"I heard that you'd been arrested; it's very good that you're free again," he said. "I said to Leona that I didn't believe for a second that you had anything to do with that murder. How did you prove that you were innocent?"

"Sören, it's a little inconvenient right now," I said. "Was it something important?"

"No, no, we can discuss it later."

After a strange look at both of us he left the office and closed the door behind him. Nina looked sharply at me.

"Who the hell was that? Not a cop, right?"

"I know, he's shady. He's a medium the agency has brought in to help out with the investigation."

"Why the hell haven't you told me about this? He sounded like he knew something."

"It was what I was about to tell you when you lied that you weren't at home."

She became quiet. We both sat silently. I had a pounding headache. I went over to the bookshelf and searched for an aspirin. These days I usually had a bottle handy.

"What the hell has happened to you, Leona? Don't you even understand what you've done?"

I sat down on the office chair again. My head was bursting. It felt like I wasn't getting any air. I reached for a glass of water that was sitting by the computer screen. My hand was shaking so much that the water splashed onto the desk. I took hold with both hands and managed to set the glass down without damaging the keyboard.

"Jesus, Leona," said Nina.

A doctor probably would have pointed out that I had signs of exhaustion. My body had taken a beating by being up at night and gambling, taking pills to be able to sleep, getting up after a couple of hours with sleeping pills in my bloodstream, and spending the rest of the day wandering around in a kind of surreal haze. Suddenly I realized how tired I was. I felt tears start to well up. They couldn't be stopped. Since I had killed Christer I had lost control over my body. I began to cry so hard that I shook. Presumably from exhaustion, I didn't know. Between sobs I tried to talk.

"I'm losing my grip, Nina. I…can't take…any more. I haven't…slept…a wink. It's horrible…what I've done."

Maybe it was horrible, I don't know. Nina apparently thought so. But I was crying for other reasons. From fatigue, from exhaustion. Nina slowly came up to me. She stood awhile and simply looked at me. Then she crouched down and placed one hand on my knee.

"You're not alone, Leona. I'm just as involved."

I didn't speak. I sobbed while Nina continued.

"This whole mess is too awful. What you've done is crazy. Christer was perhaps an idiot but he didn't deserve to die. I wish you had brought it up with me first before you got the idea that…Then I could have explained…"

Nina seemed sincerely sorry. I couldn't manage to speak. I tried to calm myself by taking a few more gulps of water.

"I understand that I'm involved in this. I should've told you about Christer but I thought I had him under control."

I nodded.

"When this is over, when the money is divided, we'll never talk about this again," I said.

"I think I have some good news among all the misery," said Nina. "I think we can make use of that recording from the prostitute in the Hooker Affair that Christer told me about."

I took a tissue out of my bag and blew my nose. Nina continued.

"It's supposed to be locked up in his childhood home, the house where his mother still lives. He gave me a duplicate key. Said that he wanted it with me if something happened to him. I got a feeling that he had been threatened. It feels like I'm reaching to say that he was threatened by the finance minister, but that was my first thought. We need to get hold of the recording."

I looked at Nina. It was hardly the right time to question the truthfulness of what she was saying. I was in no shape to do so, anyway.

SEVENTY-FOUR

The next day we drove to Christer Skoog's mother's house out in Hässelby. The yellow house looked uninhabited and like it had needed repainting years ago. The yard was overgrown and the car parked there did not seem to have moved for a long time. I wasn't comfortable with the meeting. Facing the mother whose son I brutally murdered was not exactly on my bucket list, but it had to be done. I pressed the doorbell. A faint sound of steps was heard from inside.

"Yes?"

A skinny woman in her seventies answered. Her gray-streaked hair was tied in a loose knot at the back of her neck. She held her dark-brown cardigan closed over her chest, as if she was cold.

"Inga Skoog?"

I spoke in a gentle, calm voice. She nodded. I showed my badge.

"Leona Lindberg, police. This is my colleague, Nina Wallin. May we come in?"

Inga sighed.

"I thought you were done here."

Nina and I looked at each other. There was no point explaining to Inga that we weren't the ones investigating the murder of her son.

"No, we would like to speak with you a little. We knew Christer better than the other police officers you've met."

She nodded and showed us in by backing up a few steps into the hall. I had hoped that she would be more reluctant. Somehow that would have made this easier. We left our shoes in the hall and followed her into the kitchen.

The house reminded me of my parents'. The hall was papered with cream fabric and the kitchen had old-fashioned brown-and-white wallpaper. We remained standing by a wooden bench in the kitchen. My eyes were fixed on the door. It was a door similar to the one in my parents' house. I stopped breathing. My whole body froze and became heavy. My heart was pounding.

"If you don't go down on your own you know what will happen, Leona."

Mother had unlocked the door. Stood next to it. Father was staring at us from the kitchen table. He was drunk. Didn't seem to be able to focus his gaze properly.

Cold and damp welled up from the cellar. I had tears in my eyes. Mother looked at me but didn't bat an eyelid.

"I'm not going to say it again."

She nodded at the stairs. I went closer. Looked down. The stairs were steep. I looked up at Mother again. Pleaded with my eyes. I didn't want to go down there again. Hated the cellar. I took a step back so as not to lose my balance on the edge. In the corner of my eye I saw Mother cast a glance at Father.

"Mariiita!" he said loudly and firmly.

With a firm hand she gave me a quick shove forward. I lost my balance. Fell headlong.

Down all the steps.

Down onto the ice-cold stone floor.

The sound when the door slammed shut echoed in my head.

"Please sit down. The coffee has been on since that politician was here, but that was only half an hour ago so it's probably still drinkable."

Inga pointed toward the table. I came around. Looked at Nina. She didn't appear to have noticed that my thoughts had been elsewhere.

"What kind of politician was here?" said Nina.

Without answering Inga took off into the hall and went up the stairs to the top floor. We sat down at the round, dark-brown kitchen table. When Inga came back down she was carrying a yearbook, which she set on the tablecloth between us. It was the Trollboda School yearbook. She browsed through the pages of class after class of black-and-white group photographs.

"There he is..." She spoke quietly and pointed at a boy who was standing at the far side with dark hair and bangs. "...my beloved Christer."

Her voice broke when she said his name. She took a handkerchief from her pocket and dabbed her cheeks around her eyes.

"I'm sorry. I still can't comprehend the fact that he's gone. I'm just waiting for him to step through the front door. At least once a week he comes home...or did."

She looked down, seemingly ashamed that she'd spoken about her son as though he were still alive. I looked at the boy in the black-and-white photograph. Other than the dark hair I couldn't recognize Christer.

"He was my only child."

She spoke quietly. Whispered. I avoided looking at her. Tried not to think about what it would be like to lose your only son.

Inga pointed at another boy in the middle of the photograph.

"And there is Niklas Olander, the minister for finance. He and Christer were in the same class in grade school."

I looked with surprise at the photograph. I never would have suspected that Christer had a personal connection to the minister for finance. I'd wondered why he hadn't been more eager to create a scoop with what he knew about the girl robberies. Now I understood that this meant something completely different to Christer. The question was how much Inga knew about that.

"Were they friends in primary school?" I asked.

Inga shook her head.

"Christer was extremely shy as a child. Didn't have many friends. He didn't like school, either. I had to struggle every morning to get him there. Sometimes when he cried too much I let him stay home. He missed a lot and had to repeat a grade."

Inga got the coffeepot.

"He never seemed to like Nino, as he was called back then. I don't know why. In later years Christer always used to say something sarcastic when he saw the finance minister on TV."

Inga took hold of Nina's cup and started pouring.

"Just half a cup, thanks," said Nina.

"When that business about prostitution came up I said to Christer that he shouldn't go after Nino so hard."

"What did he say then?" I asked.

Inga stopped after she had poured coffee in all three cups. She sat down.

"He said that people would finally see Nino's true colors. I never understood what he meant. Nino was always a well-behaved boy. And then he became finance minister and everything. He can't have acted that way toward a poor prostitute. I just can't believe it."

"Was the minister here today?" said Nina.

"Not him, his secretary. Nice of Nino to ask his secretary to come with flowers."

Inga got up and poured milk in a little pitcher that she set on the table.

"The secretary wanted to put the flowers in Christer's old room. He said that the minister had requested that. I said that Christer didn't have a room here anymore. He has, but I would prefer that no one goes in there. Oh, excuse me, I forgot the cake."

Inga went up to the counter, then stopped and remained standing quietly with both hands on the kitchen counter and her back to me and Nina. I could see from behind that she was crying. Her body was shaking.

"I simply can't understand why he was murdered. My dear Christer," said Inga.

I went up and placed a hand on her shoulder. She leaned her head against me. Embraced me while she sobbed.

"Inga, we're going to do everything we can to find the murderer," I heard myself say.

Over Inga's head Nina's eyes met mine. Nina slowly shook her head. Inga was sobbing against my shoulder. I felt my blouse getting warm and wet from her tears.

"He had no enemies..."

I stood quietly. Couldn't move. Wanted to get out of there...

"Of course I understood that his job as a journalist involved risks, but I never believed that something like this would happen."

I wanted to leave the house. Leave the woman who was crying in my arms, completely desperate because her son was dead.

Murdered.

By me.

Inga looked up at me with her eyes red from crying.

"Excuse me, but it feels so nice to have you police officers here. Christer must have felt just as safe in your presence."

I couldn't bear to hear her anymore. Moved a little so she'd understand we could no longer stand in each other's embrace. Nina came to my rescue.

"Inga, Christer told me that he was in the process of writing a very important article about the politician case. He is supposed to have placed a recording of a phone call in a dresser here at the house. We need to get hold of it."

"I see."

She tore a piece of paper towel from the roll and blew her nose before she showed us up to the top floor. She stood quietly a moment before the door. Her eyes closed as if she was gathering strength. Then she unlocked it. The room looked like an ordinary guest room. For some reason I had expected a young boy's room with posters of pop stars on the walls. Inga seemed to be the kind of lady who wanted to hold on to the past. Next to the bed and nightstand was a dresser.

"He said it would be in a locked case in a drawer in the dresser," said Nina.

Inga nodded at me to open it. I pulled out the drawer and searched among T-shirts and socks. Nothing. I didn't have the energy to care that in formal terms this was a house search I was doing. This was an informal meeting. No one would know that we had been there. After I searched in all the drawers without finding anything except clothes I began to think that maybe the case had already been picked up.

"Inga, did the other police officer take anything out of this room?"

Inga had gone over to the window. She shook her head.

"They said they didn't find anything that could be used in the investigation."

"Is there any other dresser he might have put the case in?" I continued.

Inga stood quietly a moment and then left the room without a word. I followed her into another bedroom. There was a dresser on either side of the double bed.

"My husband, Christer's father, always slept on this side. He passed away when Christer was fourteen. Perhaps Christer put it there."

I followed Inga up to the dresser. In the third drawer was a little black case. I picked it up. Asked Nina to bring the key over. It fit. In the case were a few documents and a USB flash drive. We had what we needed and it was time to leave Inga. We went downstairs to the front door.

"But you haven't finished your coffee," said Inga.

I excused myself and explained it was important that we try to get hold of the person who had done this to her son. Nina and I started walking to the car.

"I have my laptop with me; we can listen in the car," said Nina.

I started the car while Nina turned on the computer.

"He has a password on it, damn, he told me, but..."

Nina fell silent.

"Oh, wait a minute..."

She entered a code without saying it out loud. I noticed that, but let it be. The recording was raspy but you could clearly hear the voice of the finance minister. He was talking with a woman.

"A generous hourly rate if you spread it out over a year, isn't it?"

"Do you want anything or what?"

The dialogue continued. The minister bargained with the woman so long that finally she agreed to sex, almost for free. The voices were clear and there was no doubt what the whole thing was about, as they spoke openly about anal, oral, and other sexual acts. The recording was a gold mine.

Now we needed to prove that the minister knew about the recording and thereby had a motive to get Christer out of the way. We also needed to check what the minister was doing on the night of the murder.

SEVENTY-FIVE

After ten minutes of persuasion in the doorway, Nina and I were invited into Dina's friend's apartment on Nybohovsbacken in Liljeholmen. Dina didn't seem to have any confidence in the police, or in any authority whatsoever. She looked at Nina and me with contempt in her eyes.

"Which one of you is going to care when I'm assaulted later and raped or murdered? How can I be guaranteed protection?" said Dina.

"Why will you need protection, Dina?" I said.

Dina sighed and shook her head. She turned on the kitchen fan and lit a cigarette.

"Dina, you have to understand, we think we can put the finance minister in prison for murder with your help."

Dina leaned over and blew out smoke under the fan. I started to wonder if there was some other reason for her reluctance.

"Listen. Christer, with whom you've been in contact, has been murdered. We believe that the finance minister got wind that Christer had information about him buying sex that could convict him. For that reason we think he murdered Christer, or had him murdered. As the situation is now, he's gone free for buying sex and will probably go free for murder too. What you know may be decisive for whether we can put him away. Do you understand? We have no other evidence."

Dina hardly seemed to listen. She puffed away uninterruptedly.

"We are not after you at all. If you're guilty of something that is not, how shall I put it, on the right side of the law, we don't care about that."

She looked at me. Then at Nina. And back to me.

"You have my word on that, Dina. I'm a woman myself."

My intimation that, because I was also a woman, I could understand Dina, would presumably not have much sway. I had never understood the point of putting yourself in another person's shoes, but I could see a number of similarities between me and Dina. In some ways I admired her. She moved at the bottom level of society but was stronger than most people I knew.

Dina put out the cigarette and sat at the kitchen table across from me.

"The finance minister came here and was completely enraged."

"So he knew where you were?" I said.

Dina fell silent and then said calmly, "It's not possible to hide from those people."

I sat down on the kitchen chair. Nodded at Dina to continue.

"He said he'd found out that the journalist, Christer, had not stopped digging into the incident even though the case was closed. He's upset that I was feeding Christer information and wanted to make sure I kept quiet. I told him to go to hell. Said that I do what I want. Then he threatened me, but I was mad and yelled that I didn't care if he killed me. When that didn't work he offered me a large sum of money."

"When was this?"

Dina searched in her phone.

"It must have been on October 16."

The same day as the murder. Could that be possible? Nina and I looked at each other.

"He refused to leave until I blew him. Said he took that as a bonus for all the money he'd given me to keep quiet."

"What time?"

"Around nine or ten o'clock maybe. Then he left in his car."

"Did he say anything else about Christer?"

"Just that that fucking journalist had ruined his life. When I said that Christer was actually quite nice he got really mad and left."

"Is there anything that shows that he's been here in your apartment?"

"Annie came home right when he was on his way out but I don't think she's too eager to testify. But I have this…"

Dina started searching in her phone.

"After everything that's happened I've started recording most things on my phone. But I'm not giving out anything else, I'll just end up in more shit."

"Dina, Christer was murdered. Do you understand that you may be in danger?"

"I've been saying that the whole time, damn it! You're not listening. The minister probably already knows that you're here."

Dina parted the curtain slightly and looked out on the street below.

"Could he somehow know you recorded his conversation?" said Nina.

Dina shook her head.

"Come on now," I said. "He knew you'd recorded him previously; wouldn't he guess you'd record him again?"

"No, I said. He took away my phone and held on to it the whole time. That stupid bastard didn't realize I have two."

"The recording is extremely important. And Dina, if you testify and tell the court what you just told us, then you won't have to worry about him anymore. Do yourself a favor and end this now so you don't have to always be worried."

Dina stood up. Looked me right in the eyes.

"If you live like I do you're always worried. When someone needs you, you're never available. If I get threatened again you're the first ones I'm going to call and then I'll be demanding that you help me."

She opened the phone, took out the SIM card and handed the phone over to me.

SEVENTY-SIX

Back at the office things were messy. A new case must have dropped in while I was gone. My colleagues were frantically moving around in the corridors. I slipped quickly into my office to avoid the risk of getting involved. I closed the door and was just about to take off my jacket.

"Where have you been, Leona?"

I whirled around. In my eagerness to close the door before anyone noticed me, I hadn't noticed Sören, who was sitting very quietly with a newspaper in his hand in the corner of the room.

"Oh! You scared me."

"Nerves on tenterhooks, are they?" he said calmly.

I hung up the jacket and went and sat down behind my desk.

"What can I help you with? Have you 'seen' something?"

I tried to sound casual but his presence made me very uncomfortable. He got up and went over to my bookshelf. Looked around and picked up the framed photo of Benjamin and Beatrice. Studied it carefully.

"One and three?" he said, still looking at the photo.

"Yes, approximately. Then. Now they're three and almost five."

He set down the photo. I didn't like that he was poking around in my things. He continued walking around the office, studying every corner as if he was searching for something.

"Hard to understand that someone could do something like that to a child, isn't it?" he said, studying me.

"Yes. People are capable of anything these days. The most important thing is that we find him now."

"That's just what I wanted to talk with you about. There's something about this that doesn't add up."

Was he joking? Of course it didn't add up. Otherwise the robberies would have been solved by now and I would be in prison. I put my ID into the computer, entered the code, and waited to be logged on to the system.

"You and Nina, you know each other really well, huh?" he said.

I didn't understand whether he knew something or was simply fishing for information.

"Yes, we've done a few investigations together. Or together in the sense that I've done them and she's made the decisions. That's how it works."

He nodded.

"Why these questions?" I said.

I was starting to get irritated. Couldn't he just spit out what all this snooping was about?

"You're working according to the theory that it's a man who is behind the robberies, is that true?"

"Hmm, exactly."

I opened the computerized procedure for preliminary investigation and handling of coercive measures that was still being used for investigations until a new one was introduced.

"I think it's a woman."

I looked at him with raised eyebrows. He looked right at me with a steady gaze.

"Or more correctly stated, I'm convinced that it is a woman."

I shook my head.

"The possibility that it would be a female perpetrator is basically nonexistent. I don't know how familiar you are with the statistics on bank robberies in Sweden, or the whole world for that matter. They are dominated by men, as with the vast majority of serious crimes."

Without answering he got up and started for the door.

"How have you even come to that conclusion?" I said.

In the doorway he turned around and looked at me briefly before he continued out into the corridor.

He could think what he wanted. I just needed to keep him at a distance a little longer, until it was all over.

SEVENTY-SEVEN

"That sure took a long time."

Ronni opened the door and let me into the apartment on Sand-hamnsgatan at Gärdet. He had called me that morning and rat-tled off a lot of odd things on the phone. He'd sounded strangely upset. There had been poor reception, as well, so I'd only been able to make out something about the girl and illness. I brought the little pediatric medical kit that I always carried with me in my bag, ever since Benjamin had become ill. There were two days left until the next robbery. Nothing could go wrong now.

"It's Monday morning, Ronni. I have a job to do."

"I don't know what I should do with her. She's completely gone. Had chills all night and raved a lot."

He went ahead into the apartment and opened the bedroom door. The girl was lying on the mattress on the floor under two blankets and a down jacket. I went over, crouched down. The girl appeared to be struggling to keep her eyes open. Her pale skin was, if possible, even paler. Her hair was clinging in wisps to her damp face. I placed my hand on her warm, clammy forehead and could tell that she had a fever. I stroked her on the cheek.

"Does it hurt anywhere?" I said.

"I'm cold."

I had to lean down to hear what she said. I took the medical kit out of my bag.

"Damn, just when she was starting to get better," said Ronni, wandering around the room.

"What do you mean, better?" I said.

Without answering he continued pacing back and forth. I handed him a tablet.

"Put this in half a glass of water. It's only a pain reliever and fever reducer. We have to get the fever down. Open wide, Olivia, hold this under your tongue."

I put a thermometer in her mouth. She looked up at me with tired eyes.

"That's a good girl," I said.

I thought the girl smiled a little. Yes, she did. I took the thermometer out. Ronni came in with the tablet in a glass of water.

"It's 39.2. I see why you're cold. But don't worry. Drink this. All of it. You're going to feel better soon. I'm just going to talk with your daddy in the kitchen. Sleep a little if you can."

We left the room.

"Damn it, Leona, what if she can't do it?" said Ronni.

"She'll manage on fever-reducing tablets. The fever will go down now."

The girl was sick, but I had seen my own son in much worse condition and I knew that she would be okay.

"Why haven't you given her anything?" I said.

"I don't have a damned pharmacy here. I meant to go out and get some painkillers but she became completely hysterical when I was going to leave her. And I can't take her out, of course."

Ronni continued pacing around the kitchen.

"Maybe she can't do it anymore."

"Oh, get a grip, damn it, Ronni. Are you going to start getting soft now just because the girl has a little fever? It's nothing to worry about. All children get sick sometimes."

"If the fever doesn't go down I'm calling off the whole fucking thing and going back to Finland with her."

"In that case you're going without cash."

I didn't intend to give him a cent if he pulled out. He'd hardly seemed to care about the girl until now. It was pathetic that he'd suddenly become protective. With fever-reducing medicine and sleep she would be better by tomorrow.

"Give her two tablets every four hours," I said. "I have to go. And listen, don't forget to make sure that she finds the drain, because it's farther away this time. She will have less time, too."

I closed the door to the apartment even though Ronni was still shouting something from inside. I wasn't worried. The girl would perk up with the pills. Ronni was much too eager for money to pull out. I left the apartment feeling calm. Got into the car and turned on the radio.

P3 News.

A high-level Swedish politician has been arrested today for the murder of the journalist Christer Skoog, who was killed in his home on Wednesday the sixteenth of October. Earlier this year the politician was the object of a preliminary investigation when, along with two other public officials, he was accused of paying for sex. The prosecutor ruled that the evidence against the politician was insufficient for an indictment and the preliminary investigation was closed. The prosecutor has now confirmed that new evidence has emerged in the case, which means that the preliminary investigation regarding the purchase of sex has been reopened. The deceased journalist reportedly had information about the crimes the politician is alleged to have committed. New witness statements also show that the politician was involved in the murder.

SEVENTY-EIGHT

Olivia curled up on the floor of the car. Daddy had put down plastic so it would not get messy. He had sprayed her, too. Her skin was all red and stung a little. But that didn't matter. Because this was the last time now. Daddy had promised that.

She looked out the windows on the other side of the car, watching the roofs of buildings and light poles rush quickly past. The sky was gray, with round white clouds. The car bobbed up and down so much she had to curl up even more so she didn't get hurt. Even so, she wanted to stay there. Didn't want to leave the car.

She had finally got the teddy bear back. She hugged it as hard as she could. Her hands felt strange. Cold and numb, somehow.

This time she had two broad, black belts fastened around her chest. On them Daddy had strapped six canisters with a jumble of thin, gray cords around each other. The cords looked like spaghetti, but shorter. Like when you've cut the spaghetti a little so it will be easier to eat. Daddy said that people would be even more afraid when she had the canisters with spaghetti on her. Then everything would be easier.

"Make sure to do this right, now. Remember that you have to get away quicker this time."

Daddy was talking from the front seat. Olivia understood what she should do, but she was so tired. About to fall asleep. She had to walk much faster this time. How would she be able to? The blueness on her foot had disappeared and it was no longer as swollen, but it still hurt when she walked. She closed her eyes. Her body was briefly pressed against the front seat as the car slowed down and stopped by the curb.

"When I say so, you get going."

She tried to get ready.

"Now!"

She reached for the door handle.

"*Now*, I said. Go!"

She got the door open. Stepped out onto the sidewalk and had to stand still for a moment to get her balance. Closed the door and started walking close to the parked cars, just as Daddy had said. She tried to walk fast but still go gently on the sore foot. Soon she would get to go home to Mommy.

Lots of cars drove past on the street. Regular cars and big thundering trucks. Many people were bicycling. Some were walking on the sidewalk, too. Everyone seemed to be in a hurry. They didn't even look at her but instead looked right over her head. They held on to their clothing so they wouldn't blow away. It was lucky that Olivia had the rain cape on. Then it didn't blow on her as much. She had a new rain cape this time because the old one had fallen apart. This one was bigger. She held the hood down a little in front of her face as Daddy had shown her. Olivia tried to walk just as quickly as a man in a dark-blue coat who had just passed her, but she couldn't.

Now she was at the corner. There! She could see the entrance.

Inside the door she wriggled off the backpack and the rain cape at the same time and dropped everything on the floor. She dropped the teddy bear, too, but she picked that up again immediately and held it in her arms.

She looked around. Go to the middle of the room, he had said. It was hard to know. The room had a lot of corners, and there were little alcoves in several places. She went straight ahead. Stopped where she thought the middle was. Set down the tape recorder and pressed play. No one there seemed to have seen her as she came in. Now everyone was looking at her. The first time it had been scary to be stared at like that. Now she was too tired to be afraid. She just stood there. Her eyes half closed. Moved back and forth a little from one foot to the other to keep herself awake. She hoped the recording would end soon.

Daddy's voice blared from the speaker. She shuddered just hearing it, even though she knew it was only a recording. He could sound so horrible. All the others seemed to think so too because they looked terrified. They stood with their eyes wide open and stared. Or else they thought she was disgusting, just like Daddy thought. He had changed the tape. Added something about exploding. Olivia didn't understand. She couldn't bear to listen.

It felt like forever before the recording ended. A few old men in suits had gathered everything in bags and set it on the floor. Soon it would be over.

When the recording was done she picked up the tape player and walked back toward the exit. Set the teddy bear down next to the bags. Opened the zipper on the backpack and put in the tape recorder. Then it was time for the bags. They contained money, she knew that. She quickly picked up one bag at a time and put it in the backpack. The rustling was the only sound in the place. Only one bag left now. When she picked it up a few bundles of money fell out on the floor. Quickly she started picking up the money. The same colorful slips of paper like at home in Finland, but this particular kind she had never seen. The bundles where it said 500 on each one were violet and the rest were yellow. Olivia liked yellow and violet. They were so clean and flat, like play money. Her hands were still cold and stiff but she got the last bundle down into the bag. All she could think about was Daddy. Now he would be angry again. Because it was taking such a long time.

In the corner of her eye she saw a lady start moving. Olivia didn't understand why. Daddy had said that they would be completely still. She hoped the lady didn't come up to her the way the old man did the last time. She had to hurry. She pushed the bag down in the backpack and closed the zipper. Quickly she slipped the rain cape over her head and picked up the backpack. It had gotten heavy. She staggered but kept herself upright. Tried to get her one arm through the strap of the backpack as she started walking toward the exit. And then the other arm. Now it was on.

She felt a freezing blast of wind against her legs when the doors opened. It had started raining too, but that didn't matter. She just wanted to get away.

When the doors had closed behind her and she took a few steps, she remembered. The teddy bear! She had left it on the floor in there. She quickly turned around. Ran back to the glass doors. They closed right in front of her. When she put her hands up against the window and her forehead against the gloves she could see the teddy bear lying on the floor a little farther into the bank. She pressed her hands against the glass panes as if trying to push them to the sides. It didn't work. She heard Daddy's voice in her head, "Let that fucking teddy bear be." She kept standing with her hands against the glass and her eyes fixed on the teddy bear on the floor. She felt hot tears running down her cheeks. The lady from inside the bank came rushing toward the exit. She screamed something that Olivia could not hear. Picked up the teddy bear and ran to the sliding doors. When they didn't open the lady started to hit on the glass from inside. But they didn't open. The woman started crying. She sank down on the floor on the other side of the doors. Strange that she was crying, thought Olivia, when she had the teddy bear.

"Get out of there, fast," she heard Daddy calling in her head. She was probably late now. She turned around and started walking as fast as she could in the direction of the drain. There were fewer people on the sidewalk now. A lady with an umbrella was pushing a baby buggy farther away. In front of Olivia a mail carrier was standing with a big cart. Olivia went past the cart. The mail carrier didn't look at her but instead went into an entry with a lot of mail in his hands. The pack struck against her back with every step. She panted. Couldn't go on much longer. Her foot hurt. A car drove past and splashed water up on her legs. Cold, dirty rainwater. Only a few steps to the corner now. At the corner she would probably see the drain. She turned around. Then she saw. She stopped abruptly. Stood quietly next to the building wall. Stared at the big thing that stood there. She breathed in. Held her breath. Her heart was pounding. She didn't understand what she was seeing. What was it? Help!

SEVENTY-NINE

It was as if I knew that something would go wrong this time. That the last robbery would not be like the other two. But Ronni had made contact yesterday and said that the girl was feeling better and assured me that everything was on track. He had not been in touch this morning, which was a good sign.

I looked at the clock. It should be happening now. Something still made me feel uneasy. I moved quickly through the corridors at work. Couldn't get myself to sit quietly in my office. I repeatedly told myself that this was the last time. The last robbery.

Handelsbanken, on Renstiernas gata in Södermalm.

Wednesday, October 30.

Then it was over.

Finished.

As I passed Claes's office Sören came running out from what looked like a meeting between him and Claes. I saw Claes through the window to his office. He had a strange expression that I couldn't interpret.

"Leona, do you have a moment?"

I tried to look even more stressed, to avoid his questions.

"I've gone through all the material now. Interviews, memos, surveillance video, everything. I'd like to talk with you about a few things that I think are a little strange."

My phone rang in my pocket. Thank God, I was rescued.

"Excuse me, Sören."

I had hoped that he would go away, but he remained standing there, looking at me. Nina's voice on the phone did not sound normal. She spoke quickly and in a shrill voice.

"They're cleaning the storm drains in Södermalm today."

I didn't understand what she was saying. Couldn't make the connection.

"Hello, Leona? Do you hear me? I'm in the car. I'm listening to the traffic report on the local news. They just informed drivers that they're flushing the storm drains all over Söder today."

I completely froze. My jaw dropped. I couldn't produce a sound. I had planned everything down to the slightest detail, but storm drain cleaning? I hadn't given that a thought.

"They have several trucks out. If they're cleaning the drain then the girl will never get down into it. And if she's already down there…Well, you understand the problem."

"Thanks so much for the information," I said. "I'll arrange it."

I spoke in a formal voice. Tried to sound unperturbed in front of Sören. Now it was urgent.

"You'll have to excuse me, I have to go. We'll talk about that later."

"Is it something that has to do with the case? If so, I'd be happy to come along."

Claes had heard Sören's question and looked sharply out at me from his office.

"Uh, okay," I said. "We'll take the car."

I walked quickly toward the stairwell with Sören close behind. I had to get rid of him. But how?

"Who was that who called?" he asked on the way down in the elevator.

"It was the prosecutor, Nina. I have to stop by her office and review the case with her. Oh, I forgot the file with all the documents. Do you think you could go up to the squad and get them from my desk while I get the car out?"

It was a good plan. I could explain afterward why I had been forced to leave without him.

"No problem," he said, tapping the briefcase he was carrying. "I have everything with me."

Damn! How would I get rid of him? I jogged to the car and got in. Quickly drove out of the garage and continued out on Fleminggatan.

"Hey, is it that urgent?" said Sören.

I turned on the police radio in the car. As we drove, the radio reported a bank robbery at Handelsbanken at Renstiernas gata 18 in Södermalm, and mentioned that a girl had been seen leaving the crime scene.

"Another girl robbery?" asked Sören.

Strange that he had asked. He ought to have known already. He slowly turned his head and looked at me with his usual penetrating gaze.

"Did you already know?"

"Listen, I need to go there. I'll have to let you off. It may be dangerous. Can you make your way back to the squad yourself?"

"Sure."

As soon as he closed the car door I pushed the accelerator to the floor. I had to get to the girl before someone else did. I rushed ahead between cars, up on sidewalks. Had to get hold of the girl. Lots of police officers were certainly already en route to the crime scene. My heart raced as I heard sirens.

EIGHTY

Olivia stood as if petrified. Looked at the drain, as if what she was seeing would disappear if she just looked at it enough. Next to the drain, in the middle of the street, an enormous truck was parked. It wasn't a regular truck with a big loading platform like Grandpa used when he carted out gravel. This one had a big white barrel on it. From the barrel a long rack stuck out with a hose pointing down toward the ground. A man with bright orange clothes and white reflectors around his legs was pointing the hose down into the drain. Olivia didn't understand why he was standing there. Daddy hadn't said anything about it, so the man probably didn't know anything. He was probably there even though he shouldn't be. He had to move. Couldn't stand there. He would ruin everything. Olivia had promised that everything would be perfect this time. Daddy would get so angry if she didn't do what she was meant to.

She had to wait until the man was done with what he was doing. She looked around. A short distance from where she stood was an entranceway with an alcove. She ran there as fast as she could. Hid in the alcove. Another man with similar orange clothes came walking toward her. She made herself small against the alcove's edge, back pressed to the door. Heard the steps approach. Closed her eyes. When the steps continued going past she peered out over the area. A little closer to the drain was a big container. She could hide there and wait until they had driven away. Then she'd be close enough to run down into the drain. To get there she would have to cross the street. She hesitated. Daddy had said that she was not allowed to cross streets by herself. But if she didn't get down in the drain Daddy would be even angrier. She waited until there was only a single car left on the street before she took off.

EIGHTY-ONE

I was approaching Handelsbanken on Renstiernas gata. Saw some uniformed officers who were already outside the scene. I drove around the block toward the drain. When I came in on Kocksgatan I saw the drain-cleaning truck with its enormous tank. The truck almost took up both lanes. By the drain stood an orange-clad worker. I looked around quickly, but I couldn't see the girl anywhere. I drove slowly past the truck. The street was cluttered with two large orange dumpsters full of concrete and lumber, plus a smaller container. There were plenty of places for a little girl to hide. I was about to turn right at the intersection when suddenly I saw her in the rearview mirror, behind the container. I made a quick U-turn. If I just drove her to the apartment then I could drive back to the crime scene and the other officers as if nothing had happened.

I drove closer to the girl and braked right in front of her. Opened the door and ran out. Grabbed hold of her arm and pulled her toward the car. The girl started pulling and wriggling her body to get loose.

"What the hell are you doing? You have to come with me."

I hissed at her. The sound of the cleaning truck's pump had stopped and the street had become strangely quiet.

"I have to go down! I have to go down!"

She screamed and struggled. The skinny little girl was stronger than I would have thought. The two orange-clad workers who were now packing up looked in our direction. I pulled the girl over to the back door of the car. As I opened the door to push her in I saw a familiar unmarked car coming toward us. It slowed down and drove up close. In the car sat Minna and Sam. The two of them leaned closer to the window and looked right at me. Damn!

They had seen me.

And the girl.

Together.

There was no doubt they understood what was going on. I waved them away, indicating that they could go. That I was taking care of the girl. The plan to drive the girl to the apartment was ruined. I swore to myself. Now I had no other choice than to take her to the station.

EIGHTY-TWO

Daddy, Daddy, Daddy. Olivia couldn't think of anything else. What he would do when he found out she hadn't managed it. That she had made a mistake again.

The dumb quiet lady had come and ruined everything. Picked her up when she didn't want it. If she had been left alone to wait for the orange man to be done she would have managed it. Then she could have done everything just the way Daddy said. But the lady forced her into the car, yelled at her to give her the bag and to wrap herself in a blanket. Then she had driven off. Now Olivia would never get to go home to Mommy again.

"I don't want to. Daddy is going to be really angry."

"Quiet. As of now you do as I say. You stay completely quiet and don't say a word when anyone else is listening. Do you hear that? Not a word. This has already gone to hell. I'll take care of your daddy and say that you've been good if you just do as I say, okay? I'll make sure that you get home to your mommy too, as soon as possible, but you have to pull yourself together now. Do you understand?"

The lady took out a phone and put it against her ear. She looked at Olivia in the rearview mirror and turned quickly around.

"Where's the teddy bear?"

Olivia didn't reply. She didn't know what to say.

"Hey!" the lady yelled. "Where the hell is the teddy bear?"

She was driving fast, braking and making fast turns. Olivia had to hold on so she didn't fall down on the floor.

"Forgot," said Olivia.

"What do you mean forgot? Where?"

"At the bank…"

"Hello, it's me," said the lady with the phone against her ear. "We've run into problems. Major fucking problems. The city of Stockholm has drain cleaning so she didn't make it down. She's with me in the car. No, she hasn't caused any problems. Pull yourself together, damn it, stop blaming everything on the girl."

Olivia understood that the lady was talking with Daddy. He was mad, she could hear that.

"I'll take care of this, but it's going to take time. Don't call me. I'll be in touch before I stop by with the girl. Just don't do anything stupid, Ronni. Stay inside."

The lady hung up.

"Was Daddy mad?"

"No, just a little worried about how things were going for you."

The lady looked in the rearview mirror. It was lucky that she hadn't said anything to Daddy about the teddy bear.

"Your daddy isn't very nice to you, huh?"

Olivia didn't know how to answer. He was nice sometimes and mean sometimes. She didn't dare say that Daddy was mean because maybe the lady would tell Daddy and then Daddy would be mean again.

The lady didn't drive to Daddy's house, but instead to another place where they drove past a man who was sitting in a cage. The lady showed something from a flat black wallet that she had on a chain around her neck. Then the man in the cage let them pass. They drove down to a garage that was underground. There was a dark, scary tunnel there. Then the lady stopped the car, stared at her sternly, and said, "Now you listen to me. Whatever happens, I'm telling you, not a single sound to anyone other than me. Not a peep. If I ask you something then you look at me. If I blink two times you can answer. If I don't blink two times you keep quiet. Completely quiet. Do you understand? If you do that I promise that you will get to go home to Mommy as soon as possible. Okay?"

She nodded.

"My teddy bear..."

"I said that you should keep quiet. Not another word about that now."

The lady took Olivia by the hand through several basement passages to a room with rows of tall lockers and clothes hangers. They walked quickly past a lady who stood bent over in one of the passages, putting on a black boot. At the back of the room she stopped and opened a locker. She took out the tape recorder and then put the backpack in the locker. She locked the locker and took Olivia to two big elevators. She pressed the button. Walked once around Olivia. Opened another door and stuck her head out. Closed it again and went back to the elevator door. Olivia stood quietly.

EIGHTY-THREE

I pressed the elevator button again. Fucking slow elevators. I hoped that no one would be taking the elevator together with me and a bloody seven-year-old girl in a wig, black rain cape, with dummy bombs fastened to her body and slipper socks.

I needed time.

Time to think.

The time in the elevator was all I had.

The bag. I didn't have time to move it now. But it was securely stored in my locker in the basement. I would have to take it home after work. The elevator door opened slowly as usual. I dragged the girl in with me. The blanket from the car had fallen down and was dragging behind her. I pulled it up over her shoulders. She had forgotten the teddy bear, but that was the least of my problems right now. I pressed seven. The squad office would probably be full of people. I wanted to talk with Nina, to discuss what we should do, but now there was no time. The elevator door opened at level seven. I took hold of her hand and walked quickly out into the stairwell, pulling the card through the reader and entering the code to get into the corridor. Looked around. I needed more time to think. I pulled the girl into the restrooms that were only a couple of meters into the corridor. The handicap restroom was occupied so I quickly opened one of the small, cramped stalls and locked the door behind us.

Think, Leona.

Think.

The girl looked up at me with tired eyes. I set her quickly on the toilet seat. I crouched down and looked her sharply in the eyes.

"Now you have to listen carefully. What I'm going to tell you now is the absolute most important thing for you to remember so you'll be able to go home to your mommy."

The girl didn't say anything. Just kept looking at me. I took hold of her shoulders.

"Do you hear me?"

Her whole body tightened. She nodded quickly and looked down at the floor. I let go. I tried to calm myself.

"Sorry, sorry."

My phone vibrated in my pocket. I quickly took it out. A text. "Last one done?" it said. I couldn't answer now. I didn't have time.

"Olivia, look at me. If at any time I blink with one eye like this—" I blinked with one eye. "—then that means this has become an extremely serious situation for us. Then I want you to pretend to be really frightened. You mustn't talk at all, but just look really scared. You can run and hide, scream or whatever. But don't say a word. Do you understand? Can you do that?"

She nodded slowly. There was flushing in the handicap restroom adjacent. I whispered to the girl.

"And then you can only answer when I blink two times like I said before. Okay?"

She nodded. More than that I did not have time to assure myself that she understood.

I got up. Took a deep breath. I would take the girl straight to Anette. If I just got there I would feel calmer. Anette had that effect on me. She could make any problem disappear. I'd let her help me.

As soon as I heard the departing footsteps of whoever had been in the handicap restroom I unlocked the door. I took the girl by the hand and pulled her at a rapid clip after me through the corridor. Officers were sitting occupied, with their faces pointed right at their screens. Anette's door was only a few offices away now. No one had noticed us yet. I pulled the girl into Anette's office and closed the door.

"Leona! But dear, what is this?"

Anette looked down at the girl who now looked more miserable than ever.

"Anette! Please, you have to help me. This is the girl from the robberies. I found her at the crime scene. I can't take her into custody. She's scared out of her wits, traumatized. She needs care, warmth, and clothes. We have to get a technician down here who can check whether there is DNA from the perpetrator on her. We need a forensic examination of her, too. And listen, can you turn this recording in for audio analysis, too? I have to call Nina. The girl needs to be questioned as soon as possible. Through her we may get hold of the perpetrator. Someone must be waiting for her to show up and is probably very angry right now. Will you please contact Social Services too?"

I could hear that I was babbling. Did she even understand what I was saying?

"Of course, but my God. Poor little thing. What's your name?"

I gave the girl a stern look to remind her not to say anything.

"She hasn't said a word so far, but do try to talk with her," I said.

I crouched down.

"This nice lady, Anette, will take care of you for a while. I'll come back soon."

I went straight into my office and called Nina.

"The girl is here at the police station."

"What?"

"I had to bring her here. Minna and Sam saw me pick her up near the drain. The money is safe in my locker for now; I'll go back for it later…"

I paced back and forth around the office while I talked. Yet another message vibrated in my pocket.

"I have to question her," I continued. "She knows she's not allowed to say anything and to be honest I don't think she's going to either. She is really worried. I have to be sure to get her home to her mother now."

I was talking at a fast pace but Nina was quick to understand that the circumstances had changed completely.

"Okay. Hold a video interview with the girl for the sake of formalities. I'll arrange it so that she gets victim assistance right away. The girl's parents or, well, the mother then, must be informed. Set up a separate report and initiate a preliminary investigation of assault and human trafficking with the girl as the injured party, because formally there is reason to assume that crimes have been committed against her. I will write off everything later on the basis 'no investigation result.' And listen, Leona, take a deep breath now, we'll solve this together."

EIGHTY-FOUR

"Leona, Leona, I heard you got hold of the girl."

Sören came running after me on my way to the elevator. Damn, he was the last person I wanted to deal with right now.

"I'm on my way down to pick up the victim advocate before the interview with the girl," I said.

"I'll go with you."

I had held a small number of child interviews during my career. If this had been a normal investigation I probably would have asked someone from the Domestic Violence squad to do the interview. But this time I needed to do it myself so I could control the girl's responses. The important thing was to ask the right questions so that no one suspected anything. The girl was a victim in everyone's eyes. Even if she was the one who carried the money out and under normal circumstances would be considered a suspect, the surrounding circumstances meant that she was deemed an injured party and therefore she had a victim advocate assigned to her.

"Ingela Sundström."

The victim advocate was a dark-haired woman in her fifties. Her body language was relaxed, which calmed me somewhat. I looked at Sören. How do you introduce a medium? It's awkward to explain to an academic that police officers watch too many horror films.

"This is Sören Möller. He's working with me and, uh, analyzing interviews. He is going to be with us in the observation room."

Ingela shook his hand and turned to me.

"How is the girl doing?"

"She's been bandaged, given food and clothes. My colleague Anette is keeping her company."

On the way to the observation room I could see Sören looking at me out of the corner of my eye. If I could just get rid of him.

Anette had prepared the interview room. The plasma screen in the observation room was turned on. On it you could see the girl and Anette, each sitting in an armchair in the interview room. I turned to Ingela.

"She hasn't said a word the whole time so I don't know what we can expect from an interview. We'll go in and I'll introduce you. You can of course talk with her yourself before we get started. I'll turn off the sound to the observation room in the meantime."

"I would also really like to say hello to the girl," said Sören.

I see, now the circus was in town. I would have preferred that he didn't see me and the girl together, in case his psychic gaze saw that we were already acquainted. But refusing his request would look strange.

I opened the door and we went into the interview room. The girl was curled up with her legs close to her body and a pillow beside her. Anette had found some borrowed clothes from the holding cell, which were much too large. She had pulled the hood up on the hoodie and the pants were way past her feet.

"Thanks for helping, Anette," I said. "Did you get hold of anyone from Social Services?"

"They're supposed to send someone here as soon as they can."

Anette left the room. I crouched down in front of the chair where the girl was sitting.

"I have two very nice people with me who would really like to meet you. The man here is named Sören, and he is helping me in my work."

"Hi," said Sören, leaning down. "What's your name?"

The girl glanced up at him without changing her expression or saying anything.

"And this is Ingela, who is here to give you a little extra help."

"Hi, my name is Ingela."

Ingela leaned over and extended her hand. The girl didn't take it.

"I work as a lawyer and I help children and grownups who have ended up in situations like you have."

The girl looked at Ingela, still without saying anything.

"I thought that you and I could talk a little before Leona asks you a few questions. Is that okay?"

No reaction. Ingela gave me a meaningful look that showed she did not think this was going to be easy.

"Sören and I will leave you with Ingela for a little while," I said. "We'll be in the room next door and in a little while I'll come back again so that you and I can talk some more."

We went out. Anette was standing outside the door.

"Did she say anything to you?" I said.

"Not a word. Poor girl, either she's mute or else she's been completely traumatized by the incident. This is crazy. Only an evil person could treat a child this way."

I went into the observation room with Sören behind me. The victim advocate was talking. The girl sat quietly. I turned off the sound in the observation room, as I had promised Ingela.

"Sören, will you please let Claes know that we have the girl here."

"Of course."

He left. After a minute or two Claes was standing in the observation room with a smile.

"Nicely done, Leona. I knew you were the right person for this. Did the girl have the money on her?"

"A tape recorder and dummy bombs, but no money."

"I'll be damned. Was the Bomb Squad on the scene that quickly?"

"Uh...we didn't need to bring them in. I saw immediately that they were dummies."

Claes raised his eyebrows.

"Yes, well, it was obvious that they were just toys," I explained. "But the bank customers were presumably jittery... not to mention the girl herself...although she probably knew they weren't really bombs...but it's still a shame about her...she's had to endure so much...it was good that I got hold of her so there's finally an end to this..."

I noticed that I was babbling a little too much but I wanted to remove Claes's focus from the girl's things. I felt my phone vibrate again. Took it out of my pocket. There was a new text from abroad, asking if everything was done. I didn't have time to answer now. Clicked it away.

"So someone had taken the money from the girl before you got hold of her? Without picking her up at the same time?"

"The most important thing is that we get hold of the perpetrator now, isn't it? Through him we can trace the money. I'm just about to question the girl."

Claes looked pensive. He turned his eyes toward the screen. "Parent?"

"No. Victim advocate," I said. "We don't know who the girl is yet. Or even what language she speaks, because so far she hasn't said a word. We'll have to arrange for an interpreter, if that's needed."

Claes walked toward the door.

"Keep me informed."

"Claes, I would really like for you to stay while I interview her. I'll need your input."

"Perhaps we should turn over the interviewing to a child interrogator," said Claes. "Have you discussed that with the pros — "

"Nina wants me to do the interview. Since I know the case. We can't wait for a child interrogator to get familiar with it."

"You shouldn't underestimate the interrogators at Domestic Violence. They can familiarize themselves with a case in no time."

"Claes, this isn't the first time I've interviewed a traumatized child. The girl has to be interviewed now. We can't torment her anymore. It's the prosecutor's decision."

Claes backed off. The decision was not his. In any case, he knew that I had experience in the area.

Anette looked into the room. Behind her stood Sören and a dark-haired man in his thirties.

"Leona, the guy from Social Services is here."

The man extended his hand.

"Thomas Liljegren."

"Good. I'll start by trying to find out who she is so that we can get hold of her parents. Please sit down in here; you'll see everything on the screen. Claes and Sören can fill you in if you're wondering about anything."

I turned on the sound again and went into the interview room. Ingela stood up. Shook her head slightly, before leaving the room. I sat in the armchair by the girl.

"I know that recently things have been extremely tough for you, but I have to ask you a few questions."

The baggy hoodie made her look even smaller than she was.

"What we say here is being recorded on video so that others will be able to look at it. In the room next to this one Ingela and

Sören, whom you just met, my boss Claes, and a very nice man from Social Services are sitting by a big TV. They are sitting in the next room so they won't disturb us when we're talking, but they hear everything we say and can see us through those cameras."

I pointed at the cameras. The girl didn't move. She didn't even look toward the cameras.

"My name is Leona. What's your name?"

No answer. I put down the pen I'd been holding, looked at her, and spoke in a softer voice.

"Do you understand what I'm saying?"

Still no answer.

"Do you remember when I picked you up on the street? I did that because it's very dangerous for children to be there. You know that, don't you?"

Two blinks. Olivia nodded her head, but still didn't say anything.

"Do you remember when I told you that I wanted to take you home, to your family?"

Two blinks. She nodded again.

"To do that I need to know your name and where you're from, so I can find them, okay? So, what's your name?"

Two blinks.

"Olivia."

Her Finnish-Swedish was clear, even though she had only said her name.

"Hi, Olivia. What country do you come from?"

Two blinks.

"Finland."

"Do you know from what city?"

Two blinks.

"Tammisaari."

"How old are you, Olivia?"

Two blinks. The girl held up seven fingers.

"What are your parents' names?"

No answer. The girl was sharp, no doubt about it.

"What's your mother's name?"

Two blinks.

"Katriina."

"What's your mother's last name, Olivia?"

Two blinks.

"Tuulavaara."

"Does she know where you are?"

Two blinks. The girl nodded.

"Visiting Grandma."

I was impressed. She had followed the instructions to a tee.

"Olivia, can you wait here a moment while I go out and talk with the people in the next room. I will also call your mother so she knows that you'll be coming home soon. I'll ask my boss Claes to come in and sit here with you for a while. I'll be back soon."

I moved toward the door. Right before I left the room I turned around and winked with one eye at the girl. She had acquitted herself in an exemplary way so far. Now it was time for the real test.

I opened the door to the observation room.

"Claes, can I speak to you?" I said.

Claes came out quickly, closing the door behind him.

"Damn, that's good, Leona. It will be easy to identify the girl now."

"Yes, I'll inform the Finnish police, CIS, and investigations. We have to get hold of the girl's parents. Can you go in and be with her in the meantime?"

"No problem. I'll go right in."

I opened the door to the observation room and placed myself with my back to the screen. Nina had arrived. She gave me a look and nodded curtly from the other side of the room.

"As you heard, this is a little Finnish girl. I interrupted the interview so I could make a few calls but I also want to know if there's anything in particular you think I should have in mind before I continue?"

Ingela, Sören, Nina, and the man from Social Services did not take their eyes off the screen behind me. When I turned around I saw what was happening in the interview room. Claes was standing a little farther into the room. The girl had gotten up from the armchair and was backing away from where Claes was standing. She had started running around, as if to get away from Claes.

"Olivia, Olivia, I'm a policeman, don't worry," said Claes, holding up his hands as if to calm her.

I ran out and tore open the door to the interview room.

"Leave, Claes, I'll take care of this."

"What's happening? I don't understand," said Claes.

The girl was moving quickly back and forth between the back of the armchair and the corner at the far end of the room as she wailed.

"*Go*, Claes! You're scaring her."

Claes moved quickly to the door. I closed it behind him. The girl was sitting down in the far corner with her legs pulled up. Her head was lowered. I remained standing in the middle of the room.

"Don't worry. He's gone now."

I crouched down and reached my hand out toward her. She looked slowly up at me.

"It's just me here now."

She didn't move. I went slowly toward her.

"I'm coming up to you now. Don't worry. Take my hand."

The girl didn't move. I went slowly the whole way up to her and carefully placed one hand on her knee.

"You can sit on my lap if you want. Do you want to?"

I knew that others would criticize what I was doing. In an interview situation with children you should preferably not show too much sympathy. Not hug or pick up a child, but these circumstances were different. I needed to show that this was a situation where no more questions should be asked. I got up slowly and carefully picked her up in my arms. I sat down in the armchair with her on my lap.

"It will be all right. Soon you'll get to go home to your mother."

I rocked her. She became calmer. Perhaps no one had hugged her in a long time. I stroked a strand of hair away from her face. She looked up at me.

"We'll take a break. I think you should try some really good rhubarb juice I have in the refrigerator."

Afterward I was told by Nina that there had been a mutiny in the observation room after the girl's reaction to Claes. The victim advocate had become completely rabid and accusatory toward Claes. She refused to allow further interviews to be held without one of the girl's parents being present. Sören had frantically written things down on his notepad. After wild discussions with the victim advocate Claes disappeared into his office. Nina had taken the victim advocate's line and decided that the girl should not be interviewed more closely until the parents had been contacted and we produced more information about the case. If this couldn't happen before tomorrow they would have to cooperate with the Finnish police and make sure the girl was interviewed in Finland.

Before I turned the girl over to Thomas Liljegren from Social Services I went down to the storeroom to look for clothes to borrow. In a basket of toys were a few different stuffed animals. No teddy bear, but there was a little green dragon with small dark blue wings.

When I got back, Thomas was holding the girl by the hand. I crouched down slowly and looked her in the eyes.

"Your teddy bear that was left at the bank needs to be examined before you can get it back, but here is another little creature who needs a friend."

I handed the dragon to her. She took it slowly. Looked at me.

Thomas turned and moved toward the exit. The girl went with him.

The girl. Olivia.

She had a name.

For me, too.

I saw Thomas open the door and leave the police station with Olivia in hand. I remained standing. Frozen. I couldn't take my eyes off them.

"Wait!"

I ran to the door and out onto the stairs.

"Where is she going to stay tonight?" I asked.

Thomas turned around.

"We're trying to arrange temporary accommodation for her overnight so she can go home to Finland tomorrow."

I wasn't satisfied with his answer. Social Services were not known for arranging housing on short notice. Above all not for homeless seven-year-olds without any relatives or friends in the country.

"I think Olivia needs to be with someone she knows. Someone she has confidence in and who knows what she's gone through."

Thomas stood quietly. He didn't seem to understand where I was going.

"She can stay with me and my family tonight."

Thomas looked at me with surprise.

"I don't think that's appropriate. We have to know we are leaving children in homes that are…"

He stopped when he realized he was about to say that I would not be suitable for taking care of a child. That was true, of course, but he could not possibly know that.

"You mean that I wouldn't be suitable for taking care of Olivia for a single night? For the record, I have two kids of my own, I'm a police officer, and I know what Olivia has gone through. Do you think that at Social Services you're going to get hold of a safer family in two or three hours for a seven-year-old?"

"Sorry, that's not what I meant. It's just that things don't usually work that way."

"It's not exactly common for seven-year-olds to commit such serious acts and end up in these kinds of situations, though, is it? Then you have to improvise a little. Isn't the child's well-being the most important thing?"

Thomas crouched down and spoke directly to Olivia.

"Olivia, would you like to stay with Leona?"

Olivia looked at me, back at Thomas, and at me again. I reached my hand out toward her. Our eyes met again. In a different way than before. There on the stairs it was as if I had made contact with her for the first time. I felt overwhelming feelings of affinity with this little girl. I was overcome with humility for what she, quite unknowingly, had done for me.

It was my duty to see that she recovered from all this.

She let go of Thomas and took hold of my outstretched hand.

EIGHTY-FIVE

Olivia was shy and reserved on the way home, but was livened up a little by Benjamin and Beatrice. Beatrice looked wide-eyed at her and asked if she was the girl from TV. Olivia, who didn't understand the question, looked at me. She searched in my eyes for the answer. The answer to how she ended up here, and why. The answer to the connection between the two of us. I didn't say anything. The most important thing now was that Olivia should feel safe.

The bag with the money was still in the locker at work. I decided to bring it home tomorrow after work when everything had calmed down. I had answered the text from abroad, too. Now I was longing for a good night's sleep.

After Olivia had been fed I took her to the bathroom for a hot bath. Earlier, when we had taken off her borrowed clothes, I had been shocked, but I had thought that her body looked as it did because of the fake blood that was still on her. But when I saw the water rinse away the dye I could hardly breathe. Several bruises and two small cuts appeared on her light skin. Real injuries. She refused to tell me how she'd gotten them, but I understood.

Ronni.

Suddenly I was completely drained of energy.

I sat on the edge of the tub and stared straight ahead. I thought about what Ronni had said. That I was naive. That it wasn't easy to get a seven-year-old to do something like this. I hadn't understood. Was that it? Had I closed my eyes, not wanting to see?

Been so fixated on my goals that I hadn't taken in what Ronni was actually doing to her? Sure, I had understood that it would involve a certain degree of coercion, but this...I hadn't seen that she had these kinds of injuries. The few times I had been in the apartment she had either been in the bedroom or worn a night-gown or pajamas. Sure, she had seemed tired and skinny, but I had not seen any bruises or other injuries.

I blamed myself for letting Ronni manage everything that concerned her. The girl, as I had called her. In my thoughts she hadn't even had a name until now. Until today. Olivia. Olivia. Olivia.

Now she was so present. I was on the verge of tears. Had I cre-ated the same conditions for Olivia that I had experienced myself as a child? No, it was not the same. Or was it?

I carefully put bandages on the wounds. Wrapped a warm towel around her and lifted her up in my arms to where I sat on the toilet seat. Rocked her. Whispered to her, to myself, I did not know which.

"Sorry, sorry..."

She looked up at me with surprise. Dried my cheek with her little hand. I gave her a T-shirt that was still too big for Beatrice. Picked her up in my arms again and carried her into our bedroom. Since Peter was sleeping in the guest room now, I laid her on his side of the bed. I lay down behind her and embraced her. The last thing I remember was stroking her cheek and saying that tomor-row, tomorrow she would get to go home to her mother.

EIGHTY-SIX

Many thoughts had been whirling around in my head when I'd gone to bed, but I fell asleep from pure exhaustion. Olivia had slept calmly beside me. She woke up once during the night and asked for her mother. After I placed an arm around her, explained where she was, that she didn't need to be afraid, and that she would get to go home to her mother tomorrow, she fell back asleep.

Turning Olivia over to Social Services, who would arrange for her journey home to Finland, had been both hard and good. I had become attached to her somehow. She stirred up a lot of emotions in me. The same kind I had for my own children. Having her close to me was hard. Now she would get to go home to her mother.

After that I went straight to the office. I had just taken off my jacket and turned on the computer when I felt a vibration in my pocket.

"Leona, I have information for you about the voice on the tape. You have to hear it yourself."

Johan Östberg from the Image and Audio Analysis Group spoke quickly on the phone. I went straight to the elevators. Johan met me with a look that resembled the one my kids had when they thought they heard Santa Claus's reindeer on the roof on Christmas Eve, a kind of delight mingled with terror. He quickly closed the door behind me and put a disk into the computer.

"The voice on the recording is distorted, of course. It's a man with a Finnish accent speaking. Who it is I don't know, but right at the end there is something that was presumably included by mistake when the recording was made. Another voice, speaking Swedish without an accent. Listen here."

Johan played the recording. A short section in the middle of a sentence was heard: "...*then we're done. Now...*"

I opened my eyes wide and looked at Johan.

"Oh! Can I hear it one more time?"

He played the audio file again. I avoided looking at him, but I saw out of the corner of my eye that he was observing me attentively.

"I hardly believe what I'm hearing. How in God's name...?" I said.

I looked at Johan. Johan looked at me.

"Is there any possibility that a sound from outside, from something else, may have been left in your recorder and ended up on top of this audio file?" I asked. "You have sound samples of a large number of employees stored, I assume."

I played dumb. Of course I knew that was impossible.

"No, there's no chance of that. I don't have any employees' voices recorded just hanging around in here."

No, why should he have?

"But I don't understand," I said.

I sat down on the chair and stared straight ahead.

"How did that get onto the tape?" I said.

"Leona, I'll research this a little more. I was so shocked when I heard it that I called you at once. This is news to me, too."

I leaned with my elbows on the table and my head in my hands.

"What if people find out about it?"

Johan sat quietly a moment.

"Leona, I'm not going to say anything until I know exactly how this fits together. I'll listen more carefully to the recording. Perhaps there is an obvious explanation."

I thanked Johan. Left his office, headed back up to my squad. I had only taken a few steps into the corridor before Claes came up to me. His hair was strangely messy and he had dark rings under his eyes.

"Leona, there you are. Come!"

Claes almost dragged me into his office. He closed the door and pulled the curtain. Then he started pacing around in the room.

"The interview with the girl," he said. "What the hell really happened?"

Ah, that was why he looked like he had just gotten out of bed. He mustn't have been able to sleep.

"Nina thought there was no point in making a new attempt to question her yesterday. She didn't say a word after you...well, she was really upset after you left the room. Did you recognize the girl at all?"

Claes shook his head.

"It was as if she'd seen a ghost when I came in."

"And here I thought you were good with children, Claes. That's why I asked you to go in and stay with her. I hope you don't have that kind of effect on your own daughters at home."

Claes didn't smile. He gave me a surly look and continued pacing around the room.

"Let it go, Claes. She must have seen something in you that resembled the person who subjected her to this. It's nothing to brood about."

He frowned. Stared straight ahead. I continued.

"Considering her reaction you might say that it's a handsome, fit man in his prime who is behind the robberies. A good lead, I think."

The flattery worked. He smiled.

"Listen, by the way. Sören was here, and he said that he thought it was a female perpetrator."

I sighed and shook my head at the same time.

"I heard that. Honestly, Claes, do you really believe he has the abilities that he says he has? Are we going to start believing in trolls and gnomes too?"

"Well, the statistics don't directly argue for..."

"No, exactly," I said, stepping out into the corridor. "Speak up if he has anything sensible to suggest. Until then we'll make use of customary proven investigation methods."

EIGHTY-SEVEN

Anette called to me as I went past her office the next morning. I backed up and looked in. Even more potted plants had been added, making the room look like a small jungle. Between the plants she had placed framed photos of her family members. One of her grandchildren was wearing a jacket like Benjamin's.

"Claes asked me to tell you that he wanted to see you as soon as you came in."

There was something different in Anette's voice. It was calm. Almost a whisper.

"Do you know what it's about?" I said.

She started humming and clearing her throat.

"I know it's something important that has to do with the girl robbery but I promised Claes I wouldn't say anything. He wants to talk with you himself."

"Thanks, Anette. I'll see him right away."

I tried to prepare myself for what was coming. Had something occurred to Sören that, despite what we had decided, he'd taken straight to Claes?

Claes was on the phone but waved me in when he saw me in the corridor.

I sat down at the meeting table and waited. He was speaking calmly and collectedly. Seemed to be in no hurry to conclude the call.

I looked at the clock. I had been waiting three minutes now

and was starting to squirm. Claes put up a finger as if to say that he was almost done.

"Good, then that's what we'll do."

He hung up the phone, then stood up, went over to the door and closed it.

"I see," I said. "Either it's something really pleasant or something really unpleasant you have to say."

"Unfortunately it's more serious this time, Leona."

He sat down across from me at the round meeting table. Sighed deeply and put his elbows on the table.

"Leona, you know that I consider you one of our absolute best investigators."

I didn't answer. Tried to stay cool. Any detective would be terrified after such an introduction to a conversation with their boss. Termination effective immediately?

"I have unfortunately received information that things are not completely right with your investigation. The girl robberies."

I swallowed. Took a firm hold of the arm rests on either side of the chair. My palms had become clammy. My mouth was dry. My heart pounded in my chest. I had to concentrate on breathing.

So this was how it would end.

All the work.

All the planning.

All the dreams.

"Okay. What do you mean?"

I had no choice other than to play dumb. The exertion that was required to keep my voice steady was exhausting. My heart continued to pound.

"The head of investigations called and said that the case will be moved to II."

Now I didn't know what to think. I stared at Claes, completely speechless. II was the National Police Board's unit for internal investigations. They investigated cases where police employees were suspected of crimes. So it really was over now.

"They didn't say the reason, so we can only speculate on that."

So Claes didn't know. That was a relief. But what exactly had they found? I tried to calm down. Tried to sound unperturbed.

"Mmm...but...what conclusions do you draw from this?" I asked.

"None at all. It's not on my desk and it's not my job to sit and guess at what's behind their decision."

He suspected me. I was sure of it. I clenched my jaw. Told myself to straighten up. Not flip out now. I got up. Walked around the room, over to the window.

"But this is crazy! It's only me, Minna, Sam, and Nina who are working on the case now."

"And Sören," said Claes.

Sören, yes. Could it really be possible that he had a vision and "saw" something?

"Claes, you don't really believe that — "

"I don't believe anything," he interrupted me sharply. "I'm asking you to immediately turn over the physical files to II. None of you who have worked with the case have authority any longer to open it in the computer system."

"What about Nina?"

"The leadership of the preliminary investigation will be moved over to the National Unit for Police Court Cases. We don't know who the prosecutor will be yet. Anyway, Nina will no longer be the preliminary investigation leader."

I was mute. Had to call Nina as soon as possible. How could this have happened? What had we missed?

"I'm sorry, Leona. You've worked very hard on the robberies, I know that. But you'll have to see it as a good thing that someone looks at it with fresh eyes. And if a colleague is involved it's only good that we find out."

"Mmm…of course…"

"This changes nothing for you here. I'm sorry you didn't get to finish your work but you know how it is sometimes."

I wanted out of the room.

Out of the building.

Away from it all.

To flee to the apartment on Malta that had become my symbol for freedom and the life I wanted to live.

"Was there anything else?" I said.

"Make sure to get the physical files up to II immediately. Then you can leave for the day. I think you need to rest, Leona. You've looked tired lately."

I left the room. Sören was standing outside, talking with a colleague. Our eyes met. He inspected me in his usual strange way. I noted that he slipped into Claes's office as soon as I was down the hall.

EIGHTY-EIGHT

An hour later the whole squad had gathered in the break room. Claes had sent out an "urgent" email that he had something important to report. The only ones who knew what it was about were Anette and me. Other colleagues were speculating wildly about what might have happened. Would Claes report that he had quit, or had an old colleague passed away? Anette and I kept quiet. Claes was in his office along with the head of investigations.

"Did you hear that the finance minister wasn't indicted for the murder of that journalist?" said Anette.

Damn! I'd had so much else on my mind that I hadn't kept track of when a decision would be made on the indictment.

"I just heard it on the radio," Anette continued. "But the sleazeball appears to have paid for sex, and as luck would have it, he will be indicted for that. According to the news the prosecutor said that the evidence was there, so he'll probably go to prison for that."

"Always something," I said. "Will I have time to go to the restroom do you think?"

Anette looked into Claes's office.

"They're still talking, go ahead."

I took off. Pulled out my phone. I needed to get hold of Dina to tell her that she had to go underground for a while. No answer. Just when I had hung up, the mobile rang. Nina's name was on the display.

"I just heard," I said to Nina. "I tried to reach Dina but she isn't answering. She wouldn't want to talk with me now anyway. I'll have to contact Personal Protection and see if they can keep her safe until the trial."

"That's the only thing we can do in the present situation," said Nina. "It's important that she comes to court so that he doesn't walk."

Anette waved to me in the corridor.

"I have to go, Nina."

Claes and the head of investigations had come out of Claes's office. Everyone fell silent when they saw Claes's grave expression.

"I have something serious to tell you. I have been informed by Kenneth here that the girl robberies, which Leona has recently been working on intensively, will be transferred to II."

The room was dead silent. Everyone knew what that meant. My colleagues' eyes turned on me. I didn't bat an eyelid.

"According to II, information has emerged that one or more police employees are involved in the robberies."

Claes and Kenneth must have noticed that everyone was looking at me. Kenneth stepped in.

"We want to be clear and say that we are not speculating about this and would be grateful if you also refrained from doing so. I have extremely little information but as far as I know there is enough evidence that it is only a matter of time before someone or several people are arrested. It is now extremely important that those of you who know something about the case assist the investigators at II with all the information you have. So far the media has not gotten wind of this, but that is surely only a matter of time. Try to stick together and stand firm."

"The most important thing is that we here at the squad keep working as usual," said Claes. "There is no reason for us to look suspiciously at each other. As you understand, this doesn't necessarily concern a colleague here at the squad, or even in our district. We'll let II do their work. You can report to me if you have information that you think may be important to the investigation."

Kenneth was quick to comment, "Uh, it's better that you contact me in that case."

"Sure, perhaps that's just as well," said Claes. "Any questions?"

I stuck a finger up in the air.

"I wonder how long you've known about this? It feels a little... unpleasant, that II is snooping around in my investigation without telling me."

"For understandable reasons we can't announce that sort of thing in advance, as you all know," said Kenneth. "We found out only an hour or so ago."

I tried to interpret my colleagues' reactions. Anette looked at me with worry in her eyes. Fredrik cautiously threw out his hands as if he wondered what this was about. Sören looked away as soon as our eyes met. Had he really...?

"If there's nothing else then I'll leave you. If you have questions later I want you to contact me or II directly," said Kenneth, leaving the room.

No one said a word. I could hear myself breathing. Claes broke the silence.

"As I said, this is not something we should speculate about. Those involved are presumably colleagues from outside."

Claes got no response. No one made a sound.

"Okay everybody, let's get back to work."

I turned around and moved toward my office. Wanted out.

To breathe fresh air.

Clear my head.

"By the way, before you leave," said Claes. "Two things. First and foremost, I have received information that some of you have still not given DNA samples. That must be done before November 20. I'm not mentioning any names but Niklas, Katrin, and Leona, damn it, see about getting that done."

Claes stared at me, the only one of the three listed who was present. I had avoided having DNA taken on purpose. Wanted to delay it as long as possible. Along with many others, I had been strongly opposed to the legislative proposal that DNA samples should be stored for all employees within the justice system. But because the proposal went through and the law had gone into force on July 1, we had no choice. Since then, though, I had other things on my mind.

"Another thing. I got a message from the janitor. Because they are renovating the firing range in the basement, they needed the space where your lockers were. The lockers that stood against the wall evidently had no backs, so all your things were removed and locked in bags with the janitor. You have to go there yourselves and pick them up."

I couldn't believe it.

The locker.

The backpack.

The money.

I started walking slowly toward the stairwell. I cast a glance back as I turned the corner in the corridor and happened to see Sören and Claes looking after me. As soon as I was out of their sight I started running. I ran as fast as I could down the stairs. Two flights for every floor. A colleague from Trafficking who met me on the stairs tried to be funny and placed himself in my way in the middle of the stairs.

"Out of my way, Uffe! If you don't want to get run over."

"Maybe that would have been nice, Leona."

He laughed and moved. I kept running, one more floor. Then I forced myself to calm down, so the janitor didn't start wondering. I opened the door from the stairwell and walked toward the janitor's office. The door was closed. I looked in through the glass pane, knocked. Not a sound. I banged one more time.

"I'm coming, I'm coming," was heard from inside.

The janitor opened the door.

"Leona! I'm just on my way home. I assume you want the things from your locker?"

"I need them quickly. Is there any way you could open up again?"

The janitor gave me a shrewd look. Then he pointed at his cheek with one index finger.

"You old devil," I said, giving him a kiss on the cheek.

He laughed and went in ahead of me.

"I don't dole those out right and left," I called. "Now it will have to be extra fast."

The janitor retrieved the keys, unlocked the door, and let me in.

"The shelves are arranged by locker number. Look for yours while I finish closing up."

He left me alone in the storeroom. There were things everywhere. At first glance it looked as if everything was tossed all over the place, but on closer inspection I saw that all the things were carefully numbered. I searched for my locker number. Rummaged about among my things. Everything was there—except the backpack. I searched the piles nearby. Had someone just put it in the wrong spot? No. It was gone. Could the janitor have…?

"Did you get everything?"

The janitor stood in the doorway with his coat on.

"I'm actually missing a bag. Are you sure that everything was brought here?"

"I moved everything myself. Palle is sick today so I had to do it all myself. Typical that they decided everything should be moved just to—"

"Has anyone else been here and picked up anything yet?"

I noticed that I had difficulty appearing unaffected. I was talking much too fast and in slightly too loud a voice.

"Just one. I don't think I'll be rid of these things very soon. You know how people are, don't get around to picking up their things unless you threaten to forfeit them."

"Who was it who was here?"

"It was him…what's his name now…your squad chief."

"Claes?"

"Exactly, Claes Zetterlund. Damn, I've started forgetting names recently."

"When was that?"

"Oh, it's probably been going on for years, I don't even remember—"

"No, I mean, when was Claes here?"

"A couple of hours, three hours ago max. He picked up a few things while I ran to the john. When I came back he was gone."

"Okay, thanks."

I ran out. Back up all the stairs. Didn't have the patience to wait for the elevators. Had to get hold of Claes. If anyone wondered why I had put the backpack with money in my own locker instead of turning it in I could explain that it had been essential to get care for Olivia first. But how would Claes explain why he had taken the bag from my locker? And how could he even have known that it was there? Only I'd had that information…

And Nina.

My God, Nina!

Could she have told Claes? Was it really true that the case would be moved to II? Everything was whirling in my head. I went straight to Claes's office at a rapid clip. When I got closer I saw that the office was dark and the door closed. Damn!

"See you tomorrow, Leona," Anette called from the far end of the corridor.

"Anette, has Claes left?" I called.

"He just left. Said that he was going past Property and then home. Don't know what he was going to do there, but if you hurry maybe you'll catch up with him."

I ran. Had to get hold of him before he turned in the bag. I cursed that I had to swipe my security card and enter my code at every door. In the long corridor I saw Hampe from Property coming toward me.

"Hampe!"

Hampe stopped and smiled at me.

"Not often anyone runs after me like that anymore."

"Are you closed?"

"Yep. And I'm not opening again unless it's life or death. Your boss was just here and talked me into staying late for him."

"So he's been here?"

"Hmmm, he turned in a bag. I thought it was a little strange. You know, those big shots don't usually crawl down to us unnecessarily, much less to turn in property. I asked to be on the safe side if the bag shouldn't go in for Forensics first, but he said that all that sort of thing was done."

"So you saw the contents?"

"Contents? It was empty. Leona, what's this about?"

"Thanks, Hampe, now I know."

I turned and started jogging away.

EIGHTY-NINE

Fifty-three minutes later I drove slowly, with my lights off, into the street in the residential neighborhood of Nacka. Parked a couple of blocks from Claes's house. It was dark. The air was brisk, as usual, and the grass was wet. I slipped in through the hedge and onto the lawn. Got a brief feeling of déjà vu from when I had sneaked into Christer Skoog's house. I had hoped I would never end up in that situation again. Now, only a few weeks later, here I was. Not about to take someone's life, but the circumstances were unpleasantly similar.

I looked up at Claes's house. There were lights on in all the windows. I assumed he had hidden the money in the garage so the family wouldn't discover it.

Getting into the garage without being seen was not a problem. The problem was the family's Labrador, but I was prepared. I sneaked past the window. The whole family was sitting at the dinner table.

A little snap was the only sound when I opened the garage door. Inside, it was completely dark. I turned on the flashlight and pulled out the hot dog that I had bought at a stand on my way there. I broke it into pieces and set them behind a black plastic sack in one corner of the garage. Using the beam of the flashlight I looked through the car window into the car. Swept the light over both of the front seats and onto the floor. Nothing. Same thing in the backseat. I carefully pushed in the handle to the rear hatch. Loud barking was heard from inside the house.

"Quiet, Ozzy! Go and lie down!"

Claes's wife shouted at the dog. I stopped. Listened. I could hear the clatter of silverware, and assumed that the family was still eating. I pulled open the hatch and shone the flashlight into the trunk. There was a lot of junk. As soon as I picked up a bag the dog burst out into more loud barking. Now I heard scratching sounds at the door between the garage and the house. Steps approached the garage door. It was a matter of time before someone opened the door and discovered me.

"Ozzy, what is it?" I heard Claes say on the other side of the door.

I turned off the flashlight and quickly and quietly crawled down into the trunk, carefully closing the hatch. It was completely black. I could feel a child's seat by my head and a rubber boot on my back. I didn't know what the other things were. I heard the door between the garage and the house being opened. Paws ran around the car and then straight to the corner where I had set out the pieces of sausage. The dog gobbled up the cold hot dog I had set out.

"So what have you found now?" Claes's voice sounded tired.

"Damn, we should have gotten a Rottweiler or some other useful dog."

I heard steps around the car. They stopped. Where was he? Judging by the sound he was standing right by the rear hatch. I slowly wrapped my hand around my service pistol.

"Claes, come on. The food is getting cold," Claes's wife called from inside the house.

The paws went away. As did the steps. The door closed. I had realized that the money was not in the trunk, anyway. In that case it would have been the first thing Claes opened when he came out into the garage. I looked around in the darkness for the self-lighting safety cutoff to open the rear hatch from inside. If there wasn't one I would have to search for the tools under the mat and work open the lock of the rear hatch. But Claes's car was an American import, and a law there required all new cars to have a safety cutoff, so there should be one. I probably would have found it immediately if there hadn't been so many things in the trunk. I turned on the flashlight. Moved aside the child's seat as quietly as I could. There! I took hold of the white plastic tag that was attached to a wire. The rear hatch opened.

Now there was no time to lose.

One more bark from the dog and Claes would not give up until he knew what it was barking at. I searched in the shelves in the garage. Nothing. I turned around and happened to bump into a can with tools that was on a wooden box. It fell apart loudly against the concrete floor.

Dog barking again.

Twice as loud.

I ran to the door. Heard Claes yelling at the dog to stop, go and lie down. Just as I took hold of the garage door handle the door from inside the house opened. I kept going. I tore open the door and ran out onto the asphalt driveway away from the house. Claes came after me. He was fast.

"Leona," he shouted. "There's no point in running. I've seen you. I know what you're up to."

He was right. There was no point. I stopped. Turned around. He had stopped on the driveway by the house.

We stood still.

Stared at each other.

Should I pull my gun or bargain with him? I didn't know which.

He slowly moved his hand toward his belt. He had brought his service pistol home with him. I tried to pull mine out quicker. He was fast. Suddenly we were standing there with our guns pointed right at each other.

"Drop the gun, Leona."

He spoke in a calm voice. I was out of breath but stood completely still, my legs wide and slightly bent and my arms extended, with both hands on the gun. I didn't answer. The only thing that moved was my pounding heart. Fast. Hard. And my breathing. The angled streetlights above created a tall shadow of me along the driveway. We were standing only ten meters from each other. It was a decisive moment. My action in this situation would have major consequences.

Suddenly it was as if I woke up. I realized what I was doing. I was aiming my service pistol at my own boss. A highly regarded police commissioner, besides.

Was I out of my mind?

What did I intend to do?

I had never fired my service pistol at anyone. Only heard colleagues talk about how they felt after being forced to shoot. Several had depression, were taken out of service and unable to return. They relived the course of events in nightmares night after night and had severe sleep problems. One colleague resigned the day after an incident. I never would have believed that when I was forced to aim my service pistol, it would be at a police officer — at my own boss.

But I had gone through this once.

Killed before.

That made it easier.

But how could I explain this afterward? That Claes attacked me outside his own home? That wouldn't hold up. Was there no other way out? Could I convince him to keep quiet? Hardly. I had nothing to offer. He already had the money. We stood still facing each other. At this distance I would have no problem hit-ting exactly where I wanted. Neither would he. I was completely focused. Registered his slightest movements.

It would be him.

Or me.

I prepared myself. Index finger on the trigger. Slowly squeezed. Steady hands. Then I heard sirens. They were fast approaching. At least three cars. I remained standing with the gun aimed at Claes. I understood somewhere that it was over but couldn't get myself to put down the gun. Gripped it tightly. It was as if I was holding on to what was still left of my life. Even if only for a few more seconds. All my energy was drained. My body became heavy. The pistol felt like a big clump of lead in my hands. Tears welled up in my eyes. I saw my children before me.

Claes remained standing. Now I saw blue lights revolv-ing against the wall of the house. One, two, three cars stopped. I heard car doors opening behind me. Colleagues who shouted, "Police! Drop the gun!"

It was over. Neither of us moved. I stood as if petrified. My body would not obey me. I wanted to let go, but still I remained standing with the service pistol clenched in my hands. My fin-ger on the trigger. Everything was in the gun. My job and my personal life. The years at the Police Academy, the work out on the streets, the uniform, the corridors, the jail, colleagues, com-ing home to Peter and the children, making dinner, getting cozy in front of the TV, putting the kids to bed, everything that I so despised I was now desperately trying to hold on to.

What was I without all that, really?

The tears ran down my cheeks and prevented me from focus-ing my gaze. I heard several bolt actions behind me. Police shout-ing. I didn't understand what was being said. The sounds echoed in my ears. Those who had previously been my colleagues, police officers who had taken the same path as me, for whom I had been prepared to do anything, now aimed their guns at me. At my back.

I was in a haze.

Numb.

With one final mental charge I sharpened my awareness. I heard the officers behind me screaming.

"Claes, drop the gun. *Now!*"

Claes? Did I hear right? Before I had time to think, a shot echoed through my head. Through the entire residential area. Claes sank down to the ground. Blood was coming through one pant leg. He had been shot. By the police. I was confused. I couldn't put the pieces together. Claes was lying on the ground. Police ran past me and up to Claes. Put handcuffs on him. I slowly lowered the gun, stared straight ahead. A colleague came up and touched my shoulder.

"Leona, you can relax. It's over now. Well done!"

NINETY

Today Sweden's Most Wanted *follows up a few of the crimes we reported on earlier in the fall, where we also received tips from our viewers. This concerns the crimes that in the media came to be known as the girl robberies, where a seven-year-old girl committed three robberies in central Stockholm.*

Stockholm District Court has now convicted police commissioner Claes Zetterlund to six years in prison for having orchestrated the crimes. He was arrested outside his home under dramatic circumstances where the police were forced to shoot him in the leg after he aimed his service pistol at his own colleagues.

Presented as evidence against him in court was DNA found in an apartment at Gärdet from which the girl is said to have been kidnapped sometime before the robberies.

Sweden's Most Wanted *reported earlier on a tape recording that the girl played during all three robberies. It turned out after audio analysis to contain the police commissioner's voice. In court a video of a police interview with the girl was also shown where she reacted with such strong fear of the police commissioner that he was forced to leave the room. The girl, who was severely traumatized by the events, couldn't tell police of her involvement but instead was taken home to her mother in Finland, where she is receiving care.*

Some of the money from the robberies was confiscated from a locked cabinet in the police commissioner's office.

The case was first investigated by the squad led by the police commissioner himself but was transferred to the National Police Board's Department for Internal Investigations when it began to be suspected that he was involved in the robberies. The police commissioner was not considered to be the sole perpetrator and the police received tips from you, the viewers, that led to another man also being brought in for questioning. The man was released, however, due to a lack of evidence.

The police commissioner was convicted after pleading not guilty.

NINETY-ONE

Almost all morning I had managed to stay awake as police commissioner after police commissioner stood and rattled off figures and outdid each other in praising themselves and their own coworkers. The annual gathering for city investigators would go on all day.

The coordinator went up to the podium again. The head of investigations was welcomed. Everyone applauded.

"Thanks, I'll make this brief, but I still want to show a few examples of how we've worked during the year so that everyone will understand what amazing work we are doing."

Everyone sat quietly. Most were probably listening with half an ear, like me.

The mood at the squad had been almost unbearable over the past few weeks, starting when Claes was arrested for the robberies, right up until the verdict was pronounced. Even if a number of colleagues had been very critical of him, his leadership style, and his way of running the squad, there were few prior to the verdict who thought he really was guilty. Some made it clear, however, that they had always known there was something shady about Claes and that they had suspected he was involved the whole time. There were always police who thought, knew, and felt everything possible under the sun. They thought that now everything had fallen into place. That Claes had never revealed much about himself or his personal affairs, and thus fitted the model of the man who lived a double life. They also thought that

Claes's constant claims that he was underpaid, his repeated outbursts, and his cold attitude toward personnel proved that he wanted to get away from the agency. Added to that were the previous rumors about him as a corrupt police officer. Everyone asked me how I saw the whole thing. For understandable reasons I kept out of the discussion.

I needed Claes to complete my plan. Besides the medium, who had now been claimed for other purposes, Claes was the only one within the agency who actually had any insight into the investigation. I didn't count Minna and Sam. In order not to risk anything, it was important that I knew that Claes was where he couldn't do any damage.

Claes wasn't stupid. He realized that when I picked up the girl after the robbery, I had also taken charge of the robbery money. I wasn't really surprised that he had picked it up at the janitor's office. But neither I nor the court bought his assertion that he happened to find the money when he went to pick up his own bag, and had decided to lock it in the cabinet in his office because he didn't have time to conduct the necessary security measures for the handling of confiscated valuables or cash. On the contrary, it proved that at least some of the rumors about Claes were true.

The head of investigations showed his last image and the coordinator once again stepped up to the podium. This time the county chief constable was welcomed. Everyone applauded.

"Thanks, thanks! Dear fellow employees. It has been an over-whelming year. As always in our agency, we never quite know what's going to happen. But that's part of the excitement and what keeps us going, isn't it?"

People mumbled an "mmm." The county chief constable continued talking about how the Swedish police stood in comparison with our neighboring countries and how the cooperation between the countries looked. Cooperation with Finland had improved, and as a result several crimes had been solved. I thought of Ronni.

Nina and I had been in the courtroom during the main proceedings. The prosecutor had summoned Ronni as a witness. Nina and I had prepared him for the questions we knew would come. He conducted himself really well. He skipped his usual unpleasant attitude and exerted himself to sound credible, explaining to the court that someone had broken into his apartment at Gärdet when he was out and that Olivia had been missing ever since. The information had been backed up with forensic evidence in the form of pictures of his broken apartment door. Inside the apartment, besides DNA from Olivia and Ronni, Forensics also found the DNA from Claes that I had placed there. During the door-to-door an elderly woman had reported that she saw a man being rather heavy-handed with a little girl in the stairwell. The woman had all her focus on the girl and didn't remember what the man looked like other than that he was rather tall and well built. The lady was a little confused and couldn't remember with certainty what date she had made the observation, either. A witness who didn't remember exact appearances or days wasn't unusual, and as the woman was also elderly, there was nothing strange about it. A perfect witness, in my eyes.

Of course, the prosecutor had questioned why Ronni had not reported the girl missing. Ronni admitted that he had a criminal past and therefore didn't have any confidence in the police, which was one of the reasons he had not reported her as missing. The other was that he didn't want his former partner to find out that their daughter was missing, because he was afraid she would use that against him in a custody battle. He said that instead of going to the police, he had made use of his own contacts in the underworld to find her. When the prosecutor asked in court whether Ronni had followed the news and seen what was written about a girl who committed robberies, Ronni had answered that he had seen it, but that he didn't think that Olivia would be able to commit a bank robbery. "Who believes something like that about their own little seven-year-old daughter?" The court wrote in the verdict that a father would be expected to report his missing daughter, but that, as he had been open about his criminal past and explained his distrust of the police, and been in dispute with his former partner and therefore tried to find the girl on his own, they found no reason to doubt Ronni's story. The court also thought that parents, after learning about crimes in the media, would not expect that their own children were involved.

The prosecutor had also explained to the court that Claes had presumably not committed the crime alone, but that no additional perpetrator could be found.

As the money for the last robbery had been confiscated by the police, there was a considerably smaller sum of money for us to divide up, but that wouldn't stop me from executing my planned life change. Ronni and Nina had received their share, and Ronni hadn't been heard from since.

Up on the podium, the county chief constable seemed to be greatly enjoying the sound of his own voice. He spoke in grandiose terms about the police's basic values and visions for the future, declaring that the children and youth were our future and that the police's cooperation with Social Services was very important work for preventing young people from taking up a life of crime. I sighed. I'd heard it all before.

My contact with Social Services where Olivia was concerned had been relatively smooth. Olivia had exceeded all my expectations. That girl had something special. I would never forget that. Ronni had clearly explained to her what would happen if she told anyone what she had been involved in. Probably her brain was also doing everything in its power to repress the memories of what happened, but I didn't see any great risk that she would have difficulties because of it. She was a strong little girl.

I couldn't help but think that almost everything had worked out. The murder of Christer Skoog still gnawed at my mind. I never liked Christer, but had he deserved to die? The murder investigation had been closed when Nina and I had not managed to gather enough evidence against the finance minister, but I felt a certain satisfaction that Christer's struggle to get the minister convicted for buying sex had succeeded. Perhaps also for Dina's sake. Personal Protection had helped her until the trial. After that I heard that she had gone to live with her sister in London.

I could hardly wait until all this was over. Peter and I were still living under the same roof but only discussed practical details concerning the children. In a way I missed him. Probably not like other people miss each other, but still. I was used to our life together and I had great respect for Peter's involvement and his way of taking care of the children. I felt secure that he was there for them.

The divorce papers were submitted and the apartment was up for sale. Now Benji's operation awaited.

After that I would leave everything.

Then I would be free.

"I want to thank the previous speakers for the information about what an amazing job you all have done during the year," the county chief constable continued. "They've said it so well that I don't have much more to add other than to give you all my support and a big thank you. It is a joy to be county chief constable with so many competent colleagues."

The back-scratchers' club. I sank down a bit more in my chair. Perhaps I could nap awhile without anyone noticing it.

"Finally I want to point out an incident that occurred during the year, which in many ways was exceptional. A former colleague and close friend of mine was convicted for the robberies where a young girl was forced into committing appalling actions that have probably scarred her for life. However unbelievable I find it, there is now a verdict that I, along with those of you who worked closely with him, must accept. I therefore offer extra support to the Violent Crimes Unit and also will hand over this lovely bouquet of flowers and a gift card for the year's best investigative effort. They go to Leona Lindberg. Leona, where are you?"

I couldn't believe what I was hearing. People started looking around for me.

"Leona Lindberg," the county chief constable said again.

"What's wrong with you, Leona, stand up," Fredrik whispered, poking me with his elbow.

As I stood up the whole hall started to applaud. As if in a haze I weaved past a lot of colleagues' legs along the row of chairs out to the side aisle.

"Leona, thanks for your amazing efforts," the county chief constable continued with a louder voice in the microphone while people applauded. "You have, with great acuity and brilliant investigative methods, managed to clear up the loathsome robberies that shook our district during the fall."

I could not think clearly. Was I on my way to receive an award for having put my own boss in prison for three robberies that I had staged myself?

"Without you, Leona, yet another felon would be out free," said the chief constable.

I was out free to the very highest degree. On my way up to the chief constable at the present moment.

"Even though it is sad that a very capable colleague lost his footing and betrayed the agency, I want us all to be happy that we have associates like you, Leona, who, despite very difficult circumstances, stand up for the law and the police."

I had made my way past everyone's legs. My body was numb. Without knowing how, I moved forward along the aisle.

"From the entire Police Department I want to say — thanks!"

My legs had never felt so weak as when I took those five steps up to the podium.

The county chief constable handed over a large bouquet of flowers and pointed toward the microphone at the lectern. I took the flowers and went slowly over to the microphone. I looked out over all my colleagues. There were several hundred police officers there. I searched for some safe person to fix my eyes on. Where was Anette? There sat Fredrik. He smiled at me. Clapped his hands along with the others. The hall fell silent. It seemed like I should say something. What? I didn't deserve the prize. What if they knew?

I cleared my throat.

Sweated.

"Uh…, thanks! I want to, uh…, thank, uh, everyone who helped me with this case. You deserve flowers too. It's been a…" Suddenly I saw Sören sitting at the far end of the first row. He sat with his hand on his chin. Stared at me with furrowed eyebrows. Was he trying to psych me out? "…um…a long journey and I'm going to need a little time off after this."

I looked at the county chief constable, who nodded understandingly. I tried to think of something else to say but went blank. Empty.

"Thanks!"

Somehow I managed to make my way down from the podium and out of the hall. I went straight to the toilet and vomited.

NINETY-TWO

"What's happening? They've been in there for I don't know how long now."

I could not understand what was taking so much time. It had been an hour since Benji's operation should have been over. Why hadn't someone come and told us how it had gone?

Just like many others I was not comfortable in a hospital. I'd never become used to the clinical smell, the sterile walls, and the white coats.

"Calm down. It won't go any faster if we get ourselves stressed."

Peter always relied on people doing what they should. I did not have that faith in others. Perhaps I should have checked up on the doctors just as Mother said. To make sure there were no complaints about them from other patients, or something similar.

"Please, sit down, Leona," said Peter. "I'm getting stressed out with you wandering around."

I sat down on the chair next to Peter. Heard the phone vibrate in my pocket.

"You're not going to answer that now, are you?" said Peter.

"It's just a message," I said.

I turned the phone away so that Peter couldn't see what was there. "Leona, please confirm that everything goes according to plan." I quickly wrote, "I confirm." Moved my thumb against the send button and was about to press it when the phone rang. I looked at Peter. He stared at me. Shook his head.

"Leona Lindberg," I said with the phone to my ear.

There was a man on the other end. Not until he said his name the second time did I understand who he was. It was Martin Carlstedt, Claes's attorney.

"I just wanted to tell you that we are going to appeal the verdict."

"Yes?"

I hadn't expected anything else. It would have been strange not to, considering that Claes had been convicted of crimes he did not commit.

"Why are you calling me? I have nothing to do with that anymore."

"I have something here that I think will interest you."

Carlstedt's voice disappeared and a raspy, scraping sound was heard on the phone. A recording. I recognized the two voices immediately. My own voice sounded so loud in the phone that I had to go farther down the corridor and lower the volume so that Peter wouldn't hear. While I stood a short distance away and listened I saw a doctor in green clothing and face mask go up to Peter. He pulled down the mask and said something. I couldn't hear what. On the phone I heard a conversation between myself and Nina.

"You killed Christer. It's insane!"

"Quiet! Don't you know that this is a police station?"

Then a lot of static. I was paralyzed. Peter stood with his back to me. I tried to hear what the doctor was saying at the same time as the crackly recording blared on the phone. It was impossible to hear the doctor. The recording continued.

"When this is over, when the money is divided, we'll never talk about this again."

I saw the doctor lean down toward Peter, who collapsed on his knees in the middle of the corridor. I stopped breathing. Dropped the phone, which thudded on the stone floor. Contrary to what I wanted to do, I slowly backed away in the other direction.

Away from Peter.

Away from the doctor.

Away from the phone.

Even though my phone was broken, I could still hear the crackling sound of my own voice in the receiver from the floor as I ran toward the exit.

Acknowledgments

First of all, thank you Micke—we made it!

Thank you to all of you who have helped me with thoughts, opinions, bouncing ideas, or proofreading: my publisher Christian Manfred, author Sören Bondeson, freelance writer Victoria Larsson, and police inspector Peter Wittboldt.

I also want to thank all of you who have shown interest in my writing and have listened and encouraged me during the writing process: Pia Törnstrand, Pia Niklasson, Niklas Mårtensson, Ulrika Westlin, Sissy Hedberg Hidalgo, and Stefan Strandberg.

Thank you to my family for being there and for your support.

Finally a big thank you to my Swedish publishing house Bonnier/Wahlström & Widstrand, my American publishing house Other Press, my literary agents Jonas Axelsson and Agnes Cavallin, and to my film agent Judith Toth.

Jenny Rogneby was born in Ethiopia, but was given away for adoption when she was one year old. She grew up in northern Sweden, studied criminology at Stockholm University, and became an investigator in the Stockholm City Police Department. Her work inspired her to create the character of Leona and write this best-selling crime novel, the first in the Leona series. Before her career in law enforcement, Rogneby was a singer and member of the pop group Cosmo4.

▞ OTHER PRESS

You might also enjoy these titles from our list:

QUICKSAND by Malin Persson Giolito

An incisive courtroom thriller and a drama that raises questions about the nature of love, the disastrous side effects of guilt, and the function of justice

"A remarkable new novel...Giolito writes with exceptional skill. She keeps us guessing a long time and the outcome, when it arrives, is just as it should be." —*Washington Post*

"Powerful...A splendid work of fiction." —*Kirkus Reviews*

THE SECRET IN THEIR EYES by Eduardo Sacheri

NOW A MAJOR MOTION PICTURE STARRING JULIA ROBERTS, NICOLE KIDMAN, AND CHIWETEL EJIOFOR

A retired detective remains obsessed with the decades-old case of the rape and murder of a young woman. Absorbing and masterfully crafted, *The Secret in Their Eyes* is a meditation on unfulfilled desire and the passage of time.

"Beguiling...A complex and engaging narrative." —*Publishers Weekly*

"A brutal murder is the starting point for this strange, compelling journey through Argentina's criminal-justice system...A view of the world as a dark place illuminated by personal loyalties." —*Kirkus Reviews*

Also recommended:

THE UNIT by Ninni Holmqvist

A *WALL STREET JOURNAL* BEST NOVEL OF THE YEAR

A gripping story about a society in the throes of a cynical, utilitarian way of thinking disguised as care.

"I liked *The Unit* very much... You would be riveted, as I was." —Margaret Atwood, @margaretatwood

"Echoing work by Marge Piercy and Margaret Atwood, *The Unit* is as thought-provoking as it is compulsively readable." —Jessa Crispin, NPR.org

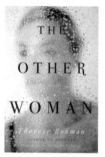

THE OTHER WOMAN by Therese Bohman

A psychological novel where questions of class, status, and ambition loom over a young woman's passionate love affair

"Bohman's characters are curiously, alarmingly awake, and a story we should all know well is transformed into something wondrous and strange. A disturbing, unforgettable book." —Rufi Thorpe, author of *The Girls from Corona del Mar*

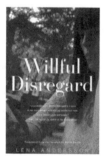

WILLFUL DISREGARD by Lena Andersson

WINNER OF THE AUGUST PRIZE

A novel about a perfectly reasonable woman's descent into the delusions of unrequited love

"Gripped me like an airport read... perfect." —Lena Dunham

"A story of the heart written with bracing intellectual rigor... a stunner, pure and simple." —Alice Sebold, best-selling author of *The Lovely Bones* and *Lucky*

mystery
ROGNEBY
2017

1474421